The Haunting of
Mitch Hamilton

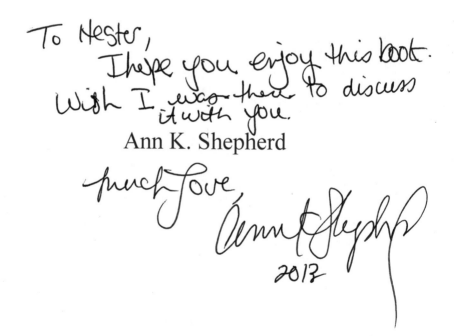

To Hester,
    I hope you enjoy this book.
Wish I was there to discuss
      it with you.

Ann K. Shepherd

much love
                    Ann K Shepherd
          2013

DEDICATION

To Marsha, my mother – Thank you for encouraging me in all things.

CONTENTS

ACKNOWLEDGMENTS

I'd like to thank my family and friends for their continuing support.
Thanks to Adam B. Shaeffer for his editing work and his enthusiasm. I'd
also like to thank Kathaleena Simonetta for creating my cover art and for
being an all-around sweetheart. A special thanks goes out to my readers.
This has been an exciting journey, and I'm so glad that you're coming
along for the ride. One final note of thanks goes to Syfy's Ghost Hunters
for keeping me in the *spirit* of things. I watched a lot of reruns while
writing this book.

Philippians 2:1-11

CHAPTER ONE

Not surprisingly, there was nothing good on television. Nothing but reality shows and angst-ridden soap operas for teens. As ASB President of Mount Vernon High School, Mitch Hamilton saw enough of that during the day. He didn't need to relive it at night. Whatever happened to good, old-fashioned sitcoms? Predicaments that were ironed out in comical ways in less than thirty minutes – that's what he wanted. But Primetime was letting him down.

With a sigh of disgust, Mitch clicked off the television and tossed the remote away. The clatter that it made as it hit the coffee table was the only sound in an otherwise silent house. That was not unusual, though, these days. His parents were gone – again – so there was no one to talk to. His homework was done so there was nothing to do. And it was too early to go to bed.

Bo-ring.

The nights were the worst. Mitch banged his head against the arm of the couch he was reclining on. Then he sighed and ran his fingers through his black hair, mussing it up for the sheer sake of having something to do. If he had any guts at all, he'd pick up the phone and dial the number he memorized three weeks ago. But what would he say?

Hey Brenna, I looked up your number in the phone book because I can't stop thinking about you.

Yeah, that didn't sound stalker-ish at all.

What he really needed was a reason to call. That would be ideal. But try as he might, Mitch couldn't drum up a legitimate excuse. The homework card was out. Brenna would know that he wasn't the type who needed help with that, and he couldn't call to ask clarifying questions, either. She would know something was up and then he'd look like a wuss for not simply being straightforward.

No, tonight wasn't the night to make that call. Not with the mood he was in – he'd probably end up sounding like he was desperate for attention. Brenna wasn't the kind of girl who'd respond well to desperation. He'd wait for the right opportunity just like he'd planned. Then he would make his move.

So, yeah. Tonight it was just him alone in his empty house.

Mitch's eyes flickered back to the remote. Maybe there would be something interesting on television now. After all, a good thirty seconds had passed, hadn't it? The thought made him laugh, but he reached for the remote anyway. And it was then, when Mitch gazed back at the black screen, that he saw the reflection.

It was distorted, but he could make out a face framed by long locks of blond hair. A girl. And she was watching him from outside the window.

Instantly on alert, Mitch sat up and whipped his head around to the window just in time to see a flash of red as the girl bolted. What he did next was probably foolish, but Mitch darted for the side door in pursuit. He flung it open and rushed out into the cool, crisp night. Logic caught up with him in that second, and the intelligence of his actions was immediately called into question. He halted a few steps past the threshold, his eyes combing the area for his mystery girl. Combing and coming up empty. There was no movement save the gentle swaying of the trees as the wind rustled through their branches.

And yet, he knew without a shadow of a doubt that he wasn't alone. She was here, somewhere.

"Who's there?" Mitch called out forcefully. "Show yourself."

Of course, she didn't. That would have been too easy. It was quiet for so long that Mitch almost thought that she was gone, but then he heard a soft, tinkling giggle.

"Listen, if you don't leave right now, I'm going to call the cops. You're trespassing."

Nothing but silence. Brow furrowed, Mitch took what he hoped was a menacing step forward. He even put his hands on his hips to show he meant business. Again, nothing. No movement whatsoever.

Was she trying to scare him? If so, it would take more than that to make him lose it. Though it was sort of creepy – the thought of someone lurking around his house at night. But he couldn't show her that she'd gotten even the least bit under his skin – assuming that she was even still out there to be intimidated by his gruff stance. She had vanished completely. And it wasn't as if there were a ton of places to hide in his side yard.

Weird.

Mitch backpedaled over the threshold and shut the door, double-checking the locks. Let her try getting through that! He flipped the light on for extra precaution. Folding his arms over his chest, Mitch willed himself to calm down.

What in the world was going on?

CHAPTER TWO

"Brenna! The Killer Klowns are invading in five minutes!" Van Vaughn shouted from the Rutherfords' living room.

Stretched out as if he owned the place, the lanky boy covered every inch of the green sofa. The remote was resting on his chest and his blue eyes were fixed on the television, which was poised to deliver cinematic greatness at the click of a button. Amazing things were lined up for this particular Friday night.

"Would it kill you to give me a hand?" Brenna's voice wafted in from the kitchen where Van could hear the microwave beeping. He detected a faint trace of annoyance in her words, which brought a smile to his face. Sometimes being a lazy scoundrel was fun.

"It just might," he replied, but he got off the sofa and trotted in to help his best friend anyway.

Standing at the microwave, retrieving a steaming bag of popcorn, was Brenna Rutherford. Since the second day of kindergarten, the two had been joined at the hip. Best friends for life, and all that. It was odd, really, because in many ways, they were complete opposites and not just in looks. He was tall with chocolate brown hair, and she was practically pocket-sized with golden hair. She was a serious student, pragmatic and responsible, and he, well, he wasn't any of those things, thank God. But instead of being driven apart by such differences, they made their friendship stronger. And it was certainly much more interesting than the average teenage relationship.

Between the buttery scent of the popcorn and chocolate chip cookies just out of the oven, the kitchen smelled like heaven. You could give the same recipe to ten different people and Brenna's cookies would be the best, hands down. She possessed that innate ability to know when to pull them out of the oven before they crossed the line from done to overdone. It could probably be attributed to her attention to detail and the fact that she'd worked at a bakery since she was sixteen. Regardless, it worked out in Van's favor. He snatched a cookie from the cooling rack and pulled it in half. Perfect chocolatey goodness.

He inhaled half of it, enjoying the way it burned the roof of his mouth. "I must say that I heartily affirm your decision to bake cookies every night of our marathon."

Brenna pulled down a plate and handed it to Van. "Put the cookies on this please," she directed as she reached up for two bowls. "Well, if you're going to do something, do it right. It wouldn't be the Halloween Horrorfest without them."

The Horrorfest, which consisted of watching classic horror films during the month of October, was something Van came up with two years ago when his parents finally agreed to let him watch *The Lost Boys*. As an avid fan of the Eighties, Van felt that by being denied such a viewing pleasure, he had heretofore been living half a life. While Olive and Max Vaughn were normally very lenient, they were surprisingly strict when it came to watching R-rated movies. Incidentally, that was why they watched them at Brenna's house instead of Van's, even though he was the one with the nice television. Max and Olive didn't want them exposing Van's little sister Chrissie to horror movies until she was older.

Brenna had agreed to the idea of a movie marathon but only if certain rules were established such as every film had to be pre-selected, it couldn't be one they'd already seen, and most importantly, no remakes allowed. After much debate, fifteen horror movies were chosen, and then five were selected at random for the first year, then the second, and the remainder saved for their senior year. Naturally, Brenna was the driving force behind the planning process. She liked having the details nailed down.

Thus the Halloween Horrorfest was born.

Brenna split the bag of popcorn evenly between the two bowls. Then she pulled two sodas out of the fridge before turning to look at her best friend. What she saw made her blue eyes twinkle with amusement. "There's chocolate on your face."

Van stuck his tongue out, probing the corners of his mouth for the yummy stain. Smiling would only encourage him, so she snorted derisively. "You're like a small child."

"Small is an interesting description coming from the midget." He patted the top of her head, emphasizing the ten-inch difference between their heights.

"Be nice or the midget won't bake cookies for you." Brenna was no fool when it came to motivating Van.

"I'm here to help." Open palms appeared stretched out before him. "My hands are willing. Give me your cookies, your popcorn, your sodas yearning to be drunk!"

Loading up his willing hands, Brenna gently pushed her best friend into the living room, where *Killer Klowns from Outer Space* was waiting for them. This was the second installment in their marathon, and one of Van's choices. Last Friday, they had watched *My Bloody Valentine*.

"I still can't figure out why you want to watch this movie. You're scared of clowns." And she wasn't just talking about spooky scared, but screaming like a little girl, pants wetting scared.

Of course, to be fair, the last time that happened was when Van was seven years old.

Looking unusually levelheaded, Van plopped down on the couch and rested his feet on the coffee table. "I prefer to think of these creatures as aliens," he clarified while munching on another cookie. "Besides, it's supposed to be an awesomely bad flick, and it's October. This is the month when getting scared is cool."

"But horror movies aren't scary. The blood is fake, the acting is horrible, and the plots are absurd and formulaic." Brenna held up her hands in mock horror, sliding her voice up an octave. "Someone please help me! I'm the hapless heroine whose boyfriend has just been tragically murdered. In a clear display of my stupidity, I've trapped myself in some secret location with the psychotic killer! But at least my large breasts look good in my form-fitting shirt!"

Van crossed his arms defiantly. "They don't all have big breasts."

Analysis unfinished, Brenna ignored the protest as she sat down next to him. "Plus, you can always tell when the bad guy is going to pop up and hack some idiot to pieces. That takes all of the suspense out of it."

The calculating look Van gave her was not unlike the one a teacher would give an upstart pupil. "So you mean to tell me that you never get scared?" There was disbelief and just the slightest hint of a challenge in his voice. Brenna could sense some kind of wager in the making. Things were about to get interesting.

"It takes more than cheap scare tactics to get me." An honest answer, yes, but one designed to provoke a reaction from Van.

It worked. Such a declaration was too good to pass up. "Oh really?" he replied, his eyes going wide with faux surprise. "Would you care to make a wager on that?"

Let it never be said that Brenna Rutherford couldn't put her money where her mouth was. It had been too long since they'd placed a friendly bet. If Van was eager to get shown up, she would be happy to oblige. "Name the terms," she charged.

"If I can make you scream, you have to make dinner for me. I choose the menu."

Brenna wrinkled her nose. "That doesn't sound like a fair exchange."

"I know!" cried the boy as he commandeered a bowl of popcorn. "Scaring you is going to be quite a challenge."

Yes, that was true. "Fine, but you get only one chance. You'd better make it count." Brenna stuck her hand out and Van shook it, each feeling confident in their odds.

The back door opened, filling the kitchen with a cool gust of wind. Abraham Rutherford stepped inside, fresh from a day's work as Chief of Police. Most likely, it had been a quiet day. Mount Vernon, Ohio wasn't exactly a hotbed of seedy criminal activity. At least, not usually. Last month, there had been a string of attacks at the high school, but that was over and done with. Life had returned to normal for the most part.

There was no one Brenna loved and trusted more than her uncle. When her mother Amelia had died, Abraham had taken Brenna in and raised her as his own in the house he had grown up in. There he was, a fresh college graduate with the promise of a bright career in the FBI, and he gave it all up for the sake of providing his niece with the parental supervision she required. This attitude of self-sacrifice had been modeled for her repeatedly as she grew up. How could she not respect and adore him for that? Her relationship with him transcended the bounds of the typical niece-uncle relationship, which was why she called him by the Italian word for "uncle" – *zio*. Everything sounded better in Italian.

Before the door swung closed behind her uncle, Brenna caught a glimpse of the fading orange sunlight and smiled. Fall nights were her favorite. "Hi, *Zio*," she greeted him cheerfully. "How was your day?"

"Pleasantly uneventful," he remarked with gratefulness as he hung up his coat.

Last month's attacks had placed him under a great deal of stress, primarily because he had been concerned about Brenna's safety. But even though the threat had passed, he still looked unsettled. Brenna didn't understand what that was all about, and Abraham typically wasn't very forthcoming about his emotions. That was a trait she'd picked up from him.

He walked into the living room, inspecting the layout. "And how was school today?"

"Good," was Brenna's reply.

"Boring with a side of inane," was Van's. That earned him a disapproving snort from his best friend, who believed that Van's boredom was his own fault for taking ridiculously easy classes.

The older man nodded as if he'd expected as much. "And what quality entertainment do you have lined up for this evening?"

Brenna held up the DVD cover. "*Killer Klowns from Outer Space.*"

Abraham leaned in for a closer look. "From 1988, right?"

Clearly impressed, Van eyebrows shot up in amazement. "You've heard of it?"

"I saw it in the theater," he admitted without hesitation. Their incredulous looks made him frown. "During my time, it was customary for teens to go to the movies. I believe that is still a common practice today."

The idea of Abraham doing something so normal, even as a teenager, was practically mind-blowing. Had he taken a girl to see that movie or gone with friends? Brenna tried to picture him as a young man, sitting in a theater surrounded by his peers. It was a bit hard to visualize. She even had trouble making his mustache disappear.

"Was it any good?" Van probed, eager to hear the opinion of someone who'd actually seen the movie.

Abraham bent down and claimed a cookie for himself. "It was absolutely ludicrous. I loved it." Atypical enthusiasm crept into his voice, empowering his recollection and making his hands come to life as he spoke. "My friends and I hadn't laughed that hard in a long time. Though I actually thought it was clever how they used balloon animal dogs to track their human prey."

"*Zio*!" cried Brenna as she clamped her hands over her ears. She shot him a traitorous look. "No spoilers!"

Mustache twitching as he fought a smile, her uncle pretended to look sheepish. "My sincerest apologies."

"The clowns aren't too scary, are they?" Van almost looked apologetic as he asked the question.

Abraham smiled. "No, but then again, I was never afraid of clowns."

"What were you afraid of as a kid?" Brenna wasn't exactly sure what prompted the question, but the thought of her uncle sitting in a dark movie theater like a normal kid had her wondering what other "normal" experiences he might have had.

A flicker passed across Abraham's face like the shadow of an old memory. "Ghosts," he replied in hushed tones. She almost laughed, thinking that he hadn't given her a real answer, but then she noticed the way his eyes darkened. He was serious. Abraham Rutherford – afraid of ghosts. How irrational.

But then his face broke into a smile. "Have fun and try to keep the screaming to a minimum."

CHAPTER THREE

As usual, *Zio* had been right. The movie *was* ludicrous – how can a movie where clowns wrap humans in cotton candy cocoons be taken seriously? – and yet, heartily entertaining. Truthfully, it wasn't exactly your run of the mill horror film, definitely more campy than terrifying, but Brenna considered it a memorable entry in the Horrorfest.

"I'm not going to lie to you," began Van as they trudged up to the gate of Mount Vernon's cemetery. "I totally dreamed that clowns were drowning me in cotton candy last night."

Of course, he *would* dream something like that. Brenna hid a smile. "Did you wake up screaming?"

"No, I woke up when I fell out of bed, and don't you dare laugh!"

His warning went unheeded. "I can't help it," she sighed when she managed to catch her breath. "The strength of your imagination is highly amusing." Brenna sensed that he was rolling his eyes from behind his Aviators. Sighing sorrowfully, Van stuffed his hands into the pockets of his acid-wash jacket as a light breeze ruffled his hair.

It was mid-afternoon on Saturday, and the cemetery was

nearly empty of living souls. If it had been Memorial Day or the Fourth of July, the place would have been crawling with people coming to pay homage to the deceased. Mount Vernon's historical society liked to place patriotic wreaths on the graves of former soldiers, some of whom had fought in the Revolutionary War. They did the same for the local politicians, including a US Senator, that were buried there as well, though some of the members were less enthusiastic about that.

But today, with the exception of a family on the other side of the lot, it was quiet. Possibly such solace, given the location, would make some people feel desolate and maybe just a little freaked out, but Brenna felt none of these things. In fact, the cemetery always brought to her a sense of peace. Maybe it was that because so many people had been laid to rest here that she couldn't help but feel restful herself. Death, while sometimes sad and tragic as she knew full well, was one of the great constants in life. As poets and writers had commented, it was the great equalizer among men. Rich and poor, good and bad – everyone had to face it.

Perhaps it was weird that she enjoyed the cemetery, but Brenna was used to being thought of as weird and wasn't about to let popular opinion diminish her way of thinking. Not only was it a beautiful place, especially now that the leaves were changing color, but it was one of the best places to take in Mount Vernon's history. Brenna's hometown wasn't exactly full of glittering lights and wild times, but it held its own when it came to charm. And the Mound View Cemetery was certainly charming.

As its name suggested, the cemetery contained its own mound, most likely constructed by the Adena Indians who lived in the area centuries ago. Skeletons had been found inside of it along with several artifacts, which Brenna had seen on exhibit. At the time, it had made her feel small in a significant way – she was just one of the thousands, maybe millions, of people who had lived here. People came and went, but the land remained, and she was just one more participant in the land's great history. Van had failed to be as impressed.

But beyond anything else, what made Mound View Cemetery so special to Brenna was that it was the final resting place of mother, Amelia.

Brenna's eyes flickered down to the red roses in her hand, and she felt in her heart the momentousness of today's trip. She used to visit her mother's grave on her birthday in August since that was the day Amelia died, but after Van had given her a diatribe on how very morbid that was, she moved it to October. Eighteen years ago, Amelia had been eighteen when the car accident that eventually took her life forced her to deliver Brenna prematurely. Mother and daughter were now the same age. Hence the momentousness of the occasion.

Today also felt extra significant since Brenna very nearly died at eighteen herself a few weeks ago. The dust had barely settled over the whole Dark Avenger fiasco but settled it had. One would have thought that Kevin Bishop and his lead pipe would have merited a longer time in the limelight, but a few weeks after his arrest and Kevin was old news. Life went back to normal as people prepped for Homecoming, discussed popular music, and gossiped about the romantic entanglements of their classmates. Jared Guthrie was still a bully. Dylan O'Connor was still an idiot. Alexis Rydell was still a witch. Only Coach Turner and Librarian Julia Bishop seemed a paler version of their former selves.

But even if they were mostly unaffected by what happened, she wasn't. Kevin's wrath and the pain that fueled it had seared itself permanently in her mind. She hadn't been one of his targets, just someone who repeatedly got in the way as he attempted to dispense his idea of justice. But she would never forget how

Kevin had pointed a gun at her, demanding that she hand over his mother or die. Thankfully, Van had been with her during those tense moments in the library, and he had been instrumental in keeping her alive. It was amazing how a few short minutes could so dramatically impact one's life. They still haunted her dreams. Drowning in cotton candy would be a welcome reprieve.

Brenna shook her head, driving away the unpleasant memory. Today didn't belong to that darkness. It belonged to her mother.

"How are you doing?" Her best friend's question pulled Brenna's head up. In a demonstration of his sincerity, Van had moved his beloved Aviators to the top of his head so he could look her in the face with no barrier between them. He meant business.

That question from almost any other person would have earned an automatic "fine," because most people didn't really want to know how you were doing when they asked that kind of question. But not Van. He deserved a real answer. So how was she really?

"I don't know," Brenna admitted, letting her voice sound as conflicted as she felt. "It's complicated. I'm the same age my mom was when she died."

Now that she'd finally said it out loud, the truth of the matter brought her up short. She stopped under the shade of a tall oak tree with fading green leaves, which stood next to one of the prettiest mausoleums in the cemetery. There were so many things that she wanted to know about her mother, questions that she wanted to ask her. But she would never get those answers in this life. For someone like Brenna, not knowing was a kind of torture.

"I'm never going to know her, and it makes me sad," she confessed. "I can't understand what her life was like, so I try to put myself in her shoes. What was it like to be pregnant while still in high school? What was going through her mind as she looked after her dying father? But more than anything, how in the world did she handle it all? I don't think I could do that."

"Yes, you could," he was quick to disagree. "She was strong. You get that from her."

It sounded so simple coming out of Van's mouth, but Brenna wasn't so sure. She desperately wanted to believe that she was like Amelia – if that was true, then she could know her in some small way – but there was no way to know for certain. She had no first-hand experience of her mother. She had to rely on her uncle to provide her with the details she so very much desired. Most people tended to speak of lost loved ones in larger than life terms, ignoring the faults and focusing solely on the virtues. While Abraham typically wasn't prone to exaggeration, Brenna believed he wasn't completely insusceptible to that. After all, she had her mom up on a pedestal, and she'd never even met her. It was true that physically she favored Amelia, but facial features didn't speak to the young woman her mother had been.

"Maybe." Her argument was half-hearted as she resumed her trek. They were nearly to the gravesite. "But maybe I'm all *Zio*." Almost as an afterthought, she added, "or my father."

Van shook his head vehemently. "No way. Your dad was a spineless coward who was afraid of responsibility. He abandoned your mom. You'd never do anything like that. You stick it out even when it's hard."

"Thanks," Brenna smiled as she linked arms with her best friend, "and thanks for coming with me."

"It's a pleasure to honor the memory of such a noble young woman." Van's smile was small but genuine. Then he shot her a glance out of the corner of his eye. "And speaking of honoring the dead, can we pay homage to the Wild Men of Borneo while we're out here?"

The Wild Men were Hiram and Barney Davis, dwarves who toured with the Barnum and Bailey Circus in the 1800's. They were billed as the twin sons of the Emperor of Borneo and the only wild men in captivity. Van, who had always considered himself a wild man, felt a certain kinship with the Davis brothers and never missed a chance to offer his respects.

Ever thankful for how her friend could improve her mood, Brenna laughed. "Of course!"

A few moments later, they diverged from the path, letting their feet carry them up a small incline and then back down again. Before she reached the grave marker though, Brenna knew something was wrong. Well, not wrong per se, but off.

Someone else had already visited her mother's grave today.

Lying in front of the marble stone were a dozen red roses, identical to the ones in Brenna's hand. Wrapped around the stems was a newspaper. It was dry which meant the flowers had been left there not long after the morning dew had evaporated. Immediately, Brenna's eyes searched the surrounding area for any sign of the person who'd come to visit Amelia, but there was no one in sight. They were completely alone.

"Who left these?" As he posed the question, Van bent down to pick up the bundle of roses. "Did Abe do it?"

Frowning, Brenna shook her head. "That's not his style."

Her uncle didn't like coming to the cemetery. Not because he didn't like visiting Amelia's grave but because he didn't like visiting her grave with Brenna. A few years ago, when they were still making the trip on Brenna's birthday, she'd realized how uncomfortable and sad it made him. Usually, Abraham excelled at concealing his emotions, so the fact that he failed to completely do so spoke volumes about their strength. He never would have admitted it, but Brenna could tell that Abe had been secretly relieved the day she'd asked to make these trips without him. She was quite certain that he made his own trips here, but he'd never come the day she was planning to, nor would he have left flowers.

No, this was someone else's doing.

And strange though it may have been, Brenna felt cheated. Her second place bouquet seemed like an afterthought since true mourners arrived at the cemetery early. Of course, to a rational mind that kind of thinking made absolutely no sense, but apparently, Brenna's mind wasn't feeling particularly rational at the moment.

Van was oblivious to her pain. He was still trying to figure out where the flowers came from. "They didn't just magically appear. Someone had to leave them. Did your mom have any friends?"

"She didn't have many friends that I know of. At least, I never met any." But even as she said it, Brenna realized that was probably false. From what she'd learned from Abraham, her mother hadn't been like him in that regard. Though quiet, she had a tender heart that drew her to others in need of comfort and companionship.

Even Van recognized that. "Well, she has to have had a friend. Who else would leave her flowers?"

Brenna frowned, tightening her grip on her own roses. Yes, who indeed? The sudden appearance of the mysterious roses called to mind the other bouquet she'd received on her birthday. No one had stepped forward to claim credit for those either. Was it possible that both bouquets were from the same person?

"Maybe whoever left these also sent me the roses I got on my birthday," she voiced aloud.

Van rolled his eyes. "Don't be so paranoid," he chided. "I already told you who those birthday roses were from."

His annoying air of superiority rankled Brenna. "Mitch Hamilton didn't send me roses! How many times do I have to tell you that?" She couldn't understand why Van persisted in clinging to such an absurd idea unless it was to irritate her.

Congratulations, it was working. As far as she was concerned, it made much more sense to think that both sets of roses came from someone unknown – no matter how unpleasant an idea that might be.

Van took in her furrowed brow and let out a nearly inaudible sigh. "This bothers you, doesn't it?"

"It's creepy," she said dully. That was putting it lightly as far as she was concerned. As someone who didn't believe in coincidences, it had to be significant. Why flowers? Why now? Did the person know she was planning to come to the cemetery today? Apparently, she was the only one who felt this way, though.

Huffing, Van rolled his shoulders, frustration seeping into his words. "Why does it have to be creepy? Why can't it be sweet and thoughtful? Why can't it be that some person remembered your mom and wanted to do something nice for her?"

He painted a pretty picture with his words. Brenna could almost visualize some sainted soul waking up with the name "Amelia Rutherford" on her lips, and moved by fondness, flying on angel's wings down to the florist to buy roses. Too bad it wasn't realistic.

"Because that's not the way people are!" Exasperated, Brenna pinched the bridge of her nose, unable to understand why he couldn't see that. No one was sitting around thinking of a dead eighteen year-old girl. Very few people in the world were that thoughtful.

"Fine. If they bother you that much, just get rid of them." With mock outrage, Van smacked her in the stomach with the roses.

Perhaps she was overreacting. No, scratch that. She was most certainly overreacting, but somehow, the irrational part of her brain refused to let it go. Casting an angry eye down at the offending bundle, she sniffed disapprovingly. The newspaper wasn't even new – it was yellow with age. So much for Van's theory about a caring mourner. This person couldn't even be bothered to get a new paper.

And then her eyes landed on the logo. It belonged to Columbia University – the very place Abraham had graduated from and where Brenna was considering attending next year.

That was weird.

"Look at this. It's Columbia University's school newspaper." Brenna showed it to her friend. "How did it end up here?" And more importantly, why did someone use it to wrap flowers in? It felt deliberate.

Even Van, who almost never found reasons to be suspicious, was thoroughly mystified by the paper's presence. But he had no helpful answer to offer so he merely shrugged in uncertainty.

Brenna peered at the paper's date and received another shock. It was April 1991. That was the month before Abraham graduated. Again, it was weird with a healthy dose of creepy. This meant something, and it definitely merited further investigation. There was only one option before her. Brenna unwrapped the roses.

"You're not really going to take them, are you?" Aghast, Van was thoroughly appalled at the idea. His voice rose sharply, highlighting his disapproval. "That's like violating your mother's grave!"

"Don't be ridiculous," she chastised, waving the now free paper in front of his face. "I'm just taking this." Brenna placed both bouquets down on the ground. "Mom loved roses. I want her to have them, no matter who put them here."

She handed the newspaper to Van, who folded it up, and then knelt in front of the marker. The stone felt cold underneath her hand. She stared at her mother's name, trying to see past the words to an image of an adult Amelia, alive and vibrant. But it was like trying to picture Abraham as a teenager. She simply couldn't do it.

My age, Brenna thought, forever my age.

If things had gone like they should have, Amelia would have been thirty-six now. What would their lives have been like if she had never died? What if her father had married her mom instead of running away? She might be living in a different town. She could have brothers and sisters like Van did. And Abraham would be working for the FBI as a profiler like he always wanted to.

A fantasy world, not reality.

"I love you, Mom," she whispered and got to her feet. To give Brenna privacy, Van had discreetly turned his back on her, so he didn't see her wipe tears from her eyes. She found herself grateful for the moment alone. Then Brenna held out her hand for the paper.

"I can't believe you're taking that," he replied with a shake of his head.

Brenna was unapologetic. "If it sits here overnight, it'll get wet with dew, and I don't want damp newspaper all over my mother's grave."

It was hard to disagree with that logic.

Once their business at the cemetery had been concluded, they headed home with Van chattering like a magpie as he drove. Brenna nodded and inserted comments when it was appropriate, but she wasn't fully devoted to the conversation. Her mind was still wrapped up in the mystery of her mother's visitor. She racked her brain, but no suitable explanation presented itself. Everything she came up with was what Van would have termed "ridiculously paranoid."

"Hey, there's Danny."

Van's sudden exclamation brought Brenna's mind into the present tense. Looking out the window, she spotted her childhood friend running alongside the road. Even from inside of a minivan, Daniel Ward, or Duke as she called him, was an imposing form. While Duke only had an extra inch of height on Van, he seemed to dwarf the lanky boy, thanks to his muscular frame. His normally dark blond hair had turned black with sweat, and his shirt was soaked through with it as well, making it look like he'd decided to shower fully clothed.

Pulling over, Van decelerated enough to keep pace with the young man. He rolled down Brenna's window, poised for a witty remark. Duke didn't even give him a chance.

"Not in the mood, Van," he stated between panted breaths.

"Preemptive strikes aren't cool, Danny," the offended boy replied. Duke ignored him, fixing his eyes on the road ahead of him. He should have known that wasn't going to work. Ignoring Van was an exercise in futility, so Brenna performed a preemptive strike of her own.

"Have you been running since sun-up?" she asked. Duke had always been a morning runner, believing the day went better when you got your exercising out of the way as soon as possible. From the look of him, he could have been running nonstop for hours. That wasn't normal. Something was wrong.

This thought was further confirmed by the way he stubbornly refused to turn his head her way. "I'm an officer of the law, Biddy," he reminded her. "I've got to stay in shape."

"That rule doesn't apply in here. Officer Fenton looks like he's about to give birth any moment," chided Van. Brenna suppressed a smile. Bill Fenton was a sweetheart but not the finest of physical specimens.

"I should give you a ticket right now for driving so slowly," Duke replied, deflecting the focus of the conversation off of himself. "You're impeding the flow of traffic."

That was a joke. They were on a quiet residential street. There were no other vehicles on the road. Van eyed him shrewdly, "Dude, who soured your milk? Did Kelly dump you or something?"

Duke made a face, clearly upset by the question.

"Oh man, she totally did!" Letting out an exasperated cry, Van slapped the steering wheel in dismay. "Why do you put up with that crap?"

Duke had been dating Kelly Stokes on and off again since high school. Unfortunately, Kelly had the rather nasty habit of dumping Duke for random, ludicrous reasons and forcing him to do a certain amount of groveling before taking him back. This cruelty would have been reason enough for Brenna not to like her, but Kelly was also shallow and obnoxious. Somehow, though, Duke saw none of her flaws. Apparently being in love made you a blind fool.

Shaking his head, Duke sighed. "It's complicated."

It was an effort for Brenna to keep her mouth shut. She'd had too many fights with him about his relationship with Kelly, and she wasn't looking for another one right now, especially since he was feeling so surly. Fortunately, Van felt no such compunction.

"No, it isn't!" he countered. "Just take your spine back and join the ranks of your liberated brothers! Say goodbye to tyrannical, emasculating women!"

How was it possible that Van could say such things and only get an eye roll from Duke? Such a declaration coming from her would have started World War III.

"This from the guy who has never been on a date," Duke replied.

Van shrugged unapologetically. "Whatever. I'm a free agent and much happier than you right now."

Since that assessment couldn't be refuted, Duke clammed up entirely, so they left him to continue running the Marathon of Emotional Suffering. As the van pulled away, Brenna watched her friend growing smaller in the rearview mirror with thoughtful eyes. It boggled her mind that Duke would so willingly subject his heart to that sort of trauma. He was absolutely miserable when Kelly dumped him, and yet, he was never able to break the cycle of their dysfunctionality. Love made people do stupid things like that. It was irrational and from what Brenna had observed, not worth the effort in most cases.

"Don't ever let me get stupid over some boy," she charged Van.

"I think there's something wrong with you if you never get stupid over a boy," he threw back. His hands drummed against the steering wheel as Van Halen, the band for which he was named, played through the speakers. "But I will promise to not let a guy treat you the way Kelly treats Danny."

Though the odds of that ever happening were slim, she thought that sounded fair. "I can accept that," she replied.

When Van dropped her off a few minutes later, Brenna took the stairs up to her room two at a time in her enthusiasm. She'd decided to ignore her homework in favor of further exploring the newspaper she had taken from the cemetery. It had to mean something – someone visiting her mother's grave on the same day she did and leaving behind a Columbia University paper. The odds were too great to be coincidental. The answer was waiting for her in one of the articles. It had to be.

She took it to her desk and unfolded the front page. The headline immediately grabbed her attention: *Student Beaten to Death*.

Unbidden, images of the broken bodies of Jared Guthrie and Coach Turner flooded Brenna's mind. The phantom stench of blood assaulted her nostrils, making her stomach churn. With a shake of her head, Brenna refocused her attention on the article. This had to be what she was supposed to see.

On Tuesday night, Eliza Kent was found dead in her off-campus apartment by fellow senior, Abraham Rutherford.

What? Brenna's eyes were arrested by the text. Her uncle had discovered a dead body? Who was this girl and why had Abraham never mentioned her? For a moment, she sat stunned and then she devoured the article. The police believed Eliza had been beaten to death when she interrupted a robbery in her home. There were no suspects at the time the article was printed. And Abraham was described as a "close" friend of the victim.

Close friend – what did that mean? Had Eliza been his girlfriend? *Zio* had never, ever mentioned dating anyone before, but surely he must have. And if he'd dated Eliza, loved her, and she died, well, no wonder he never married or showed any inclination to date anyone else. He could still be mourning her.

There was a picture of Eliza, of course. She was a raven-haired beauty with a charming smile. Brenna could tell that this was someone she could have been friends with. She could see it in her eyes – they were kind.

Now, Brenna's natural inclination would have been to find out more information about the murder of this poor girl. Had the killer been caught or was he still at large? A quick search on the Internet would probably tell her everything she wanted to know. After all, she knew a thing or two about launching her own investigations. But it felt different this time, like she was snooping into her uncle's private affairs. That was the only thing that kept her from switching on her computer to find out. Maybe he had a reason for keeping this a secret.

Wait, was it possible that Abraham had been a murder suspect?

Brenna's mind reeled at the thought, because, of course, he was innocent. However, for those who didn't know Abraham, it could have been a possibility. A young man studying criminology would have known how to cover his tracks. He could have staged a crime scene. At the very least, the cops would have questioned him. That's what she would have done. But he had to have been officially cleared, right?

Suddenly, her curiosity was raging. The mystery was too alluring. She had to at least try to find out. Perhaps there was a way to pull the information out of Abraham?

Brenna's eyes rolled of their own accord at such a thought. As if *Zio* had ever been tricked into revealing something he didn't want her to know. But they weren't dealing with Christmas presents this time, and he had been anticipating her efforts then. He would have no idea that she knew anything about Eliza. She might be able to catch him off guard.

Which naturally got Brenna wondering…

Why did someone want her to know about Eliza Kent's murder? She couldn't help but acknowledge the similarity between it and the Dark Avenger's modus operandi. Was that the point? If so, what did it all mean? Why bring it up now after Kevin Bishop was behind bars? Who knew this intimate detail of her uncle's past? He was such a private man, and she felt she was one of the few people who knew him quite well. Obviously there were some things he'd kept hidden from her.

But evidently not from the whole world.

Chapter Four

"So I've been thinking about college," Brenna announced a short while later at the dinner table. It had taken some thought, but she'd devised what she considered to be a clever strategy to get Abraham to talk about his past. As long as she didn't tip her hand, maybe she could learn a few things.

Her uncle flashed her a wry smile. "Really? You don't say."

Ignoring the subtle sarcasm, she pressed on. "Yes, and since I'm considering Columbia, I have a few questions for you. After all, you are a member of its distinguished alumni."

Was she imagining it or did he actually look apprehensive? She thought his eyes flickered, but it was hard to say. Abraham quickly wiped his mouth with his napkin, and in doing so, wiped all emotion from his face as well.

"Fire away," he encouraged.

Quickly, Brenna ran through the list of questions she'd come up with and plucked one out to get the ball rolling. "What did you like best about attending there?"

She watched her uncle as he sat back in his chair. Everything about his posture screamed serious contemplation. He even had that faraway look in his eyes, suggesting that he was sifting through old memories. And if Brenna hadn't been on guard, she might not have thought anything was off. As she studied him, though, his behavior struck her as completely rehearsed. Like he already knew what he was going to say but wanted her to believe that he didn't have a predetermined answer.

But there would be no reason for such a performance unless he had something he wanted to hide. Something like Eliza Kent, maybe?

"My classes," he finally said. "I always enjoyed learning, and I found that my professors challenged me in every way possible."

What a boring answer. Believable, yes, but boring. On any other day, the thought of a challenging learning environment would have excited Brenna, but today it paled in comparison to the mystery she'd been presented with. To be fair though, she couldn't honestly believe that with one simple question *Zio* would let loose with all the sordid details about Eliza Kent.

So how about something a little more pointed? "What was the social scene like?"

If she wasn't mistaken, the look he shot her was a mixture of incredulity and suspicion, which wasn't too surprising. After all, that wasn't typically the sort of thing she cared about. Brenna tried her best to look uncalculating, just curious.

"I haven't been there in over eighteen years," he reminded her with a smile. "I'm sure things have changed."

"Well, you know how much I love history," came her casual reply as she propped her chin up with her hand. "Humor me."

"I know this will come as a great surprise to you, but I spent most of my free time studying in the library."

Yes, this was an image of *Zio* that could be conjured up easily. She could see him perfectly – head bent low over some thick and dusty volume as he dutifully tuned out the world around him. Perhaps it was an easy picture to visualize because she knew that in less than a year, she'd be doing the same thing. More than likely, she'd have no Van encouraging her to engage her energies in anything other than studying. Everything would change when they graduated, but rather than be depressed by this, Brenna accepted the inevitable change as a reality in life.

"The apple isn't falling far from the tree in that respect," she observed wryly, "but surely you weren't solely focused on studying. You and your friends had to have taken advantage of all that New York had to offer."

There was no way he didn't see his fair share of museums. *Zio* appreciated culture like Van lived for the Eighties. He was just a bit more subdued about it.

Abraham helped himself to more salad. "If I remember correctly, there was a student discount to the Metropolitan Museum of Art and the Museum of Natural History. I did visit there on more than one occasion to get a break from work. Of course, Central Park was across the street so I spent time there as well. I particularly enjoyed reading near the fountains."

All of this was quite fascinating, but it wasn't the kind of information Brenna was looking for. Where were the people? From the way *Zio* spoke it sounded like he lived in a vacuum devoid of humans his own age. Most normal people would talk about their friends and what they did together because such emotional ties enhanced memories.

Maybe that was the answer then. Maybe her uncle had no fond memories of his time at Columbia or enough bad ones that they overshadowed the good ones. Now *that* was a sad thought.

But instead of leaving it alone, Brenna pressed a little harder. "That sounds lovely, and I bet it was nice finding friends who appreciated the same things as you." Grandfather Rutherford hadn't exactly been someone who understood or cared about learning or culture. How his children managed to escape that

Philistine gene was somewhat of a mystery to Brenna.

Abraham's eyes shot up and back down so quickly that she almost missed it. And she'd done it. She'd pushed too hard and now he was officially on guard. He knew her questions were anything but casual.

Which meant that she'd never get the answer she was looking for now.

"Is there something you'd like to ask me, sweetheart?"

Great. A straightforward approach that openly acknowledged the fishing she'd been doing. The odds of getting something to show for her efforts hadn't been great anyway. Nothing she did ever escaped his attention. *Zio* was just that good. So maybe she should just ask it – who was Eliza Kent? Why had he never mentioned her before? But if she did that, he would want to know how she knew about Eliza and she'd have to show him the newspaper, which was the same as effectively handing over the mystery to him. Brenna wasn't ready to let go of it yet.

So she did the next best thing – posed a legitimate scenario that could explain her motives.

Brenna set her fork down. "You never mention any friends from your childhood or college days, and it makes me sad. I worry about what's going to happen to you when I'm gone."

She'd said something wrong. She could tell by the way Abraham refused to meet her eyes. Remorse flooded her, and she dropped her gaze. Causing him pain hadn't been her intention. It had been foolish not to consider that a possibility.

"You needn't worry about me," he assured her with a small smile. "I've never been the kind of person who required a lot of friends. I did have a few in college, but relationships like that are hard to maintain, especially when raising an infant alone."

That was a true enough but incomplete answer, Brenna felt. It was only fair as she wasn't being totally honest with him either.

Uncle and niece seemed to reach an unspoken agreement where they realized the other wasn't saying all that could be said but leaving it at that for now.

"So you're blaming your lack of a social life on me?" Brenna was all smiles as she said this, trying to dispel the grey cloud that had settled between them.

"On the contrary, I am thanking you," Abraham amended lightly. "You saved me from countless hours of tedium."

And on that light note, conversation steered towards pleasanter waters. Brenna considered herself very fortunate to have her uncle for a guardian. She'd been thinking so much lately about how her life would be different if Amelia was still alive, focusing on the things she didn't have that other people her age did, that she neglected to consider what she'd be giving up. Dinners like this for one thing. Her relationship with her uncle would be completely different – probably reduced to polite, superficial conversation around the dinner table at holidays. For as much as Brenna missed having a mother, the mere idea of giving up her relationship with Abraham was abhorrent. The whole thing struck her as a "be careful what you wish for" kind of thing. Sure you might get good things but you never knew what you might lose in return.

After dinner, Brenna went out to her darkroom, which was located over the garage, to give Van an update on her lack of success with Abraham. Her best friend had been against any such inquiry in the first place and took this opportunity to remind her of that.

"He obviously doesn't want to talk about his past. Even I can see that. I've been at your house every week for over a decade, and I can probably count on both hands the number of times he's brought up stories from his childhood that didn't include your mom," he stated with authority over the phone. Then he paused for a breath. "It makes sense though."

It made sense? That was a loaded remark that she didn't understand. "What do you mean by that?" she pressed.

For a moment, there was silence on the other end of the phone. Van was probably trying to find a way around what he'd said without getting in trouble. In the end, he realized how futile his efforts were, so he exhaled heavily before trudging on.

"Abe has always seemed sad to me. Not pathetic-sad, but tragic-sad," he clarified. "You know?"

No, she didn't know. Sure, *Zio* was quiet and reserved, but that didn't mean he was sad. If that was the determining criteria for sadness, then she could be considered sad, too. And she most definitely wasn't sad. "I don't see that," she replied firmly.

"Of course, he isn't sad with you. He wouldn't want you to know," he hurried to assure her. "But think about it. His parents are dead and so is his sister. He's got no social life. All he has is you."

Okay, all of this was true. She'd said as much to her uncle's face at dinner, but that didn't mean he was miserable. "I think you're projecting. You're misconstruing his behavior as sad because that's how you'd feel if you were in his situation. That's just his personality. I'd be the same way if I didn't have you."

The sigh Van let out this time was one of exasperation. She was frustrating him, which was an unusual turn of events. Usually he was the one doing the frustrating. It might have been entertaining if the happiness of her uncle wasn't being called into question.

"Okay, I know that you are usually right about most things, but you gotta trust me on this one. There's more going on here than just a reclusive personality." Van was starting to get worked up. Brenna could hear the eagerness in his tone. "I can see it in his eyes. The man is the personification of tragedy especially if you're right in thinking that Eliza Kent was his girlfriend. His *murdered* girlfriend. You're probably the only thing that has kept Abraham Rutherford going for the last eighteen years."

As difficult as it was to do, Brenna had to admit that Van might be right. It wasn't so much that she didn't like being wrong, but rather that she'd failed to put the pieces together on her own. There had been sadness in his life. There was no denying that, but there was a difference between experiencing sadness and being sad continually. And the latter was what Van was proposing. If that was true, she'd been blind for years. Trust Van to pick up Abraham's emotional state when she couldn't. No, she was better with logic, rational motives behind people's actions, brains not hearts. But when it came to sorting out feelings, Van had her beat – probably because he was so very free with his own. There was a good chance that he could be right on this one.

Zio was the most important person in her life. If Brenna had failed to pick up on this, what else had she missed about him?

CHAPTER FIVE

"Question-Question. A movie is being made of your life. What genre is it?"

Van's eyes went misty as he contemplated Brenna's question. The sleeves of his trademark acid wash jacket were rolled up to mid-forearm and his Aviators were hanging from the collar of his t-shirt. And his hair, oh the hair. Today, the boy was paying homage to the Fifties with a grand pompadour hairdo. This was one of Brenna's favorite styles. Classic yet fun. Clad in jeans and a red shirt, she didn't look half as exciting as her best friend, but she was quite comfortable letting him outshine her in the area of fashion.

Van snapped his fingers. "I got it! Picture this," he announced with excitement. He threw his hands up in front of him to cast the vision. "A zombie musical as a thinly veiled commentary on the public school system. I'm thinking big, flashy dance numbers with the nimble undead. Can't you see it now?"

He spread his arms wide, gesturing to the crowded halls of Mount Vernon High School. In all honesty, it didn't seem too far off. Most people weren't thrilled by the prospect of being there and were doing whatever they could to deny the harsh truth that another school day was minutes away from starting.

Dylan O'Connor was yawning, his mouth stretched so wide that he could have stuck his fist into it. Brittany Cooper was tugging at his shirt, attempting to get his attention, but the football player had his eyes on Alexis Rydell. Compact in hand, the redheaded bombshell was touching up her makeup. At least, that's what she wanted everyone to think. In reality, she was using the tiny mirror to spy on her ex-boyfriend and former quarterback, Lucas Nash.

Last month, when the Dark Avenger was terrorizing the school, Lucas had staged a fake attack on himself to get out of playing football. No one had taken the truth well, least of all Alexis, who'd promptly dumped him in a very public, very humiliating way. Lucas would probably still be a social outcast were it not for Hannah Davenport. She was the kind of person who couldn't stand to see anyone suffer, so she'd befriended the lonely soul when no one else would.

So that was the reason why Lucas was surrounded by Hannah and her friends – now his friends, too – laughing and thoroughly enjoying himself. That made Alexis furious. Her compact closed quickly with a loud snap, and then her cold eyes landed on Brenna. The look on her face screamed of hatred.

It didn't go unnoticed by Van. He let out a low whistle. "Wow. It doesn't look like Alexis has forgiven you for the whole Lucas situation."

Technically, it hadn't been Brenna's fault. She'd merely put the pieces together and confronted Lucas, but Alexis didn't care. The cheerleader was determined to make Brenna pay for ruining her life.

Hardly intimidated by the threat, the girl shrugged. "She'd make an excellent zombie queen in your musical. I give you a ten for that answer, by the way. That's totally you."

"I know," he sighed drearily. "I think three-day weekends are a horrible tease. They give you just enough time to start getting that vacation vibe and then wham! They pull the rug out from under your feet. Half of our classmates need another three days to recover from the weekend. Just look at Mitch. He might actually *be* a zombie."

It was true. Mitch, who was usually put together, looked like he hadn't slept in days. His black hair was ruffled and not in the way that suggested it had been done on purpose. Dark circles were under eyes that he could barely keep open. Brenna suspected that if he moved away from the lockers he was reclining against, the boy would fall over.

"He's got a lot on his plate with the Halloween carnival," Brenna reminded Van. The carnival was one of those safe alternatives for local kids and since the ASB hosted it, that basically meant that Mitch, as president, was in charge. It had everything from the standard games to a dunk tank to a large maze built out of bales of hay. "I'm sure it's not easy coordinating all the games and volunteers."

"Speaking of Halloween, Chrissie needs you to come over for a fitting."

At age thirteen, Van's little sister was a budding clothes designer. A few years ago, they'd commissioned Chrissie to design their Halloween costumes. While some of their peers might turn their noses up at the thought of dressing up, that couldn't be said of Brenna and Van. They'd worn complementary costumes since the first grade when they'd dressed up as Thing 1 and Thing 2 from *The Cat and The Hat*. Last year, it had been Alice and the Mad Hatter. The Halloween carnival gave them a legitimate reason to indulge themselves now that they were past the trick-or-treating age.

"I can come over after school tomorrow," Brenna offered.

Van leaned against his locker, looking smug. "I must say, I feel this year's costumes are highly appropriate. It's almost as if I was psychic or something."

Brenna sighed. Of course, Van would take credit for something like that. "You know, I've been wondering if we should change our costumes," she mused. "It might seem like we're making light of recent events or tooting our own horns."

"For the sake of our friendship, I'm going to pretend like you didn't just say that," the boy replied with a shake of his head. "*Scooby Doo* is an iconic cartoon, and I've been looking forward to portraying Shaggy for over a year. Let's just consider our recent foray into amateur sleuthing as getting into character."

The bell for first period rang with a note of finality, putting an end to the discussion. They joined the throng of students reluctantly heading off to their first class. When they entered the room, their English teacher was standing at the whiteboard. Winsome and engaging, Mr. Rose flashed them a warm smile. Automatically, Brenna felt the corners of her mouth turn up in reply.

"Suck up," Cameron Irby muttered as she headed to her seat. Automatically, she looked down at the curly-haired boy as he sneered up at her. Competitive to the core, Cameron was bucking for valedictorian and was doing whatever he could to put Brenna off her game – even verbal attacks weren't beneath him. She was doing what she could to not be bated, but the idiot was hard to ignore. If arrogance could be bottled and sold, Cameron would be a millionaire.

"Intellectual poser," Brenna fired back.

"Frizzy-haired hobgoblin," added Van.

Brenna slid into her seat with a grin that turned into a giggle when she saw Cameron's red face. Perhaps it wasn't wise to laugh. After all, the boy had a temper, but he was so obnoxious that she couldn't help it.

"Ten points for stumping the chump. He never knows how to respond to your comebacks," she told Van, holding up her hand for an appreciative high-five, which he met with a resounding smack.

He shrugged. "It's one of the perks of being outlandish. You baffle the uncreative."

On a normal day, English would pass by with both Brenna and Van paying rapt attention to every word coming out of Mr. Rose's mouth. Normally a devout slacker, Van renounced his ways and was completely focused in English, taking extensive notes that rivaled Brenna's. As he figured it, if he paid extra attention in this class, that gave him license to be catatonic in his second and third periods – he got extra points since English was an Advanced Placement course. Fourth period was a bust because it was right before lunch, and his hungry stomach was more powerful than his brain. Since eating usually made him sleepy, it was too hard to focus in fifth period even when he was sitting next to his best friend. And who really paid attention during sixth period when the sweet taste of freedom was so near? That was the Philosophy of School according to Van.

He by no means got bad grades, so either he studied secretly or he was the world's biggest intellectual sponge. The jury was still out on that, but deep down, Brenna suspected that he was full of crap when it came to all this anti-school talk. She, on the other hand, subscribed to the "listen hard, study hard, work hard" way of life as handed down to her by Abraham.

Today, though, Brenna was finding it difficult to pay attention. The book they were discussing, *Tess of the d'Urbervilles*, was the worst book she'd ever read. Even Mr. Rose couldn't make it interesting. Her mind drifted to more fascinating topics like her teacher's hair. His dark curls were getting thicker and more pronounced, which meant it was just about time for him to get them cut. That was too bad, really. The curls were nice. Not at all unmanageable like Cameron's – his looked like he'd stuck his finger in an electrical outlet.

The bell rang, jolting Brenna out of her stupor. "Glad that's over," she murmured as she picked up her binder. "This book is utter agony. Who cares why she was wandering around so aimlessly? If you're going to wander, wander with a purpose or sit down."

Van brought his head up sharply. "Surely you jest."

"Hardly," she replied. "I'm heartily against book burning, but I might make an exception in this case and *Ethan Frome*," she added. "I hate spineless men."

Patting his copy of the book, Van muttered, "Don't worry, Tess. I won't let the unenlightened girl hurt you." Affecting the air of an offended man, Van turned his back on her and strode away with his nose held high.

Though smiling, Brenna didn't try to catch up. Let him have his moment of superiority. They were few and far between. She was at the door when someone intercepted her.

"Brenna?" Mitch called her name tentatively. He beckoned her over to the side, out of the immediate flow of hall traffic. Shoulders hunched like he was trying to collapse in on himself, the boy hugged his binder to his chest. This was atypical posture for the charismatic ASB President.

"What's up?" She wondered what he wanted. It had been a few weeks since they'd spoken last. For a while, Mitch had seemed to be everywhere she was, eager for conversation, but lately, he had kept his distance.

Up close, Brenna could see more clearly that life seemed to be taking its toll on Mitch. To say the boy looked uncomfortable would have been an understatement. He turned suddenly, indicating that he wanted to keep walking.

"I want to talk to you about something," he said.

Okay, a preamble was hardly needed for that. Why else would he have called her over? Brenna gestured for him to proceed, but he shook his head.

"Not at school."

"Well, I'm working at the bakery this afternoon. You could stop by."

Mitch hesitated. "No, it's not safe. It needs to be someplace private."

It wasn't safe? What did that mean? What could he possibly have to say that demanded such secrecy? She halted in her tracks and looked up at him. "What is this about?"

Looking uncertain, he bit his lip. "I'm having some trouble, and I think you might be able to help me." When she didn't automatically jump at his vague request for help, he sighed, resigned. "Look, I'm going nuts, and I don't know what else to do. Will you at least hear me out?"

Brenna got the feeling that Mitch was about two second away from getting down on his knees and begging in the middle of a crowded hall. That image was enough to make her agree in order to spare his pride. And if that wasn't enough, her curiosity had officially been piqued.

"I'm meeting Mr. Rose after work to go over my college entrance essay and then I have dinner."

Mitch's face dropped. "Oh."

"But you can come over after that," she finished, pulling out a pen. "Around seven. Let me give you my address."

He looked – if possible – even more awkward. "No need. I know where you live."

Brenna politely overlooked his discomfort. "Okay, I'll see you then." She turned from him, intending to race off to her next class, but he grabbed her wrist.

"Please don't tell anyone," he entreated.

That had to be code for "don't tell Van." Her affirming nod earned her a relieved smile. Releasing her wrist, he bid Brenna a hasty farewell before darting away, leaving her to wonder what in the world was going on with him.

CHAPTER SIX

As Brenna sat in her chair, she was keenly aware of Mr. Rose as he leaned over her shoulder to read her essay. Normally, she had no trouble focusing when she wanted to, but his close proximity had seriously called that ability into question. If she angled her head slightly, she could watch his lips move as he read what she'd written. Wow. He even mouthed words with perfect clarity. Was there anything he couldn't do?

Brenna's heart started to pick up. Maybe fixating on her teacher's lips wasn't a great idea. Her eyes found his face instead. He really was good-looking. Most students might have turned nauseous at such a thought, but it was true. Or maybe he just looked better in comparison to the other teachers at the school. Still, Avery Rose didn't seem to belong in a classroom. On the silver screen maybe but not helping students with college entrance essays. Van had kidded her more than once about having a crush on her teacher. Maybe there was some truth to his joke. There usually was.

Tonight was their last session, which disappointed Brenna more than she cared to admit. She liked discussing intellectual things with him. In truth, they should have been done a while ago, but she'd taken some time off after the Dark Avenger fallout. Mr. Rose had been very understanding.

"You've done exceptional work, Brenna. If it were up to me, I'd admit you on the spot," Mr. Rose declared with a smile. He turned her way, catching her in mid-stare.

Brenna felt her cheeks flush but tried to ignore the sensation and play it cool. "Thanks for your help."

He straightened up with a laugh and stepped away from her. "You didn't need my help. You've always been successful in whatever you've undertaken."

Such praise coming from him made her blush again. She ducked her head to hide her cheeks from view while stuffing her work into her backpack. She got to her feet quickly.

Up at his desk, Mr. Rose was staring in dismay at a pile of spiral-bound notebooks. "You know, it seemed like such a good idea to have the sophomores write weekly expositions, but finding the time to go through them all and do everything else is a challenge."

"Can't your TA help you?" Brenna asked. Mr. Rose was one of those teachers who always had students – usually girls – volunteer to be his teaching aide. He was very popular.

The man sighed. "Normally, yes, but I don't have one this year." As he reached down to pick up his shoulder bag, his elbow caught the stack of notebooks, knocking them to the floor.

Automatically, Brenna bent down to lend a hand in picking them up. "I could help you," she offered before realizing what she was doing. She placed the notebooks in his waiting arms.

"I couldn't ask you to do that," he said, shaking his head. "You have too much on your plate."

He wasn't exactly wrong there, but she brushed it off. "It's nothing I can't handle. I have excellent time management skills." Did that sound too eager?

Mr. Rose gave Brenna a smile that no doubt had her grinning like an idiot in return. "I can't deny that I need the help. Thanks, Brenna." Notebooks collected, he stood up again and stuck them in his bag. "Let's keep it simple, though. Shall we stick with the same day and time?"

Brenna nodded. "That works for me."

They left the building together. Ever since she'd gotten tangled up in Kevin Bishop's attack on Coach Turner, Mr. Rose hadn't felt comfortable letting her walk to her Vespa alone. Of course, Brenna didn't mind. Any excuse to keep talking to him was good for her.

"So what are your plans for this evening?" Mr. Rose inquired as they exited the building.

"Just dinner with my uncle and homework." And a secret meeting with a very troubled Mitch Hamilton.

Her answer amused him. "What? No dates?"

How many times had she blushed this evening? It was embarrassing to feel so ridiculous. Thankfully, the cover of darkness concealed it. "I don't do that. Boys aren't really interested in me. They tend to think I'm weird." Having reached her beloved Vespa, Brenna reached for her helmet, grateful for an excuse not to look at her teacher.

"I'm going to tell you a secret." His voice dropped to a conspiratorial whisper. "High school boys are idiots. Don't waste your time with them." She grinned as he headed for his car. "Have a good night, Brenna," he called in parting.

"See you tomorrow," she said. She hopped onto her Vespa and drove home. It wasn't long before she arrived. Her stomach was rumbling as she bounded up the steps, thankful that dinner was waiting for her. When she stepped inside, there was an unexpected person in the kitchen.

"Good. You're here," Duke said by way of greeting. He was

setting the table. "We can eat now. I'm starving."

"So lovely to see you too," she replied with an eye roll and a grin. Setting her backpack down, Brenna went over to investigate the smell coming from the oven. Pot roast. Yum. She turned back to her friend. "To what do we owe the privilege of your company this evening?"

"It's compensation for working on my car," Abraham answered upon entering the kitchen. Translation: *Zio* wanted to occupy Duke's mind until his mood improved with two of the young man's favorite things – eating and working on cars.

Long before Duke joined the police force, Abraham had a vested interest in him. Almost fourteen years ago, Abraham had been the unfortunate officer who'd had to deliver the news that Duke's parents had died in a car crash. Winter had been especially bad that year, making the roads treacherous. Duke's grandparents, Henry and Carrie, had been watching him for the weekend. They'd also been babysitting a four-year-old Brenna while Abraham was at work.

Naturally, her uncle didn't like talking about that night, but a few years ago, he had given Brenna a detailed – for Abraham – account. Hat in hand, he'd stood on the doorstep, and though he'd kept his face as calm as possible, Henry Ward had known the truth from the moment he opened the door. Especially since it wasn't time for Brenna to be picked up yet. Abraham remembered how Duke, then a skinny boy of nine years, had put on a brave front when his grandpa had explained that his parents had gone to heaven. Carrie had been crying her eyes out on the couch when Duke climbed into her lap, kissed her cheek, and promised everything was going to be okay. That's when Abraham realized he was in the presence of a remarkable young man.

Maybe because the boy's situation reminded him so much of Brenna's or maybe because he knew what it was like to lose someone so tragically, but Abraham went out of his way to pay attention to Duke from that moment on. While Henry was an excellent role model, Abraham had the eyes of a younger man, one who was closer in age to the boy's deceased father. It was especially easy and natural for their relationship to develop since Grandma Carrie looked after Brenna.

As Brenna ate, she listened to the pair talk about work. With Duke's personality, there was a good chance he would have become a cop anyway, but it was knowing, and in some ways idolizing, Abraham that solidified his career path. But this respect hadn't transformed him into carbon copy of the older man. Their approach to the job couldn't have been more different. Her uncle was rational, holding tight control over his emotions while Duke was reactionary, relying heavily on gut instinct.

Though in a dour mood when dinner started, Duke grew happier with every bite. Subsequently, the happier he grew, the happier Brenna became. Nobody had a smile like him – it shined brighter than a million watt light bulb on a dark night. It was a shame that Kelly could make it disappear so quickly.

For a while, the conversation was dominated by shoptalk. Not the gritty details of ongoing cases – like there were any such remotely interesting tidbits – but the boring day-to-day stuff like speeding tickets, Officer Jones never changing the coffee filter, etc. Duke also shared the latest chapter in the ongoing saga of Mrs. Watson, an elderly lady who called the police every week with some outrageous claim. This week, she was convinced that someone was trying to catch a peek of her in her unmentionables. When she had confronted her neighbor, Mr. Lafferty, the old man had laughed right in her face. Duke wasn't sure if the call was about lodging a Peeping Tom complaint or because she'd been insulted.

"Maybe she's hoping you'll do a stakeout tonight," Brenna

suggested. "She heard you were single and wants to sink her cougar claws in you." She made a swiping motion with her hand.

Duke's napkin hit her squarely in the face. Its thrower was grinning. "Don't tease," he said. "You know she's got her sights set on Abe."

Abraham smiled. "When the competition is Mr. Lafferty, it's not hard to look dashing." If Brenna didn't know better, she would have thought he was embarrassed.

With that, the conversation steered away from age-appropriate girlfriends to a much safer topic: baseball. All Abraham had to do was ask Duke what he thought the St. Louis Cardinals' chances were of making it to the World Series, and the young man's mouth was off and running, giving them a play-by-play analysis of the season. Originally from Missouri, the Wards had Cardinal-red encoded in their DNA. A while back, when Duke had been antagonizing her, Brenna thought it would be amusing to cheer for the Chicago Cubs. Duke refused to speak to her for a week. But what had started out as a joke turned into an actual appreciation for the franchise. There was something so endearing about such a pathetic team. For his part, Abraham kept things lively by rooting for the Cincinnati Reds.

But even though conversation was enjoyable, Brenna couldn't help but track the minute hand's progression towards seven o'clock. She'd be lying if she said that the thought of Mitch and his mystery didn't excite her. She'd been thinking about it on and off again all day. Had she consulted Van, her best friend would have considered this a ruse in order to get some alone time with her, but that thought had never crossed her mind. So when the knock sounded on the door a few minutes shy of the appointed hour and Duke went to answer it because her hands were submerged in dishwater, it suddenly occurred to Brenna what Mitch's arrival might look like to others.

Upon opening the door and finding the dark-haired boy standing there, Duke struck an imposing stance, one arm resting against the doorframe as he leaned forward slightly. Caught off-guard momentarily by the presence of this unexpected young man, Mitch hesitated.

"Yeah?" Duke's tone was proprietary and a little suspicious.

Mitch was spared having to reply by the timely appearance of Brenna. She ducked under Duke's arm, bumping him out of the way with her hip.

"Hi, Mitch. Come on in." Taking his arm, she pulled him over the threshold. She waved dismissively at Duke with her free hand. "Just ignore him."

Without a pause, Brenna led Mitch through the kitchen to the back door. "*Zio*, Mitch and I are going to be out in the darkroom for a while." She allowed her uncle a moment to give Mitch that penetrating stare – the one that said he was committing the boy's face to memory so he'd better not try anything funny. Brenna would have been hard pressed to say who made Mitch more nervous – *Zio* or Duke.

He didn't speak again until they were alone and halfway up the steps to the garage's second story. "You have your own darkroom?" he asked.

"*Zio* put it together for me a few years ago. He likes to encourage my hobbies." As long as they didn't include running after pipe-wielding attackers, that is.

When he walked inside, Mitch glanced around with appreciative eyes. "This place is so cool. I knew you liked photography, but this is some hardcore dedication." Fascinated, he ran his fingers admiringly over the enlarger. "What does this thing do?"

"It's the enlarger. It prints the image on the photo paper. You can raise it or lower it depending on the size of photo you want."

She demonstrated for him.

The photos hanging up on the line captivated his eyes next, and he darted over to them. It was a photographic study of hands at work. The first few were of Berthal, her boss at Honey B's, her black hands dusted with flour as she baked, manipulated fondant, and iced a cake. The next were of Chrissie as she worked on Brenna's Halloween costume, followed by a set of Van with his video game controller in hand.

"These are amazing. You have a great eye." Mitch leaned in for a closer inspection. "What do you do with the photos you take?"

Brenna walked over to his side. "Some get framed or given away. The others end up in my photo album." She knew what he was doing – stalling. His fidgetiness and inability to meet her eyes gave him away. Before he could pepper her with more questions, she said, "While I could talk photography with you all night, I don't think you came over here to discuss my hobby."

Defeated, Mitch sighed and rubbed his forehead. "I think I'm being followed," he blurted out with warning.

Whoa. That hadn't even been on her radar. "Why do you think that?"

"I keep seeing this girl everywhere."

One thing Brenna had picked up from cop shows that seemed consistent with real police work was the playing of devil's advocate. She applied the technique now. "Mount Vernon isn't big. It's not unfeasible that you'd run into the same people every now and then."

Not to be discredited, Mitch shook his head. He took up pacing around the small space. "This is different. It's not like I'm running into her at the grocery store. She's watching me, following me like a shadow." He stopped pacing long enough to stare at her, emphasizing his point. "She's been to my house,

Brenna."

Okay, that was sort of creepy. She could see why Mitch would be upset. "How do you know it's the same girl?"

"She wears the same clothes. A red hoodie with a patchwork trim around it, a yellow skirt, and blue leggings."

That was a memorable outfit, and therefore, probably significant, but she couldn't remember anyone dressing like that at school. Walking over to the counter, she opened her notebook and retrieved a pen to take notes.

"What does she look like?" Brenna glanced up from her work.

Mitch shrugged helplessly. "I haven't been able to get a good look at her. She has long blond hair, and she's thin. That's about all I can say for sure."

"Have you ever seen her at school?" When Mitch shook his head, she took a different tack. "Have you tried to talk to her?"

The boy flushed, looking suddenly uncomfortable. "Every time I try to get close to her, she disappears."

A warning bell went off in her head, and Brenna latched onto the word that stuck out. "Disappears?"

Mitch's discomfort intensified, like he'd said something incredibly embarrassing. She thought that meant something, so she filed it away for further analysis. "She ditches me, I mean," he clarified.

Okay, so this girl wanted her presence to be known, wanted Mitch to recognize her, but wasn't interested in talking to him. So was she friend or foe? Admittedly, the girl had a stalker vibe about her. She had to ask the standard textbook question. "Is there anyone who would want to harm you?"

Poor guy. He looked really upset now. "Not that I know of."

Brenna decided to take a step back. Maybe she was looking at this far too seriously. Maybe this poor girl's intentions were being misconstrued. "Maybe she has a crush on you and is too shy to come forward. Are there any girls pining for you?" Her question made the boy's cheeks turn red.

He cleared his throat. "I don't think that's what's going on here, and even if it is, I want it to stop. It's creeping me out."

"And you want me to help you do that," Brenna summed up.

"Will you?" He looked as if his very existence hinged upon her saying yes. "You're good at this stuff. You figured out Kevin was the bad guy after all."

Bringing up the Dark Avenger case probably wasn't the best way to convince her. After all, she'd sworn not to go investigating things again since Abraham and Duke had been so concerned with her safety. To give herself more time to think, Brenna said, "If you think someone's stalking you, we should really be talking to my uncle."

"I can't do that. What if I'm overreacting or something? I'd be so embarrassed."

Maybe there wasn't any harm in checking things out. This was different. Property wasn't being destroyed and people weren't getting attacked. This was simply helping out a friend. She sighed. "Okay, but if things take a violent turn, I reserve the right to go to my uncle."

"If that means you'll help, then yes." Mitch looked relieved.

She held up a finger. "One more thing. I have to bring Van in on this. We're a package deal. He may not look like it, but he's completely trustworthy and discreet." Plus, she wasn't sure how she was going to keep something like this a secret from him.

Enthusiasm slightly abated, Mitch nodded. "Okay, I trust you."

With the deal struck, Brenna rubbed her hands together. Time to get serious. "Constructing a strategy will take me some time, so for now, why don't you tell me about your weekly schedule?" She walked over to the whiteboard and picked up a marker. "What does an average week in the life of Mitch Hamilton look like?"

Smiling, he opened his mouth, but instead of the sound of his voice, loud music filled the air. It was coming from below them – the sound waves made the floor vibrate. And if that wasn't obtrusive enough, someone started singing in an unabashedly-monotone-and-proud-of-it way.

Duke. Brenna wrinkled her nose in annoyance.

"What's that?" Mitch asked.

"It's supposed to be Johnny Cash's *Folsom Prison Blues*, but it's being mangled as only Duke can mangle it!" Brenna shouted the last few words, stomping her foot with emphasis. As if that would do any good.

Looking politely confused, Mitch folded his arms over his chest. "Duke. Is that the guy who answered the door?"

"Yeah, sorry. His name is Daniel, but I call him Duke because he calls me Biddy. It's this whole thing." She waved her hands dismissively over their history. "His grandma was my babysitter so we go way back, and now he works for my uncle."

"So he's around a lot?" Mitch shifted awkwardly.

Brenna shook her head. "Not a lot. He's really good with cars so *Zio* is having him fix his. He likes to put Duke to work so he doesn't sit around and mope constantly when he's having relationship woes. Normally, I'd be sympathetic, but right now, my compassion is lacking." She stomped her foot again. No change whatsoever.

"So he's like an older brother-type?"

"No way," she sniffed. "He's more like a really annoying third cousin." Why were they still talking about Duke? There were more important things to deal with like stalkers.

But it appeared that Mitch had other ideas. "Look, why don't I write down my schedule and give it to you tomorrow? We can get together at a better time."

"I'll make him turn it down. You don't have to go."

He smiled to show her he was fine. "Thanks, but it's okay."

"While you're at it, write down every time you've seen her, where you were, what you were doing. That sort of thing."

After they exchanged cell phone numbers, Brenna walked Mitch to the door. He lingered for a moment, trying to ignore the racket coming from below. "How's your entrance essay coming?"

"Great. I just finished tonight."

Mitch's face brightened. "So now you don't have to stay late at school? You're free to do other things?"

She shook her head. "I'll still be there. Mr. Rose doesn't have a TA, and I offered to help."

He looked disappointed by her answer. "Okay, well, thanks again for your help, Brenna."

"Don't worry. We'll get to the bottom of this," she promised. "If something happens or you need to talk, give me a call. Otherwise, I'll figure out a game plan and get in touch with you."

He nodded and flashed her a somewhat wistful smile. "See you tomorrow." Poor Mitch. She didn't like seeing him so upset. Hopefully, she'd be able to help him.

Once he was gone, Brenna walked down the steps and reclined against the open door of the garage. The hood of Abraham's car was up, and Duke was hunched over the engine, pretending he hadn't been watching.

A moment later, he looked up with feigned surprise. "Did your friend leave already?" The obvious stress he placed on "friend" had her frowning.

"No thanks to you," she replied, pointing at the stereo.

"Is my music too loud?" Duke inquired, moving to lower the volume. As if he didn't already know that. "You could have just asked me to turn it down, Biddy."

Fighting a smile, she shook her head. "You're like a small child. No, an abnormally large child."

He grinned impishly. "What did he want anyway?"

"Mitch is interested in photography." Should it be concerning her how smoothly that lie came out?

Duke snorted in obvious disagreement. "Yeah, okay." He fiddled with something in front of him. "So he always looks like that then?"

Brenna frowned. What was wrong with the way Mitch was dressed? She thought he'd looked quite good in his button-up green shirt. "What's that supposed to mean? He looked nice."

"He looked like he was going on a date."

Duke was trying to be annoying on purpose, Brenna decided, so she refrained from comment. Instead, she walked into the garage and leaned over the engine. "What are you doing?"

"I'm trying to determine where Abe's oil leak is coming from."

"Show me, please," she requested.

Eager to share his wisdom, he spent the new few moments schooling Brenna in Car 101. She soaked up his knowledge and got her hands filthy as he walked her through basic car maintenance. All the while, glimmers of the old Duke resurfaced. His moodiness, as well as his obnoxious immaturity, vanished. All he needed was to be distracted by something he loved.

"Kelly doesn't like this stuff." He gestured to the car. "It bores her when I bring it up."

There were so many replies Brenna could have made now that Duke had willingly opened the door, but she managed to keep herself in check – for the most part. "Kelly doesn't like things that get her dirty, but I don't mind."

Duke raked an exceptionally grimy thumb down her cheek, giving her the first genuine smile she'd seen since his breakup.

She grinned back. The brevity of the moment didn't last long.

He sighed. "You know why she broke up with me this time?" Brenna shook her head. "Because I forgot our anniversary." That statement earned him a confused look.

"But it's October. You guys got together in the spring."

"I know! But apparently when we broke up the last time, she considered it permanent. When we got back together, it was like starting over. I failed to get that memo." Looking weary, he wiped his brow with the back of his hand and waited. "This is usually the part where you tell me how better off I am without her and all that. It's no secret that you don't like her."

"I don't," she admitted. "I can't stand how she mistreats you. But at the same time, I don't like seeing you so upset. How can I call myself your friend if I take pleasure in what makes you sad?"

Falling silent, Duke looked back down at the engine. "So you gonna help me fix Abe's car or what?"

"No," Brenna declared, her eyes growing bright with excitement. "I'm going to take pictures as you work." She darted away, and in a moment, she was back with her camera in hand.

Together, they worked in silence, and while their hands were occupied, their minds were left free to ponder what had been said and consider the future.

Chapter Seven

"So let me get this straight," Van prefaced the following morning at school. He kept his voice low to prevent anyone from overhearing them, a skillful trick given that students were crowding around the locked classroom door. Mr. Rose was running late. "Mitch approached you for 'help.' He got you to invite him over to your house and give him your cell phone number without producing any evidence that his 'mystery girl' actually exists?"

"I find your use of air quotes offensive," was the only reply he got from an annoyed Brenna. His tone, the look in his eyes, the not-so veiled meaning of his words – they were making her feel incredibly dim-witted, and she wasn't even sure why. Mitch would have no purpose for concocting such an elaborate scheme. What cause did Van have to doubt him?

Her best friend's eyebrows went up in astonishment. "Wow. Mitch is more cunning than I realized."

"Of course she's real! He has no reason to lie." That earned her a condescending smile from Van. Tired of his antics, she threw up a hand. "Fine. You don't have to help. I just assumed that you'd be up for some excitement. Clearly, I overestimated your sense of adventure."

"And clearly I overestimated your ability to keep your word," he retorted mercilessly. "I thought you retired from the investigative life. What was all that talk about sparing your loved ones? I expected more from you, Brenna Pearl."

"This is completely different." Only Van could simultaneously tease and accuse someone. That was both the blessing and curse of having him for a best friend. "I told Mitch that if things got dangerous, I was going straight to *Zio*." She resisted the urge to add a "so there" at the last second. No need to resort to childishness.

"Well, okay, then. I'm sure this won't be the last time you prove me wrong." Van's words were all graciousness but the twinkle in his eye was devilish.

The most exasperating aspect about his behavior in all of this was that it highlighted the fact that she was missing something, and he stubbornly refused to illuminate her. No, making fun of her was more diverting. It couldn't have been anything too serious, though. Van had no grudge against Mitch – she would have known if he did – so there was no reason for him to be giving the boy, or her, such a hard time.

"Whatever it is that you keep hinting at, just spit it out already," she demanded, poking a finger into his chest. "I'm sick of your little comments that weigh a ton."

"I can't," Van said with a shake of his head. The annoying smile he wore was too big for his face.

"Why not?"

"Because Mitch is coming." He nodded to the boy in question as he made his way through the throng to join them. "I hear you're having some women trouble, Mr. President."

Mitch grimaced. "More like a really irritating shadow."

Van clamped his hand down on the boy's shoulder. "Well, you're in luck then, because Brenna excels at dealing with irritating things."

"I'm sort of counting on that." Mitch gave Brenna a smile that had Van hastily rearranging his features to keep from laughing. Then he looked back at Van. "Thanks for your help, too. I really appreciate it."

Reaching into his binder, Mitch pulled out an envelope and handed it to Brenna. "Here's the information you wanted." She stuck it in her backpack as the bell rang.

Right on cue, Mr. Rose, looking as if he'd burned the midnight oil to get caught up on his work, came rushing into view. "Sorry guys," he said by way of greeting as he fished his keys out of his pocket. He fumbled with his shoulder bag and books as he unlocked the door. Finally, he pushed it open with a triumphant cry.

"Enter, young minds." The teacher ushered them inside with a smile. "Learning shall commence momentarily."

One good thing about Mitch's mystery girl was that it gave Brenna something to think about during class instead of attempting – and failing – to focus on another lecture about Thomas Hardy's wretched book. To maintain a studious appearance, she jotted down possible motives for stalking someone in the side margins of her notes while the normally engaging Mr. Rose droned on about symbolism.

Despite what Mitch might say, romantic fixation was topping the list. How many cop shows had she seen where some poor person, albeit usually a girl, was getting stalked by some love-crazed psycho? Of course, "psycho" wasn't a word she'd want to use around Mitch. He didn't need to feel more uncomfortable than he already was. Plus, those shows usually climaxed with the victim being physically terrorized by their stalker. Again, not something Mitch needed to dwell on. Her goal was to prevent that from happening.

The second motive she'd written down wasn't any better either. Malicious intent. Had Mitch done something to incur her wrath? If so, she could be intent on doing him harm. Maybe she was playing a cruel game, driving Mitch to the edge before pushing him over it. In many ways, psychological torture was harder to get over than the physical kind.

Brenna tapped her pen lightly against her paper as she thought. Aside from those two options, what other choices were there? Maybe the girl had something to tell him, an important message of some kind – but if that was true, why wasn't she attempting to speak to him? Why did she run away when he tried to approach her? Running away implied that she didn't want to get caught, which naturally had Brenna thinking that the girl's motives were far from innocent.

Or maybe there was some sort of guardian angel thing going on. What if the girl thought Mitch was in danger? What if she wanted to be on hand to protect him? Admittedly, that seemed far-fetched. Plus, they'd have to come up with a reason for why Mitch would be in life-threatening trouble in the first place, and if he already didn't know why someone would want to hurt him, he'd probably have no idea why someone would want to protect him either.

No, as far as Brenna could tell, the best motive by far was romantic infatuation bordering on obsession. If that line of thinking was pursued aggressively, perhaps they could scare her out into the open.

"You know who would make a great stalker? Zack Perry," Van proposed at lunch. He balled up his empty bag of potato chips and stuffed it into his sack. "He's the personification of creepy."

Brenna shifted her gaze over to where Zack sat with Cameron. With small, black eyes and a twitchy nose, Zack reminded Brenna of a large rat – the kind that mutated over the years and emerged from the sewers to feast on human flesh. Sensing her gaze, he turned his beady eyes in her direction and stared at her. Holy crap but he was sideshow freaky.

"How does he always know when we're talking about him?" pondered Van. "Maybe he's got super hearing. Maybe he's a vampire."

She snorted in contempt. "You've been reading too much gothic fiction."

"Vampires are all the rage now, Brenna. And who knows? They could really be among us." With exaggerated suspense, he grabbed his best friend's arm. "Maybe The Vampire Perry wants to take control of your mind! Avoid his gaze or he'll turn you into his vampire baby mama!" Van threw up a hand to shield her eyes.

Laughing, Brenna knocked it away. "The stalker is female, and while Zack may not be buff, I don't think Mitch would mistake him for a girl."

"Okay, so let's see what we got." With amazing dexterity, Van hopped onto his chair and planted one foot on the lunch table like an explorer surveying the land. "I see no red hoodies or blue leggings. Maybe Stalker Girl is absent today."

Brenna tugged at his hand. "I already told you. Mitch has never seen her at school, and you can't call her that. It's disturbing."

With a thud, Van plopped back down in his seat. "I hate to break it to you, but this whole thing's already disturbing. An overly precise moniker is the least of our troubles."

"Let's just stick with something a little more toned down like Mystery Girl, okay?"

"Yes, she's your kinder, gentler stalker." Van playfully batted his eyes. "The kind that wants to bake cookies and keep house while Mitch is chained to the bed."

The mental image his words conjured sent a shiver up

Brenna's spine. "Don't even kid about stuff like that. It isn't funny."

"I didn't say it was." Shaking his head, Van pulled a marker out of his back pocket and began drawing on his sneaker. "There's nothing more dangerous than a love-struck female."

Yeah, she wanted to say, because boys could never, ever fixate on girls. They could never stalk after their prey like lions. They never made themselves an unwanted presence in a girl's life. The truth of the matter was that males were far more likely to brutalize females, but there were bigger issues at stake here than the difference between the sexes. That wasn't at the heart of the matter.

"What you're describing isn't love. It's obsession," Brenna clarified. "Unfortunately, most people our age can't distinguish between the two."

Resting his forehead against his knee, Van groaned. "You're not going to give me the lecture on how Romeo and Juliet weren't really in love again, are you? Because I left my dueling blade at home."

"Well, they weren't!" she huffed, feeling the urge to defend her position in the great debate once again. "In lust is more like it. They were horny teens who were too stupid to see their way out of a problem so they killed themselves."

"But that's why it's a tragedy," he pressed. "It didn't have to end that way for them. It gives the reader a taste of a love that could have been, should have been, but never was allowed to flourish. Hence, the tragic-ness of it."

"Idiotic, not tragic," she countered. "It's absurd that they're counted among great couples like Elizabeth and Mr. Darcy."

Sliding out of his seat, Van placed his hand on Brenna's chest. He cocked his head, listening. "Hmmm. That's funny. I *think* I feel a heart beating in you, Tin Man."

Half growling, she pushed him away. "My heart works perfectly fine, thank you very much."

"I pity the boy who tries to win your love," sighed Van. "Contending with your ignorance will be quite the challenge."

The "discussion" that followed those fighting words was one of the most heated they'd ever exchanged. An intellectual like Brenna didn't like to be called ignorant of anything, even when it came to something as abstract as love, and Van was too amused by her fury to let it go. They were still at it when they arrived at their Childhood Development class. Aside from English, it was the only class they had together. Being an elective, there wasn't much to it – show up breathing and you passed – which was probably why Van wanted to take it in the first place. That and he was one of two males in the class.

As she slid into her chair, Brenna couldn't help but assess the other females in the room. Could any of these girls be Mystery Girl? Penelope Dyer definitely had the right hair color, but she was so tall and muscular – surely Mitch would know if an Amazon was stalking him. Maybe not, though, since he'd never gotten up close and personal with her. The quiet and unassuming Amy Duncan might be a better choice, personality-wise. Brenna had never seen her speak more than two words to a boy.

Her analysis was put on hold when Mrs. Johnson, their grandmotherly teacher, called the class to order with an announcement. "Congratulations! You're all expecting! Next Tuesday, you'll be given your very own baby to care for and cherish. Batteries included."

Next to Brenna, Van squirmed in his chair. He'd been looking forward to this assignment since he signed up for the course. Perhaps because it was the closest thing to getting to play with toys for homework that he could find. He claimed, though, that taking care of a baby, even a robot one, would make him look sensitive to the female population. Nothing drew a woman's sympathies like a single father. Brenna tried to say she didn't think the same was true when the guy was carting around a glorified baby doll, but he would have none of her negativity.

Up front, Mrs. Johnson was oblivious to the boy's excitement. "In addition to your reading, you must think of a first and middle name for a girl and a boy baby. I want to know how and why you chose your names. The better the reason, the better the grade." She gave them a calculating look that dared them to pick names at random. "I also want to know what your plans are for the nursery. Two pages total and it's due on Friday, which is when you'll find out the sex of your baby."

Brenna appreciated the effort Mrs. Johnson went to simulate the pregnancy – forcing them to actually think about naming choices, and the practical task of preparing the nursery, even if it was imaginary. Being a planner by nature, attention to detail was something Brenna obsessed over – Van's words, not hers. While the rest of the class seemed stuck on the page length requirement, she was already drawing up nursery plans in her mind.

This project was going to be fun.

CHAPTER EIGHT

A few hours later, Brenna stood on a stool with Chrissie kneeling at her feet. The girl was busy adjusting the hem of Brenna's purple dress, which was a perfect copy of Daphne's outfit. Brenna had had some reservations about dressing as the hot member of the Scooby Doo gang, but Chrissie had encouraged her to be brave, stating that Halloween was the perfect time to step out of one's comfort zone. Van was stretched out on his sister's bed, keeping mum for once as he tossed a rubber ball in the air.

"I don't think simply tailing Mitch is an option," mused Brenna.

After being sufficiently diverted by Childhood Development, her mind returned to the problem at hand: Catching Mystery Girl in the act. She felt confident that if she could just get a good look at the girl, she'd be able to identify her and then they could confront her. So with that in mind, Brenna had been trying to figure out how to make that happen.

"If Mystery Girl is paying attention, and given her stalker status she probably would be, she might notice that there are two other people following Mitch." The blonde tapped her chin thoughtfully. "But if one of us was with him, providing our girl with a distracting ruse, then the other one could spy on her. Getting him out at night would be best, given her nocturnal proclivities."

Chrissie stood up abruptly. "Wait, is this *the* Mitch?" She looked to her brother for confirmation, and Van flashed her a thumbs up. Brenna didn't understand what that meant, and the younger girl didn't bother to clarify before continuing. "So let me see if I got this straight. Mitch has a stalker – possibly a love struck gal looking to make him her boy toy – and you want to get her sufficiently distracted so you can catch a glimpse of her face?"

Brenna nodded.

"It's completely obvious what you need to do," she stated matter-of-factly. "Go out on a date with him."

Her abrupt answer caught Brenna completely off guard. Go on a date with Mitch?

Chrissie rolled her eyes. "It's just pretend. If she shows, you'll be able to assess her reaction to you, which will help you determine her motivation. If she's crazy jealous, you'll know she's interested in Mitch."

Upon hearing the young girl's logic, Brenna could detect a kind of simple beauty to her plan that was highly appealing. "Van could tail us then," she thought out loud. A potential problem occurred to her. "But will Mitch agree to a charade like that?"

"Oh, I'm sure he won't have a problem with it," Van said from the bed. His little sister snorted.

Brenna's temper flared. All of these veiled remarks about Mitch were getting real old, real fast. "What?" she demanded. "How do you know that?"

The Vaughn siblings shared a knowing look. "She's so cute, isn't she?" Chrissie's voice was overwhelmingly condescending and incredibly irritating.

Grinning impishly, Van swung off the bed. "Brenna, you

know I love you more than my own hair, so don't take this the wrong way, but you're being very stupid about this whole Mitch thing."

His words brought her up short. That was twice today that he'd questioned her intelligence. Two times too many as far as she was concerned. "What? Do you have a better idea to catch Mystery Girl?"

"And that just proves my point." Sighing dramatically, he stood in front of her, meeting her eye level without stooping thanks to the stool Brenna was standing on. With the air of one about to impart a great secret, Van placed his hands on her shoulders. "He's interested in you. Romantically. You make his heart go pitter-pat." The last words oozed out of his mouth like molasses, slow and deliberate. "You said it yourself, remember? The guy's been hanging around since school started. Boys only do that for one reason, which, incidentally, would be the same reason why he sent you roses on your birthday."

Oh. *Oh.*

"That's why you've been laughing so much!" She gave him a shove, annoyed by his antics. "Why didn't you tell me?"

"You're supposed to be smart and observant. I thought you'd figure it out." He shrugged without pity. "Plus, it was really fun to watch the two of you. It's like watching television. Will he ever muster up the courage to confess his love? Will she ever clue in? Tune in tomorrow!" He laughed and collapsed onto the bed as Chrissie dissolved into a fit of giggles on the floor.

Ridiculous wasn't a broad enough term for how Brenna felt. In fact, she thought a new word should be created to encapsulate how embarrassed, stupid, awkward, and yes, ridiculous she felt. What was she supposed to do with this information? She had no idea what to say or how to feel. She hadn't thought of Mitch in that way, but if she were to look at it objectively, he was a pretty good catch. He was great – smart, kind to others, outgoing, confident. While she liked him a lot, she wasn't sure that meant anything. It also made their potential plan problematic.

"It doesn't seem right," she said, "asking him to go on a pretend date with me when I don't know how I…" She broke off, looking bashful. "It just feels wrong."

For once, Van was rational and calm. "Look, just float the idea by him, and let him make the call. He's a big boy, Brenna. He can make up his own mind. And if he says yes, that'll give you an opportunity to do some figuring out of your own."

That sounded like a reasonable solution. As long as she was clear that it wasn't a real date, she wouldn't be misleading him. It could work, and with any luck, they'd have the case solved in short order.

"Okay," she agreed resolutely. "But what should I do about the whole 'feelings' thing? Should I bring it up, let him know that I know?"

Chrissie was on her feet again. "You're not required to do anything. It's not like he's confessed his undying love for you. He'll make his move and when he does, all you have to do is be honest. Just don't be heartless in the meantime."

In other words, don't exploit his feelings. She could do that. Shooting Chrissie an appraising looking, she said, "You're very knowledgeable for a thirteen-year-old."

"And you're very naïve for an eighteen-year-old," the girl replied. "Honestly, Brenna, you're completely backwards when it comes to anything remotely connected to romance. Your brain just doesn't even consider it. I bet Van knew a date would be the perfect diversion for your stalker well before you did."

Both girls turned to him for confirmation. He shrugged guiltily. "The thought crossed my mind during sixth period. I just wanted to see how long it would take for the genius to come up with such a simple solution."

"I hope you two savor the humor you've had at my expense tonight," Brenna replied gruffly, crossing her arms over her chest.

Chrissie wrapped her in a tight hug. "Don't be mad for keeps. We rarely get to enjoy moments like these."

Even as she huffed, Brenna felt her confidence return, and a plan began to take shape in her mind. "Assuming Mitch agrees to this, our date will need to be someplace public where Van can blend in." The exact location was unclear in her mind, but she could see it swarming with people, especially people her own age. But if it was crowded…

"We're going to need some sort of signal to let you know if Mitch sees her." She turned to Van. "I think it might be helpful to have an extra set of eyes." Her own eyes flickered to Chrissie.

The girl held up her hands in protest. "I will carry your secrets to the grave, but I'm not gonna spend the night on a public stakeout with my brother. Not when I'm cultivating a genuine social life for myself."

Van jerked on the end of his sister's ponytail. "Just hem the dress, and let the adults talk." When Chrissie dropped back down to the floor, he put his hands on his best friend's shoulders. "I'll take care of my part. You just get Mitch prepped."

An hour later, Brenna was up in her darkroom, calling Mitch's cell phone. She'd gone over what she was going to say a dozen times in her mind, self-editing as needed to make sure there would be no misunderstanding. It was a good thing she was prepared, because she didn't even have time to pace. He answered on the first ring.

"Hi, Brenna." It sounded like he was smiling, which, for some reason, made her want to smile, too. "I assume you're calling with a plan in mind."

Relieved by his straightforwardness, she launched into a summary of her discussion. If someone could just get a good look at Mystery Girl, then they could identify her. Therefore a legitimate reason was needed for them to be seen in his company on a regular basis. So how did he feel about pretending to be a dating couple?

"I think that's a great idea," Mitch affirmed enthusiastically.

Brenna felt the need to make sure he completely understood that it was just a charade. "It's just that she probably goes to our school and is probably watching you there, too. We need her to think that our relationship isn't about detective work because we don't want to tip her off."

"And if we pretend that we're dating, that looks normal," he concluded. "Plus, it might lure her out into the open more readily if she does have a crush on me." He sounded very much like he doubted that. "But it's all for show."

She exhaled slowly, feeling better about their plan now that she was sure he understood it wasn't real. "It needs to look authentic, though, so we need to play it up at school."

"So I guess you'll be seeing a lot of me during the day." She could tell he was smiling again.

Brenna bit her lip. "That's part of it, but if we're really going to sell our Saturday date night, it needs to be perfect."

There was a pause. "And what does that mean exactly?"

"We have to convince my uncle."

CHAPTER NINE

The first part to setting the stage, while the easiest, was potentially the most critical to their success, because if her uncle felt something duplicitous was going on, it could throw a kink in the entire investigation. All Mitch had to do was call the Rutherford home and ask to speak to Brenna when Abraham answered. Fortunately, it would fall to Brenna to deal with the immediate aftermath, and she felt reasonably certain that she could handle it.

The timing of the call had to be perfect. Abraham needed to be in the kitchen by the phone so it would be only natural for him to answer it. Right before dinner was ideal, and then uncle and niece could discuss the turn of events. While most girls might shudder at the thought of their parental figure answering calls from boys on their behalf, Brenna thought this was the best course of action. Trying to hide the charade would only make him suspicious. It was best to lay it all out for him and be as honest as possible. Hide the lie with as much truth as they could and Abraham might miss it.

Maybe.

Plus, she had another reason for wanting to bring up the subject of dating. It would give her the perfect opportunity to probe him for more information about Eliza Kent. Brenna's love life was a natural segue into discussing his. Given her previous failed attempt, her uncle would probably be on guard to protect his past – if it even *needed* protecting – but she would try regardless.

Downstairs, she could hear her uncle making dinner in the kitchen. Any second now, the phone would ring. Brenna tapped her fingers against the surface of her desk, keeping time with the thudding of her heart. Being this nervous wasn't something she'd anticipated, so why was she? She didn't think it had anything to do with convincing Abraham of the legitimacy of Saturday's date, though perhaps she should have been more concerned about misleading him. No, it had more to do with the thought of being out alone with Mitch. Yes, she knew it wasn't a real date, and so did he, but that still didn't change the fact that she'd be by herself for an extended period of time with a boy who had feelings for her.

Assuming Van was right about that.

If that was true, why hadn't Mitch asked her out yet? Why would a boy who was confident and popular, who could lead the student body with ease, have trouble asking a girl out? After all, it's not like he had competition. Boys weren't exactly beating Brenna's door down. He saw her every day at school, so why hadn't he been making his intentions known? Or maybe…maybe Van was right at lunch. Maybe Mitch *was* trying but "contending with her ignorance" made things a lot more difficult.

The phone rang, and she held her breath, waiting. "Brenna!" Abraham raised his voice to get her attention. "Telephone!" A moment later, when she entered the kitchen, he elaborated. "You have a gentleman caller."

Brenna tried her best to look puzzled as she took the phone from him. "Hello?"

"Hi, Brenna, it's Mitch," the boy greeted jovially. "Now, you should probably say 'hi, Mitch,' for your uncle's benefit."

There was something incredibly winsome about his voice. She felt like she was playing a game with him, and her face split into an automatic grin. "Hi, Mitch."

"That's excellent," he approved. "Now if I was really going to ask you out, I would need to summon the courage, so I would give myself more time by asking about your afternoon. How was it? Do anything fun?"

Her grin grew wider at the boy's enthusiasm over the subterfuge. She pivoted on her foot, turning her back on the kitchen and her uncle, and leaned against the doorjamb. She could hear Abraham rustling behind her and knew he was listening.

"It was great. I did some homework and got fitted for the costume that I'm wearing to the carnival. How about yours?"

"Very monotonous but thanks for asking. I realized that we didn't hash out any date details so I took the liberty of coming up with some. I'm thinking that I'll pick you up at six o'clock on Saturday, and we can go to Harvey's Soda Shoppe. I thought that seemed like a stalker-friendly venue."

Harvey's was one of those 1950's-inspired diners where carhops served meals on roller skates for those patrons inclined to eat in their car. When she was younger, Brenna used to beg her uncle to take her there because they served the best ice cream sundaes. It had probably been a good six months since they'd last dined there.

And he was right. It probably would be very easy for Mystery Girl to keep an eye on them with all the comings and goings.

"I love Harvey's," she replied with genuine sincerity. "That sounds like fun."

Mitch was grinning – she was getting quite adept at picking up the slight lift to his voice. "I was hoping you'd say that." There was a pause like he wanted to prolong the conversation but wasn't sure how now that the task was done. "Well, I guess I'll see you tomorrow. I'll come find you at your locker before school so we can get the rumor mill spinning."

"I'm looking forward to it."

When they'd said their goodbyes and Brenna turned to put the phone back in its cradle, the smile on her face was authentic. So were the brightness in her eyes and the slight blush in her cheeks. She ducked her head, feeling embarrassed by her reaction. After all, it wasn't even a real date.

But as far as convincing Abraham went, she'd scored a success. He arched an inquisitive eyebrow, prompting his niece.

"I have a date on Saturday," she confessed.

"So young Mr. Hamilton finally made his move? I'd been wondering when he would."

Brenna had become quite used to her uncle knowing and seeing everything, but this was too much. She folded her arms across her chest defensively.

"How could you possibly have known that? You've only met him a couple of times."

"I could tell the moment you brought him into the kitchen yesterday, and if that wasn't enough, I saw the two of you talking at Back to School Night before Dylan was attacked." Abraham shrugged and pulled out two bowls for the soup he'd made. "And you're not the only one Van talks to." He flashed her a slightly roguish smile.

Exasperated, Brenna scowled. "He tells you, he tells Chrissie, but I have to practically beat it out of him. Holding this over my head has been way too much fun for him." She went to work filling up the glasses and setting them on the table.

"So the idea of me dating, does that terrify you?" she asked once they were seated.

"There are many things that terrify me, but the thought of you dating takes me to a whole new level of paralyzing fear." He gave his napkin a hearty snap before placing it in his lap.

Brenna grinned.

"You like this boy, then? I haven't heard you talk a lot about him." Her uncle was wearing his infamous calculating look, the one that brought lesser folk to their knees. Fortunately, she was ready for it.

"I've always liked him in a friendly sort of way, but he's been around more, which has led to interesting feelings and thoughts of late." Very late, actually. Like two hours ago. "I would like to explore that."

He nodded, accepting her logic. "Perhaps we should have the 'talk' again?"

"Absolutely not," she replied. "I remember it vividly. Little boys are made differently than little girls. I got it." Actually, it hadn't been that bad. It's amazing how blasé the topic of sex became when you approached it calmly and rationally.

"Maybe I should have the 'talk' with Mitch," he mused. Probably armed while the poor boy was behind bars.

"Your soup is getting cold, *Zio*," Brenna reminded him as they shared a smile. She devoured a few spoonfuls of tomato soup in silence, delighting in its flavor. It wasn't the strange orange paste that most places claimed was tomato soup but a savory broth with chunks of tomato and herbs in it.

"Where are you going on this date? Did I hear you mention Harvey's?" Man but he could play it cool. Other parents would be demanding facts, but his inquiry was so casual, almost as if he were merely feigning polite interest. Brenna knew better. Internally, he was probably suffering his own brand of a panic attack.

She nodded. "I've always liked that place. He chose well."

"I still remember when I finally let you order that large chocolate sundae. I turned my back on you for ten seconds, and when I looked again, you were covered head-to-toe in it. It remains a mystery how exactly you did that. Poor little thing in her pigtails and overalls." He tapped her nose affectionately with his finger. "You cried and cried."

Brenna groaned. That night was forever seared in her memory as it was responsible for her abhorrence of food mess.

"Try not to let that happen on your date," he teased, eyes crinkling with suppressed laughter.

"I'll give it my best shot," she promised, sarcasm dripping from her tongue. She made lazy circles in her soup with her spoon, willing herself to stay casual. "So, do you have any dating pointers from your no doubt varied experience on the subject?" A jaunty smile was tacked on at the last second in an attempt to convey innocence.

"Yes, because I am the Don Juan of Mount Vernon."

Brenna put her spoon down to challenge him. "You're saying that you never dated? Ever? I don't believe it. Girls had to have been after you in college. I've seen pictures. You were quite handsome. Still are, in fact."

Abraham held up a finger. "I didn't say I never dated, but merely implied I didn't do it much."

"Didn't take to it?" she prompted lightly.

He shrugged. "I think that some people aren't meant to marry."

Her uncle was smiling but there was definitely an air of sadness about him that seemed to confirm her suspicions. *Zio* wasn't a bachelor by choice. He was one because the woman he loved was dead. Murdered. Suddenly, she felt very cruel for attempting to pry information about Eliza Kent out of him. He didn't want to talk about her because that wound hadn't healed completely. Van was right – he *was* a tragic figure.

"I understand that, but you shouldn't count yourself out yet," she told him. "You would make some woman very happy."

Abraham nodded, took a sip from his glass, and promptly changed the subject.

CHAPTER TEN

"Body language is critically important if you want to sell this thing," Van told her the next morning, keeping his head bent low towards hers so no one could overhear him. They stood next to Brenna's locker, waiting for Mitch to show up. "You gotta look coy."

"Coy?" The word sounded foreign in her mouth. Almost as much as the thought of actually behaving that way. How was she supposed to do that? She'd never once tried to make a boy think she was interested in him.

"Yeah, it means affectedly modest or shy especially in a playful or provocative way." He sounded like an obnoxious dictionary.

She thumped his chest. "I know what it means! I just don't know how to do it." She hadn't done anything and already she felt extremely self-conscious.

"Come on! You're a girl! This stuff should be second nature to you." When she didn't respond, he pinched the bridge of his nose, mustering patience. He rattled off a few suggestions. "Bat your eyelashes, bit your lower lip like you're trying to hide a smile, keep your body close to his, find excuses to touch him, laugh if he tells a joke, and don't look at anything but him. Stuff like that."

"Did you take Flirting 101? How do you know all that?" It was hard to hide how impressed she was. She tried to picture herself doing those things. In her mind, she looked like a fool.

He shrugged. "I have a little sister who likes boys."

"It's embarrassing that a junior higher knows more about this stuff than I do," she admitted with a sigh. "I feel relationally stunted."

"Quit the defeatist talk. Brenna Rutherford has never failed at anything." He gave her shoulder a shake. "Besides, you're not doing this alone. Mitch is your co-conspirator. Just play off each other, and we'll have the whole school buzzing by lunch."

Class wasn't due to start yet but the hall was rapidly becoming populated with students. One of the best reasons for staying near Brenna's locker was that key players in the social life of Mount Vernon High tended to congregate in the general area. If you wanted to get people talking, do something noteworthy in front of Alexis Rydell and her cheerleading squad or one of the ASB members. And while Brenna herself might not be worthy of public attention according to someone like Alexis, Mitch certainly was. The cheerleader would notice and she would talk.

Glancing to her left, Brenna spotted Mitch heading her way. She hadn't really noticed it before but with his popularity, walking down the hall was something of a challenge for him. Nearly ten different people tried to engage him in conversation before he stopped in front of her.

"Is it always like that?" she asked by way of greeting. "Your fleet of well-wishers?"

"Pretty much." Exhaling, he shook his head. "Most of them mean well, but it gets overwhelming at times." Casually, he took a step closer, letting his arm brush against Brenna's.

Van patted his pockets in an exaggerated way like he was

searching for something. "I seem to have misplaced my pen. I'd better go to my locker." He waggled his eyebrows suggestively and added quietly, "Sell it, kids." He pushed lightly past Sara Xavier and ran off so he could monitor the reactions of their fellow students.

Now alone, Mitch rested his forearm against the locker, next to Brenna's head, and leaned in so their faces were quite close. She tried to remember all of the coy cues Van had given her but breathing steady was hard enough as it was. Being this physically close to a boy who wasn't her best friend or Duke was a little unnerving. Brenna was a fan of her personal space. But she wasn't herself right now. She was a girl in infatuation – she refused to say love – and the last thing a girl who felt like that would want is for the object of her affection to move away from her.

Maintain eye contact. Smile.

"You look nervous," he observed, grinning. He looked perfectly comfortable, which wasn't fair. He was the lucky one with his back to the crowd.

"That's because I am," she replied. It was very hard not to turn her eyes away.

His grin became more pronounced. "You don't have to be. We're just two people talking. Tell me something. What are you doing this weekend besides going on a stakeout date with me?"

Two people talking. Two people talking. Okay, she could do that. Feeling slightly more at ease, Brenna bit her lip, smiling. "Van and I are viewing the third entry in our Halloween Horrorfest tomorrow night. We watch one horror movie every Friday during October."

"Sounds like fun. What are you watching this weekend?" he inquired.

"*Cujo.*"

Mitch nodded approvingly. "Stephen King is the master. *The Shining* scared the crap out of me the first time I watched it. You've seen it, right?"

"Yeah, we watched that last year. We tried to mix classics like that in with more eccentric entries like *Killer Klowns from Outer Space*."

That struck him as funny. "Never heard of it."

"Exactly." It was amazing how every student, every sound had faded to background noise as they talked. She felt better, more confident. This wasn't so hard. After all, she liked Mitch. He was easy to talk to – even in spite of the pretense they were putting up.

"I wouldn't have pegged you as a fan of horror movies," Mitch confessed. He frowned like he was having trouble summoning up a visual.

She shrugged. "I suppose I'm not a fan in the strictest since, but they're so preposterous that they can be fun, especially around Halloween. They can be spooky." She wiggled her fingers in front of his face for emphasis as he laughed.

"Maybe we could watch one," he suggested. "If we have to keep hanging out, I mean."

The clarification brought on a small, unexpected twinge of disappointment, but she smiled all the same. "Sure. That sounds like fun."

Hannah interrupted their conversation momentarily so she could get into her locker. Her eyes were bright and cheery as she flashed the pair a particularly large parting smile – clear indicators that Hannah believed what her eyes were seeing.

"Do you think anyone's watching?" Brenna asked. It was hard not to check to see if someone else was paying attention to them. What a shame it would be to go to all of this effort only to have no one else notice. Hannah wasn't the kind of person who liked to spread juicy details.

"I hope so, but just in case, I'm going to step it up."

She shifted her gaze so that she was looking up at him from underneath her lashes. She batted them playfully a couple of times. It must have been effective because Mitch faltered briefly before managing a grin. Actually, this coy stuff was kind of fun.

"Show me what you got," she challenged.

"I'm going to whisper sweet nothings in your ear, so get ready to react appropriately." When his hand found her waist, she covered it with her own, remembering that Van had told her to touch Mitch when she could. He put his lips to her ear and whispered, "Nothing, nothing, nothing."

Mitch's breath tickled, so when Brenna giggled and pushed him away, it was a natural reaction. He caught her hands and pulled her close to his chest. It was strangely exhilarating to be held in such a way. It made her pulse race, and she was sure that she was blushing.

"Be careful," she warned, her eyes locked on his, "or we'll get in trouble for too much PDA. I don't want to have to explain that to my uncle."

He laughed and let all but her elbow go. He tugged on it lightly. "Let's meander slowly to class for the benefit of others."

Mitch turned and bumped into Lucas Nash. While the two boys exchanged a few polite words, Brenna caught the eye of Keiko Martin. During the Dark Avenger crisis, Keiko had played an instrumental role in Brenna's investigation, and her work had earned her the respect of the young detective. As she stood with her best friend, Paige Conklin, and Autumn Winters, Keiko gave the blonde an appraising look. Brenna winked.

She felt Mitch's hand at the small of her back, encouraging her forward. He kept it there as they headed for Mr. Rose's class.

"What are you doing tonight?" he asked.

"I'm being a girl and going shopping for a date-appropriate

outfit." The words had no sooner left her mouth when she pitched forward unexpectedly as Alexis crashed into her shoulder. Mitch steadied her with both hands.

"Watch where you're going," the cheerleader spat over her shoulder and continued striding down the hall. Brenna allowed herself a couple heartbeats to glare after the redhead, knowing that it had been a deliberate move. Probably because the sight of Brenna and Mitch together annoyed her. But Brenna could take a bit of negative attention while resting in the satisfaction of knowing the charade was working.

Now that they were on the move, it was impossible not to notice the reaction of their fellow classmates. It wasn't about her, Brenna knew that. Mitch was the popular one. People noticed him automatically – the girl he was with was irrelevant, really. They would talk no matter who she was. If Mystery Girl was one of their classmates, she was definitely going to hear about this. That was good to know.

"We're creating a sensation," he whispered to her.

"You are," she corrected. "The exact flavor of your arm candy isn't important to them."

She felt his thumb brush across her back. Goosebumps emerged instantly. "It is to me," he stated with an intensity that drew her gaze to his face. There was something in his eyes, a weightiness he was trying to communicate to her. Now that she had been warned about his feelings, it seemed obvious what he was trying to convey. How many times had he looked at her like this and she'd been completely oblivious to it? Hotness flooded her cheeks, and her mouth went dry. Oh boy.

The bell rang, startling them both. They lingered in front of Mr. Rose's door, neither of them quite ready to part company. They engaged in small talk, discussing their thoughts on *Tess of the d'Urbervilles* – Mitch wasn't a fan of the book either – and the upcoming essay they had to write on it. They stayed outside until the last possible moment, and then Mitch ushered her into the room.

As they parted near Cameron Irby's desk, the boy pulled a scowl and muttered, "disgusting" loud enough to be heard. They ignored him.

Van was squirming in his chair when Brenna slid into her seat as the bell rang. "Mission accomplished," he told her. "People were gawking openly. You were very convincing, so much so that you almost had me fooled."

"Was it too much?" she questioned, feeling suddenly uncertain.

He shook his head. "Nah. Just don't stick your tongue down his throat. Unless you want to, that is." He grinned devilishly. Brenna swatted him with her binder.

When lunch rolled around, Brenna made a beeline for the library instead of the cafeteria, so she could pick up a book on baby names. Van would laugh at her commitment to her homework, which was why she chose to go now before he knew what she was doing.

Setting foot in the library, after what happened a few weeks ago, wasn't easy. It was all she could do to keep from replaying that whole terrible scene in her mind. But if Julia Bishop could come into the library every day after her son had tried to kill her, then Brenna could go in long enough to check out a book. It was healthy to face your fears. How else would you defeat them?

Her backpack hit the table with a heavy thud as she deposited it there. After English, Mr. Rose had asked her if she could come back at break to pick up some sophomore essays that needed to be looked at, and of course, she'd been more than willing. Naturally that meant she had to carry them around with her since she hadn't had time to put them in her locker. Adding an extra few pounds of paper to an already full backpack wasn't fun. She disappeared into the stacks, thankful for a moment to spare her aching shoulders.

There was one section in the library that every student knew about. The room itself wasn't a perfect square – the far corner wall had a bit of a stair step design. In that little spot, the bookshelf that ran along the wall and the row parallel to it were capped off by a small shelf that nestled against a portion of the stair-step wall, making a perfect little nook. It was there that the human reproduction books were housed. Whoever decided to put books like that in a quiet, secluded spot was just asking for trouble. People got caught back there all the time while doing a whole variety of things under the guise of research. Thankfully, it was free from amorous couples when she arrived.

There were a few baby names books to choose from. Instinctively, Brenna was drawn to the fattest one since it contained the most information. She could have researched names online, but that felt sort of like cheating. She missed the feel of a book in her hands, liked being able to flip through its pages and familiarize herself with it like a friend. Sometimes, the Internet was too impersonal.

She pulled it off the shelf and turned to leave when a recognizable voice wafted her way. "Brittany," it called out teasingly. "I'm coming to get you."

Dylan. Crap. Getting trapped by the sex books with the boy who couldn't take no for an answer wasn't her idea of a good time. There was nowhere to go unless she wanted to climb the bookshelves. Somehow, she didn't think Mrs. Bishop would like that. The football player strolled around the end of the row and halted in his tracks.

"You're not Brittany," he stated dully.

"Wow, Dylan. Nothing gets past you, does it?" Brenna strode forward, hoping to brush right on by him but at the last second, he stepped in her path. She ran into his muscled chest. Really, the boy was built like a brick wall. On the football field, that was a good thing, but now, it was nothing short of problematic. Taking a step back, she glared up at him. "Please move."

Smirking, he ignored her. "What are you doing back here? Waiting for someone?"

"No, I'm getting a book. That's what you're supposed to do in a library." She hugged the book tightly to her chest as a shield against his advances.

"That's not what I do in here," he replied suggestively. Brenna had absolutely no trouble believing that. "Are you sure you're not meeting someone here? Like Mitch, maybe?"

There was no way Brenna was going to deign that with an answer. She stepped to the left, but he was there. She went right, but to no avail. Trying to outmaneuver a linebacker was impossible. Maybe scaling the bookshelves wasn't such a bad idea after all.

"It breaks my heart that you'll go out with Mitch, but you say no to me on a regular basis. What does he have that I don't?"

He took a step forward, and she took one back automatically before she could think. He ran a hand over his buzz cut and then dropped it casually on her shoulder. Disgusted, she pulled back from him, and he took another step forward. Ah, now that was a surprisingly clever strategy on his part. A few more moves like that and she'd literally have her back against the wall. The urge to fight back simmered underneath her skin.

"A brain, manners, good personal hygiene, kindness – take your pick. Now, get out of my way." She pushed against him using her book. It did no good, of course. All he did was smile bigger as he looked down at her. He plucked the book out of her hands.

"Baby names," he practically crowed with amusement as he read the title. Brenna snatched it back from him, but the damage was done. "Now, why would you need a book like that unless, no, wait! Did you let Mitch put his bun in your oven?" He leaned in his face close to hers and looked her up and down. "I knew you were a bad girl."

"You like bad girls?" she asked, anger rising.

Licking his lips, he nodded.

"Then I'll show you bad." Without warning, Brenna smacked Dylan across the face with the book as hard as she could. The momentum carried him into the shelves. Feeling thrilled with herself, she darted away, leaving the boy swearing behind her.

Grabbing her backpack, she hotfooted it to the front desk to check out her book. It was as Mrs. Bishop was scanning the bar code that Brenna realized her backpack was unzipped. She hadn't left it that way. There was a moment of internal panic before she ascertained that everything was still there.

But something had been left behind. Sticking up out of her copy of *Tess of the d'Urbervilles* was a white note card. She pulled it out. There was one sentence on it: *Stay away from him.* Well, well, well. So Mystery Girl was staking her claim on Mitch, was she? This was promising.

"Done," Mrs. Bishop declared, thrusting the book back at Brenna.

Eager to show the note to Van and Mitch, she left the library and made her way to the cafeteria. She found them sitting across from each other at her usual table. She sat down between them

"Where were you?" her best friend asked.

"Library," she replied a touch breathlessly, "and look what someone left for me. I found it in my copy of *Tess*." She smacked the card down on the table so they could both see it.

It didn't produce the same feeling of accomplishment in the boys. Mitch actually turned green. "Whoa. This is bad," he declared.

"No, it's good!" Brenna contradicted. "First, this tells us for certain that Mystery Girl is one of our classmates. Second, it tells us that her motive for stalking you is romantic in nature because she's threatened by the thought of us as a couple. Third, because of the threat I pose, we can be sure that she'll show on Saturday. Now we can plan accordingly."

With growing concern, Mitch turned to Van for help. Her best friend leaned across the table and tapped the note card with one finger. "Brenna, this is essentially a threat. She might try to hurt you. Stalkers don't like obstacles to their affection."

"I know what it means," she told them, rolling her eyes. "I'm not an idiot. But Saturday night now has serious potential for success. We can end this long before anyone gets hurt."

"No," Mitch shook his head. "I don't want to risk it. What if we don't get her and she comes after you?"

Brenna exhaled slowly. "We have to go through with it, because I'm not the sort of person to be scared off by something as trivial as this." She cast a disparaging eye at note. "I have to stay true to my character. It's not a specific threat anyway. We've seen nothing to indicate that she's capable of carrying out actual violence. She doesn't appear to like confrontation. Also, I'm going to be protected that night. I have you and Van watching out for me. We're already going to be on guard."

She placed her hand over his and ducked her head to find his eyes. He'd been looking at the table. "If you want her to stop, we have to catch her. To catch her, we have to set a trap. This is a good plan. Van will be on the lookout for us, and he won't be alone. That's four against one. Those are good odds."

"Fine, but you made me promise that if things turned

dangerous, we'd bring your uncle in," Mitch reminded her. "I'm holding you to that as well." He squeezed her hand.

"Agreed," she nodded. She turned to Van, who was trying not to stare at the handholding taking place. "Who are you recruiting to help you that night?"

Van waved his hand vaguely. "Don't worry about it. I'm working on it."

The tension passed and the casual dining experience resumed. One would have thought that the addition of Mitch to their normally private time would have felt odd, but it didn't. Brenna found that she enjoyed listening to him talk because he was so unlike Van in a lot of ways. She could never really tell what was going to come out of his mouth. The mystery he presented was rather intriguing.

"Uh, Brenna," Van began conversationally, "do you know why a furious Dylan O'Connor keeps looking over here?"

She turned her head, spotting the football player sitting not too far away. He looked murderous, which, of course, gave Brenna immense satisfaction. She waved at him. "Because I hit him in the face with a book of baby names."

The boys laughed out loud, tossing looks over their shoulders that only made Dylan more upset. "And what did he do to merit such a beating?" Van inquired when he could breathe again.

"He had me cornered in the human reproduction section of the library and said some inappropriate things. I let him know such talk wasn't appreciated." She shrugged like it was no big deal, but Mitch frowned, looking very much like he wanted to finish what Brenna had started. She tugged on his sleeve. "I do not need my honor defended. I think it'd be overkill now, anyway."

"I can't believe you checked out a baby names book." Van shook his head in disbelief. "Only you would do something like that, Brenna Pearl."

"Naming a baby is important," she told him, ignoring his sarcasm. She then explained their Childhood Development homework assignment to Mitch. He seemed intrigued by the idea of taking care of a robot baby.

"It's a good thing you don't have one yet, though," he said. "Otherwise, we'd have to take that thing on our date. That'd be weird."

Picking up a carrot, Brenna shook her head. "I would have gotten a babysitter. A stakeout date is no place for an infant."

Van looked at his best friend like she was crazy. "You take your homework far too seriously."

"You already knew this about me," she complained, lobbing her carrot at him. "You should be used to it by now."

CHAPTER ELEVEN

When shopping for a dress in Mount Vernon, young ladies weren't presented with very many options. There were no department stores, but there were a few small shops and boutiques to which shoppers could avail themselves, the most popular being Trendsation. The aptly named store was stocked with the latest in fashion trends, including accessories, at pocket-friendly prices. It was the place Chrissie Vaughn went to for design inspiration, and it was where she demanded Brenna go to find something to wear on her date with Mitch.

Brenna was grateful that Chrissie had agreed to accompany her to the shop after her shift at Honey B's. Clothes weren't her thing. Previously, her only criteria had been that it fit and was comfortable. Now, she had to look at things with a boy's eye – what would Mitch like her to wear? What was appropriate for the situation? As Brenna was dealing with these questions, she realized that she had no one her own age to turn to for guidance. Not having girlfriends had never been a problem before, but now, it was nothing short of inconvenient. Thankfully, though, she had a clothes-savvy little sister she could borrow.

So when Brenna entered the shop with Chrissie in tow, she felt very much out of her element. Everywhere she looked, Brenna saw something different. Short dresses with low-cut necklines. Dresses that clung to the body like a second skin. Dresses that were meant to be worn big so they draped off the body. Dresses that shimmered in the light. Dresses that were two-toned. Dresses that had geometric shapes cut out of the material in strategic places. Dresses for formal occasions or a fun night out. Plus, there was a wide variety of tops and skirts that could be mixed and matched depending on one's preference.

It was sensory overload.

"I don't know what to do." A wide-eyed Brenna confessed to Chrissie.

The young girl took her by the arm and led her over to the nearest rack. "Okay, let's be rational about this," Chrissie suggested. "Forget what you see and just answer the questions. Skirt or dress?"

"Dress."

"Bare or covered shoulders?"

"Covered." This wasn't too bad. It was almost like a test, and she was good at those.

"Actual sleeves or some sort of jacket or sweater?"

"Sweater." The faint image of a dress started taking shape in Brenna's mind. She almost knew what she wanted.

Chrissie nodded approvingly. "Form-fitting or more relaxed?"

"Relaxed," Brenna said. "I think it's best to keep things light and fun. A tight dress is too sexy, and that's not really what I'm going for right now." She didn't need to add that dressing suggestively might send the wrong impression to Mitch.

"Okay, then, let's get started with those parameters in mind."

They separated to search for the perfect dress. As her eyes roamed the merchandise, Brenna wondered if she hadn't misjudged the whole shopping thing. It was sort of like a treasure hunt. She knew what she wanted was here somewhere. All she had to do was keep digging until she found it.

And suddenly, the stars aligned and it was right there before her eyes.

It was periwinkle blue with spaghetti straps and a mid-calf length skirt that would have been ideal for twirling if she was so inclined. The small sweater that accompanied it had a crocheted look to it with holes big enough to show some skin, but not big enough to make her feel self-conscious. It was short, stopping above her waist, so the skirt could flare out appropriately. She could definitely see herself wearing a dress like that. It was innocent with a splash of flirtiness. And they had one left in her size. Heaven had smiled down upon her.

"Can I help you?"

The familiar voice brought Brenna's head up. Missy Jensen, one of Alexis' cheerleaders, had stepped up to assist Chrissie. Though not as popular as Alexis, Missy held a well-deserved title as one of Mount Vernon High's Most Fashionably Dressed. Her trendy dresses and strategically styled brunette curls made it look like Missy was perpetually one stop away from a nightclub. Why one felt they needed to dress like that in the middle of Ohio, Brenna wasn't sure, but the girl looked good. It was a style that Brenna didn't think she'd ever be able to pull off.

"I'm looking for a dress for my friend." Chrissie gestured in Brenna's direction. Upon seeing her, Missy frowned unpleasantly. The frown intensified when she saw the dress in Brenna's hand.

Chrissie, on the other hand, squealed in delight and rushed over to examine it. Enraptured, she carried on for two minutes about what a perfect color it was, that it set the right tone for the entire evening, and how amazing it would look on her. An annoyed Missy unlocked the dressing room for Brenna, who wasn't completely sure what she'd done to deserve the contemptuous look she was getting. A few moments later, Chrissie's enthusiasm increased when Brenna stepped out of the room. Thankfully, Missy had disappeared.

"Finding a dress can't always be this easy," observed Brenna.

"Usually it takes forever, but every now and then, a girl gets lucky." Chrissie eyed her with deep satisfaction. Then she leaned in to whisper, "Fake date or not, you're gonna knock Mitch dead in this thing. If he doesn't make his move on Saturday, then he's an idiot."

For a moment, the Brenna in the mirror was wearing a decidedly goofy grin, but then she frowned. "I don't know what I'm going to do if he does make a move. It's too early for me to sort out how I'm feeling."

"And how's that?" the younger girl pressed.

"Really nervous with intense heart palpitations. I've been smiling more than usual, too."

"Then you're progressing nicely with your first romance," Chrissie concluded. "Give it a few more days, and I think you'll know what to do."

How she could be so certain of such things, Brenna didn't know.

Once again, Chrissie was all business. "Change out of that – if you can bear it – so we can accessorize." She pushed Brenna back into the dressing room and didn't wait for her to reemerge before dashing off to look at jewelry.

Missy was back when Brenna finished changing, waiting for her by the door. She put her hand on the hanger. "I'm sorry," she stated in a tone that indicated otherwise, "but you can't buy this dress."

She tugged on the hanger, but Brenna wasn't about to let it go. What did Missy think she was doing? Who in their right mind refused a sale? "Why not?"

"There's a design flaw in this particular dress. I had to pull the others from the floor, because it wouldn't be right to sell them."

Of course, it was a lie. There was absolutely nothing wrong with the dress. Missy simply didn't want her to have it. There was no bad blood between them that she knew of, so why the sudden hostility? Did this have something to do with Alexis and the threat she'd made a few weeks ago to destroy Brenna? If so, she wasn't going down that easily. She loved the dress and wasn't going to leave the store without it.

"I think you're mistaken. The dress is perfect, and I'm going to buy it," Brenna said, tightening her grip on the hanger. "If you have a problem with that, I'd be happy to discuss it with your supervisor."

It felt like one of those classic showdowns in a western with two opponents eyeing each other before a quick draw. The air was taut with tension as neither girl backed down. It was irrational to behave such a way over a dress, but Brenna wasn't the kind of girl who let injustices go by undefended. She had every right to buy it, and no upstart cheerleader was going to stop her.

"Do my eyes deceive me or is that Brenna Rutherford in a dress shop? I didn't think you even knew what those were." Alexis Rydell appeared from behind the clothes rack, looking highly amused at the sight before her. She looked down at the outfit the girls were fighting over. "Brenna, did you pick that dress out? It's so adorable. I bet you look precious in it."

The cheerleader's sugary tone and kind words had Brenna instantly on alert. Alexis had never, ever said anything nice to her before. Her demeanor wasn't to be trusted. Something devious was going on here.

"Thank you," she answered, maintaining a white-knuckled grip on the hanger. "I'm looking forward to buying it."

Missy's hand shook with determination. "You can't have it."

The high, lilting laugh Alexis gave only increased the tension between the two girls. "Missy, no one likes a bitch," the redhead teased, casually flicking a strand of her hair off her shoulder. "Let her have the dress. It's no big deal."

A furious Missy shot Alexis a look of betrayal before she shoved the dress at Brenna. "Fine. Take the damn thing," she spat. Pivoting on her heel, she stalked away with her nose in the air. Alexis laughed again like it was the funniest thing she'd ever seen.

"Thanks," Brenna said, attempting to be polite while maintaining her defenses. Alexis did favors for no one. She stepped around the redhead as if she were a poisonous snake that merited a wide berth – which was basically true. She could feel Alexis following her and sighed, wondering what manifestation the coming torment would take. Still fuming from her encounter with Missy, Brenna felt ready to tackle anything Alexis threw her way. Her eyes scanned the room for Chrissie and found her on the other side of the store, examining the various accessories along the wall. She felt quite capable of handling Alexis on her own, but it was always nice to know where your back-up was, especially when it took the form of the feisty Chrissie Vaughn.

Brenna stopped at the counter, studiously examining a rather pretty scarf. It wouldn't go with her dress, but it was very nice, and it gave her an excuse to ignore the enemy behind her. But Alexis wasn't in the habit of going unnoticed.

"You know why Missy hates you, right?" the girl inquired, a smug look on her face.

Of course Brenna didn't know, but she didn't want to hear anything that the cheerleader had to say. She turned away from her, fixing her attention on the assortment of necklaces. Alexis was not so easily put off. She sidled up to Brenna and placed a porcelain elbow on the counter.

"Missy and Mitch had a thing last Christmas," she whispered in a tone reserved specifically for the best gossip. "It didn't last long, but it was hot."

"Hot?" The word escaped her mouth before Brenna could stop it.

Knowing she'd successfully captured the blonde's attention, Alexis' grin grew more pronounced. "Yeah, 'all the way' hot. Mitch scored a home run faster than I would have thought him capable."

It took Brenna a second to realize what Alexis meant, and then it hit her – Mitch slept with Missy. Of course, there was no way to know if she was lying or not. Brenna couldn't ever remember hearing Mitch's name attached to a girl, but then again, she hadn't really been paying attention to his love life until recently. Even if it were true, though, why would it matter to Missy who Mitch dated? They hadn't been together for almost a year, and she had a very attentive boyfriend now.

"Last I saw, Missy seemed pretty fond of Tate. I don't think she's pining over Mitch."

Alexis smiled, fingering the dangling necklace that Brenna had been admiring. "Oh, Missy and Tate are joined at the, um, hip." She grinned wickedly at some mental image her mind had conjured. "But you never forget your first, especially when he dumps you the next day. You know?" Alexis smirked, leaning down to whisper in her ear. "No, I guess you wouldn't."

Brenna's cheeks went crimson. She felt no shame in being a virgin, but the way the cheerleader launched her parting shot made it sound like it was because no boy in his right mind would ever touch Brenna.

"See you around," Alexis said as she departed, feeling quite pleased with herself.

At the counter, Brenna was left to battle her emotions. Well played, Miss Rydell. The girl had a finally found a way to get under her skin. Who would have thought a boy would be the key to her success? The idea of Mitch sleeping with Missy upset her tremendously. So much so that she didn't know what to do with herself. She wanted to believe it was lie, but it probably wasn't. Alexis would have more fun telling the truth, reveling in the fact that Brenna would ask Mitch about it, and enjoying the aftermath of confirmation. With a bomb like that to drop, no wonder she told Missy to let her have the dress. She probably assumed that Brenna wouldn't want it anymore.

Sad. Brenna was sad. But did she have any right to be? After all, she wasn't dating Mitch. She had no claim on him – just the unverified suspicion that he was interested in her. He wasn't hers, but there had been the possibility of it. Now she didn't know what to think. Alexis would have her believe that he was looking to make her another notch on his bedpost, but that didn't seem in line with Mitch's character. But if he really cared about Missy, why did he dump her the next day? It didn't make sense. To get to the truth, she would have to ask Mitch – as Alexis knew she would. What Brenna did next would hinge upon his answer. It was only fair that he be allowed to speak.

"So, what do you think of this?" Chrissie appeared at her side, holding up a simple, short necklace of white beads shaped like roses.

Brenna gave it a cursory glance. "It's great. Let's get it."

Chrissie deflated like a balloon. "What's wrong?" she asked. "I thought you were having fun."

"I am," she replied, injecting enthusiasm into her words. "I've just spent enough time shopping. I've got so much homework that I need to do. Besides, I'm happy with my dress and I think the necklace you picked is perfect. Why waste time when you've found what you're looking for?" That was a very Brenna-ish answer.

The younger girl remained unconvinced, but she reluctantly agreed to leave. Both Brenna and Missy refused to meet each other's gazes while Brenna's purchases were rung up. Once the transaction was completed, the blonde practically ran out of the store, dragging a bewildered Chrissie with her.

CHAPTER TWELVE

When she went to school on Friday, Brenna told herself that she wouldn't let the Mitch-Missy love connection get in her way of her mission to uncover Mystery Girl's identity. She needed to remain focused and rational. The crowded hall was not the place to ask Mitch about his history with Missy. Furthermore, she'd wrestled the entire evening with whether or not she should even pose the question. Why did it bother her so much? What did she hope to accomplish from a conversation like that?

One part of her brain argued that it was her business to learn all about Mitch in order to figure out who was stalking him. Missy didn't seem the stalker type. Plus, she wasn't blond, and the red hoodie-blue leggings combo didn't sound like an outfit Missy would be caught dead in. But maybe Mitch had other girlfriends in his closet – ones who fit the description of Mystery Girl. As much as she tried to rationalize it, Brenna knew that wasn't really it, though. Something inside of her was warming up to the idea of a relationship with Mitch, and she didn't know how this revelation factored into their future. Of course, right now they had no future because the boy had yet to do anything to secure it.

In spite of what Brenna told herself, it was hard to stand in the hall with him, feel the closeness of his presence, stare into his eyes, and let him touch her without thinking about it. What had brought Mitch and Missy together in the first place? They didn't seem like they had much in common. Sure, they were both in ASB and they both dressed nice, but that was about it. Maybe that coupled with raging hormones was enough.

"You're quiet today," Mitch observed, leaning into her. "Everything okay?"

No, not really.

Brenna nodded. "I'm just a little tired, I guess." She wished Van had stayed with them. Something to divide her attention from Mitch would have been nice.

"Did you find a dress last night?"

Hmm. Maybe she could do a little probing with the open door he'd unintentionally given her. "Yes, I found it at Trendsation, that store where Missy works," she added, watching his face. Did her eyes deceive her or did he flinch at the mention of Missy's name?

If he did, he recovered quickly, slipping a small smile onto his face. "I look forward to seeing it tomorrow."

An awkwardness settled between them, which confirmed in Brenna's mind that there definitely had been something between the two. Unlike yesterday, when the crowd around them faded from view, Brenna was highly aware of the students lingering in the hall. Jared Guthrie was being studiously ignored by a more confident-looking Benny McBride. Hannah and Lucas were pouring over a math book, discussing the intricacies of numbers. Fisher Brown was flicking the end of Sara Xavier's brown ponytail as she fiddled with her flute case. Paige was talking nonstop – most likely about some pressing issue like fair trade – to an inattentive Autumn, who was busy drawing on her arm with a black permanent marker. Brenna didn't see Keiko, who was usually with them.

And then there was Missy. The thoroughly delighted girl was getting groped in public by her boyfriend, Tatum Powell. They were an odd pair – the perfectly coiffed Missy and Tate with his baggy jeans and t-shirts. He wasn't especially good-looking with his nearly orange hair, large blue eyes, and big nose, but he was built well and an incredible guard on the basketball court. He might not be exceptionally bright, but he was amiable, and Missy seemed quite taken with him. But that didn't mean she couldn't still be nursing a serious grudge against Mitch. Most girls were quite capable of emotional multitasking when it came to boys.

"She showed up at my house last night," Mitch quietly confessed.

For one terrifying moment, Brenna thought he meant Missy, but then she dismissed the idea as ridiculous. There was only one "she" he could be referring to.

"Why didn't you call me?" Brenna sounded a little more demanding than she'd intended, but hadn't they established a protocol for a reason? What if Mystery Girl got aggressive or something and no one knew that Mitch was in trouble until it was too late?

Embarrassed, he ducked his head. "I was going to, but then I wondered if maybe she showed up because of what we did yesterday."

"But that's why we're doing it," Brenna reminded him. "We want to drive her out into the open."

He nodded. "I know, but then I got to thinking, what if I called you and you came over and that made her mad."

Mitch was thinking about the note. He was afraid she was going to get hurt. Instead of being annoyed over his concern for her safety, she decided to let it slide. After all, Mystery Girl's presence at Saturday's date was what they were shooting for.

"Exactly what happened?" she questioned, stooping down to

find his eyes. "Tell me, please. This is important stuff."

He closed his eyes, exhaling through his teeth. "I was up in my room, and I just happened to look outside the window. She was there, down on the ground, looking up at me."

Standing there as bold as brass, was she? "For how long?"

"I don't know," he replied with a shake of his head. "I didn't want to be the first to look away, like I was intimidated by her or something, but then my cell phone rang. I picked it up, and when I looked again, she was gone."

Mitch's distress was evident, though he tried to downplay it. Looking at his face, Brenna felt herself divide in two. The Brenna who was upset about Missy was pushed to the back seat while the Brenna who cared about Mitch, who got excited every time he drew near, took control of the situation. Wanting to encourage him, she took hold of his wrist. "This is going to stop. We'll catch her, and she won't bother you again. I promise."

The rest of the day fared better as Brenna beat her emotions in check. Mitch responded well to the change in her mood. Their cover as a newly established couple was secure. Still, she was glad when lunch ended and she could take a break from seeing Mitch until tomorrow.

"What names did you pick out for your baby?" Van had been pestering Brenna on and off during the day, trying to get her to come clean. She stubbornly refused under the argument that he'd tease her mercilessly about it, but he was nothing if not persistent. "Come on. We're handing the assignment in today for crying out loud."

Brenna sighed, giving in. "Fine. When we find out the sex, I'll tell you. That way you can only make fun of one name."

Savoring victory, Van pumped his fist in the air. "I'm naming my baby Lloyd Dobler."

"You're naming him after John Cusack's character in *Say*

Anything?" Really, that shouldn't have surprised her. Of course Van's baby would have an Eighties-inspired name. "I would have thought that you'd stick with your family's custom of using musician names."

"Nah, I'm bucking tradition." Van held his notebook over his head with two hands in tribute to that famous scene with the boom box. "I want to teach my progeny to shoot for the stars when it comes to love."

"And if you're having a girl?" she inquired, feeling ready for almost anything.

"Lloydette Doblerina," he replied without hesitation.

Anything but that. "You can't name a baby that!"

"I can name her whatever I want," Van declared superiorly. He leaned forward. "You do remember that these aren't real babies, right? These names don't really matter in the grand scheme of things."

Brenna frowned. "I still hope you get a boy."

Fortune smiled down on Van's robot offspring, and he pulled out a blue diaper pin. Brenna pulled out a pink one.

"Awww. Baby Girl Rutherford," Van cooed. "Now spill her name."

"Sophia Irene, which mean 'wisdom' and 'peace.'" Brenna waited for the laughter, but none came. Instead, Van looked thoughtful.

He tapped his chin. "Sophia Irene Rutherford is quite a mouthful for poor Lloyd Dobler, so we shall call her 'Sir' instead."

Only her best friend could take a meaningful name and twist it into something ridiculous. She figured the best way to kill his fun was to ignore him, so she did for the rest of the class period despite his persistent attempts to get her attention. The Van Embargo might have persisted through the evening just for fun if they hadn't had a standing date with a rabid dog.

"I always wanted a dog," Van stated glumly as he situated himself on the couch. *Cujo* was cued up and ready to go.

"A dog would have been good for you," Brenna replied as she walked into the living room, movie snacks in hand. "It would have made you more responsible. Too bad Stevie Ray is allergic."

Allergic was a bit of an understatement. Van's older brother couldn't be in close proximity to a dog without developing hives.

"I petitioned to get one when he went away to college, but Mom was all 'but then he could never come and visit.' I didn't see anything wrong with that," he muttered. Despite his words, Van got along swimmingly with his big brother – for the most part.

Brenna joined him on the couch. "*Zio* and my mom had a Great Dane when they were kids. He was a menace." Grandfather Rutherford had liked big dogs, because he'd felt that they increased his status as a man. Of course, he liked what it represented more than the animal itself. It had fallen to his children to keep the animal in line, which was difficult for them to do given that the dog was practically twice their size.

"So what was up with you today? You were tense every time Mitch came around." Van's insightful question came out of nowhere, unsteadying her nerves. She hadn't told him what Alexis had divulged to her because it had been too embarrassing at the time, but now, she felt like hearing his opinion.

"Mitch slept with Missy," she blurted out, cheeks flushing.

His eyes went wide with shock. "Last night?"

"No, last Christmas and then he dumped her the next day," Brenna clarified. "At least, that's what Alexis told me yesterday. We crossed paths while shopping."

Comprehension dawning in his eyes, Van nodded. "So that's why you were in a hurry to leave the store. You know she could be lying."

Yes, Brenna had told herself that repeatedly, but she didn't believe it and neither did Van. They knew Alexis too well.

"It bothers me, the thought of them together like that," she admitted, rubbing her fingers across the fabric of the couch. Her eyes concentrated on the pattern so other, less pleasant images didn't materialize in front of them. "If he dumped her the next day, that makes it seem like he's a certain kind of guy, and if he is, I don't want to get caught up in that. At the same time, though, that doesn't seem like him."

Van ran his hand through his hair, deep in thought. He knew what she was asking without asking it. As a guy, what did he honestly think of Mitch? Guys were different, unguarded, when they were around each other. She wanted to know if he'd ever seen anything in Mitch's behavior that might indicate him capable of such a despicable act. Van exhaled heavily and leaned forward, resting his elbows on his knees.

"Okay, I've logged plenty of time in the guys' locker room, and I've heard things that would curl your hair. But not from Mitch. What you see is what I've seen. He doesn't boast about sexual conquests, participate when guys start analyzing the finer points of female anatomy, or talk about who he wants to nail. That's not the kind of guy he is, but that doesn't mean he's immune to the physical. He has the same urges that Dylan has."

This was starting to sound like the "Little boys are made differently" speech that *Zio* had given her a few years ago, but she let him proceed without interruption.

"My guess is that he got caught up in a moment of weakness that he regretted, but that's just my gut talking." He shrugged, a gesture that conveyed both sympathy and uncertainty. "If you want answers, you gotta talk to him, but you already knew that."

Yes, she did. Closing her eyes, Brenna pinched the bridge of her nose. "That is not a conversation that I'm looking forward to having."

"It's real life. Everyone has baggage to deal with." He leaned back against the couch, relaxing now that the deep thinking part of their talk was over.

There was a knock at the door.

"Did you invite Mitch?" Van asked as Brenna got up to answer it.

She shook her head. The thought had crossed her mind earlier in the day, but she'd decided against it because she was tired of feeling self-conscious.

The person at the door was Duke. Shoulders hunched, he gave Brenna his best impression of a kicked puppy. "Grandma turned me out of the house," he announced dejectedly. "Apparently she finds me depressing."

"Can't imagine why," she replied with an eye roll.

"Tell me about it." Deliberately ignoring her sarcasm, he spread his hands. "The old woman has a heart of stone."

"So you decided to grace us with your presence?" She was torn between pity and laughter.

"Where else am I going to go? Besides, I think watching some good, old fashioned horror will be good for my soul," he told her, blinking his green eyes at her. "Aren't you going to let me in, Biddy?"

Brenna sighed and pulled him inside. "Come on, Sunshine," she said, "but if you eat all of our movie snacks, I will have to hurt you."

"Did you make cookies?" he inquired, perking up. She nodded, pleased that he wasn't too far gone to fail to get excited about food.

Van snorted when he caught a look at Duke. "Danny, if you're gonna keep moping around like that, I'll have to revoke your Man Card."

"Says the boy who spends half an hour on his hair each day,"

Duke shot back, grabbing a cookie as he sat down. "What are we watching anyway? Better be something terrifying."

"*Cujo*," Brenna told him as she disappeared into the kitchen for more soda. She could hear the two debating whether or not a man-killing Saint Bernard qualified as terrifying. According to Duke, it didn't even if Stephen King did write the book. Van declared that Duke's judgment was impaired by his women troubles because Stephen King was a genius when it came to horror. When she came back, Van was leaning forward on the couch, his face uncharacteristically sullen.

"Actually, before we start the movie, I think there's something that we should to tell you, Danny. Brenna and I have some big news," he said, getting to his feet. Brenna almost missed the sly wink he gave her right before his eyes misted over and he slipped his arm around her. "We're expecting." In a natural move, Van placed his hand on Brenna's stomach while she dropped her head to his shoulder, eager to play along.

For a moment, a wide-eyed Duke sat immobile in his chair, a cookie sticking halfway out of his mouth. Then Brenna giggled, and the young man's heart restarted. "That isn't funny!" he all but shouted as he wiped his mouth. The scoundrels begged to differ as they collapsed on the couch amidst gales of laughter, Van nearing hyperventilation.

"Technically, it's true. We're going to get our simulation babies soon," Brenna clarified once she recovered. "We have to pick out names and the whole nine yards."

Still furious, Duke glared at her.

"Oh, lighten up, Captain Gloomy," Van cried, wiping tears from his eyes.

"Don't pull that on Abe unless you have a death wish," Duke advised.

"I couldn't do that to him now, what with him stressing about

Brenna's date tomorrow."

And like that, the cat was out of the bag. She'd been sort of hoping that she could get through Saturday without Duke finding out about her date with Mitch. Now he was going to get annoyingly overprotective and want to know all of the details.

"You're going on a date? It's with that boy, isn't it? The one who came over the other night?" Duke pressed, getting serious. He sounded irritated. Great.

"His name is Mitch," she nodded, a tad defensive.

"I knew he was sniffing!" he declared with passion, jabbing his finger into the air. "I hate sniffers. They're no good. When did you plan on telling me about this?"

Brenna crossed her arms over her chest and shot Van a thank-you-very-much look. "I don't tell you everything that's going on in my life, and it's only a first date. It may not go beyond that."

Even as she said it, Brenna felt a very telling pang of disappointment. She hadn't considered the kind of havoc the charade would play on her emotions. Her heart had been all over the spectrum the past few days, and she still wasn't completely sure where she'd landed on the subject. Perhaps the faux date hadn't been the wisest of moves.

Duke didn't look hopeful. "What are you and the Sniffer going to do?" His voice was heavy with a suspicion that Brenna didn't feel she deserved.

"Oh, just the usual stuff – drink copious amounts of alcohol and engage in inappropriate touching before we meet up with his coven for the ritual sacrifice," she replied, earning her a disapproving look from Duke and a hearty guffaw from Van. "We're eating dinner. What do you think we're going to do?" She shook her head, reaching for the remote. "As fascinating as my love life is, we have a movie to watch."

The credits rolled and the terror commenced. Unlike last

week's movie, this one was a bona fide nail-biter. Brenna sat on the couch, knees drawn into her chest so her eyes could hide if needed. She wasn't scared so much as thoroughly delighted by the genuine thrill of dread coursing through her veins. Compared to her best friend, she was a picture of calmness. Van was on his feet for almost the entire movie, preparing to bolt the second the Saint Bernard magically appeared in the living room. Despite his antics, he was hardly a sufficient distraction from the suspense. And Duke, who had deigned to judge the movie before seeing it, jumped more than once.

"So, do you still wish you owned a dog?" Brenna inquired of her best friend when the movie was over.

Van had his head in his hands, trying to steady his breathing. "Sure," he said, looking up. "Why not? Poor, sick Cujo isn't the villain in this story. The blame belongs to his owner for not vaccinating him."

"That's funny coming from the guy screaming 'shoot him!' every time the dog appeared on screen," Duke replied, cleaning up the popcorn he'd spilled during a particularly tense moment.

Van ignored his comment.

The great thing about the horror movie was that it had them all too keyed up to go back to the subject of Brenna's impending date, which was just fine with her. She had no desire to be further grilled by Duke. They cleaned up the living room, taking their dishes back into the kitchen and straightening up the couch. A few minutes later, Brenna said goodbye to Duke. He had a slight spring in his step, which delighted her to see.

"You'd better get some sleep tonight," Van said, "or you'll look all nasty on your date."

Scowling, Brenna thumped his shoulder. "You never told me who you got as your partner tomorrow."

"Keiko." He was taken aback by the surprised look on her

face. "What? She's already proved herself to us. It just made sense."

Brenna couldn't disagree with that logic.

"Oh, I haggled on your behalf. You owe her two dozen chocolate and peanut butter chip cookies." Van leaned in, smirking. "Hope you have sweet dreams." Laughing, he bounded down the sidewalk and out of her reach.

Chapter Thirteen

The hours leading up to her stakeout date with Mitch went
abnormally fast in Brenna's opinion. The butterflies in her
stomach weren't fluttering like they normally did when she was
nervous. No, these butterflies were having some sort of rave.
Playing loud, pulsating music and dancing their tiny hearts out.

And it wasn't even a real date – how many times had she told
herself that? This was strictly business, but in her heart, she knew
it was far more than that. Tonight held a tremendous significance
for both her investigation and her possible future with Mitch that
couldn't be ignored. Talking with Van, even briefly, had solidified
her decision to ask him about Missy. The way she was feeling,
torn in two by her emotions, was unacceptable. Only tackling the
issue head on would bring Brenna any amount of peace.

But when to do it? Surely not at the beginning of the date. A
question like that could ruin the entire evening, depending on how
he responded. No, she needed to wait for the right moment.
Hopefully, she'd be able to sense it when it arrived. Until then, she
had to keep calm.

Taking a hot bath helped. Her muscles relaxed as she closed
her eyes, her mind drifting away to the classical music that she'd

turned on. She stayed in the water as long as she dared before deciding it was time to get ready. She'd decided to wear her hair down and unadorned. Chrissie had tried to convince her to wear makeup, but Brenna wanted to keep it simple. She did agree to wear a delicate shade of pink lipstick, though.

As she did some final primping in front of the mirror, Brenna felt faint traces of pride in her appearance. Her amazing dress fit her perfectly, and her golden hair glowed vibrantly. Now she understood why girls took so much time to get ready to leave the house. Feeling pretty felt good. She wasn't sure the sensation was enough to make her completely change the way she dressed, but it was nice to indulge in it once in a while.

There was something about seeing herself so put together that helped Brenna keep cool even when the doorbell rang. Her uncle opened the door and invited Mitch inside. Upon seeing him, she nearly laughed as it looked like the two had coordinated their outfits. Mitch was wearing a light blue shirt with khaki slacks. He handled small talk with Abraham well, not looking the least bit flustered at being politely interrogated by the Chief of Police.

When he had been satisfied, Abraham sent the couple on their way. Mitch found Brenna's hand as they walked to the car. She smiled, knowing her uncle was watching them from the window.

"You look amazing," Mitch told her, eyeing her dress.

"Thank you," she replied. Funny how three small words could start the rave in her stomach going again. "You're pretty dashing yourself. I feel quite certain that no one will be able to see through our disguises."

As Mitch opened the car door, he leaned his head down to her ear. "We are far too cunning for our own good."

Once safely inside, Brenna pulled out her cell phone and sent Van a text: *Leaving now. Meet you at Harvey's.*

His reply was almost instantaneous: *Roger. Commencing with*

Operation GBALL now.

"What's GBALL?" inquired Mitch as he peered over Brenna's shoulder.

She flushed, keeping mum as she put her phone in the cup holder. Operation Get Brenna A Love Life was something Van in his infinite immaturity had come up with. She'd refused to acknowledge it. "Some acronym Van devised," she said dismissively. "I don't remember what it stands for."

"So let's go over the plan once again," Mitch suggested as he drove. "We'll go to dinner, eat food, and chat like a normal couple, all the while looking for Mystery Girl. Van and Keiko will be doing likewise. If we spot her –"

"When we spot her," Brenna clarified with an upraised finger.

"When we spot her, we'll give them the signal and head off to the Kokosing Trail, where they'll endeavor to trap her."

She nodded.

"But how can we be sure that she'll follow us to the trail?"

Not wanting to emphasize the creepiness of Mystery Girl's actions, Brenna chose her words carefully. "If she follows you to Harvey's, she'll follow you to the trail. She won't like the idea of you taking me to a private place like that. She'll have to know what you're doing with me."

Gripping the steering wheel, Mitch opened his mouth only to close it and then nod in understanding.

She continued, "Theoretically, the plan should work, but even if some unexpected turns should occur, I feel quite confident in our ability to punt."

"Keiko seems like an odd choice for Van to recruit. I didn't realize you were such good friends with her." Mitch pulled out onto the interstate that connected Mount Vernon to the neighboring town where Harvey's was located. Traffic was light as his car sped silently down the road.

At first blush, Brenna felt the same way. Truthfully, she hadn't given much thought to who Van would get to accompany him, so after she'd gotten over the shock of it, she realized that Keiko was the perfect person.

"Technically, we aren't, but she helped us last month during the Dark Avenger investigation. I have great respect for her abilities." Brenna gave him a quick rundown of the services Keiko had provided. "That's all strictly confidential," she added with a smile.

Mitch shook his head, his voice full of false condemnation. "As your ASB President, I am shocked and appalled by your blatant disregard for the privacy of your classmates."

"I know, I'm such a rebel," Brenna remarked dryly.

Once business was concluded, conversation drifted into casual waters, which suited Brenna just fine. She wanted to learn more about the boy she was sitting next to. Did he like to go to parties? No, he was more of a homebody. Which kinds of movies did he prefer? Comedies because they were unrealistic. Did he read a lot? Yes, especially historical biographies. So did that mean history was his favorite subject? Yes, it did. Did he play video games like Van? Not since he was a sophomore.

The more they talked, the more his answers became more telling of his personality and what his life was really like. The stream of conversation paused only when they had to order dinner. Like it had been the first day at the lockers, talking with Mitch was easy and comfortable despite the change in setting. They kept their eyes open for Mystery Girl, of course. Neither of them could forget the reason that brought them together.

"My dad runs the Cincinnati branch of a Manhattan investment company," Mitch told her when the topic turned to home life. In his lap was a half-eaten hamburger. Brenna quietly chewed her own as he talked. "Don't ask me what he does exactly.

All I know is that it's super stressful and he travels a lot."

"Mount Vernon to Cincinnati is a long commute," Brenna observed. It was nearly three hours. She couldn't imagine anyone wanting to make that drive every day. Sometimes going to and from school was enough driving time for her.

"The company owns an apartment in the city. He stays there a lot during the week, because he doesn't like to be in the car that much in one day."

There was something in his tone that made Brenna think that Mr. Hamilton didn't come home much on the weekends either. She felt bad for Mitch. She wouldn't like it if *Zio* stayed away like that. Of course, that was assuming that Mitch even liked his dad. She remembered that day in Honey B's when Mitch talked about college. He'd been quite vehement in his desire to leave Ohio. Maybe it wasn't the state he wanted to get away from.

Looking down at her basket, she picked up a fry. A light breeze blew threw her open window out through Mitch's. It was a beautiful night, though marred slightly by neglectful parents. She tried to keep her voice free of the sadness she felt. "What about your mom? Does she work?"

"Not technically, but she's big into philanthropy. She's got significant ties to some of the major charities in Cincinnati. Volunteering and attending board meetings take up a lot of her time."

The passing of a carhop caught his attention and he watched her progress as she skated past the car, black ponytail streaming out behind her like a flag. Harvey's was hopping with people, which would provide Mystery Girl with the perfect opportunity to blend in – if she bothered to show up. So far, there had been no sign of her. A few rows behind them, Van and Keiko were probably bored out of their minds. Brenna tried not to let it worry her. The night was still young. There was plenty of time for

Mystery Girl to show up.

But as for Mitch, she understood what his words meant. "She stays in the city with your dad." He nodded.

All of that time spent to help others and there was none to be spared for her own child. Was she completely devoid of motherly sentiment? Apparently, Brenna decided. In essence, Mitch lived alone with his parents behaving more like guests than residents when they finally turned up at home. That might seem like a pretty sweet deal to most people their age, but Brenna could tell that Mitch didn't care for the arrangement. His downcast eyes coupled with his determined chin were a dead giveaway to the conflicting desires he felt – to be a self-reliant young man and to have his parents behave like they were supposed to.

Why would the Hamiltons choose to live in Mount Vernon when their work kept them in Cincinnati and away from their son? It didn't make any sense unless they'd wanted a child only for the sake of being able to say they had one while making small talk at dinner parties. Brenna could just picture Mrs. Hamilton, hobnobbing with some socialite at a fundraiser, bragging about how her son was a stellar student and ASB President, or Mr. Hamilton declaring him to be a chip off the old block – as if either parent could take credit for how their son turned out. He basically was raising himself these days. She frowned, not thinking very much of Mitch's parents.

"You're probably wondering why we moved here in the first place," he guessed, swirling a fry in his ketchup. He hadn't been born here. Brenna remembered when Mitch showed up at school in the second grade. They didn't get too many new faces, so they tended to take note of who was new. "My parents didn't want to raise me in the city. They liked the small community feel of Mount Vernon."

It was also a safe place to leave your kid for days on end.

That was a crappy reason in Brenna's opinion, but she kept her mouth shut on that particular point.

She nodded. "It's a great place to be raised. That's why my uncle stayed here when I was born." Maybe mentioning *Zio* hadn't been the best idea. It would only be natural to draw comparisons between him and the Hamiltons. Actually, there wasn't much of a comparison to be made.

"Your mom," he started delicately, "how did she die? If you don't mind my asking."

The boy had basically admitted to being abandoned by his parents, so of course, she didn't mind. Brenna thought that she was much better off than him when it came to parents. At least her mother hadn't left her by choice. Her dad had been a deadbeat prior to her birth, so he didn't even merit consideration.

"She was in a really bad car accident, and she died giving birth to me."

He hadn't been expecting that. His face clouded over with sadness. "I'm sorry. I shouldn't have asked."

"It's okay, really. I like talking and thinking about her," Brenna told him. "She was pretty great. In fact, she's the reason that I work at Honey B's."

As anticipated, Mitch latched onto the happier topic and peppered her with questions. Brenna explained that Amelia, even at a young age, had been an incredible baker, going so far as to invent a few recipes of her own, and that interest had apparently been genetic. Brenna turned up at Honey B's the day she turned sixteen to see if Berthal was hiring. Technically, the baker hadn't been, but she'd been impressed by the young girl and took her on as an apprentice of sorts.

Of course, talking about baked goods got them in the mood for sundaes. As much as Brenna was enjoying her evening – the ice cream was every bit as good as she remembered it – a dark cloud hung over her head in the form of Missy. Time was running out for her to ask about Mitch's relationship with the cheerleader. But as she was wondering how to broach the subject, Mitch provided her with the perfect opportunity.

"So you and Van, you spend a lot of time together," he stated casually after their sundaes had arrived. "It's obvious that you guys are close. I was just wondering how he feels about this." He gestured to the car as a representation of their date. He was trying to play it cool, but Brenna had a fairly good idea of what he was getting at.

"He's not jealous, if that's what you mean," she said, knowing that it was. "It's not like that between us. It never has been. I mean, we love each other, but it's more like a brother-sister relationship."

Most of their classmates probably thought they were secretly in love with each other. When you saw two members of the opposite sex hanging out so much, it would be natural to assume that they either were or wanted to be a couple. She didn't fault Mitch for wanting to clarify her availability. In fact, she appreciated his concern for Van.

Nodding thoughtfully, Mitch stuck his spoon into his chocolate ice cream. "Good. I like Van, and I wouldn't want to upset him like that."

And speaking of romantic complications...

"There's something I need to ask you," she began, stomach churning. This wasn't a conversation she was looking forward to having, but there would be no peace of mind until the air was cleared.

Mitch nodded encouragingly. "You can ask me anything, Brenna."

"It's about you and Missy." She watched his features pale, and she wondered if he was regretting his eagerness. Oh man, how should she phrase this? "I heard that the two of you were intimate."

He didn't answer right away, unless you counted closing your eyes and pinching the bridge of your nose an answer. "Yeah, we were," he said after a moment. His voice was barely above a whisper as if speaking softly would lessen the blow. "We only did it once, though."

And that made it so much better.

Brenna folded her hands in her lap and looked away. "Oh."

The tiny word held incredible meaning for Mitch, who responded in near desperation. "Last Christmas was a really dark time for me. I felt like I was all alone. When Missy showed an interest, things happened fast and one thing led to another before I had time to think." He sighed and dropped his hands on the steering wheel. "It was the biggest mistake of my life, and there's not a day that goes by that I don't wish I'd waited for the right girl." There was no mistaking the significance of the look he gave her.

"I also heard that you dumped her the next day." In spite of how it seemed, Brenna wasn't trying to be cruel, but the truth had a way of hurting.

Again, he looked defeated. "I know how that looks, but believe me, that wasn't my intention. I didn't know how to fix the mistake I made, so I broke it off. I knew I hurt her, but I would have hurt her more if I'd continued in the wrong relationship. Missy and I weren't good together; we weren't even friends."

She could see his logic, but that didn't make the scenario any better. Honestly, she didn't see any way for him to make the end result better other than not having had sex with Missy at all. But that wasn't exactly something you could undo.

Her continued silence brought him pain. When he could take it no longer, he spoke up, "Brenna, I don't mean to trivialize what I did, but is this something we can get past? I've really enjoyed the time we've spent together, and I'd like to do more of it." His shoulders sagged under the weight of the moment. "I don't want to lose you."

Didn't want to lose her – that was the closest he'd come to admitting his feelings for her. It was a shame that it took a situation like this for him to verbalize it. Brenna could see the contrition on his face and knew his regret was genuine. But there were some obstacles that couldn't be overcome in a relationship and some situations that were better avoided altogether. So where did this one fall?

Fact: No one was perfect. Everyone made mistakes. The goal was not to wallow in one's mistakes but to deal with the pain and move forward. Mitch was trying to do that, and it should be encouraged.

Fact: She cared about him. Definitely as a friend and possibly more than that. The excitement she felt when they talked as well as the sting of sadness she'd been nursing over the past few days only drove that truth home more intensely. If she rejected him, his presence would leave a void in her life. But it wasn't a pain that couldn't be healed with time.

Fact: One couldn't retroactively stake a claim on a boy and remain a rational person. Even if they did start dating, Brenna couldn't punish him for having girlfriends before her. It wasn't fair, and it accomplished nothing. His past was his, not hers. Sure, it'd have ramifications on their future, but she couldn't hold it against him. He hadn't cheated on her or anyone else. He'd slept with the girl he was involved with, and while not the wisest move, unfaithfulness wasn't an issue.

Fact: Choosing to be with Mitch didn't mean she had to change her views on sex. Being the child of an unwed girl, Brenna had some pretty hard-nosed rules when it came to physical intimacy. She wasn't having sex until she was ready to deal with all of the possible ramifications, like pregnancy, which basically meant that she wasn't having sex until she was married. Period. If Mitch or any other boy didn't like that, they were free to move on to someone else. Her resolve was firm.

Based on that logic, the answer became clear.

"The short time we've spent together has impacted me more than I thought it would," she admitted, choosing her words carefully. In the spirit of fairness, she didn't want to say anything that wasn't true. "I would be sad if it ended." She smiled at his evident relief. And like that, the serious atmosphere was dispelled and happiness settled around them.

The feeling didn't last long.

"Awww, aren't you two just the sweetest thing?" Alexis appeared out of nowhere, leaning against the passenger door, ice cream cone in hand. She hunched down, resting an elbow on the door so she could stick her head inside the car – and give Mitch a perfect view of her breasts. There was a serious amount of cleavage on display. Brenna feared that at one false move, the girl would burst free from her top. For his part, Mitch was trying very hard not to stare. He seemed to be focusing on the cheerleader's forehead.

No one should be allowed to lick an ice cream cone like that in public.

"Imagine running into you two lovebirds here," she cried with false surprise. Truly, the girl had no shame. "Mitch, don't you just love Brenna's dress? I ran into her the other day at Trendsation. It was so cute how excited she was about her outfit."

Furious, Brenna didn't trust herself to speak. Instead, she shot Mitch a look, demanding that he take care of the situation. Immediately.

"I think Brenna looks beautiful," he replied, giving the object of his compliment a significant smile. Then his eyes took on a steely glint as they flashed back up at Alexis. "We're actually in the middle of a private conversation, and while I appreciate your kindness, we'd prefer to be alone."

Brenna marveled at Mitch's diplomacy. Clearly, being ASB President had taught him a few things about diffusing sticky situations.

"Oh, of course!" the offending girl replied as if she only just realized her error. "I just wanted to come say hi, and oh no!" In a swift, cunning move, Alexis upended her ice cream right on to Brenna's dress. "My total bad," she declared, laughing lightly. Reaching down, the redhead made a show of scooping up the chocolate ice cream while smearing it over the fabric as much as possible. The stain it left was huge.

Brenna couldn't let herself do it. She couldn't cry in front of Alexis Rydell. Not over a dress. No matter how much she wanted to. She clenched her hands into tight fists, channeling all of her emotions out through the tips of her fingers.

Her work done, Alexis departed with a satisfied smile on her face. Mitch leaned over to help, paper napkins in hand. "I'm so sorry," he offered unnecessarily. "What can I do?"

"It's okay. It's just a dress," she replied, staring at the brown smear that went from her waist nearly to the hem of her skirt. Only the single most perfect dress she'd ever owned. "I need to wash it out before it sets in. I'll be right back."

She escaped from the car before he could reply. She walked as fast as she could without actually running, ignoring the pitying looks from the patrons. Thankfully, the bathroom was empty. As Brenna set about trying to salvage her dress, she didn't try to fight it as a few treacherous tears escaped. Never before had she felt so capable of violence. She wanted to strike back at the cheerleader, but she knew that would only escalate things. No, she had to stay calm or at least pretend to be calm. Reacting would only show

Alexis that she'd won.

And really, what had the girl done but mess up her dress? Yes, that had been humiliating, but Brenna wasn't so superficial that she couldn't get over it eventually. An ice cream stain had no bearing on her relationship with Mitch, either. Still, she was frustrated that it affected her so much. Alexis' insults and slights had always rolled right off her back, but now that there was a boy involved, it was hard to remain impervious to such things for some reason. As she washed the stain out, Brenna consoled herself with the thought that some day, Alexis Rydell would get her comeuppance. That would truly be a day of celebration.

She sighed, looking down at the massive wet spot she was left with. The sight of it annoyed her almost as much as her self-pity. Slapping her hands down on the counter, she stared at her reflection.

"Pull yourself together," she commanded the face looking back at her. "Brenna Rutherford doesn't get flustered by such unimportant things. Get your head on straight."

That's when she noticed the other reflection in the mirror. Her heart kicked into high gear. Someone was peering into the girls' bathroom, watching her. The window was frosted so any distinguishing details were obscured for people on either side of it, but there was no doubt in Brenna's mind that it was her. Mystery Girl had finally shown herself.

Keeping her face impassive, Brenna headed back to the car, feeling grateful for the girl's timely appearance. Now she had something upon which to focus her energies instead of nursing her bruised ego. She slid into Mitch's car with an exceptionally large smile, which he returned. He was pleased to see her mood had improved.

"She's here," Brenna told him quietly.

"Where?" he asked, fighting the urge to scan the crowd for

her.

"She was looking in the bathroom window. I saw her in the mirror."

Mitch pulled a face. "She was watching you?"

The implication of this bothered him more than it did her. He looked like he was trying to figure out how to form words. Brenna didn't feel this was the time or the place to have that discussion, though. "You need to give Van and Keiko the signal now."

"Right," he nodded. "Lean towards me like we're having an intense moment, and give me a minute to make it look casual."

Brenna complied, smiling as their faces drew close. "Are you ready for phase two?"

He nodded. "It's not that complicated. Our part in all of this is pretty easy."

"I know. It seems unfair. I feel like I haven't done much to help," Brenna confessed.

"Trust me, you've done plenty." With delicate fingers, Mitch brushed the hair out of her face and tucked it behind her ear. Even though the gesture was staged, it still brought a blush to Brenna's cheeks. Embarrassed, she looked away, biting her lower lip. Down in the cup holder, her cell phone vibrated with an incoming text from Van.

Signal received. Time for phase two.

CHAPTER FOURTEEN

Later, Van would describe his night as surreal.

He hadn't really given much thought to being alone in a car with Keiko Martin for the evening. He was supposed to be on lookout, so he'd assumed that he would be spending his time looking out – looking at the patrons, looking for red hoodies and blue leggings, but not looking at Keiko. Not that there was anything wrong with her face. In fact, the combination of Caucasian and Japanese features made her almost exotic. And her hair, which was by far the most important feature on anyone, was amazing. How did she get it to glisten the way that it did? Was it natural or did she use a special hair care product? Depending on how the light caught it, there was almost a blueish tint to the sheen that was absolutely fascinating. He was curious about the texture of it, too.

But that was a second-place detail. Looking for Mystery Girl was the priority. Keiko, however, saw a flaw in his plan.

"We're not in a tinted van in a dark alley," she told him, frowning.

"Ah, but we *are* in a van," the boy cheekily interjected, holding up a finger. A rather unglamorous van that had seen too many road trips. There was nothing state-of-the-art about it, but it did offer them a slightly elevated position from which to people-watch.

She gave him a look that told him exactly what she thought of his interruption and continued, "We can't just sit and watch everyone like a hawk or people will notice and start to watch *us*. Our goal is to see everything without being seen."

Keiko then suggested that, using the rear view mirror, they divide the windshield in half, and she would be in charge of watching the portion in front of Van up through the driver's side window. Doing it like this would allow her to position her body so it looked like she was talking to Van while she monitored the area. She recommended that he do the same on her side. Upon considering it, Van approved of her suggestion. Mitch and Brenna were two rows ahead of them and two cars to the right. He had a perfect view of them.

"I can't believe Mitch has a stalker," Keiko said, wrinkling her nose in distaste. "I can't believe she goes to our school!"

Her sudden intensity made Van jump. "Relax. She's not stalking you. Besides, we're going to catch her."

"I know, but still! First, bullies are getting beaten with lead pipes, and now, our good-natured ASB President is the subject of a made-for-television movie. What is going on this year? We're seniors! We should be having fun! Not being scared for our lives!" Wide-eyed, Keiko's voice grew more high-pitched with each word that flew out of her mouth.

"Woman, please! No one's life is in danger, so calm down!" Van shot back with more assurance than he felt. His mind suddenly flashed back to the threatening note, and he wondered – again – if his best friend knew what she was doing.

Keiko buried her head in her hands.

"Are you wishing that I hadn't asked for your help?" he asked, curious given her outburst.

She shook her head, her silky hair swishing from side to side in an intoxicating way. Unbidden, Van's head moved, mimicking the movement. His hair didn't swish quite as well.

"No, I want to help. I just wish there wasn't a reason that my help was needed. You know?"

Yeah, he understood that completely. He'd much prefer it if there were no stalkers or angry students prone to violence, but unfortunately, that wasn't the case.

"I know what will make you feel better," he said as he rolled down the window. "A satiated stomach will make things feel less dire. Do you know what you want?"

Keiko bit her lip, tugging on a lock of her hair. It was looking especially blue at the moment. How *did* it do that? It was mesmerizing. He wanted to reach out and touch it. "The grilled chicken wrap," she said, frowning.

He pulled a face. Why were girls so uptight when it came to eating in front of guys? She didn't want to eat that any more than he did. Why couldn't she just order what she wanted? He of all people, with his hair and his wardrobe, couldn't give a crap about what she ate.

"Is that what you really want?" he pressed.

"I want a cheeseburger," she admitted, "but I shouldn't have it. I'm supposed to be on a diet."

His eyes automatically looked her up and down, which was unnecessary since – being a male with eyes – he'd checked her out when he picked her up. She'd looked great in her jeans and knit top. Did she have that I'm-so-skinny-that-I-look-like-a-pre-pubescent-boy look going for her? No, but he didn't find anorexia attractive. Was she petite like Brenna? No, but that wasn't a look he went for either. Keiko was soft with delicate curves that made her look like she should be the subject of a Botticelli painting. If

Van was a painter, he would paint someone like her. Maybe clad in a dark blue gown, standing on a rock in the middle of the stormy sea as her hair billowed around her.

Man, he really had to cut down on reading so much gothic fiction. It didn't matter if it was Halloween.

"You say that," he voiced aloud, "but I can't see any reason why you need to be on diet."

Disheartened, Keiko sighed. "You don't live with my mom, and you don't have Nana Martin's body type." She puffed out her cheeks and rounded out her arms like she had blown up like a balloon.

"Nana Martin sounds hot." He waggled his eyebrows, earning him an eye roll as she tried not to smile. "I'm going to order you a cheeseburger."

"No onion!" she was quick to say as he leaned out of the window to press the intercom button.

After Van placed their order, they sat back in their respective positions and watched, not talking about anything that required more than half of their brain like the public school system in America. Van rattled off a few of the major flaws he saw while Keiko countered with what she considered to be the pros of it. The discussion then gave way to video games, whether or not eating sushi could kill you, and why ketchup was so hard to get out of the bottle.

"I don't understand what's going on here," Keiko announced after their food had arrived.

"Well, this is called a cheeseburger." Speaking carefully, Van pointed to her basket. "You eat it and it gives you energy to go about your day. It's not incredibly nutritious but it tastes great."

Fighting a smile, she huffed. "I meant I don't understand this," she pointed vaguely at him. "I don't understand you."

"That's because I defy explanation." He shot her a wicked

grin.

Brows pinched together, Keiko regarded him thoughtfully. He could almost hear the gears of her mind turning. It was unnerving to be stared at like a bug under a microscope.

"What?" he demanded, annoyance setting in.

"I always thought you were an idiot. The way you dress, wear your hair, and behave – it's comical," she admitted with brutal honesty. "You act as if you're irresponsible, but you're not."

"And how do you know that?"

"Because someone like Brenna – who was born responsible – wouldn't put her life in your hands if she thought you wouldn't have her back. You're very serious about taking care of her, and I'm not just talking about now. You did so during that confrontation with Kevin."

That was not an event upon which Van liked to dwell. He looked away from the girl's piercing stare, focusing on what was going on outside.

"A few weeks ago, I wouldn't have thought you capable of such things," Keiko continued.

"And now?" he pressed.

"Now I know better," she concluded. "You can be counted upon during trying times."

Van shrugged, downplaying the real way he felt about her compliment. It was hard to do since he was used to hearing everyone talk about how ridiculous he was. "I'm so glad I meet with your approval," he said with as much humor as he could muster.

"You should be. I'm very judgmental."

He could hear the teasing in her voice, and he flashed her a smile, which she returned. She was hard to put your finger on, this Keiko Martin with the lovely hair.

"How's your burger?" he asked, stealing another glance at her as she savored a bite.

Keiko sighed, delighted. "Yummy. I'm so glad I listened to you." There was a wistfulness to her tone that Van didn't understand until he saw the longing look that she was trying not to give his onion rings. She obviously wanted one but was either too polite or too self-conscious to ask. To compromise for getting a cheeseburger, she opted against a side dish. That was clearly a bad decision.

He held out his basket to her. "Would you like some?"

Keiko's hair swished from side to side again, indicating no. He didn't buy it. "You know you want some. Why don't we share?" He picked up a handful and deposited them into her basket.

The look she gave him made Van feel extremely self-conscious. "What?"

"Don't you like those?" she asked.

"Yeah, they're great," he affirmed, wondering what the big deal was. It was onion rings, but she was staring at them like they were priceless diamonds.

"No one has ever shared food with me before," she admitted. "My family hordes food like gold. Well, Dad does. Mom tosses out the leftovers of anything we like the second our backs are turned. When it comes to eating, the Martin motto is 'You snooze, you lose.'"

Van could just picture the Martins stabbing each other for the coveted last potato. It would have been funny if Keiko hadn't looked so serious. He was feeling self-conscious again, so he gave a dismissive wave. "Oh, well, it's the opposite in my family. When we find something we like, we want everyone to enjoy it."

And she *did* enjoy them. It was fun to watch her eat them – more fun than watching for Mystery Girl at any rate. The girl was nowhere to be seen. Brenna and Mitch didn't seem to mind that she'd yet to show. They were talking nonstop, which he found highly amusing. Truth be told, he had felt bad for Mitch. On the surface, the intellectual, rational, straight-laced Brenna was quite intimidating even for a guy with a strong pedigree like Mitch. But then add in the fact that the girl was completely indifferent to your every advance, and Van marveled that Mitch was even still trying to get her.

Of course, now it was different since she knew she was being an idiot. Now she realized what the poor boy had been trying to do. Now she was responding to his advances. It was funny to watch Mitch transform from someone she liked well enough to someone she truly cared about. There were some feelings there, Van could tell. In fact, he'd been surprised how quickly they seemed to bubble up. Brenna was usually more measured than that, but matters of the heart – even her heart apparently – worked differently from the brain. Those two were about three steps from locking lips.

"You're in serious contemplation mode. What are you thinking about?" Keiko asked.

"I'm wondering how soon it will be before Brenna and Mitch start making out," he confessed.

His honesty surprised her. "Oh, does it upset you that much?"

Van was about to ask why when he realized what she meant. Keiko thought that he had feelings for Brenna. "No, because I'm not in love with her."

"Oh," she repeated, blinking rapidly as she processed his words. With that expression, she kinda looked like a robot – a half-Asian robot with really amazing hair and an irrational fear of obesity. "Why not?"

"Because that'd be like dating my sister, and incest is disgusting and wrong," he replied, his eyes sweeping across the windshield until they naturally came to rest on Keiko. "We're perfect best friends for each other, but as a couple, we'd be horrible. My quirks wouldn't be half as charming as they are now."

"Okay, so are they really dating or not?" she asked, brows pinched together in confusion. "It looked real at school, but now I know it's a ploy. If they start making out though, that seems like a big concession for the sake of staying in character, so to speak."

"Mitch is practically in love with Brenna," Van told her, "so it's real for him even though he knows it's just for show. Brenna didn't realize how he felt until a few days ago, so now she's sorting out her feelings. It's been rather difficult guiding her through the whole process."

Her curiosity satisfied for the time being, Keiko nodded as she looked out the window again. "I've seen red sweaters, red sweatshirts, blue jeans, and blue skirts, but no red hoodies or blue leggings. What are we going to do if the stalker doesn't show up? How much longer can they sit there?" She gestured vaguely to Mitch's car.

"No need to panic," he promised. "They haven't even ordered ice cream yet. There's plenty of time."

No sooner had the words left his mouth than Mitch leaned out his window to order dessert. Van followed suit and a few minutes later, both he and Keiko were slurping chocolate ice cream cones. So far, this stakeout sure beat the only other one he'd been on. Sitting outside Cameron Irby's house for hours until Brenna made it home safely had been nothing short of coma inducing. That had been dreadful, but this, sitting in a van with a girl, eating junk food – this was the kind of stakeout he could get used to.

"Why do you love the Eighties so much?" Keiko asked without preamble. "You weren't even born in that decade."

Her blunt practicality was beginning to remind him of an uncensored Brenna. It was oddly comforting. "Everything was larger than life back then. Big hair, big clothes, big angst. It's a decade that screams to be noticed. Plus, people weren't afraid to be who they were. That appeals to me because I'm weird."

"You are weird," Keiko confirmed but not in a way that made Van think it was a bad thing. "Your parents didn't give you much of a chance, though, with that name of yours."

Highly offended, Van wrinkled his nose. "And what is wrong with Van Halen?"

"It's a rock band, not a name you give a baby."

"For your information, my name holds great significance for my parents. They met at a Van Halen concert, and the rest, as they say, is history."

Keiko snorted. "How romantic."

"It is for them," Van countered. "Romance is what you make of it."

They got back to business, but the only girl that caught Van's attention was Alexis Rydell, a femme fatale if ever there was one. The cheerleader was slinking her way towards Mitch's car, wearing an outfit no self-respecting hooker would be caught dead in. The look on her face was nothing short of devious.

"Crap," he muttered. This was an unforeseen complication. "What does she want?"

"She's hell-bent on evil," Keiko observed coldly, her eyes narrowing into slits. "Should we intervene? I'd be happy to drop her like a ton of bricks."

The girl's enthusiasm made him smile as the mental image played out in his head. As appealing as it was, he knew that wouldn't be what Brenna would want. It went against his every inclination not to try to help, but Van shook his head resolutely. "No, we're supposed to avoid being seen together. Brenna wouldn't want us to sacrifice the mission to save her from a spot of torment."

They watched Alexis' head disappear inside the car, and when it reemerged a few minutes later, the cheerleader was smiling like a Cheshire cat. Not a good sign.

"Where did her ice cream go?" he wondered.

Taking a guess, Keiko spat waspishly, "I'm betting she dropped it on Brenna's dress."

A moment later, Brenna exited the car. Van couldn't see his best friend's face, but the set of her shoulders and the restrained way she walked told him that she was upset. Very upset. He pulled out his cell phone and sent a quick text message, asking what had happened. Mitch responded, confirming Keiko's suspicion.

Next to him, Keiko let out a righteous huff of indignation. "Alexis should be destroyed. You don't mess with a girl's dress." She began describing some very clever ways in which revenge could be won against Alexis Rydell. He laughed as she waxed poetically on the matter but took note of the savage glint in her eye that told him just how dangerous it might prove to cross Keiko Martin.

When he caught sight of Brenna again, Van sat up straight. "Something's happened," he remarked, his hand reaching automatically for his phone.

To casual observers, there was nothing about her appearance that would launch them into action, but Van knew his best friend's body language better than his own. The way her brow pinched together to form a tiny W, the way her lips were pressed into a thin line, how her shoulders rounded forward – these were signs to convey her continued distress over her confrontation with Alexis. But they were lies, for underneath them, she was practically aglow with excitement. Before she disappeared into the car, Van caught the tiny smile that managed to break through her mask.

"She's seen Mystery Girl," he told Keiko.

"How do you know that?" she demanded, her eyes searching the area.

Van stared intently at the pair in Mitch's car. "Trust me, I'm an expert in deciphering Brenna Rutherford. Now watch for the signal."

Not ten seconds later, Mitch brushed Brenna's hair behind her ear. "Ha!" Van shouted in triumph. "I told you!" He hastily sent the appropriate text response and watched as Mitch pulled out of his parking spot. Van's hand inched towards the keys dangling in the ignition.

"We can't leave yet," Keiko reminded him. "We're supposed to give them a ten minute head start."

That had been Brenna's idea. She said that they needed to give Mystery Girl enough time to get to her car and follow them. If Van and Keiko moved too quickly, she might get suspicious and abandon pursuit. He'd argued against waiting that long, but Brenna wouldn't hear it. She'd given him clear instructions on where he could find them. The couple would be taking a leisurely stroll down the Kokosing trail, which would provide Mystery Girl, Van, and Keiko with plenty of cover to stay hidden as they snooped.

"I know that," he replied, letting his hand drop into his lap. Glancing down at his phone, he marked the time. It was going to be a long ten minutes.

"We need to catch her tonight, Van." Keiko's voice was thick with unspoken implications. "She showed herself to Brenna. That's a first, right?" She turned to look at him. He nodded. "Then we have to catch Mystery Girl before she branches out even further."

Brenna painted a big target on her back. He knew that's what Keiko was thinking because it was the same thing he was thinking, too. It was the Dark Avenger all over again, he could feel it. Mind racing, Van drummed his fingers on the steering wheel. Well, he wouldn't let it get that far. Failure was not an option tonight. He and Keiko would see to that.

Eight minutes passed before Van started the engine. Keiko kept silent at his eagerness. Silence persisted as he drove, his foot nudging the accelerator when traffic permitted. In short order, he was parking his van next to the trail. They hopped out and stepped into the brush.

"We must move quickly but with a cat-like tread," Van instructed in a whisper. Around them were trees and tall bushes. Van kept the trail on his left as they moved forward. It was a quiet night and there weren't many people out. Just the occasional biker and jogger. They kept walking, knowing that Brenna had promised to linger by the first mile marker.

Thankfully, they didn't actually have to walk a full mile. From where they entered the trail, it was roughly a quarter of a mile until the rendezvous point. He knew it would take a few minutes to get there – he'd been out earlier in the day to time the trek – but at the rate he and Keiko had to go to keep quiet, a few minutes turned into nearly fifteen. Every little sound, the snap of a twig or the rustle of the wind through the trees, brought them to a standstill.

Van's heart thudded dully in his chest. His breathing had accelerated and his palms were sweaty – dead giveaways to his anxiety, but part of him was loving every minute of it. Kinda like the rush he and Brenna got watching horror movies. Yes, he was concerned for his best friend's safety. Yes, there was a very real chance that Mystery Girl was a dangerous psycho. But they were about to catch her and catching the bad guy was always awesome.

The last of the daylight had faded on their drive to the trail, so all they had now was the moon to guide their way. Trudging through the brush during the darkness of night to catch a ıysterious figure – it was a scenario that enticed Van's imagination to run wild, and he was eager to let it. He stole a glance at him companion.

Thanks to the moonlight, Keiko's hair was blue again, which in turn made her skin look like it was glowing. She was otherworldly – the ghost of an ill-fated lover straight from the pages of gothic literature. In such a story, he wouldn't be the hero. No, that would be Mitch, even though he wasn't Byronic, and Brenna would fall into the role of the damsel in distress. Van figured he would be another link to the spiritual realm. Perhaps a young priest. Stirred from sleep by a thunderstorm, he walked the church grounds with his heart heavy with heavenly concern. Thereupon he encountered the very ethereal soul walking alongside him, who shared her tale of woe and how she was constrained to walk the earth unless she could rescue a young man and his lover from the villain who caused her demise. Joined together, they would save the couple and the ghost would be released to Heaven.

Whoa. Maybe he should write that down. Then he shook his head. Okay, Vaughn, get your head in the game. Now wasn't the time to get distracted by anything other than Mystery Girl.

A twig snapped behind them. Keiko's icy fingers clamped onto his wrist. Van pressed his finger to his lips, indicating for the girl to remain quiet, and pivoted stealthily on his foot. He saw nothing out of the ordinary. It had probably been a small animal scurrying away from the sound of their approach. They moved forward but Keiko didn't let go of his wrist. It made him smile that she was spooked.

Van sensed that they were nearing the rendezvous point and intentionally slowed his steps. Keiko mimicked him. He motioned for her to stop, and he stepped up to peer behind a large bush. There, leaning against a tree, was Mystery Girl. Though she was shrouded in darkness, Van recognized the outfit from its description. She hadn't heard them approach, so intently was she watching the young couple talking on the path. That was good. Maybe she wouldn't realize they were there until they were ready to grab her. He waved for Keiko to join him, which she did. Then he took a step forward.

A twig snapped like a firecracker under his foot. Mystery Girl whirled at the sound, and Van's heart stopped.

Horror! Shock! Terror! And any other appropriate gothic utterance!

What was wrong with her face? She didn't have one! No, that wasn't quite it. There was a spot for a face on her head, but the features were obscured, indefinable, like they weren't there at all. Forget about who she was. Van's mind was suddenly racing to figure out *what* she was. Mystery Girl didn't look completely human.

But debating the matter was out of the question because she was running away. Van tore after her with Keiko bringing up the rear. Mystery Girl was nimble, darting through the trees and bushes like they were old friends, whereas Van kept stumbling to keep her in sight. Running through a forested area was a lot easier to do in a video game than real life. Behind him, the sound of Keiko's footfalls diminished. The girl was having even more trouble navigating the terrain than him, but he didn't have time to spare any concern for Keiko when his quarry was getting away. He nearly panicked every time he periodically lost sight of Mystery Girl behind the brush only to be relieved when she darted back into sight.

Crashing through an abnormally large bush, Van darted into a small clearing. It was completely still. Swearing internally as he panted, his eyes searched for some sign of disturbance. He saw nothing. He'd lost her.

"Which way?" A winded Keiko appeared next to him, holding her side.

Van threw up his hands. "She disappeared!"

"How is that possible? You were right behind her!" Frustration crept into her words. All that work for nothing. Van understood the feeling.

Someone giggled behind him. Distinctly female and young, it was the kind of laugh a girl would make after pulling a prank. So the joke was on them, was it? Van and Keiko whirled around, looking for Mystery Girl. Nothing.

Another giggle came on their left, then the right, and behind them again. Wait, how was she moving so quickly? He couldn't even hear her footsteps! Then giggling erupted from the same three spots at once. The hairs on the back of his neck stood up as a cold shiver ran down his spine. It wasn't possible, but his ears weren't deceiving him. Mystery Girl was everywhere, seeming to move as rapidly and silently as the wind.

"Van," Keiko whispered, her voice filled with dread. He knew her thoughts were in line with his – something unnatural, something befitting a gothic tale, was going on here.

A large shape moved through the trees, disturbing the foliage as it moved. It had to be her. Van was on the move again, grateful for something tangible to pursue. He didn't get far, though, before he heard Keiko cry out behind him. Van applied his brakes, using a tree to help him stop, and ran back for his partner.

She was on the ground, not ten feet from the clearing. Her shoe was caught in a hole and she was having trouble dislodging it. "I'm stuck!" the panic-stricken girl told him. Staying silent and amazingly self-possessed, Van knelt down to free Keiko's foot. Grimacing, she sucked her breath in sharply through her teeth.

Keiko grabbed his hand. Their eyes met and an understanding passed between them. Their fear and suspicions were the same.

"We have to get out of here," she said. "Now."

As if to mock them, the giggling resumed, softer but just as unnerving. Were Van's ears deceiving him or did it sound more menacing this time? There was movement in the trees behind Van – the sound of someone running. Keiko, her eyes fearful, shoved him. "Go!" she hissed. "Leave me! Save yourself!"

No matter what she said, it was clear from the look on Keiko's face that the last thing she wanted him to do was leave her alone. Not with that inane giggling getting louder and more persistent. Not with an unknown figure running in half-moons in front of them. Not when every snap of a twig and rustle of a tree branch sent her jumping.

Van had signed on to catch a girl, but this he was unprepared for. He had no idea what he was dealing with, except that it was clear Mystery Girl was playing a game with them. Therefore, he wasn't about to leave a frightened, injured girl alone. And yeah, he was more than a little freaked himself. There was safety in numbers, and he was officially calling the evening a bust.

"We're done," he concluded, sliding his hands underneath her body.

Keiko struggled in his arms as he lifted her. "Put me down!" she all but pleaded.

"Your ankle's twisted. Possibly sprained," he told her. Ignoring the giggling and Mystery Girl's blatant attempts to lure him back into the chase, he headed for the trail, bypassing the clearing altogether. "The last thing you need to do is cause further damage by walking on it."

"But I'm too heavy!" she insisted.

"For a weaker man, maybe, but not me." He smiled at her, enjoying the feel of her hair on his bare arm. He'd been right. It *did* feel silky.

The more distance they put between themselves and the tiny

ıring, the more things returned to normal. At least from a ᵕtuational perspective. The giggling stopped and no one was moving in the brush but them. But Van's mind was still reeling from what he'd seen and heard. He had no explanation save the one his gut was telling him – and Brenna wasn't going to like it at all. She'd fault his over active imagination and his current obsession with gothic literature. He wouldn't blame her, and yet he knew what he saw.

Mystery Girl had been everywhere tonight, moving like a female Flash Gordon. She had the ability to move without making a sound, which she seemed to employ when she wanted to be mischievous. She could multiply the sound of her voice. If the tricks she pulled were the only things she could come up with when caught off-guard, Van hated to see what she could do if she had time to plan.

Nothing about the situation had felt right, because she, Mystery Girl, wasn't right. She could perform inhuman feats because she wasn't human. And despite what rationality and common sense told him, Van knew the reason why. Mitch wasn't being stalked. He was being haunted.

CHAPTER FIFTEEN

Van had been right. Brenna hated his theory.

It was dinnertime on Sunday, and Brenna, Van, and Mitch had joined Keiko at The Cherry Blossom. They'd arrived to find the injured girl, leg propped up, at the cash register instead of waiting tables, because life as a restaurateur's daughter didn't stop with a sprained ankle. She was granted a reprieve and joined the trio at a booth to discuss the previous evening.

Closing her eyes, Brenna willed herself to stay calm. This was easier to do when she didn't have to look at the two people sitting across from her. "Why don't you tell me again what happened last night?" she urged.

"It's like I said, we waited at Harvey's for the allotted time and then headed to the trail. Everything went according to plan. We found Mystery Girl watching you from behind a tree. She heard me coming, turned, and nothing." Van moved his hand across his face like he was wiping it clean.

"But it was dark," Mitch insisted. He hadn't been any fonder of the ghost theory, but unlike Brenna, he couldn't dismiss the idea so easily. "You said it was hard to see. Her features were probably obscured by shadows."

Anticipating such a reply, Van and Keiko exchanged a look.

t wasn't *that* dark," Keiko replied, "and we know what we saw or didn't see, rather."

"Please continue." Brenna extended a hand to her best friend, endeavoring to be polite.

"We followed her to a clearing, where she promptly disappeared. Then we heard laughter all around us, but we couldn't hear her moving. Then we saw her and she took off again. We both pursued her, but Keiko got hurt and things were weirder than I anticipated, so I threw in the towel." Van rubbed his forehead. "How many times do we have to go over this?"

"Until you start making sense," Brenna countered. "Ghosts don't exist."

"You weren't there. You didn't see what we did or else you'd be singing a different tune."

Brenna snorted, looking at Mitch for affirmation, but he was absentmindedly twirling a fork in his hand. "You're not seriously buying this, are you?"

Grimacing, he cast a wary look over his shoulder to make sure no one was too close. "I don't know, Brenna," he admitted with a shrug. "Lots of people have claimed to see ghosts. Strange things happen sometimes, and they can't be explained. Like how every time I try to go after this girl, she always eludes me, and I can't figure out how."

Brenna's head shook in silent disapproval. Was there not one other rational person at the table? She expected periodic foolish from Van, but Mitch? He seemed too steady to believe in something so preposterous.

Just then, one of the waitresses, a young woman named Meg, brought over a couple of sushi rolls and set them down on the table. "I took the liberty of ordering dinner," Keiko told them as she passed out a set of chopsticks to everyone. "Don't worry.

They're on the house."

Van blinked at the food before him. Sushi wasn't on his list of approved items for consumption. "What am I supposed to do with this?"

"This is called sushi." Keiko spoke carefully as she pointed at the roll. "You eat it, and it gives you energy to go about your day. It might look intimidating, but it tastes great."

The pair shared a smile that made Brenna curious, but instead of getting distracted, she channeled her curiosity into the matter at hand. She turned to Keiko. "You're a researcher. You hack databases and organize data in a comprehensive and intelligent way. How can you possibly believe in this nonsense?"

"Belief in the immortality of the soul can be traced back to the Stone Age," Keiko replied as she trapped a piece of the roll with her chopsticks. Van was still looking at it with wary eyes like he expected it to attack him. "Just look at the Egyptians! They're obsessed with the afterlife."

The girl's argument held truth, but Brenna couldn't see what it had to do with anything. "I'm not suggesting that the soul isn't immortal. In fact, I agree that it is, but it's a long stretch to take that into a belief in ghosts."

Keiko shook her head. "Not really. If you believe that the soul exists after a person dies and goes to Heaven or Hell, why couldn't that soul get stuck on its way to the next place?"

"Like the Soul Taxi broke down, leaving the soul stranded on the side of the road, so it has to hitchhike to the next plane of existence," offered Van. Keiko gave him a smile while Brenna rolled her eyes.

"Lots of cultures perpetuate a belief in ghosts," the dark-haired girl continued without the slightest hint of embarrassment. "Even the Japanese. In fact, my grandma used to tell me the story of the *Kuchisake-onna* before bedtime."

She uttered the name in a hushed tone that naturally attracted the interest of those at the table. The girl certainly knew how to draw people in. Brenna could almost believe that they were huddled together around a campfire on a dark night. While she believed Van's ghost to be nonsense, who couldn't appreciate a good scary story?

"The *Kuchisake-onna* is the spiteful spirit of a vain young girl," Keiko began.

"Wow. A spiteful female, who would have thought?" Van observed wryly.

Brenna pinched his hand. Wincing, he yanked it away. "That's for interrupting the narrative flow," she chastised. Next to her, Mitch chuckled behind his hand.

Tossing her hair over her shoulder, Keiko continued, "Anyway, she was the wife, or some versions say concubine, of a samurai in the Heian period. He suspected her of unfaithfulness, so he disfigured her and taunted her, saying 'Who will think you're beautiful now?'"

With the air of a true performer, the girl's voice dropped an octave and hardened with cruelty like she knew exactly how the samurai had spoken. No doubt that was how her grandma had told the story. Without being aware of it, the listeners were leaning forward to hear more – even the skeptical Brenna was captivated. She could see the samurai, his sword flashing in the moonlight as he dispensed his own brand of vengeance.

"Legend has it that she wanders through the fog, her face covered by a mask, seeking solitary children and young men and women. When she finds them, she asks, 'Am I beautiful?' If they answer 'yes,' she tears off her mask and asks again. Those who are brave enough to say 'yes' again are spared. If, however, they run screaming, she pursues them and when she catches them, she butchers them!"

Keiko sliced the knife she'd been concealing through the air, making the boys lurch away from her with great speed. Brenna laughed, appreciating the storytelling.

Setting her knife down, Keiko clarified, "Actually, she just butchers the boys. With a young girl, she mutilates her, turning her into another *Kuchisake-onna*."

"Your grandma told you that before bedtime?" Van panted, hand over his heart. If one of Van's grandmas had pulled a stunt like that with him, he'd have been up all night, wide-eyed with terror.

Keiko nodded. "She wanted to teach me the importance of being polite to strangers." Her eyes turned to Mitch. "So if Mystery Girl asks you if she's beautiful, say 'yes' no matter what."

"Duly noted." Mitch tried to laugh it off, but the effect was rather unconvincing.

"Wow. This is amazing," Van half-moaned. At least, Brenna thought that was what he said. It was hard to figure out what he was saying with his mouth full of sushi. "What am I eating?" he asked. Then he held up a hand. "Never mind. It's probably best that I don't know."

Brenna shook her head, amazed by her best friend. She'd been trying to get Van to eat sushi for years. Apparently bonding with Keiko over ghosts had made him more adventuresome. He was right, though. Keiko had chosen the best rolls on the menu. Brenna was already halfway through hers.

"Of course, you don't have to go to Japan to hear good ghost stories. There are plenty closer to home," Mitch reminded them. "Kenyon College in Gambier is supposed to have multiple hauntings. They say nine students were killed in a fire in 1949 and that they still haunt the dorm where they died. People have seen ghostly figures floating down the hall, woken up to pounding noises and cries to be let out, and the lights turn off and on. Also, smoldering candles have been found next to 1949 yearbooks that have been opened to the pages containing the victims' names."

Not to be left out, Van added, "The Knox County Poor House is supposed to be haunted, too. There are cold spots and disembodied voices – the works!"

"And don't forget Sarah," Keiko breathed. That was a story most everyone was familiar with. Sarah was a self-proclaimed witch and devil worshipper, who had been decapitated by her husband when he discovered that she'd been cheating on him. He'd put her head in a jar and buried it alongside the road before committing suicide. Sarah's headless corpse had been spotted along the road, searching for her head, and her home supposedly had a death curse on it due to the black magic she practiced.

Feeling the need to bring the group back to reality, Brenna resumed her questioning. "Okay, we've heard about what you saw, but there's an aspect that we've neglected to go over."

"And what might that be?" Van posed, mimicking his best friend's business-like tone. It was rather annoying to be mocked by someone who was claiming that a ghost was playing games with them.

"State of mind," she replied. "Keiko, can you please tell me how you were feeling upon arriving at the trail? What were you thinking about?"

"Don't answer her." Van leaned over to advise his partner. "She's trying to discredit you."

Brenna smacked her palm against the table. "It's not a cross-examination! I'm just trying to get an accurate picture of the evening. You're the one who's always talking about how important emotions and feelings are!"

"I object!" Van interjected, holding up a chopstick. "You're using my words against me."

"It's okay, Van," Keiko promised before Brenna could weigh

in again. "She's right. I was upset in the slightly scared sense of the word. I was thinking about how Mystery Girl had shown herself to you and what that might mean. Plus, it was dark and we were creeping around." She folded her arms on the table, resigned. "My body was definitely in a heightened state of awareness."

Brenna nodded, appreciating her honesty. "Do you think that being in that frame of mind might have skewed your perspective on what actually happened?"

She didn't want to say yes – that much was obvious – but Keiko was nothing if not reasonable, belief in ghosts aside. "To be completely fair, I suppose one would have to consider that a possibility."

Smiling, Brenna looked pleased while Van looked betrayed.

"Don't look at me like that," Keiko replied, wounded. "I still stand by my account and will until Brenna proves otherwise."

Mollified, Van shot his best friend a challenging look. "Go ahead and ask what I was thinking about."

"I don't need to," she answered, self-assured. "Your mind was gothically-inclined. I'd bet ten bucks that ghosts or spirits had already crossed your mind in some fashion before you ever saw Mystery Girl."

The look on Van's face made Mitch laugh for real this time, but Brenna's being right had no impact on Van's certainty. "I'm right," he stated firmly. He folded his arms across his chest. "We told you what we saw and how we felt. It's up to you to prove we're wrong."

"Shouldn't be a problem," she smiled, confident that she could make them see reason. She swirled her straw around in her drink, deciding to humor them. "Let's just say that you're right, and Mitch is being haunted. What possible motives would a ghost have for doing so?"

"Well, ghosts can haunt their killers," Keiko began. "You

haven't committed any murders lately, have you, Mitch?"

"Ah, not that I'm aware of." Managing a small grin, he leaned forward to rest his arm on the table so that it touched Brenna's. The tactile contact made goose bumps rise on her skin. She fought to keep the smile off of her face.

If Keiko noticed what was going on, she politely ignored it unlike Van, who had his face half-concealed behind his napkin. Brenna kicked him under the table, and he pulled himself together as Keiko continued.

She folded her hands. "I think it's for more likely that she's seeking Mitch's help to catch her killer."

"And that'll do what? Release her spirit or let her go into the light or whatever?" Mitch finally sounded properly skeptical to Brenna. He shot her a look, which got him a shrug. Ghostbusting wasn't her area of expertise.

Keiko nodded. "Yeah. Hauntings like that usually end once justice has been administered and the ghost finds peace." She leaned forward and dropped her voice down to a whisper. "You must be close to the killer or at the very least, uncovering the truth. Have you been doing anything out of the ordinary? Meeting new people?"

Frowning, Mitch shook his head. "There's the Halloween Carnival, I guess, but aside from that, it's business as usual."

"Maybe the ghost is tied to the carnival somehow," suggested Van.

"But there are a ton of people working on it, and no one else has complained of being stalked," the other boy was quick to point out.

"Yeah, but you're in charge. You're doing most of the work," Van reminded him. He ran his hand through his hair. "She's picked you as the best person to help her. Probably because you're brushing shoulders with her killer."

That was an honor Mitch would have preferred to forego. He drummed his fingers on the table.

"There is one other possibility." Keiko spoke quietly into the silence. She refused to look up from her hands. "She could be a death omen."

Brenna had a feeling that she knew where this was going but wanted to hear the words from Keiko herself." "Which means?"

A heavy sigh passed through her lips. "Which means Mitch's life is in danger. The same person who killed her is, or soon will be, after Mitch. She's trying to warn you." Her dark eyes flickered to Mitch, who shifted uncomfortably.

"And Brenna," he added. "If the ghost appeared to Brenna, then she's in danger, too."

Keiko nodded.

An uncomfortable silence fell on the group. Well, not on Brenna since she considered the whole idea to be hogwash. But Keiko had given her plenty to mull over. It was interesting how the ghost's motives were so similar to the human ones Brenna had come up with: punishment, seeking aid, and warning. In essence, the investigation hadn't shifted too much. Except now the suspect pool had widen to include the dead – at least in the minds of Van and Keiko.

Something occurred to Brenna. A tidbit so critical that she was annoyed that she hadn't remembered it sooner as she was certain it would put an end to the ghost talk.

"You're forgetting one thing," she said. "What about the note I found in my book? The one telling me to stay away from Mitch? Are you telling me a ghost is responsible for that?"

Having no answer, Van looked at Keiko for help. She didn't disappoint. "It's totally possible. Some ghosts have the ability to manipulate objects. There are accounts of them communicating via computer, written word, and even the telephone. Some can even manifest corporeally for a period of time."

Astounded by Keiko, Brenna shook her head. "You have an answer for everything."

"Now you know what it's like being around you," Van quipped. "Annoying, isn't it?"

"But why would the ghost tell Brenna to stay away from me?" Mitch asked, pressing the issue.

"Maybe she was hoping to scare Brenna off before it was too late. A preemptive strike of sorts," suggested Van, "but it didn't work, and now it's too late. Brenna's in the killer's crosshairs now, which is why she appeared to her."

Brenna buried her face in her hands. "This is absurd."

"Did the note actually mention Mitch by name?" asked Keiko.

"No," admitted Mitch. "It just said 'him.'"

"Then it's possible that the ghost was referring to the killer. Brenna was wandering into his path on her own." Keiko's eyes widened as if she was suddenly seeing Brenna for the first time. "You're blond. So is the ghost."

Van paled. "Holy crap. You're his type. You could be the next victim."

"And the ghost wants Mitch to save you," Keiko practically gushed, clasping her hands together. "That's so romantic!"

Brenna was too astounded to be embarrassed by the girl's statement. "You're forgetting that we haven't had any high school girls murdered here in years!" she reminded them.

"The location of the crime doesn't matter, especially if the killer kept a souvenir of his victim. She'd be linked to him, and where he went, she'd go, too." Van was right. The speed at which Keiko could shoot back an answer *was* annoying.

"We have to tell Abe," her best friend announced.

This was too much for Brenna. "Tell him what? A ghost is haunting Mitch so he can save me from a serial killer?"

Van nodded. "Absolutely."

"That's it!" cried Brenna, tossing down her napkin. She slid
out of the booth. "I'm going to the car where I will wait until you
recover your senses. There is a real person behind all of this,
you'll see. There is no such thing as ghosts. What we have here is
a good, old-fashioned stalking." She turned to Mitch, hand
outstretched. "Keys, please."

He handed them over without a word, and Brenna left the
restaurant.

Mystery Girl was not a ghost, and Brenna would prove it. If
for no other reason, she was grateful for the red herring, because it
forced her to look harder at the living, breathing girls of Mount
Vernon High. One thing was certain – playing at romance with
Mitch wasn't enough. She had to be more proactive if she wanted
to put an end to all of this nonsense.

During the car ride home, two things became clear to Brenna.
First, her best friend was certifiably insane. Van refused to let the
ghost matter drop until both Mitch and Brenna agreed to meet at
the library tomorrow night to research dead girls. She agreed
because she'd sworn to herself that she would have concocted a
second phase of the investigation by tomorrow that she could work
on while Van "researched" his theory.

Second, she realized that she was going to have to continue
pretending to date Mitch. When the plan had been devised
originally, Brenna had assumed that they'd only have to go on one
date in order to catch Mystery Girl, but with their suspect still on
the loose, they'd have to maintain the charade. She was sort of
wishing that they'd never come up with the plan. It had been great
on paper, but in reality, it was complicated and confusing.
Primarily because Brenna was developing some very warm

feelings for the boy that made it difficult to concentrate on the case at hand.

After Mitch dropped Brenna off at home, she found her uncle in the living room, doing something he very rarely did – watching television. Actual television. Not the news, which he watched out of civic duty, or some sporting event, which he kept an eye on so he could participate in casual conversation with his officers, but full on Primetime. Brenna wondered if the world was spinning out of control. First ghosts and now *Zio* was watching a glorified medical soap opera. Usually he stuck his limited Primetime viewing to procedural crime shows so he could have a laugh or two at the fantastical way crime solving was portrayed.

"You do realize that this isn't one of those legitimate medical shows were they operate on real people, right?" she teased as she sat down on the couch.

"It's quite engrossing, actually. The brilliant surgeon is faced with an ethical dilemma. He's realized that the visiting African dictator has been misdiagnosed. If he doesn't speak up, the dictator will die, but if he does speak up, he's dooming the dictator's people to years of continued persecution. Look at him brood." Abraham pointed at the devastatingly handsome man whose brows were furrowed to convey the depth of his emotional torment. "And if that weren't enough, he's just learned that his alcoholic brother's liver is failing."

Fortunately for the handsome doctor, distraction in the form of a hot nurse arrived. She was quite willing to give him something much more pleasant to think about. In the end, the surgeon decided to save the dictator, but the man died anyway through no fault of his medical treatment. The dictator's liver was given to the alcoholic brother and the hot nurse announced she was pregnant.

"And who claims that television isn't realistic?" Brenna cried with a flourish. "Let there be happy endings for everyone but the bad guy!"

Chuckling, Abraham switched off the television. "Did you have a nice time with your friends?"

"Yeah, but it was a bit unusual," she admitted with a frown, her mind replaying the discussion around the table. "We got sidetracked by ghosts."

"Ah, the Halloween spirit has truly descended," he observed with amusement. "Let me guess. You're a nonbeliever but Van is open-minded." Her uncle knew Van almost as well as she did. Brenna nodded. "And young Mr. Hamilton?"

Fiddling with one of the couch's pillows, Brenna remembered how there had been barely concealed terror on Mitch's face about the idea of his being haunted. "He was on the fence. Keiko was a diehard believer, though, which surprised me. I thought she was more rational than that."

Contemplating her words, Abraham crossed his arms over his chest. "Many rational people believe in ghosts. It's one way that they explain unexplainable things."

A memory from last week resurfaced – Abraham confessing that he had been scared of ghosts as a child. At the time, Brenna had assumed he was joking, but now, she wondered. If someone like *Zio* believed in ghosts, maybe she had to rethink her hard lined stance.

"You know, someone like Keiko might say that our house, given how old it is, might have ghosts in it." She dangled the idea in front of his nose, seeing if he'd bite.

He did but not like she expected. "Well, more than one person has died in this house, including your grandfather, so, yes, some people might look at our house, hear the creaks and groans that it makes periodically, and claim it was haunted. However, people like us take such sounds to be the mundane things that they are."

It pleased her that he'd lumped himself into the nonbeliever crowd. That made it easier for Brenna to hold her stance on the matter.

Her uncle frowned over memories from long ago. "Besides, I think we'd know for certain if your grandfather was still lingering about. Life would be far less pleasant."

Brenna snorted, grateful to be spared such torment. "So were you really afraid of ghosts as a kid?" The idea that he could be frightened by the supernatural even as a child still boggled her mind.

"For a few years, yes," he admitted without embarrassment. "I was studying the area's history and realized just how many abandoned places there were here, many of which claimed to be haunted. I was more than a little obsessed with the idea. I spent a lot of time visiting places late at night, hoping to see something but absolutely terrified about what would happen if I did."

"How old were you?" She shifted on the couch, resting her back against its arm, and leaned forward in eagerness. Abraham Rutherford, Ghost Hunter – Van would be over the moon at the very idea.

"Around ten, I think."

It was fascinating to hear him talk about this detail of his young life. While Abraham had always been forthcoming with information about Amelia, he kept details about his own childhood close to his chest, claiming that they weren't that interesting. He was wrong though. Brenna felt he'd been holding out on her.

"Did you ever find anything?" she inquired.

He shook his head. "Nothing but trouble. An officer picked me up one night and took me home. Your grandfather didn't take kindly to my hobby and lectured me quite thoroughly on the folly of my ways. I had no choice but to give it up, and not long after that, I came to realize for myself that a belief in ghosts was irrational. Like all phases, it passed."

That sounded very typical of Grandfather Rutherford. He was a hard, stubborn, and prideful man. How Abraham managed to avoid that crippling combination of personality traits was nothing short of miraculous.

Not ready to shut the door on the past, Brenna asked, "What was my mom afraid of the most?"

Looking almost sheepish, he scratched his face. "She was claustrophobic. Probably because I used to lock her in the closet."

"*Zio!*" she cried, aghast. "How could you?"

He spread his hands apologetically. "That's the sort of thing big brothers do." He propped his elbow on the couch's other armrest and with a furrowed brow, regarded the scandalous look his niece gave him. "I'm hardly the saint you think I am, Brenna. I have my fair share of black marks."

Almost instantly, the face of Eliza Kent swam into focus in her mind. She wondered, yet again, what Eliza had meant to her uncle, if he'd been a suspect in her murder, and if the killer had been caught. Now was as good a time as any to ask. He'd basically given her an open invitation to explore his past with that last comment. In the face of his honesty, Brenna was confronted by her own duplicity. She didn't like misleading, which really was just a polite way of saying "lying to," her uncle. With Mystery Girl, Mitch, and Eliza Kent, there were simply too many secrets that she was keeping. It was time to put one issue to rest.

"Who was Eliza Kent?"

It was the first time that Brenna could ever remember catching her uncle completely off guard. He sat immobile, staring at her with eyes the size of dinner plates. Speechlessness wasn't a trait she liked to see on him. It made her extremely uncomfortable. Maybe bringing Eliza up hadn't been the best idea.

"How do you know that name?" he asked once he had recovered. His voice was careful and quiet like he was speaking to a gravely ill person.

Brenna's stomach twisted in knots like it had the few times she'd been in serious trouble. In her mind, she knew she hadn't done anything wrong – except, perhaps, for not bringing it to his attention sooner – but she still felt a slight reluctance to answer him. "When I went to Mom's grave, someone had left roses. They were wrapped in a Columbia newspaper, and the cover page was about her murder."

Without warning, he was on his feet. "May I see it, please?"

She got to her feet and led him upstairs. The newspaper was in her desk drawer, underneath a pad of paper. Pulling it out carefully, she handed it to him. Abraham opened it and when he saw the picture of Eliza, he ran his fingers lovingly across it. That simple action spoke volumes about her uncle's feelings for the murdered girl.

When he finally spoke, his voice was so quiet that Brenna almost missed it. "She was my fiancée." He looked up at her, clearing his throat. "Or would have been if she hadn't died. I had intended to propose that night. We were supposed to meet at her apartment, but she got home earlier than expected."

For days, she'd been wondering about the truth, and now, having it confirmed made her sick with grief. The harder he tried to maintain control over his emotions, the more Brenna felt herself unraveling. She wrapped her arms around herself.

"I'm sorry," she offered helplessly. "Did they ever catch her killer?"

He shook his head, folding up the paper again. He didn't give it back, but Brenna hadn't expected him to.

"*Zio*, someone put that on Mom's grave. Who did it? What does it mean?"

Abraham's eyes flashed with anger. No, that wasn't a strong enough to word to describe what she'd seen. It was hatred, pure unadulterated rage – the kind she'd seen in Kevin Bishop's eyes. But then he blinked and it was gone.

"It's nothing other than a childish prank." His voice had a hard edge to it that smacked of finality. "I shall take care of it. You needn't dwell on it."

They regarded each other in silence for a moment. She knew he wasn't being completely honest and he knew that she knew it, but she decided to let it go. Not that she wasn't raging with curiosity. Of course, Brenna wanted to know who left it, because obviously whoever it was had meant to involve her. But she had secrets of her own. Now niece and uncle were even.

And it was time to change the subject.

"Thanks for letting me use the car for the next couple of weeks. Sticking a baby on the back of a Vespa isn't too practical, even when she's fake." Brenna hoped her attempt at brevity didn't sound too false. Abraham had obligingly agreed to drive his police cruiser to and from work while she was playing "mother."

He wiped a hand across his brow, sweeping away all traces of sadness, and smiled. "It's my pleasure and quite fortuitous given the weather forecast." The weatherman had predicted that a massive thunderstorm was due to roll in some time tomorrow. Brenna had already arranged to take Van to school so he and his bike wouldn't get swept away in the torrential downpour.

"I suppose I'd better do some homework," she said almost begrudgingly.

"Yes, you have been out gallivanting quite a bit this weekend." He shot her a frown that was meant to convey a disapproval he didn't really feel. Then he put his hand on her cheek and leaned over to kiss the top of her head. Brenna wrapped her arms tightly around him.

When he released her, he turned to go, but she called after him. "Oh, I'm going to get home late tomorrow," she informed her uncle. "After work, Van and I are meeting Mitch at the library."

Abraham fixed her with a calculating stare. "That's three days in a row that you'll be spending time with him." She knew he didn't mean Van.

Nothing else was said, but she had a fair idea what he was going through his mind – a caution against excessiveness with a highlight of the perils of getting too close too fast. There was probably some truth to that given that a week ago, she hadn't even considered dating Mitch and now she was fantasizing about kissing him. If it wasn't for Mystery Girl, Brenna could pace herself, but that wasn't a luxury she could afford herself when a stalker – not a ghost – was on the loose.

"It's not a date," she assured him. "We won't be alone, and we weren't alone tonight. It's just hanging out. Plus, I'll have my own car."

Shaking his head, he raised his eyebrows as if to indicate that he hadn't meant anything by the remark. She fought a smile. "Just promise to bring him over for dinner before you get engaged," he replied with an uncharacteristic smirk. "Don't stay out too late, either."

CHAPTER SIXTEEN

"I have a good feeling about today," Van announced on the way to school the next morning. As usual, he was decked out in his acid wash jacket and wearing his Aviators even though the sun was obscured behind some seriously dark clouds. The only concession he made to the weather was to forego styling his hair.

"How so?" Brenna asked.

He smiled cheekily at her. "Not only are we going to get our robot babies, but I'm pretty sure that by the end of the day, we'll have a solid lead on our ghost's identity."

She matched his smile. "Yes, I, too, feel optimistic about uncovering Mystery Girl's identity. I have a plan that will require your specific expertise."

Last night, Brenna had devoted a significant amount of time to coming up with another way to identify Mystery Girl. Since Van claimed that she didn't have a face that made things tricky, so she would focus on what they all knew she *did* have – hair. Once that had been decided, a plan quickly fell into place.

"In which field?" he questioned.

"Hair," she told him. "I'm going to take as many pictures as I can of girls with blond hair, and later at the library, we'll go through the photos to see if you can find a girl with the same hair as Mystery Girl while ignoring her face."

Van tapped his chin, considering the scenario. "A case study on hair. I love it!" he cried with enthusiasm. "Even though we'll never find the perfect match since we're dealing with a ghost rather than a living girl, I'll be happy to placate you."

Rather than be annoyed, Brenna was curious about Van's own plan of attack. "And just how do you suggest we uncover your ghost's identity?"

"Keiko texted me with some ideas – most of which involve internet research," he shrugged. "Once we know who we're dealing with, we can be proactive and start hunting instead of waiting for her to pop up. Technically, we could start hunting now, but it'd be wiser to get as much information as possible before going in with guns blazing."

Brenna suddenly envisioned the two of them decked out in camouflage and hunting rifles, which was idiotic given that ghosts were already dead. "How does one 'hunt' a ghost?"

"Well, there are several detectors that are useful in finding ghosts, such as the classic Electromagnetic field meter. You can use air ion counters, infrared proximity detectors, and temperature-reading equipment, too."

"Awesome, I'll bring the thermometer and you find the rest of that stuff," she replied with a shake of her head.

"Hey, nonbeliever," he said, jabbing a finger into her shoulder. "Don't make me shun you. This is interesting stuff and you know it."

Brenna would never admit it, but he wasn't exactly wrong about that. If she wasn't careful, Van and his interesting, detailed answers were going to pull her down the rabbit trail, befuddling her mind until she didn't know which end was up. Maintaining a firm grasp on reality was critical to defeating Mystery Girl, not picking up EMF readings. She let him blabber on, though, since she found him entertaining. Also, it'd be good to know all of this in case they were in fact dealing with a ghost.

Tightening her grip on the steering wheel, Brenna banished the thought. Ghosts didn't exist! Period.

"So I asked *Zio* about Eliza Kent last night," she stated as a way of changing the subject.

That got Van's attention. "And you're just now mentioning this?" he chided, looking wounded. "What did he say?"

"It was as we suspected. Eliza was his girlfriend," she said, fighting hard to keep her throat from closing up as she remembered the look on Abraham's face. "He was going to propose the night of the robbery. They were meeting at her place. The police never caught the killer."

Deflated, Van let his head fall back against the headrest with a thud. "Man, poor Abe. You couldn't pay me to be that guy." He looked at his best friend. "Did he have any thoughts on who left the paper behind?"

"I think so. He tried to hide it, but I could tell he was livid," Brenna said, suppressing a shudder. Making *Zio* that mad wasn't something she ever wanted to do. "He told me not to worry about, and that he would take care of it."

"I'm assuming that his words have had no effect on you," Van surmised flatly.

Brenna shook her head. "Actually, I'm going to let him have this one," she said, ignoring her best friend's shocked expression. "Since I'm currently keeping a few secrets of my own about Mitch and Mystery Girl, I figure I can let it go at the moment."

"You must really be feeling guilty about lying to Abe," he replied.

Gritting her teeth, Brenna turned into the school's parking lot. "I'm trying not to think of it as lying but more of a temporary deception."

Van snorted. "We can play the word game all you want, but it won't change anything."

"I hate it when you do that," she snapped.

"Do what? Speak with the voice of your conscience?"

She replied with a sigh. "When it's done, I'll tell him about Mystery Girl," she vowed as she parked her car.

They parted ways then, Van heading leisurely to his locker while Brenna made a record quick stop at hers before heading to Mr. Rose's class. As promised, she'd looked over the sophomore essays and was eager to get them out of her backpack and into his keeping. Mr. Rose was sorting through papers at his desk, savoring his final moments of silence before class began, when she arrived.

"Hi, Brenna," he greeted with a perfectly charming smile. It was almost criminal for a teacher to be so adorable.

"Hi," she said, embarrassed by how breathless she sounded. Embarrassment turned to guilt as a thought of Mitch rolled through her mind. Focusing on her task, Brenna sat her backpack on a desk and opened it. "I finished looking over the essays," she said, handing the stack of notebooks to him. "They were, um, interesting."

Interesting was a bit of an understatement. There was one, maybe two, well written essays, which had Brenna questioning the work she'd produced as a sophomore. Had she been as bad only to improve dramatically in the span of two years? Or was Mr. Rose dealing with an especially sub-par group of students?

Sighing, her teacher crossed his fingers. "Here's hoping for some marked improvement by the end of the semester." He took the notebooks from her. "I really appreciate your help, Brenna. I hope you didn't spend all weekend looking over these."

"No, I was able to get out." Almost immediately, she felt her cheeks flush. What was wrong with her? There was no reason she should feel so self-conscious. Dropping her gaze, she made a pretense of picking an invisible piece of lint off her shirt.

"Ah, so the rumors I heard were true then." When she saw Mr. Rose's sly smile, Brenna thought her face might actually catch fire. Rumors were spreading around the school, were they? Clearly, she deserved an award for the performance she pulled last week. "Well, I certainly hope he was a gentleman."

Brenna didn't have time to answer, because the gentleman in question darted into the room, looking every bit as breathless as she'd been a moment ago. "There you are," Mitch said, stopping at her side. "I have the camera. Hey, Mr. Rose." He gave the teacher a cursory nod before tugging Brenna gently over to his desk.

"I cleared the memory card last night, so there's no way you're going to fill it up," he told her as he unzipped his backpack. The camera he retrieved easily fit in the palm of Brenna's hand or would have if Mitch had given it to her. Instead, he held it up to his face and said, "Smile." She barely had time to comply before the flash went off.

"What was that for?" she asked, still smiling.

He shrugged nonchalantly. "You're blond. Seemed only fair." He placed the camera in her hand, eyes dancing.

"Show me how to use this thing," Brenna requested, examining the foreign device. Sure it was light and compact, but she missed her trusty old camera. With bells and whistles like automatic focus, she felt she had no control over the final product.

Stepping behind Brenna, Mitch put his arms around her, so he could lean over her shoulder to give her a tutorial. He was quite thorough, pointing every setting out and showing her fingers where to go, but Brenna had to work extra hard to absorb any of it. She would have much preferred to enjoy how her back fit perfectly

against his chest, the way his hands held hers, how his breath
raised goose bumps on her skin, listen to the slow steadiness of his
voice, and yes, when he raised the camera to her eyes, savor the
pressure of his cheek next to hers.

When Mitch had finished his lesson, he didn't let her go.
Brenna craned her neck to find his eyes, blushing furiously when
she finally did. She knew that they were a couple now in the eyes
of their fellow students, so this kind of behavior was expected, but
it felt more real today than the pretense they'd put up last week.
Ironically, the whole Missy discussion seemed to have brought
them closer as it allowed them to speak truthfully about their
blossoming relationship. If Alexis hadn't interrupted their date,
who knew where the conversation would have led? Deep down
inside of Brenna a yearning was growing for such touches to be
genuine. She knew that Mitch had feelings for her, but she wasn't
sure he would be wrapping his arms around her if it weren't for the
charade. The uncertainty she felt would rapidly become thought
consuming if she wasn't careful.

She'd never been one to sit around thinking about the boys she
liked. In fact, Brenna couldn't remember ever consciously liking
any boy – schoolgirl crushes on a teacher didn't count. Simply put,
she had better things to do than fixate on them. Yes, she
appreciated a fine-looking guy when she saw one, but when he
passed by, he passed right out of her mind as well.

But it wasn't so easy to cast a fleeting glance at Mitch and not
just because they were playing at being a couple. He wasn't like
any other boy her age. Responsible and hard working weren't
words she'd associate with likes of Dylan O'Connor. They were
qualities that caught Brenna's eye, making Mitch appeal to her in
ways she hadn't considered before.

Not only that, but she was starting to think that she had
misjudged his level of cuteness. While not as attractive as Duke,

The Haunting of Mitch Hamilton

Mitch certainly wasn't woefully plain like Benny McBride. She had thought him slightly above average until she noticed the hypnotizing way the sun glinted off of his black hair. And his smile – the charmingly crooked one that he pulled out whenever he felt especially happy – had the power to draw one out of her as well.

Perhaps this was what dating was like – sliding a perspective suitor under a microscope to discover his intricacies and determine if they meshed well with your own. It boiled down to simple science and the careful study of a subject's nature. Okay, so maybe she was being too practical and not leaving her heart open to being swept away by passion, but practicality was woven into the fabric of her being. It wasn't something she could simply shut off, and she wasn't sure she wanted to. While physical attraction and romance were important, if there was nothing solid to ground the relationship on, it was doomed to fail. No, a slow, deliberate course of study was a safer route. There was no need to rush into anything, especially given the investigation. At least, that's what Brenna continued to tell herself.

"I'm going to be sick," an obnoxious voice declared, shattering their focus and reminding them of exactly where they were. Clutching his stomach dramatically, Cameron shot Mitch an exasperated look. "If you insist on touching her, don't do it in front of me, or I just might have to kill myself."

"Well, that's reason enough for me," Mitch replied, holding Brenna closer to him. She was fighting a losing battle, trying not to laugh.

"Mr. Rose! Make them stop fondling each other!" Cameron whined plaintively.

The older man sighed at his desk. "Guys, it's Monday and class hasn't even started yet. Show some mercy on your poor teacher."

Muttering an apology, the couple separated and moved away from the annoying Cameron Irby. Mitch sat down next Brenna in Van's currently unoccupied seat. In a hushed whisper, she went over the details of what she planned to do with the camera. Mitch leaned across the aisle, listening with rapt attention as he rested his arms on her desk.

"Think it'll be helpful?" he asked, rubbing absently at a spot on her binder.

"It's a step in the right direction," she said, careful not to make any promises.

He looked up at her, dropping his voice even lower. "But what if she's, you know, dead?"

Brenna wanted to roll her eyes, but his face was so pathetic that she couldn't bring herself to do it. "Do you really think that's true?" she inquired.

"I dunno," he shrugged. "She's so fast and disappears so quickly."

Mitch's words triggered a memory from the night he came over to her house. He had specifically described Mystery Girl as "disappearing" every time he tried to get close to her. She had thought it odd at the time, but now, given where everyone's minds seemed to be heading, it was illuminating.

"You thought it was a ghost all along, didn't you?"

Brenna sounded more surprised than judgmental, but that didn't stop him from looking embarrassed all the same. He avoided her eyes. "It crossed my mind," he admitted through a mumble. "I didn't think you'd help me if I told you I was being haunted."

"I would have," she insisted, slipping on a smile, "just to prove that you weren't dealing with a ghost."

Looking relieved, he grinned. A moment later, the bell rang, and Van entered the room. The sight of Mitch draped over

Brenna's desk and the comfortable ease at which she accepted his closeness had his eyebrows threatening to disappear up underneath his hair. Brenna caught his meaningful glance, but it was gone by the time Mitch saw him. The boy stood up and thumped Van on the shoulder in a friendly yet masculine way before heading to his own desk.

Van slid into his seat and then promptly leaned toward his best friend, his voice slightly above a whisper. "With the aftermath of Mystery Girl, we never actually discussed your date."

"There's nothing to report," she shrugged, disappointment settling in the pit of her stomach. The highs and lows of romance were wearing on her nerves. "I think we were going to have the conversation, but Alexis showed up and then Mystery Girl. We never got back to it."

"How hasn't he said something?" Van muttered, half-exasperated. "He's had countless opportunities by now." He looked back at her. "Is it because of the Missy thing? Did that come up?"

She nodded. "We talked about it, and we're moving forward." Other students were trickling into the room now, and even though Autumn Winters, who had just taken her accustomed seat in front of Brenna, wasn't showing the least bit of interest in her conversation, she felt embarrassed. "Later," she hissed at Van.

Brenna proved hard to pin down after that, though she wasn't deliberately trying to avoid her best friend. The second phase in her plan to catch Mystery Girl had her moving quickly through the halls, snapping a picture of any blond girl she saw. She made an effort to be purposeful and yet discreet about the whole process. No one paid much attention to her since most students were accustomed to seeing her with a camera. Being alone helped her fly below the radar as well. Whereas people usually noticed Van because he was born to stand out or Mitch because he was popular,

Brenna blended into her surroundings like a chameleon.

A similar plan was adopted during lunch. When Brenna felt satisfied with her work, she joined Van and Mitch at their table. "I think that does it," she said.

"You couldn't possibly have photographed every blonde on campus," Van remarked.

"Probably not," she admitted, "but I feel that I got the most likely suspects. I focused on seniors since they know Mitch the best, then targeted ASB girls, and went from there."

Exhaling, Van puffed out his cheeks, unimpressed by any tactic that didn't support his ghost theory, but Mitch liked her reasoning. "How many pictures did you take?" he asked.

Uncertain, she shook her head. "Maybe a couple hundred. I didn't really keep track."

"Wow," Mitch replied. "You're fast."

"That's our Brenna Pearl," Van interjected as he shredded his napkin. "Driven by an intense passion for the truth or in this instance, an intense desire to prove that she's right and I'm crazy."

Leaning over, she patted his cheek. "Oh sweetie, I already know you're crazy, but you're still adorable." Eyes going misty, she quickly pinched his cheek before Van swatted her hand away.

Conversation steered away from Mystery Girl, ghosts, and other investigation-related topics. They taught Mitch how to play Question-Question, which led to a discussion on world travel. Brenna was elated when she learned that Mitch had traveled to Italy last summer with his parents and seen many of the things that she was planning to see when she went there after graduation with Abraham. She peppered him with questions, though the boy didn't seem quite as enamored with the country as she would have liked. Given the little she knew of Mitch's home life, she suspected that traveling in close quarters with parents he hardly ever saw wasn't his idea of a good time.

As they walked to their next class, Mitch took hold of Brenna's hand. Once again, she felt that same yearning to know for certain that it was an authentic gesture rather than merely keeping up appearances. When they reached the door to her Childhood Development class, Mitch kept her from entering after Van.

Knowing the bell was about to ring, Mitch cleared his throat. "So the Halloween Carnival is coming up, and being President, I have to sit in the middle of the maze and hand out candy. I was wondering if you'd like to sit with me." He looked up at the last second to gauge her reaction.

Immediately, Brenna felt pleasantly warm all over as she smiled. And then her brain kicked in. What about Van? This was their special holiday – they had coordinating costumes for crying out loud! But she really wanted to say yes now that Mitch was finally asking her to do something that had a decidedly non-Mystery Girl vibe. He needed all the encouragement he could give. Then she remembered something else.

"I thought that the Vice President was supposed to sit with you as a sort of ASB solidarity thing," Brenna said. "Won't Hannah be disappointed if I take her place?" She mentally crossed her fingers as she said this, though which outcome she was hoping for was a little fuzzy.

Mitch waved dismissively with his free hand. "Hannah won't mind at all. She'll be just as happy sitting at the start of the maze."

Unfortunately, that didn't make her decision any easier. "Look, I'd really like to sit with you, but I need to talk to Van first. Halloween is a big deal for us, and I don't want to let him down."

Smiling, he nodded, though Brenna could hear the disappointment in his voice. "Yeah, sure, I understand. Just let me know, okay?" Then he departed quickly with a promise to see her at the library later that night. She watched him go, feeling like she'd done something wrong.

"Lloyd Dobler and Sir are in there," Van declared happily, pointing at a large box on the floor. He was too distracted to notice her listlessness as she sat down in her seat. "We get to play with robot babies for a grade!"

Brenna sincerely hoped that Mrs. Johnson was going to pass out the dolls at the beginning of class, because she wasn't sure Van could handle the suspense. At least he wasn't the only one excited. Several of the girls were chatting animatedly with each other or asking Mrs. Johnson questions. Even Penelope Dyer was hovering around the teacher's desk – a place she typically avoided – for the mere chance of peeking inside the box.

After Mrs. Johnson had explained the assignment, including how to "comfort" the babies – a process which required the student to stick a key into the doll's back when it started crying and keep it there until it stopped – the teacher passed them out. They were identical, the only method of distinction being that the boys wore a blue top and the girls wore pink.

Brenna examined Sophia Irene, trying to imagine her as a living infant. It wasn't easy. Like most dolls, she was larger than a normal baby, and heavier, too. Her eyes had been painted blue and her tiny mouth was permanently fixed into a smile. So what if Sophia Irene was real? What if she were solely responsible for her wellbeing? What exactly would that feel like? She had just gotten the doll and already she was picturing how different her life would be if this wasn't a simple class assignment. Of course, not everyone was thinking along the same lines.

"Lloyd Dobler looks just like me," Van declared after performing a similar examination of the doll in his hands. "But as you can see, he's inherited his hair genes from his mother's side. Male pattern baldness strikes the men in her family very early on." He patted Lloyd Dobler's smooth head affectionately. "Don't worry, son. We will find some nice hats for you."

The baby promptly burst into tears.

"Great," Brenna said, throwing up a hand in mock outrage. "You've given him a complex already."

"Then I guess I'm on my way to being a stellar parent," he retorted.

"Our first crier!" Mrs. Johnson exclaimed, delighted, as she walked over to examine the process. "Now, everyone, let's watch Van as he attempts to soothe his baby."

All eyes were on Van as he fumbled to put the key into Lloyd Dobler's back while the doll was resting against his shoulder. The crying lasted less than a minute, but it might as well have been an eternity for Van, who shifted under the weight of so many eyes on him. That wasn't the kind of attention he enjoyed. It was like being called up to the board to answer a math problem.

When it was over, Mrs. Johnson gave him an approving smile. "Well done, Daddy," she said, turning to address the class. "Remember, Baby must feel secure in your arms. Security equals love. Also, if you treat Baby like a doll and bang him around, he'll cry more often. My goodness!"

The sky boomed with a tremendous amount of thunder that echoed as loudly as if it had been in the room with them. Seconds later, the heavens ripped open and rain poured down on the school in buckets. The promised thunderstorm had arrived, and it didn't let up. Even though they had come prepared with raincoats and collapsible umbrellas, Brenna and Van still got fairly soaked as they ran through the flooding parking lot to the car. They barely had time to warm themselves up before they were running through the rain again to get inside of Honey B's.

"Man, it is really coming down out there!" Van declared, shaking his head like a dog. Drops of water flew everywhere. He walked over to the ovens and stretched out his hands, feeling the heat. "I think Lloyd Dobler and I might camp out here today."

"Knowing you, you'll probably end up melting your baby," Brenna observed dryly as she hung up her raincoat. Sophia Irene watched demurely from the counter.

The kitchen door swung as Berthal Bean stepped inside. Immediately, her eyes landed on Van and Lloyd Dobler. "Honey, you're too old and too male to be playing with dolls."

"Doll?" Van's eyes went wide with feigned outrage. "This is my child!" He darted over to the baker and held his son up for her to see. "Can't you see the resemblance? Lloyd Dobler, meet Berthal Bean. If you behave nicely, maybe she'll give you a cookie."

The old woman snorted derisively.

"Don't laugh at me. You have no idea the pressure I'm under as a single parent," he cried dramatically. "It nearly killed me when his mother left. Of course, deep down I always knew that one day she'd shed her human form and rejoin her wolf pack. The call of the wild was stronger than our love. She just had to run free."

His antics made Brenna laugh while Berthal, amusement dancing in her eyes, pointed a finger at Lloyd Dobler's tiny chest, and stated, "Honey, your daddy is crazy."

"Crazy awesome," Van corrected.

"True enough," Berthal admitted with a smile.

A few minutes later, Van was seated at a table, making a feeble attempt to do his homework, while Brenna worked behind the counter, alternating between serving the patrons that trickled in every so often and icing cookies. The man who'd placed the order had asked that they ice the cookies to look like jack o'lanterns. In true Halloween spirit, Brenna had come up with a couple of different face designs, ranging from happy to frightening. She sat Sophia Irene up against the wall, so the little girl could "learn."

She was admiring her handiwork when Van sidled up to her.

"So I'm thinking that the reason Mitch hasn't made a move is because he feels guilty about dragging you into this haunting business and possibly thrusting you into the path of an evil ghost or a vicious serial killer," he announced. "If the ghost or a serial killer murders you, it'd be his fault."

"Okay, seriously? The insanity has to stop," Brenna growled in frustration. "You want to say it's a ghost, then fine, but you can't keep vacillating on the details. Is she a ghost with malicious intent or a death omen? Should we be afraid of her or her killer? Is Mitch the target or am I? Pick a theory and go with it until it's disproved."

Huffing, Van crossed his arms over his chest. "You have different theories, too."

"True, but I'm still operating under the first theory that Mystery Girl is a living girl who is romantically obsessed with Mitch and doesn't like that I'm dating him. That is the most rational scenario based on everything I know thus far."

"Why are you so cranky?" he pressed.

"I am not cranky!" she all but yelled, smacking her hand against the counter. "You're driving me nuts with your ghost talk!" Van regarded her with superior eyes that knew better. Giving up, she sighed. "I'm feeling a lot of pressure with this whole Mitch-thing. I know we said it wasn't real, but it feels different now. Part of me wishes we'd never started the pretense. All it's done is confuse me. I thought we wouldn't have to keep it up this long." She massaged her temple, trying to ease her frustration. "If we just had some private time together, when we didn't have to pretend because no one was watching us, I think we could sort things out quickly. But the investigation keeps getting in the way."

"You want your relationship to be real," Van stated in

conclusion.

Brenna bit her lip, considering her answer. "I want to know where I stand with him. I mean, you say that he likes me, but he's never actually said that. Maybe you're wrong, and he's just a really good actor."

Van rolled his eyes at her insecurity but didn't verbalize his certainty on the matter. "I could play the protective best friend card and talk to him. Find out what his intentions are."

Part of Brenna desperately wanted to say yes to Van's proposal, but it felt like a junior high move. She shouldn't need a go-between to find out how Mitch really felt about her. She shook her head. "No, it's my problem, and I'll take care of it." And that provided the perfect lead-in for the carnival. "He asked me to sit in the maze with him."

"Well, that's something!" he declared, patting her on the back like she'd done something noteworthy.

"I told him that I had to ask you first," Brenna added.

Van buried his face in his hands. "You are so dim-witted, Brenna Pearl! No wonder he hasn't said anything!"

"Hey! I was trying to be a good friend! We have a standing engagement," she reminded him. It was cruel of him to make her feel foolish for not wanting to be rude. "I didn't want to blow you off!"

"But that's what you're supposed to do! You're supposed to blow me off, which will make me mad, and we'll fight about it."

Almost sulkily, Brenna crossed her arms over her chest. "But I don't want to fight with you."

Van placed his hands on her shoulders and bent down to meet her eyes. He spoke with the kind of deliberate slowness reserved for those of below average intelligence. "When the boy you like asks you to do something, you say yes. You do not put him second to your male best friend. That's altering the time-honored way the game is played."

If that was true, Brenna wasn't sure she was interested in playing. She didn't want to turn into a rude, thoughtless person because of a boy. She shook herself free from his grip. "Well, please accept my sincerest apologies," she replied saucily. Pausing, she shuffled her feet. "Does that mean you're okay with me sitting with Mitch?"

"Holy crap, yes!" Van raised his hands to the ceiling. "Text him. Text him right now before it's too late!"

Brenna complied, texting as fast as her fingers could fly. Mitch must have sensed that it was coming because she got a reply from him in under a minute. He was quite pleased that she would be joining him in the maze.

"Crisis averted," Van sighed, wiping his brow dramatically. "You know, if you manage not to screw things up anymore, we just might get you kissed before graduation rolls around."

CHAPTER SEVENTEEN

Mitch got to the library before Brenna and Van. They found him sitting at a desk console, his laptop plugged in and ready to go. During the drive over, Brenna had firmly ordered herself to stay focused on uncovering Mystery Girl's identity and ignore her feelings for Mitch. However, now that she was near him, she found it hard to keep from noticing small details about him – like how the beads of rain caught in his hair sparkled in the light. Really, this should have frustrated Brenna, but she was finding it hard to care.

When Mitch saw what they were carrying with them, he chuckled. "Wow," he said. "Those babies are pretty life-like. What did you name them?"

"Lloyd Dobler," Van announced, holding his baby up for Mitch to see. Then he gestured to Brenna's. "And that's Sir."

Mitch shot her a questioning look. "You named your baby Sir?"

"I most certainly did not. Her name is Sophia Irene." She crossed her arms over her chest, hugging her baby over her heart, and then immediately uncrossed them upon realizing that she looked like a little girl pouting over a doll – which was sort of true.

"Sophia Irene Rutherford or Sir." Van's smile was far too big to be allowed. "Guess which one me and Lloyd Dobler prefer." He then promptly dumped Lloyd Dobler on the desk space behind Mitch's laptop. Brenna huffed and pulled up a chair for herself next to Mitch.

"Aren't you supposed to treat those things like real babies? Shouldn't you hold him or something?" Mitch asked, peering at the discarded doll. He couldn't help but compare Van's treatment of his baby to Brenna's, who had Sophia Irene sitting happily in her lap.

Van shrugged haphazardly. "I don't believe in coddling. He needs to learn self-reliance." He plopped into a chair on the other side of Mitch. He rubbed his hands together. "Let's get this pointless exercise over so we can get to researching dead girls."

Brenna ignored his comment and handed over the camera to Mitch, who plugged it into his laptop. While Van chatted idly as they waited for the pictures to upload, Brenna was painfully aware of just how close she was to Mitch. Both her breathing and her heartbeat were erratic, and no matter how many times she told herself to calm down, her body refused to listen. Her palms felt clammy and her eyes lingered on his face, which – thankfully – was angled in Van's direction. It was dangerous, the close proximity. It caused crazy thoughts to fill her brain such as what it would feel like to touch his hair or stroke his cheek. If her hands had any say in the matter, they would have found out the answers, but Brenna's mind still had some control over her actions.

The computer beeped, signaling that the upload was complete. Grateful for something else to focus on, Brenna leaned forward eagerly. The first few pictures passed without much commentary from either boy, not that she expected anything from Mitch. Hair pretty much looked the same to him from one head to another.

"Stop," Van commanded.

Brenna glanced at the girl in the picture and frowned. It was Brittany Cooper. The cheerleader's face was frozen in a look of confusion, not unlike the one she normally wore. The idea of her being able to stalk someone without giving herself away was ludicrous. Almost as much as the idea of Mitch being interested in the girl at all. At least Missy had some brains.

"Is Brittany secretly in love with you?" she teased, feeling the urge to be genuinely coy for the first time in her life. She decided to go with it for the sake scientific exploration.

The pair had unconsciously been leaning towards one another so when Mitch turned to address Brenna, his mouth was brought shockingly close to hers. If she moved an inch nearer to him, they'd be kissing. A week ago, she'd have been embarrassed by such a thought, but now, she found herself more than a little curious to see what it'd be like. He flashed her a crooked smile like he knew exactly what she was thinking.

"If she is, then she's out of luck." There was a fair amount of teasing in Mitch's voice, too.

"Oh yeah?" she pressed, eyebrows raised. "Why's that?"

He shrugged playfully. "Not my type."

"You're not into blondes," she concluded with a nod.

"I like smart girls."

Who knew how long the banter would have continued if Van hadn't cleared his throat? He rolled his eyes for his best friend's benefit. Properly chastised, she sat back. What had gotten into her? Her current behavior was so atypical that she almost didn't know what to make of it. Focus, Brenna. They were here to uncover a stalker's identity, not flirt.

"I'm not suggesting Brittany is Mystery Girl," Van corrected. "I'm merely doing what was asked of me, which is focusing on the hair rather than the actual girl." Reaching across Mitch, Van picked up a thick clump of Brenna's hair. "This hair is healthy, shiny, and soft to the touch. Go ahead and see for yourself."

Mitch was all too happy to oblige, but instead of touching the lock Van was holding, he trailed his fingers down Brenna's hair all the way from her scalp to where it stopped just below her shoulders. She flushed but managed to hold the boy's gaze. "It feels great," he admitted heartily.

Behind Mitch's back, Van smirked and shook his head. "Yeah, it's awesome, while Brittany's isn't. It's been treated so much that it has lost its shine and softness. It just looks dull and coarse." He pointed at the screen.

Now that he'd pointed it out, Brenna could see the difference. "So you're suggesting that Mystery Girl has dyed her hair one too many times?"

"Or styled it without replenishing the nutrients," he added. "From what I could see of it, her hair didn't look super healthy." He sniffed as if that were a greater offense than stalking a classmate.

"That's an excellent observation," Brenna praised him. She appreciated his commitment to the task even when he thought they were dealing with a ghost and was about to say so when he added, "I guess hair care products wouldn't be useful to the dead. Though I feel like if I were a ghost, I'd still be very concerned about such things."

She rolled her eyes. "Let's just focus on the living for the time being." She was about to suggest that Mitch move on to the next picture when she was reminded of the last time she was in a library – the day Dylan cornered her.

"Wait a minute," she said. "Remember when Mystery Girl slipped that note in my backpack? The one telling me to stay away from Mitch?"

Smiling, Mitch nodded. "And you smacked Dylan in the face with a book."

"He thought I was Brittany," she told them. Maybe they shouldn't discount the cheerleader after all. "What if she came in to put the note in my backpack?"

Neither one of them seemed keen to buy her theory, and honestly, Brenna wasn't ready to commit to it just yet. Dylan could have had a prearranged meeting with Brittany that the cheerleader had simply been late for or he could have simply mistaken Brenna for his favorite make-out buddy. It wasn't like Dylan was the sharpest knife in the drawer anyway. Still, Brittany was worth keeping an eye on. She added the girl's name to the previously blank list of suspects.

They continued searching through the photos, pausing momentarily when Lloyd Dobler burst into tears and required Van's attention. Sophia Irene made not a peep, which delighted Brenna to no end. But as for finding Mystery Girl, they hit a brick wall. There were a couple of possibilities that she added to the list, but none that Van felt confident about. Mitch felt that this particular aspect of the investigation was out of his element, but he contributed as best he could.

Lloyd Dobler made his presence known two more times before drawing a librarian's attention. She ambled over in her orthopedic shoes and dangling glasses to tell Van that he'd best take his doll outside because they weren't on the playground. He hustled off to the bathroom with his crying baby.

"What are the odds that his doll is defective?" Mitch wondered as he watched Van leave.

Brenna shrugged. "I think it's rather poetic."

He twisted in his seat, angling his body her way so that their knees touched and leaned forward slightly. Brenna found herself mimicking the position automatically. Mitch's face was so close that she could feel his breath on her lips.

"Thanks for helping me," he said quietly. Unlike previous

times, Brenna had no desire to turn away from the intensity of his gaze. In fact, she felt drawn to him like her body was being pulled into his atmosphere. No one was nearby. They were all alone in their private corner of the library. They were free to be honest with each other.

"It really means a lot that you'd put so much time and effort into fixing my problem." Amused by his own word choice, he pulled out that crooked grin again.

"I'm happy to help," she assured him. "You're my friend." She hesitated over the description, not certain it was accurate anymore yet not bold enough to claim a deeper connection.

"Friend?" Eyebrows raised, Mitch gave the word a twist like it left a bad taste in his mouth. He took her hand in his own and pulled it into his lap. Very softly, he brushed his fingers back and forth against it. "Do friends hold hands?"

Heart hammering in her chest, Brenna managed a playfully grin. "Sometimes I hold Van's hand."

Without breaking eye contact, Mitch touched the side of her face, letting his thumb brush across her lips and down the length of her neck. "Do friends do that?"

Coming up with a witty rejoinder was suddenly very difficult. She was trying to gather her thoughts when the unexpected presence of a familiar face brought her up short. Automatically, a red-faced Brenna yanked her hand out of Mitch's while uttering a sharp cry of "Mr. Rose!" The only thing worse than getting caught by a teacher right before a potential first kiss would have been getting caught by her uncle.

"Hey guys," their teacher greeted with a wave. He pretended not to notice how quickly the guilty couple separated from each other. "Working on a project?"

"Something like that," Mitch mumbled, disappointment etched on his face.

Running into teachers outside of school was surreal. It didn't seem like they belonged in the real world. "What are you doing here?" Brenna asked, noticing the papers in Mr. Rose's arms.

"I'm taking advantage of the peace and quiet," he told them. "My neighbor's dog hates thunderstorms. Barks like a maniac. So I'm going to hide here until they kick me out. Hopefully I can get some work done." He flashed them a smile and headed off to find an empty table.

A thin-lipped Mitch followed the man's departure with annoyed eyes before turning them on Brenna. Much to her frustration, she could see the disappointment in them. Recapturing the essence of the moment felt like a lost cause to Mitch. Her sense of loss was palpable. It didn't seem right for him to keep her hanging on like this.

Of course, maybe Mitch could say the same thing to her. With the whole maze debacle, Van seemed to think that she, with her dim-wittedness, was the reason that things were progressing so slowly. Maybe she was sending mixed signals without even knowing it. Maybe she should be bolder. Encourage him with small but meaningful gestures.

"And we're back!" Van cried, arms outstretched. Lloyd Dobler dangled by his tiny arm out of Van's right hand. "What'd we miss?"

"Nothing," Mitch sighed.

"Well let's move on to our deceased options, shall we?" To the untrained eye, Van's behavior would have made him appear oblivious to Mitch's emotional state, but a keen observer would have caught the quick glance he shot his best friend and the tiny frown it received.

The rest of Brenna's night didn't get any better from an investigative standpoint. Van's mood deflated noticeably as the search for dead girls came up with nothing. As Brenna had suspected, there were no hot murder prospects for them to investigate. There hadn't been an unsolved murder of a teenage girl in their area for a long time. Missing girls didn't turn up a whole lot of options either as none of them fit Mystery Girl's description.

Still, Van pressed on. Brenna had to give him credit for his determination, even if it was to prove her wrong. He had taken up the lead at the laptop when Mitch surrendered his chair. The distance between them made it difficult to send an encouraging gesture Mitch's direction. Difficult but not impossible.

Ever so slyly, Brenna rested her arm on the back of Van's chair, but instead of letting her hand hang in empty air, she touched Mitch's back. He responded immediately, leaning into her hand. She brushed her thumb across his shirt, a little surprised by the hardness of the muscle beneath it. His eyes found hers and he smiled. That seemed promising.

"This stinks," Van declared, banging his fist against the table.

"Well, what did you think was going to happen? The Internet would immediately cough up the name of your ghost?" In the midst of some successful flirting, Brenna could afford to be humorous.

"Yes," the boy replied with blatant honesty.

Fighting a smile, Brenna patted his shoulder in a condescending way. "That's okay, sweetie. It's hard to find something that isn't there. Mystery Girl is a living, breathing person. We need to be looking at girls with pulses."

"Yeah, and how's that going for you so far?" Van retorted. Then his eyes brightened. "Maybe we're not looking back far enough. Her clothes looked kinda vintage. Maybe she was killed in the 1970's or something."

"That would make her killer almost sixty, if he had been her age, or older." She poked Mitch's shoulder, eyes twinkling. "Are you volunteering at the senior center?"

Grinning, he shook his head.

"You shouldn't be making jokes, Brenna Pearl. This is serious." Van shut the laptop with a resolute snap and rubbed his eyes. "I think that we should be done for the night. It's past Lloyd Dobler's bedtime."

He got to his feet, stretching. Feeling guilty, Brenna quickly moved her arm before Van could figure out what she'd been doing behind his back. Here he was, working hard to find a lead, albeit a ridiculous lead, and she was trying to attract a boy's attention. What was wrong with her? She seriously needed to kick her brain into gear or they'd never solve this puzzle. They gathered their things and headed for the exit. Van led the way, discreetly giving them some privacy.

"We will figure this out," Brenna vowed to Mitch. "What Van said about her hair will be helpful, I just know it."

Mitch caught her wrist, forcing her to stop and look at him. His eyes were serious, concerned. "Look, I'm not saying that I'm being haunted or whatever, but this whole thing is totally screwy. I don't want you getting hurt because you're helping me. I wouldn't have asked you if I thought I was putting you in danger."

"No one is going to get hurt. Not you and not me." Brenna promised, twisting her wrist so that her fingers could entwine with his.

He held on tightly as if the mere touch of his hand could protect her. "Just be careful, okay? If you get a bad vibe, stumble into any cold spots, or think something's coming after you, get out of wherever you are. Trust your instincts. If they tell you to run, then run. Don't take anything for granted."

Brenna had underestimated just how worried Mitch was for her safety. She squeezed his hand. "Now you listen to me," she began firmly. "There is no ghost haunting you. There are no death omens following you around. There are no serial killers looking to make you or me their next victim. All we're dealing with is a stalker, and when we figure out who she is, she'll never bother you again."

He chewed his lip, contemplating what she'd said before exhaling heavily. He hadn't been converted to her rather optimistic view, but he nodded all the same. "In the meantime though, remember what I said."

The rain was still coming down when they ran to their cars. A thoroughly drenched Mitch stared after her, making sure she reached her vehicle before bothering to climb into his own. Seeing him like that, so openly concerned for her safety, was new. It reminded her of Duke and his natural protectiveness. She wondered if all boys developed a similar streak when it came to the special girl in their lives. Truthfully, it was sweet knowing that he cared so much.

Inside of her car, Brenna gave a wave that she wasn't sure Mitch could see through the rain and started the engine.

"I can't take hanging out with you two anymore," Van announced without preamble.

"Why not?" she asked.

He rubbed his hand across his face. "There's just too much unresolved sexual tension. The 'will they, won't they' business is driving me nuts." He slumped down in his seat, the strain clearly wearing on him. "Do me a favor and make out with him already so we can all relax."

"I didn't realize it was that bad," she said, trying to downplay her self-consciousness. That was a trick that never worked with Van, though.

He snorted. "It was like something straight out of a teen movie! Don't think I didn't know what you were doing with your arm resting on the back of my chair!" He shook his finger at her.

"I half expected to find you two rolling around on the floor when I got back from the bathroom."

"We probably would have been if Mr. Rose hadn't distracted us."

"You wanton hussy," Van smirked. Abruptly, he changed the subject. "Has Sir cried yet?"

"No, Sophia Irene hasn't cried," Brenna corrected through pursed lips. "She clearly feels very secure and loved. Don't you, sweetheart?" She threw a smile over her shoulder to where her baby sat upright and with her belt buckled. Lloyd Dobler was face down on the floor. "Maybe you need to work on your parenting skills," she suggested a touch smugly.

"Maybe I need to take his batteries out," he countered.

Brenna gasped, appalled. "How dare you even suggest such a thing! That'd be like murdering him! You have to love your baby in spite of his difficult personality." Lloyd Dobler punctuated her remark with a wail, earning him a growl of annoyance from his father.

Slapping on a stricken face, Van snatched the baby from the ground and held him aloft. "You must stop this, Lloyd Dobler! All the crying in the world won't bring Mommy back!" he wailed at the doll. "She would have taken us to her home planet, but humans can't survive in its atmosphere! But at least we have each other!" He burst into fake tears and hugged Lloyd Dobler to his chest while simultaneously sticking the key into his back.

"I shudder at the thought of you raising actual children," Brenna said, shaking her head.

Like the crack of a whip, Brenna sat straight up in bed, heart pounding like a runaway freight train. One hand clutched at her sheet while the other flew to her chest in an attempt to calm her nerves. The nightmare had felt alarmingly real. Mystery Girl had chased her through the woods, preventing her from finding Mitch. No matter which way Brenna turned, her enemy was always hot on her heels, unshakable as an evil shadow. She hadn't been terrified for herself but for Mitch. His petrified screams were still ringing in her ears. Even though it had just been a dream, she never, ever wanted to hear that sound again. But even as she sat panting for breath, she knew instinctively that it was not her nightmare that had pulled her so brutally from sleep. It had been something else.

Had it been Sophia Irene? No, Brenna couldn't hear the baby's cries. She wondered vaguely if there was something wrong with her doll since she still hadn't cried.

Not the thunderstorm, either. The rain continued to come down hard, the deluge punctuated by tympani-like rolls of thunder and flashes of lightening. While such weather might bother some people, Brenna loved it. It was beautiful, really, and nothing that would cause fear to flood her veins like it did now.

Something was wrong. Danger was near. There was no logical explanation for such an assertion, but she sensed that it was true. It was the reason she couldn't calm down.

A bright, white light lit up her window for a moment before disappearing abruptly. Definitely not lightning. Succumbing to instinct, she hopped out of bed and dashed to the window to see what was going on down below. She wiped her hand across the glass, clearing it from icy condensation. The thunderstorm made it terribly hard to see anything clearly. Brenna pressed her face to the window, eyes straining to see past the veiled curtain of the rain.

There, on the ground by the trees, she saw it. Movement. *What* was moving though? The exact shape was indiscernible. All that she could tell was that it was black, and she was pretty sure that was because it was dark outside rather than it being the object's actual color. Was it the bushes whipping in the wind or something else? A stray dog seeking shelter from the storm? Brenna mashed her face harder against the glass as if that would magically assist her eyes. Of course it didn't. But then the thunder rolled and oh, bless it! There was the lightning, illuminating the night for only a mere fraction of a heartbeat, but it was enough.

She saw red. Literally. It was Mystery Girl's red hoodie. She was down there.

Anger flooded Brenna. Who did she think she was, this girl? What gave her the right to terrorize Mitch? He hadn't done anything to deserve such torment, and now she had the gall to lurk outside of Brenna's home! What did she hope to accomplish? Frighten Brenna into staying away from Mitch? Well, she wasn't the type of girl to get scared so easily. No one messed with her friends and got away with it. Whatever game Mystery Girl was playing was going to end.

Now.

Brenna ran to her bedroom door, yanked it open, and pounded down the steps. She navigated the dark house with relative ease, only knocking over one kitchen chair. It clattered to the floor as Brenna ripped open the back door and darted out into the rain. Only as her feet touched the wet grass did she register the fact that she wasn't appropriately dressed to give chase, but there was no stopping her now.

She ran to the trees, eyes searching for her enemy. The rain was blinding! It was even harder to see now that she was down in it. She couldn't see anyone or anything that was out of place. Frantic, she continued searching, running across the yard and back again.

"Where are you?" she called into the night. "I know you're out here! Show yourself, you coward!"

The rain pelted her unmercifully as she waited for an answer she knew wouldn't come. Mystery Girl had vanished into thin air just like – no! She refused to entertain the idea that she was dealing with a ghost. Mystery Girl had probably seen her watching at the window and run away. She would have had time, especially since Brenna had lingered in the backyard. Or maybe she simply moved to a different location. Not ready to give up, Brenna ran around to the front of the house to see if there was anything noteworthy – a suspicious car, a figure fleeing the premises.

Nothing.

She ran to the back yard again, back to where she thought she'd seen Mystery Girl. Upon closer inspection, there was nothing to indicate that anyone had ever been there, but there was something red. A red, plastic bag tangled up in a bush. Could that have been what Brenna saw? The lightning hadn't given her much time to see anything clearly. Maybe her eyes saw the bag but told her brain it was a hoodie because she wanted it to be a hoodie. Maybe Mystery Girl had never been out here, and she'd risked getting pneumonia for no reason. But what about the white light she'd seen? Merely the headlights of a passing car, her brain reasoned.

She remembered what *Zio* had said about ghosts – people saw what they wanted to see. After waking up from a nightmare, maybe Brenna had seen Mystery Girl because the girl had been the antagonist in her dream, so she was subconsciously looking for payback. Disappointed and suddenly freezing, Brenna wrapped her arms around her soaked body.

A hand clamped down on her shoulder. Fist ready, Brenna swung automatically to fend off her attacker and barely missed punching her uncle in the face as he jerked his head back. Holy crap but his reflexes were good.

"I'm sorry!" she shrieked, hands raised in dismay. Guilt flooded her as she wondered how much noise she'd made running out of the house. Probably enough to give him a small heart attack.

Abraham took her by the arms. There was something akin to panic in his eyes. "Brenna, what are you doing out here?"

Eyes darting around wildly, she shook her head. "Something woke me up, and I thought I saw someone down here!" Maybe she should have mentioned Mystery Girl, but she kept quiet. She wasn't ready to hand over her investigation to her uncle, and she wasn't completely certain that she was in danger. Mystery Girl had done nothing but make herself a nuisance.

"And so you ran out into the rain by yourself? What were you thinking?" He was angry. No, not angry. Scared, and why wouldn't he be? It was crazy and reckless, what she'd done.

Brenna opened her mouth, uncertain of what to say. She was confused, freezing, and now thinking her brain had still been trapped in her nightmare when she looked out the window. "I had a bad dream," was the only sure answer she was able to give him.

Her uncle's eyes relaxed. He thought it was all a misunderstanding motivated by nocturnal terrors, and maybe it was. Brenna couldn't say. She was almost absolutely certain that she'd seen Mystery Girl, but a kernel of doubt was all it took to keep her second guessing herself. She let Abraham usher her back inside the house. Out of the elements and without her adrenaline rush, Brenna was shivering all over. Joints practically frozen solid, she collapsed into a kitchen chair as Abraham darted away. Drawing her knees into her chest, Brenna pressed her jaw against her knee to keep her teeth from shattering her skull with their incessant chattering. She hugged herself tightly, trying to warm her core up.

All of this ghost talk was driving her around the bend, contributing to her nightmares and giving her hallucinations. She blamed Van. The wildness of his imagination was catching. He would surely laugh at her behavior tomorrow. That or be horrified by her boldness. He probably would think that the "ghost" had been out there, trying to lure her to her death or some other such nonsense.

No one was out there.

You're safe. Soaking wet but safe.

Get a grip on reality, Brenna.

Something warm fell across her shoulders – a towel. Her uncle was back. He wrapped her up in a soft, dry cocoon before scooping her into his arms. Without a word, he carried her up the stairs just like he used to when she, as a small child, would fall asleep in front of the television. She felt bad for the trouble she'd caused. *Zio* was no doubt concerned about her mental health. The poor man was every bit as cold as her and yet he was putting her comfort above his own. Just like always.

"S-s-s-sorry," Brenna managed to squeak out. She gave a sheepish smile.

The fear he'd been feeling outside was gone. He grinned back at her, water running off his mustache in two thin lines. "Just save some hot water for me," he instructed as he set her down in front of the bathroom. The shower was already running. "I set some dry clothes out for you."

Shutting the door behind her, Brenna stripped out of her wet things and hopped into the shower. The water was scalding at first but as her body warmed back up, it became absolutely delightful. It eased away her tension and embarrassment until all that was left was a very weary girl. She would have liked to stay in longer but knew *Zio* was politely waiting his turn.

Abraham was standing sentinel at her window, eyes fixed on the ground below as if he expected to see something. Amazingly, he was still in his wet clothes. Brenna thought that he would have changed out of those at least, but all he'd done to warm himself up was drape one of the towels he carried her up in over his shoulders.

A thought flickered across her mind as she took note of his assertive stance. She'd scared him, running out into the night like that. Sure, the sound of someone running through the house was bound to get his blood pumping, but his fear had seemed more intense than the average adrenaline-induced panic. But why? *Zio* wasn't prone to overreaction, which naturally got her thinking that maybe there *was* something to be frightened of. After all, someone had used her to send a message to Abraham about his past. What if he thought the person who left behind the information about Eliza Kent was interested in doing something more devious?

Then again, maybe she was being overly paranoid. After all, he'd been pulled from sleep to find his niece screaming in a thunderstorm. Surely, if he was concerned about her safety, he would say something.

He turned at the soft padding of her feet. "Feeling better?" he inquired.

"Feeling foolish," she admitted, drawing a soft chuckle from him as she climbed into bed.

Drawing near, he smiled down at her. "There are far worse things to feel foolish about," he said, patting her wet head. "But the next time you think you see someone outside, come wake me up before you go running off to investigate. After all, I *am* an officer of the law." With that, he planted a kiss on her forehead and left.

Exhausted wasn't quite a strong enough word for how Brenna felt, but in spite of her weariness, sleep was harder to catch than Mystery Girl. She'd been more than foolish tonight. It seemed that she'd lucked out, but what if her enemy had been out there? What if Mystery Girl had been trying to lure her outside so she could attack her? She would have played right into the stalker's hands. Just like those stupid girls in horror movies. After all the complaining she'd done about those girls, it turned out she was none the wiser. Well, that would be true no longer. She would use her brain. Think intelligently and be rational.

Ready to be done with such thoughts, Brenna flipped onto her stomach. She straightened her wet ponytail so that it laid nice and politely on her back even though she knew such efforts would be in vain. It would end up drying funny, making it look like a failed attempt at curling her hair.

Curling her hair. Wait a second.

If Brenna could curl her hair, why couldn't Mystery Girl straighten hers if necessary? Especially if it would help her from being recognized? And Van had said that the girl's hair had looked dull and coarse, which could be the result of using a hair straightener. Given that anonymity was important, if the girl in question had curly hair, she probably didn't go around straightening it on a regular basis. But maybe she would on special occasions.

Once again, Brenna jumped out of bed, this time dashing to her bookshelf. She switched on her desk lamp and knelt down by the shelf, searching. There it was – last year's yearbook. She flipped through the book to the junior section, scanning the faces until one stood out. A pleasant-faced girl smiled up at her with eyes that exhibited kindness. Her normally curly hair hung straight, draped strategically over one shoulder.

"No," she breathed as her heart kicked into high gear. "Not possible."

It couldn't be Hannah Davenport, could it?

Chapter Eighteen

"There's no way," Van declared with definitive assurance.

"Absolutely not," Mitch agreed with a hearty nod.

It was hard for Brenna to press her argument in the face of such certainty. The three of them – five if you counted Sophia Irene and Lloyd Dobler – had hidden themselves in the library before first period to discuss her latest brain wave since it involved the actual naming of a suspect.

"I don't want to believe that it's Hannah either," Brenna replied. She held up the yearbook for them. "But look at the hair. It's just like Van described."

Van gave the picture a cursory glance. "The quality of the photo renders your analysis obsolete." Such a smart aleck remark earned him a reproachful look. "Fine," he sighed. "In the spirit of honest investigation, I concede that you have a point about the hair. The girl, however, is wrong."

"Brenna, I've worked in ASB with Hannah since I was a freshman," Mitch told her. "She's the sweetest person I've ever met. She wouldn't hurt a fly let alone stalk me."

"Your history with her is what concerns me," she admitted. "Maybe she's been trying to get close to you, and you simply haven't noticed, so she's trying a new tactic. A girl like Hannah wouldn't make the first move."

Looking uncomfortable, Mitch shuffled his feet. "I agree with that last comment, but the rest? I've never gotten that vibe from her, and we interact a lot. She's my Vice President for crying out loud. She's one of the people I know best at this school."

"I'm shocked that you could you even accuse her of such a thing! Her dad is a pastor!" Van was the very picture of condemnation.

A wearied Brenna sighed as she massaged her forehead. "Do I honestly believe it's Hannah? No, I don't, but then again, I wouldn't have thought Kevin Bishop was the Dark Avenger. Sometimes people are really good at putting up a front."

Therein lied the real trouble. How did one sift through the genuine people to find those with dark, ulterior motives? Right now, the only answer Brenna could think of was to put Hannah to the test. Let her actions prove her innocence. Speaking of which....

"How did Hannah take it when you told her I was going to sit with you in the maze?" she asked.

"She was happy," Mitch said with a shrug. "She even suggested that Van sit with her at the entrance."

Hannah either knew all the right answers, or she was the kindest soul in the world. Brenna was praying for the latter. "Look, none of us want to think that Hannah is Mystery Girl, so let's find the evidence to exonerate her. To do that, I need to observe her closely when she's around you."

Mitch nodded, getting the picture. "You should come to our ASB meetings."

"Isn't that for members only?"

"Not right now. We're working after school every day for the next two weeks for the carnival. We could use extra hands," he told her.

"Besides, Brenna's your girlfriend. What the President wants, the President gets, right?" Van smiled, smacking the boy on his back. He gave his best friend a roguish wink. It looked like Van was going to do his part to help her relationship along whether she wanted it or not. Great.

Puffing out his chest, Mitch smirked. "You know it, brother." They high-fived each other, laughing like the silly boys they were. Brenna rolled her eyes, fighting a smile.

"Okay, I'll come to tomorrow's meeting," she said, attempting to get the conversation back on track. She would have preferred going today after school, but she had to work.

Mitch sobered up. "You can help Hannah with the maze layout. It's the perfect opportunity for you to see that it's not her."

Brenna held up her hands. "I'm quite pleased to consider this an exoneration exercise. I know it's not her, but we need the evidence to back it up."

Her words seemed to appease them as neither one wanted to think that Hannah Davenport was Mystery Girl. They rested more comfortably knowing that Brenna wasn't a hardcore believer in her theory. She waited, watching them converse with each other as she contemplated her next move. She'd debated over and over again whether or not to tell them about her midnight foray into the rain. Primarily because she wasn't sure whether or not Mystery Girl had been out there or not. In the end, she decided that her uncertainty was irrelevant. They needed to know.

"So I can't say for certain, but I think Mystery Girl might have visited me last night."

Their horror might have been comical if it wasn't directed at her. The more she said, the worse they looked. She got through her story without interruption probably because they were too stunned by her stupidity to speak, but when they finally did, the power of their emotions gave yesterday's thunderstorm a run for its money. Van's outrage was nothing compared to Mitch's. He demanded that Brenna not go out at night, especially by herself, or do anything at all that called for her to be out alone until Mystery Girl was apprehended. He even went so far as to state that she shouldn't stay after school to help Mr. Rose.

Now part of Brenna was quite annoyed with his anger and demands, believing that he was completely overreacting since it wasn't even for certain that she'd been in any danger. She wanted to defend herself and let her temper air itself out. But she kept quiet, taking his judgment with a brave face because she knew that it was out of fear for her safety. He cared for her and was upset that she'd been reckless. She had been stupid and his anger was deserved. If this was the worst result of her foolish actions, then she was quite fortunate.

The bell rang and they headed to class. As was becoming his custom, Mitch took her hand as they left the library. Mr. Rose's door was shut when they reached it. Their teacher was running late again.

"This is going to be the longest day ever. I can feel it." Van rubbed his hand across his face and gave his head a shake.

"Did the thunderstorm keep you up?" Brenna asked, taking in her best friend's haggard appearance.

Van held Lloyd Dobler up for her to see. "No, this baby kept me up. I swear that he's got some internal sensor in him that sets him crying every time I fall asleep. I think he's broken or something."

"Sounds like he works just fine to me," Brenna laughed, hugging Sophia Irene to her chest.

"Oh, what a cute doll! I didn't realize you two were in Childhood Development," exclaimed Autumn Winters as she walked over to them. She touched Lloyd Dobler's hand with the tip of one of her black fingernails. "What did you name him?"

"Well, his mother originally wanted to name him Francois after her father, but I refused to let my son be named after a Frenchman who's never read Victor Hugo. So we went with Lloyd Dobler, instead." He shrugged like that was the most natural choice.

Autumn laughed and looked at Brenna. "Sophia Irene," she quickly supplied before Van had a chance to answer on her behalf. The goth girl then peppered the two with questions about the project.

"Man, I wish I had signed up for that class! I didn't realize it was going to be so cool. I love babies," sighed Autumn. It wasn't the kind of comment Brenna would have expected from the girl, who was usually so sullen and reserved. The black she always wore was more indicative of her general mood than a fashion statement.

The final bell rang, and Sophia Irene started wailing.

"Now, I know that's your baby," Van replied. "Only your kid would cry because her eagerness to learn was being thwarted."

Letting go of Mitch's hand, Brenna ignored Van and concentrated on inserting the key into Sophia Irene's back. Once accomplished, she looked down the now deserted hall. Where was Mr. Rose? He'd never been this late before. She wondered if maybe they should go tell Mr. Elliott. None of her classmates seemed put out by their teacher's absence, except for Cameron, but Brenna was pretty sure that the contemptuous look on his face was for her benefit.

"If he's ten minutes late, that means we get to leave for the day, right?" Van asked hopefully.

"Yeah, that's not exactly how it works," Mitch grinned. "Besides, he's coming up the stairs now."

He was right. Mr. Rose came bounding up the steps, doing his best impersonation of a drowned rat. It looked like he'd decided to swim to work instead of drive. His mood was nothing short of foul as he opened the door and ushered them inside. Though when he caught sight of Brenna lingering in the hall with a crying baby in her arms, he managed to smile while shaking his head.

"Sorry," she replied sheepishly.

"It's okay. Come in when it's done." He let the door close behind him.

After what felt like an eternity, but in reality was probably only twenty seconds, Brenna joined her classmates just in time for a surprise quiz on *Tess of the d'Urbervilles*, which she suspected was inspired by their teacher's mood rather than his lesson plan. There was a fair amount of grumbling about it. People seemed to think that the continuing thunderstorm gave them an excuse to whine. Unappreciative of their behavior, Mr. Rose quipped that life wasn't fair and passed out the quizzes. Truthfully, it was harder than it should have been. If she failed, Brenna was going to blame Mystery Girl for keeping her up half the night.

Half of the quizzes had been turned in when the power went out. Suddenly, the thunderstorm became a thing of beauty. It was so dark in the room that Brenna could barely make out a teacher-shaped form throw its hands in the air in surrender.

"I think Mr. Rose might be nearing a nervous breakdown," Van mused, scooting his desk closer to Brenna's. "I've never seen a teacher lose it before. Could be interesting."

"He's super stressed this year, and his neighbor's dog hates thunderstorms," she told him. "Fate appears to be conspiring against him."

Mitch arrived, bringing a chair with him. He sat down, legs underneath Brenna's desk so they bumped against hers. She twisted in her seat to give him more room and subsequently gave him her back. He leaned one arm on the desk and rested the other where the desk met the chair, creating the effect of wrapping his arms around her without actually doing it. Her right shoulder was already touching his chest, and she had to fight the urge to lean further into him. It was a good thing the power was out. Brenna was sure that she blushing like an idiot. Add that to the goofy grin that was most certainly on her face and Van would never let her live it down. And there, as they sat together, so close to each other and yet so far, an epiphany occurred.

Without a doubt, Mitch had crossed the line, passing from friend into something more. She couldn't exactly pinpoint when the moment occurred – maybe while they were at the library – but the line was a faint blur in the distance now. He made her heart flutter, filled her with the urge to giggle like a schoolgirl – and she liked it. She wanted to blush when he confessed his feelings for her, talk with him about anything and everything, and sit with him under the stars. And yes, she really wanted to kiss him.

Wow. Was this what a serious crush felt like? Was that light-as-a-feather feeling normal? It was spectacular, even if it did make her feel a little nauseous. It was hard to believe that she had never felt this way before. Okay, maybe a little bit when she was around Mr. Rose, but what she felt now blew those feelings out of the water. Clearly, she'd misjudged the whole romance thing. Of course, it was easy to criticize what one hadn't experienced.

As the boys conversed, Brenna's mind wandered off of its own accord, building fairy tale castles that only a young girl in the throes of her first crush can do.

"Okay, I didn't want to say anything while Lover Boy was around, but it seriously bothers me that you're not more concerned about this ghost-stalker business." Van leaned across the counter to peer at his best friend as she cleaned the display case.

The girl shrugged. "I already explained this. I wasn't even sure she was out there, so why should I be freaking out?"

"Brenna, you saw something that had you running out of your house into a thunderstorm in the middle of the night. She was there." How he could sound so definitive when he hadn't even been present was a mystery to her.

"The only thing that I'm certain of is that you've corrupted my imagination with your paranormal nonsense. I had just woken up from a nightmare and was seeing things. And it's all your fault." Getting to her feet, she slammed her hands down on the counter on either side of his head for emphasis.

Van flipped over, staring up at her with a smirk. "If it really was my fault, you'd be properly terrified."

Biting back an angry sigh, Brenna pinched the bridge of her nose. "This whole thing is very frustrating. With the Dark Avenger, it was much simpler."

"Yes, people were only nearly getting beaten to death."

She smacked his chest. "You know what I mean! We had multiple suspects and figured out the motive. You could see a logical progression in what Kevin did, and in the end, we were able to anticipate his final move. With Mystery Girl, I have no idea what's going on. Sure, I have possible motives, but it's hard to go after someone who refuses to come out of the shadows."

"That's the trouble with ghosts," Van said, shifting to recline against the counter. They regarded each other, heads propped up on their elbows. "They *are* the shadows."

Unintentionally, he was emphasizing her problem. There were so many theories that they were making it impossible to see things clearly. Brenna felt as if her mind was being pulled in twenty different directions – and that was without factoring in her blossoming romance with Mitch. How could she possibly find the answer with her focus split?

"It's weird, but I feel like all the answers are right in front of me and yet completely out of my grasp. The only thing I'm getting closer to is having a boyfriend."

Van snorted into his palm.

"All joking aside," she prefaced, holding her best friend's blue eyes securely with her own. "Do you really think that we're dealing with an actual, honest-to-goodness ghost?" It wouldn't have been the first time Van had clung to the absurd for the sake of driving her nuts.

He drummed his fingers on the counter while his brow furrowed, indicating just how seriously he was contemplating his answer. "All joking aside, yeah, I think I really do. I don't know how else to explain what I saw." He shook his head, still mystified. "I know you're into logic and all that, but what I saw defied logic."

"Okay," Brenna said slowly as she tried to convince her mind to go with his line of thinking for the moment. "If she's a ghost and if she was outside my window last night, what was the purpose of that? What's your favorite theory?"

Van didn't even hesitate. "She's warning you that you're in trouble. My guess is that she's manifesting when the person who's trying to hurt you is near in order to put you on your guard." Brenna could tell he'd deliberately shied away from Keiko's 'death omen' term. "Think back to last night. Was there any sign that someone else had been outside your house? Forget Mystery Girl."

Brenna's mind transported her back to the moment she'd stepped out into the rain. It had been so hard to see anything, and she'd specifically been searching for Mystery Girl's red hoodie. Her eyes hadn't stayed long on anything that wasn't red. Just because she hadn't seen something didn't mean it wasn't there, though.

She shook her head. "I don't know. I was so focused on her.

The only thing that I can't account for that might indicate the presence of someone else was the white light that lit up my room." That had been weird, and now that she really thought about it, it was probably too bright to be mere headlights. "It was like someone had shined a light right into it."

"Maybe that was her. If she can manifest, maybe she can show herself in other forms like white light, which would have served the dual purpose of waking you up and scaring the bad guy away."

"Okay, but why was he out there in the first place? Was he going to break into the house or just merely stalking his prey?" Van held up his hand to indicate his ignorance, which was frustrating. It would be so much easier if he had all the answers figured out. She posed another sticky point to his theory. "Continuing in this vein, it seems strange that Mystery Girl would start out haunting Mitch and then switch to me. If I'm the one in danger, why wouldn't she just start with me?"

"How do you know she hasn't been haunting you all along?" he asked.

She frowned. "I would have seen her watching me just like Mitch did."

"Maybe she wasn't appearing in the same form. Maybe she was a shadow or a mist."

Instead of getting annoyed, Brenna exhaled heavily and went with it. "Okay, so if she was haunting me this whole time and I'm just now seeing her, why haunt Mitch at all? Is his life in danger, too?"

"I think it's like Keiko said. She wants him to save you. Maybe he's the only one who can do it."

"But why?" How was it possible that only one person could save her? Surely there were far more qualified rescuers like Abraham and Duke. It was their sanctioned duty as cops to save people. Why not task one of them with the responsibility?

"Because he's in love with you."

His matter-of-fact tone made Brenna straighten up, her cheeks flushed. Unconsciously, she put a hand over her stomach to try to calm the sudden flutter of activity. It was a beautiful thought, thinking that someone was in love with her, but a lot to deal with at the moment. After all, she had just gotten used to the idea of having a crush on him. Thankfully, Van wasn't expecting her to respond.

"Sometimes history repeats itself until it gets it right," he said by way of preamble. "Once upon a time, Mystery Girl was alive and in love with a boy. Then along came the evil man who picked her out, preyed upon her, and eventually killed her. Her boy tried to save her but failed. Fast forward to today and Mystery Girl, now a trapped soul, is watching her own tragic history start to play out again. This time, she's determined that love shall prevail. She's haunting you both in order to bring you together and stop the killer."

Brenna stood quietly, absorbing his words. The scene he depicted sounded more like a movie than real life, but there was something magical about it. She liked the idea of love conquering all. Still, the whole thing didn't seem plausible.

"She's incredibly omniscient," Brenna replied.

Van shrugged. "She's a ghost. Why shouldn't she have psychic insight as well?"

Since they were currently camped out in the realm of the hypothetical, Brenna figured she could allow his reasoning. All in all, he'd given her much to think about. Van had clearly put some thought into it. Honestly, of all the ghostly theories they'd kicked about at The Cherry Blossom, this one was the most logical – though one initially had to accept the irrational idea that ghosts were real. Aside from that, she could follow Van's line of thinking and felt satisfied with his answers for now.

"So if Mitch saves me and the killer is caught, Mystery Girl gets to move on," she concluded.

He nodded. "I would think so."

Feeling that they'd exhausted this possibility, Brenna turned her thoughts to the living. "And if Mystery Girl has a pulse? What was she doing outside my house last night? What is her motivation?"

"She's a crazy psycho who's going to eat your heart out," he supplied without batting an eye.

"Awesome," she stated blandly. "So I'm in danger either way."

"Pretty much," he agreed. Concentration waning, he made Lloyd Dobler dance across the counter like a ballerina. "Upholding the spirit of absolute honesty, do you really think it's Hannah?"

Brenna closed her eyes, trying to envision a psychotic Hannah Davenport. The very idea was laughable. "No, but I've got to start somewhere. By eliminating her, that gives me one less girl to worry about."

Talking things out with Van was really helping her sort through the case. This was a conversation that should have been had a long time ago, but she'd been too focused on Mitch. For days, they'd thrown so many ideas and tangents around, but now, those were being twisted and refined into solid, complete theories. So maybe she couldn't put an actual name to Mystery Girl yet, but if she could understand the girl's mind, she'd be one step closer.

"All right, so we have here a girl who's obsessed with Mitch. She stalks him and wants him to see her. He's gone after her, but she always eludes him."

"How very female," quipped Van. He held Lloyd Dobler up to his face. "Learn this lesson now, son. The word 'girl' is synonymous with 'tease.'"

The second he said it, something clicked into place in Brenna's mind. "That's it," she breathed. "She *is* a tease! She's like Alexis, strutting down the hall in her tight skirt and high heels, wanting every boy to take note of her. Except Mystery Girl only wants Mitch's attention. She wants to be noticed by him, to be pursued by him, and eventually, to be caught by him."

Yes, things were making sense now. She could see her in her mind's eye – a poor girl who pined for a boy who hadn't noticed her. "My guess is that she's around Mitch all the time, but she's not the sort of girl who attracts boys' eyes. He's probably never really seen her. Sure, he might talk to her, but he's not giving her the deep focused attention she wants. She's probably shy or withdrawn, so cue the theatrics! Suddenly, she's at the forefront of his mind. He's always on the lookout for her, which pleases her to no end, because the boy she wants is finally noticing her."

"Great plan except all that did was throw him into your arms," Van replied.

"Which is why she's targeting me now," Brenna agreed. Admittedly, that had originally been part of the plan. Make Mystery Girl jealous so she slips up and reveals herself, but the girl was proving hard to trap. Perhaps, now that Brenna had a better understanding of the type of girl she was, she'd be able to spot the culprit out of her costume.

Wait. Costume.

"Van, we are idiots," she announced, throwing her hands to the ceiling. "She's not simply wearing some weird ensemble just to get noticed. It's a costume!" Smiling, she looked at her best friend expectantly. "Maybe her clothes aren't the only thing about her that's a costume."

He blinked and then it hit him. "She's wearing a wig! That's why her hair looks awful! It's fake!" They high-fived each other.

"Of course, you realize that now instead of eliminating suspects, we've increased the pool dramatically."

"I don't care!" she cried, feeling light-hearted.

"But wait, what about her lack of a face? How did she pull that off if she's a real girl?"

The question Van posed was a tricky one, but then again, if Mystery Girl was wearing a costume, who was to say that she hadn't been wearing something over her face to hide her features?

"*Zio* and I watched this crime show where these criminals all wore the same clear mask. It hid their features, making them look identical. The victims couldn't tell them apart. Maybe our girl has a similar mask to keep her features from being recognized."

Van nodded, admitting that her theory had merit, which was a big concession on his part since he was still holding to the "it's a ghost" theory. "And what about all that giggling? How'd she pull that off?"

"I don't know, but there's probably a logical answer," she admitted. "Maybe she can tell us when we catch her."

Brenna felt a considerable weight lift from her shoulders. She had a suspect profile and the knowledge that Mystery Girl liked costumes. All she had to do was find girls who had the right personality and watch them interact with Mitch. With Brenna in the picture, Mystery Girl was probably desperate now, trying to get his attention in any way possible. In reality, the culprit had two costumes: Mystery Girl and her real identity. It seemed that the first one was exclusively being used for her benefit now – Mitch hadn't seen a red hoodie since the middle of last week – which probably meant that she was approaching him as herself now. Brenna could use the girl's need to be noticed against her.

"She's got to be in ASB or at least in one of his classes," she mused, tapping her chin as she shifted through a sea of female faces. With this revelation, Brenna felt that Hannah could most likely be ruled out since she didn't fit the profile. While she wasn't into chasing boys, Hannah was definitely not shy. However, she was going to take nothing for granted. There would be no Kevin Bishop repeats, which unfortunately meant that no one got the benefit of the doubt anymore. She flashed a smile at Van. "I am very much looking forward to school tomorrow. This girl's desperate, I can feel it. Desperate people screw up sooner or later."

Van crossed his fingers. "Let's hear it for sooner!"

"You always help me think better," she told him with heartfelt sincerity. "I'm ashamed that we didn't have a conversation like this a week ago. I was too caught up in catching her rather than thinking about her as a person."

"Plus, there's Mitch. Romance always complicates things."

At the sound of Mitch's name, Brenna felt herself sigh with delight and her mind went momentarily fuzzy as she pictured his face. But when she heard Van's chuckle in spite of its lowness, she snapped back to reality.

Cheeks an embarrassing shade of red, she slumped back down on the counter. "Am I turning into one of those silly girls who can only think about boys?" she asked dejectedly. "I don't want to forfeit my intelligence just so I can have a boyfriend."

"I'll admit that you've been a little silly of late," Van said with only a small amount of hesitancy. She found his honesty refreshing as it helped put her behavior into perspective. "But you're venturing into new territory so of course it's going to take some getting used to. It's actually been fun to watch you fall for him. Makes you seem more human." Laughing, he jumped back to elude the hand flying in his direction.

"It seems kind of sudden, these feelings that I have for him," Brenna admitted. "Shouldn't they take longer develop? Does that mean they aren't genuine? Maybe mere infatuation that will fade as fast as it came on?"

Van shrugged. "While I think that, ultimately, only time will tell, I know you would never act on thoughts or feelings that you didn't think were real. So I say, relax and enjoy your new relationship."

Relationship. That was such an intense word, especially when it was emphasized in the way Van had with such seriousness. It was a label that made weaker people high tail it for the hills. And while its implications made her a little nervous, Brenna was more than a little excited at the prospect. She tried to play it cool, though.

"I don't think you can call it a relationship when you haven't had an honest-to-goodness conversation about your feelings for each other," she mused. But that wasn't for lack of trying. Every time things seemed to be heading that way, they got interrupted.

"I can't believe you want to have a conversation about your feelings," sighed Van. "You're turning into such a girl."

CHAPTER NINETEEN

Not long after their discussion had waned, Chrissie ran into Honey B's to collect her brother while lamenting the weather's treatment of her hair. Naturally, this got her brother up in arms about his own tresses, which Brenna found mildly amusing given that he'd just accused her of being girlie. With brave faces, the siblings left the bakery, running at full speed to where their mother, Olive, sat waiting for them in the family mini van.

When it was Brenna's turn to leave an hour later, the heavens offered her a temporary respite from the rain. She couldn't help but smile as she headed to her car with Sophia Irene tucked safely under her arm. They were going to unmask Mystery Girl soon – she could feel it. Still grinning, Brenna slid inside her car and headed back to school. It was impossible to shake the giddiness she felt at her cerebral breakthrough. Add that to the fluttering excitement that came upon her when she saw Mitch, and Brenna didn't even have to pretend to be a doting girlfriend.

"Hi!" she greeted him jovially as she all but launched herself, baby and all, into his arms.

Mitch caught her, laughing. "What's with the unbridled enthusiasm?" he inquired, holding Brenna to his chest. "Not that I mind, of course."

Her arms were already around his neck, so she gently tugged his head down, bringing his ear to her lips. "My brain is officially working again."

"Which means?" Mitch pulled back so she could watch him raise his eyebrows in curiosity. He looked as excited as she felt. She was suddenly wishing that she didn't have to help Mr. Rose. Spending time with Mitch would have been more fun. If Brenna hadn't been governed by a strong sense of responsibility, she would have blown her teacher off.

"Which means that I'll call you later," she murmured, tapping his nose with her finger.

Smiling, he stared into her eyes. "This new mood of yours," he began, tightening his hands around her waist. "I like it."

"Better get used to it." Brenna's smile was most definitely coy.

Something passed between them, an understanding that things were changing in all the right ways. Of course, there were still words that needed to be said, but this was neither the time nor the place for such a conversation. They would have to remain unspoken. For now.

Rather reluctantly, Mitch pulled away with an entreaty for her to call when she got home. She made Sophia Irene wave a goodbye to him, and he chuckled. Then she turned to find an exhausted Mr. Rose frowning. He caught her looking at him and he started to smile but it morphed into a yawn.

"Sorry," he said. "It's been a rather long day."

"Maybe you should go home," she suggested, thinking about catching Mitch before he left so they could hang out instead. "I can take some additional things with me."

Unfortunately, he shook his head. "I'd love to, believe me, but that'll simply put me farther behind than I already am."

With that, they set about trying to knock a dent into the work, but neither one of them seemed very into it. Brenna tried to focus on the papers in front of her, but it was too easy to get distracted by her own thoughts since none found in the notebooks were very original. She even tried to make a game of it, trying to see how many mistakes she could find, but to no avail. It was no wonder Mr. Rose didn't want to read them. How a person in an honors English class could fail to know the difference between there, their, and they're was beyond her.

Mr. Rose wasn't helping her concentration either what with his constant yawning and muttering. Brenna had never seen him so agitated. She felt bad and wondered if Van might be right, and maybe he *was* nearing some kind of breakdown. Sleep deprivation could do that to a person. To keep himself awake, he started pacing, which was even more distracting. She didn't understand why he couldn't just cut himself some slack and call the night a wash. Even Brenna recognized that she needed a night off every now and then, and she was, as Van liked to point out, abnormally responsible.

Finally, the teacher gave up and sat down in the desk ahead of the one Brenna was in. He twisted to look at her. "A wise man must know when to concede defeat," he stated dully. "This is me conceding."

"I think that's a good idea," Brenna agreed, capping her pen. "Maybe you can catch up on some sleep."

"Not likely with that stupid dog barking all hours of the night," Mr. Rose grimaced as he stretched.

"Maybe they could put him in the garage?"

"You'd think," he replied with uncharacteristic sarcasm. He shook his head, dismayed by his inconsiderate neighbors.

Brenna hesitated, mustering the boldness to ask the question that had been lingering in her mind. "This probably borders on prying, but is everything okay? I can't recall you ever being this stressed out before."

He paused for a moment, weighing his answer and then sighed, defeated. "I'm going through a very difficult break-up, and unfortunately, it's wreaking havoc on my state of mind. She's having trouble moving on."

His answer, combined with his frankness, took her aback. Brenna hadn't even known Mr. Rose had a girlfriend. "That's too bad," she said with sympathy. "I wish there was something I could do to help."

"You are helping, Brenna," he smiled, gesturing to the notebooks. Then he rubbed an eye while his other hand pointed at the doll. "What did you name her?"

"Sophia Irene," she told him.

"Knowing you as I do, I'm assuming that the names have some sort of significance."

She grinned. "Wisdom and Peace, respectively."

"Ah, wonderful," the teacher asserted. "It's nice that you gave it some thought whereas my own mother named me after a character in a book she read during her pregnancy."

Brenna searched her memory, trying to think of a book with an Avery in it, but came up blank. "Which book?"

"*Love's Fiery Embrace* or some such inane title. It was about a firefighter, I think. Mom loved her romance novels." He rolled his eyes dramatically. "She thought Avery Rose was such a dreamy name."

"My mom named me after a little girl she babysat for. My uncle said they were as close as sisters. My middle name is in honor of my grandfather's nurse. She helped my mom through that rough time, but also at the beginning of her pregnancy." Brenna shrugged. "I know some people might not think my name's classy or whatever, but I'd much rather be named after people my mother loved than have it be trendy."

"I agree completely," he stated, fixing her with a suddenly serious gaze. "I really appreciate what you've been doing for me. You have no idea what a relief it is to entrust these into your care." Smiling, he tapped the notebooks.

Not too long ago, a comment like that would have had her blushing from head to toe, but now that she had Mitch, her infatuation with Mr. Rose was fading fast. Brenna figured that was a good thing. "I'm happy to do it," she smiled back.

"There's something I want you to have," he said, going to his desk. He opened his bag and pulled out a worn copy of Homer's *The Odyssey*. Coming back, he handed it to Brenna. "My high school English teacher gave this to me when I graduated, and now, I'd like to pass it on to you. I thought about holding onto it until graduation, but I wanted you to have it now as you're prepping for your journey to college."

As a girl with an affinity for old things, Brenna could appreciate the significance of the gift. Its hard backed spine was slightly worn from serious use, its pages yellow with age. No one in his right mind would keep such an old book unless it meant something special to him. When she opened it, she saw two inscriptions:

> *Avery,*
> *May you always avoid the pitfalls of temptation.*
> > *-Mr. Bond*
> *To Brenna, a cunning girl who could give Odysseus a run for his money.*
> > *-Mr. Rose*

"Thank you," she said, clutching the book to her chest. It was an honor that he would pass on something so meaningful to her. It sort of made her wish that she had something to give him in return.

He patted her shoulder. "Come on. Let's get out of here."

Unfortunately, the rain was back with a vengeance, and Brenna realized belatedly that she'd left her umbrella in her car. Mr. Rose had his, though, so they huddled together underneath it as they rushed through the parking lot. With the way the rain was coming down, the umbrella didn't provide them with much protection. Brenna had her backpack – with Sophia Irene stuffed safely inside – clutched tightly to her chest in effort to keep it dry. The part of her that wasn't covered by the umbrella or her rain jacket was soaked in a matter of seconds. Avoiding puddles wasn't possible since the smaller ones had joined forces to create one massive puddle that seemed to span across the entire parking lot.

As they were walking, something caught Brenna's attention. It was music, possibly from a flute. It was so hard to hear above the rain that she turned her head, trying to pinpoint the location. Then out of the corner of her eye, Brenna saw something that made her halt in her tracks – a flash of red. Automatically, her head whipped around to follow it, but she saw nothing. It being day didn't make it much easier to see through the rain, and there were more places to hide out here. She turned to look behind her.

"Brenna!" Mr. Rose all but shouted over the storm. He doubled back to cover her with the umbrella. "What is it?"

She hesitated, eyes and ears still searching. Yes, there was definitely flute music in the air. "Do you hear that?"

Mr. Rose looked confused. "Hear what?"

She hesitated, suddenly uncertain. If Mr. Rose couldn't hear it, maybe her ears were playing tricks on her. "Sorry," she cried over the rain. "I thought I saw someone."

Frowning, he looked up, mimicking her behavior. He looked concerned as he was no doubt remembering Brenna's run-in with the Dark Avenger during Coach Turner's attack. "Do you know who it was?"

She shook her head. It wasn't like she could explain Mystery

Girl to her teacher, because then he'd get concerned and want to talk to her uncle about it. Then *Zio* would get involved, which would open up a can of worms regarding Mitch that Brenna wasn't ready to deal with yet.

"It was nothing," she assured Mr. Rose. "It's too hard to see anything clearly out here anyways."

They walked briskly to her car. He held her backpack as she opened the door and then wished her a good night when he closed it. At that point, Brenna deliberately slowed her actions, using the extra time to search for Mystery Girl as she got ready to leave. She felt uneasy, like an army of spiders was crawling across her skin. The girl was here – Brenna knew it – but what to do? She could acknowledge the sensation, try to find Mystery Girl, or she could ignore it. Van and Mitch would be mad if she tried to go after her alone. It didn't matter that it was daytime. They wouldn't want her to put herself in danger. There was also Mr. Rose to consider. If she bolted from the car, he'd probably chase after her to see what was wrong.

Now that she thought about it, Mystery Girl had probably been trying to bait her – daring Brenna to come after her. If Brenna ignored her, that just might ratchet up Mystery Girl's sense of desperation. She wanted to be noticed. Maybe they could force her hand if neither Mitch or Brenna paid attention to her.

Okay, so ignoring it was the way to go then.

Once safely at home – and dry – Brenna made her promised call to Mitch. She repeated the conversation she had with Van at Honey B's and was pleased by his enthusiasm that the clearer picture of his stalker had been established. He still had no idea who it was, though.

"Don't feel bad," she soothed. "Now that I know what I'm looking for, I'll find her. I'm thinking that she might be someone in ASB, so it's good that I'll be there tomorrow. Just do what you would normally do during a meeting. I'll stick with Hannah and observe you from a distance."

"I can do that," he said. There was a pause and then he cleared his throat, indicating a change in topics. Brenna felt her heart begin to race. "So I was wondering if you'd like to come over to my house on Saturday and watch a scary movie with me. We can set pretense and stalkers aside for a while and just be us."

It was exactly what she'd told Van that she wanted – time alone with Mitch so they could speak honestly instead of uttering lines designed to mislead. The only trouble would be waiting until Saturday to get it, but waiting was better than wafting in uncertainty. Grinning broadly, she replied, "That sounds perfect."

"Great. It's a date then." He sounded relieved, and Brenna wondered how long he'd been angsting over the whole situation.

"I think Mystery Girl was at the school when we left," she announced suddenly. Before he had a chance to react, she quickly explained what she'd experienced. "Have you ever heard a flute playing when she appeared to you?"

Mitch was quiet for a moment. "I don't think so," he replied hesitantly. "What do you think it means?"

That had been bugging Brenna, too. She'd been able to come up with a few ideas that she shared with Mitch. It was either some sort of weird scare tactic, another clue to be able to identify her, the song held some sort of significance, or it was a random coincidence unrelated to the case.

"If I had to guess, I'd say that the song was significant or it was a scare tactic," Brenna answered. "I can't believe Mystery Girl would deliberately give us a clue to her identity when she's gone to such extremes to hide it."

"Unless she's a ghost. Then she'd want us to identify her," Mitch put in.

Brenna rolled her eyes. "You're as bad as Van."

"Hey, I'm just trying to maintain a full perspective. Remember, we have two working profiles – a psychotic living girl intent on doing you harm and a deceased girl trying to protect you."

"Are you suggesting that I was in danger last night?" she asked.

"I don't know. I wasn't there. Maybe her presence saved you."

Brenna snorted. Was he really being serious? "I don't think so. No one was out there last night. If there was any danger today, it was the presence of Mr. Rose that saved me. No one's going to attack me while I'm standing next to a teacher."

Mitch fell silent again. "Brenna, just be careful, okay? I don't like you being out like that when I'm not with you."

That was almost laughable, given that Mystery Girl wouldn't even be harassing Brenna were it not for Mitch. She kept her mouth shut, though, since she didn't want to hurt him. Most likely, he didn't need to be reminded of that sticky issue.

"Well, I'll be with you tomorrow. You can keep all the eyes on me that you want," she replied, smiling.

She could detect his grin when he spoke again. "I can't wait."

Like most student body associations, Mount Vernon's contained some of the most popular kids on campus. They represented a broad spectrum of students from athletes to thespians to band members to brains and everyone else in between. Some of them were great people and others, as Brenna soon discovered, were varying shades of evil.

Take Doug Porter. Last year, the blond boy had run for ASB President against Mitch and suffered a humiliating defeat. Brenna couldn't decide whether he was bitter that he knew he never stood a chance or because he had actually thought he might win. Regardless, Doug made it his mission in life to make Mitch's presidency hard. That included blatantly attempting to engage his fearless leader in open debate about the decisions being made. It didn't matter what Mitch proposed, Doug was automatically against it. Mitch took it all in stride, though, and took to compromise like a seasoned professional. Nothing fazed him, which, of course, irritated the crap out of Doug. Privately, Brenna thought it was pretty funny.

Missy Jensen was harder to find humorous. She was rapidly climbing the list of people Brenna disliked most at school, coming third only to Alexis and Cameron.

"Why is *she* here? She's not one of us." Missy pointed an accusing finger at Brenna. All twenty pairs of eyes automatically turned to look at the outsider, who wondered vaguely if she needed to drum up some sort of public defense.

Mr. Rose sat in his chair, watching the scene unfold. He tapped his pen against his desk as if weighing the options of interceding before things got really unpleasant. Yesterday's bad mood had persisted, and he looked ready to lay a verbal smack down if the group didn't straighten up.

But Mitch wasn't upset. "Brenna volunteered to help Hannah with the maze design."

"Yay!" Hannah gave an enthusiastic cheer and waved at the subject of the inquisition. "You're my hero, Brenna."

"Shut up, Hannah," Missy barked. "We don't need her. I can help with the design."

Instead of getting mad, Mitch folded his hands in his lap and nodded. "Okay, I think it's great if you want to flex your math skills."

Missy looked confused. "What?"

"You have to be proficient in math to design the maze," Mitch politely informed her. "You have to calculate how many bales of hay are needed based on the height and length of the walls and the size of the space we have to work with. I'm sure they would appreciate your help."

From the look on Missy's face, Brenna could tell that the cheerleader hated math even more than Van. Tossing her brown curls, Missy gave a sanctimonious wave. "Whatever. Put her massively annoying brain to work if you want. What do I care?"

A couple of people snickered at her obvious displeasure. If Brenna had known that her presence was going to cause Mitch this much grief, she might not have come. It was hard to track the other girls' responses to her presence when Missy was drawing so much attention to herself. Brenna wondered vaguely if the cheerleader wasn't Mystery Girl after all, but then promptly dismissed it. The profile just didn't fit her.

"But still, she's not a member of the ASB, so she shouldn't be here," Doug pressed. "Or do the rules only apply to the rest of us? Maybe I would have brought my girlfriend today if I'd been given the opportunity."

"Inflatable girlfriends don't count, Doug," quipped Nick Anders. A laughing Shane Duffy punched him appreciatively on the shoulder. No one was super fond of Doug.

The boy shot a murderous glare Nick's way, but Missy cut in before he could reply. "Yeah, I would have brought Tate."

"By all means, bring him," Mitch stated generously. He extended his hand in open invitation. "You're all welcome to bring anyone with you. As Doug mentioned, our meetings are normally closed to the rest of the student body, but the Halloween Carnival is a school-wide event. Yes, the ASB hosts it, but we recruit volunteers from our peers to run the event. That recruitment can extend to pre-event preparation, so please, bring your friends tomorrow. The more hands we have, the faster we can get all of this done. Let's get to work."

It was the equivalent of breaking huddle. Everyone split into groups and got to work. Brenna and Hannah made decent progress on the design that first day. It probably would have gone faster if Brenna had done it alone given Hannah's tendency to doubt her math skills for no apparent reason. But the girl was so cheery and amiable that Brenna found it hard to be frustrated. In fact, Hannah's many deliberations gave her the opportunity to keep an eye on Mitch and the other girls in ASB. A few of them were automatically dismissed.

Not Missy, Brenna thought with a decisive shake of her head.

Not Hannah, either. She was too caught up with her work. She hadn't even noticed Mitch. Plus, she was perfectly at ease with Brenna. If Hannah was Mystery Girl and therefore, out to get her, then the girl was the best actress in the world.

Not Paige Conklin. The girl couldn't keep her mouth shut even when there was no one within earshot. Everyone noticed her because she made herself by known, inserting herself into conversations whenever she felt like it.

Not Gwen Pickens. She was too busy flirting with Nick Anders, and not in a way designed to make another boy jealous. No, any extra attention she had was devoted to Nick.

Actually, Gwen's attitude summed up the response of the majority of the girls. They weren't all flirting with Nick, but several of them were displaying obvious signs of attraction to some boy in their general vicinity. To be fair, the boys were just as bad as the girls. High school was a veritable hotbed of sexual tension. While quite intriguing, none of the flirtation Brenna witnessed clued her into the identity of Mystery Girl.

"Let me apologize for the unpleasantness earlier," Mr. Rose said quietly as he leaned over to check her work. Hannah had run off to use the bathroom. "Usually the kids are better at minding their manners."

"It's okay," Brenna assured him. "I just feel bad for Mitch."

"He's all right. He's used to getting a hard time from Doug," the teacher replied with a roll of his eyes. "Missy is a completely different matter."

"Yeah, I think that's my fault." Brenna felt a bit sheepish, uncertain how much Mr. Rose knew about his students' love lives.

Apparently, he knew enough because he shook his head, and sighed, "It's always tricky when a relationship like that ends and then you still have to work together. Truthfully, Mitch could have handled that whole situation better. You gotta be careful who you give your heart to."

Mr. Rose shot her a quick look that immediately set Brenna on her guard. It felt like a warning or a caution to be careful, meaning he obviously didn't want her to end up like Missy. Well, he needn't worry because she had no intention of jumping into bed with Mitch.

Brenna felt a hand on her shoulder and looked up to see Mitch smiling down at her. "How's it going over here?"

"Good, I think," she replied, trying to concentrate on his words instead of the feel of his fingers running through her hair. Finally, she gave up and let herself smile. The sensation was too pleasant to be ignored.

At that moment, Hannah returned and Mr. Rose beckoned Mitch away for a private word. The girls didn't finish the layout but they got close, and while Brenna was disappointed that she couldn't find Mystery Girl among the female ASB members, it was a relief to be able to scratch some names off the list. Brenna could only hope that tomorrow's meeting would be more illuminating.

About thirty extra people showed up to help after school the next day. Since Mr. Rose's classroom was too small to accommodate them all, they headed to the cafeteria where people could spread out the posters and game backdrops they were preparing. The turn of events was both a blessing and a curse as Brenna figured a desperate Mystery Girl might jump at a chance to spend extra time with Mitch but now there were more people to watch and a larger space in which to watch them. She was sure that she was going to miss something important.

As she promised, Missy brought her boyfriend, Tate, as well as Alexis and Brittany. While Tate was a hearty worker, the same couldn't be said of the girls. They seemed more content to lean against the wall and gossip. Paige recruited Keiko and Autumn to work on the banners she was designing. Since they were working at the opposite end of the cafeteria as Brenna, Van, who had agreed to come so he could be another set of eyes, spent most of his time lingering near them. Fisher Brown showed up with some of his DJ equipment and soon everyone in the cafeteria was rocking out to the current Top 40 hits.

Choosing to work at the table where she normally ate lunch with Van was strategic as it afforded Brenna with an excellent view of the cafeteria. A steady stream of words poured forth from Hannah as she worked, but it wasn't the kind of inane chatter that would have driven Brenna up the wall. On the contrary, Hannah made several interesting observations about school and life in general that set Brenna back on her heels as she pondered them. She had always known that Hannah was kind, but the girl had a very astute mind that made Brenna wish she'd spent more time with her over the years.

"So how are things going with you and Mitch?" Hannah asked casually, her head bent over her calculator.

How could such a simple, innocent question be so difficult to answer? Truthfully, she and Mitch were just going through the motions, enjoying each other's company and eagerly anticipating their first real date on Saturday. Brenna couldn't very well say that to Hannah, but she didn't want to lie either.

"We're taking things a bit slow," she said, which was true enough. "Just hanging out after school, usually in groups like today. We've only been on one date, but we have plans for Saturday."

"Oh, I was hoping you'd say that," Hannah declared, looking up. "I hated the idea of him spending his birthday alone. His parents are gone again."

Saturday was Mitch's birthday? Why hadn't he said anything?

Her confusion must have been evident for Hannah immediately looked embarrassed. "Didn't he tell you he was turning eighteen?" When Brenna shook her head, the girl sighed, turning her eyes to the heavens. "I guess he didn't want you to feel obligated to do something for him since you just started dating. Plus, he's so private. I blame that on his being left alone so much."

That may have been the first marginally uncharitable thing Brenna had ever heard Hannah say. "I know what you mean," she said, allowing herself a moment to frown. How could his parents miss his birthday? Didn't they care? Brenna wasn't sure which was worse – forgetting or ignoring it.

"Thanks for telling me about his birthday. I'll make sure we celebrate." Her mind was already kicking around ideas. Cake. There would definitely be cake involved.

"I'm so glad Fisher's deejaying for the carnival," Hannah said, admiring the boy from afar. "He's the best DJ in Mount Vernon."

Brenna snorted. "DJ Ghost is the *only* DJ in Mount Vernon." They laughed and waved to Fisher, who held up his hand in acknowledgment. The guy might have been a little weird, but he was certainly a lot of fun.

Their focus waning, Brenna's eyes turned of their own accord to where Mitch was, his feet planted in a chair as he leaned his body over a table to paint. A streak of blue was running up his arm and his brows were pinched together in concentration. What a diligent worker he was! And pretty darn cute, too. Seeing it made her smile. She could sit there and watch him paint all day.

She shook her head to clear her thoughts. No time for cute boys, Brenna! She had to focus on Mystery Girl. If the girl was here, she was probably lingering near Mitch. She scanned the surrounding area, but everyone was either working hard or flirting with someone else. No one was watching Mitch.

No, wait. That wasn't quite right. Someone *was* watching him.

A few tables away, Sara Xavier hovered in the exact position as Mitch over her own poster. Her head was turned, eyes clearly on the ASB President. But was she watching him because she was obsessed with him or because she was examining his technique? After all, she was working on her own sign. Maybe she was using him for artistic direction.

Brenna had been surprised to see Sara show up to help. She was a quiet girl with few friends, none of whom seemed to be present. With plain features and a small, frail frame, Sara wasn't the kind of girl who was noticed by boys. In other words, she was a good fit for the Mystery Girl profile. But she didn't necessarily *look* like a lovesick girl.

"And we're done!" Hannah announced joyfully, calling Brenna's attention back to the official task at hand. She looked down, admiring the work they'd accomplished. There were plenty of twists, turns, and dead ends to keep the kids entertained for a while.

"This is a pretty incredible maze if I do say so myself," she replied. "Nice job, Hannah."

The girl wrapped her arm around Brenna and pulled her in for a side hug. "Couldn't have done it without you, partner. Let's go show Mitch." Brenna barely had time to grab Sophia Irene's hand before Hannah took hers and pulled her away.

Mitch glanced up at the sound of their approach and smiled. "All done?" Hannah nodded and handed him the design. His eyes went wide. "Wow, this is great! Good job, ladies."

"It was all Brenna," Hannah confessed. She leaned in and whispered, "Later, you really ought to properly thank her for volunteering to help."

"Trust me, I will." Mitch winked at his Vice President, who giggled and nudged Brenna in the ribs.

A grinning Brenna shook her head. "You're so silly, Hannah."

"I can't help it. Seeing you two together makes me happy."

"You know what would make me happy?" Mitch inquired as he returned to the pumpkin he was painting. "If you two grabbed paintbrushes and helped me out with this thing. My artistic skills are lacking today."

Brenna examined his work and pointed to the pumpkin. "What are you talking about? I can totally tell that's supposed to be a pineapple." Laughing, she darted out of the reach of Mitch's hand. "I'll be right back. I want to get my camera."

She casually turned her head and noticed that Sara wasn't looking at Mitch anymore. In fact, she was having a conversation with Ricky Garcia who had come over to help her with her poster. Hmm. Maybe Sara's watching of Mitch had been innocent. Maybe not. Regardless, the girl merited closer scrutiny.

Her backpack, and therefore her camera, was still in Mr. Rose's room, so Brenna headed back down the hall to retrieve it. She hadn't realized just how loud of a racket they were making until she left the cafeteria. People were definitely having fun in there. Brenna hoped that with the large turnout, they'd get all of their work done early and Mitch wouldn't have to work so hard next week. There were plenty of other things that they could do to fill the time, assuming that everything went well on Saturday. Brenna allowed herself a mischievous smile at the thought.

She had every intention of getting back to Mitch as soon as possible, but as she was leaving, she ran into Mr. Rose, who recruited her to help him raid the art teacher's supply closet for more paint – of course, Mr. Foster had granted him permission. The only trouble was that someone had already visited the closet, so they climbed into the teacher's car and headed off to buy more. It was refreshing to see her teacher returning to his old self as his foul mood dissipated. She didn't like seeing him so upset. Now that the rain had passed, he was probably sleeping better, which would help his state of mind a lot.

When Brenna returned, she found Alexis with Mitch. Apparently, he'd just told a joke because the cheerleader was laughing and touching his chest. Looking nothing short of annoyed, Mitch shuffled back a step. Brenna wondered how long he'd been getting harassed. Seeing them together irritated her, not because she thought Mitch could be tempted but because it looked like they were never going to get any peace from Alexis. What did the redhead think she was doing anyway? She was never going to come between them.

So who could fault her for being a little rude? Brenna strode purposefully over to them and stepped between them with her back to Alexis, completely ignoring her. "Hey, hon," she greeted, taking his hand. "I need your help with something. Sorry," she threw over her shoulder at a furious Alexis.

"Where did you run off to?" Mitch asked when they were safely out of earshot. He pulled her close and whispered, "Van and I thought something bad had happened when we couldn't find you."

"I'm sorry. I should have told you where I was going. Mr. Rose and I went to buy more paint." She rubbed soothing circles against his back. She was going to have to get used to this – keeping him apprised of her whereabouts, especially with Mystery Girl still on the loose. When they pulled apart, Brenna saw Mitch glare angrily at Mr. Rose, no doubt displacing his frustration when it should have been directed at her.

She poked her finger in his side, calling his attention back to her. "Show me what you're doing."

He escorted her over the table to show her his poster for the pumpkin seed-spitting contest. It was covered with pumpkins, vines, and airborne seeds. All that he had left to do was trace over the words with black paint.

"You amaze me," she smiled, squeezing his hand. "Is there anything you can't do?"

"No, I don't think so," he replied with a grin.

She gave him a light push forward. "Get over there and finish your poster. I want to take your picture. I have no lefties in my study of hands at work."

To write or paint, Mitch's left hand curled in on itself almost like it was attempting to form a claw. He started on the right side of the poster and moved left instead of the other way around so he wouldn't smear the paint. It was fascinating to watch. Eager to use up the roll, Brenna shot some pictures of the rest of the students as they worked. Then Hannah managed to wrestle the camera from her so the girl could snap a picture of Brenna with Mitch, and then one of the two of them with Van and Mr. Rose.

"I think we're going to be ready for the carnival sooner than anticipated, assuming that everyone who showed up today comes back tomorrow," Mitch said as they left the building. He had his arm draped casually over Brenna's shoulder, the other holding her backpack. His own was on his back. Van was trailing about twenty paces behind them, chatting with Keiko. He seemed to enjoy having someone to commiserate with since she was the only other person who knew exactly what was going on with Brenna, Mitch, and Mystery Girl.

The couple stopped in front of her car, and Mitch moved his hand from her shoulder to her waist, keeping her close. He let her backpack drop to the ground with a thud. Sophia Irene didn't protest the treatment.

"I wish I could help tomorrow, but I have my shift at the bakery," she reminded him. Usually she worked on Thursdays, but this week, Berthal had asked her if she could switch to Friday. One of the other workers, Mary Jordan, had a couple of family events planned on back-to-back weekends. "Van will keep an eye on you, though."

"That's okay," he assured her. "It'll just make me more excited to see you on Saturday."

Upon learning that Saturday was Mitch's birthday, Brenna had concocted a plan to celebrate it. What she'd come up with wasn't much, but it allowed them to spend more time together, which she suspected was all that Mitch would have wanted.

"Say, I heard you tell Hannah that you hadn't picked a costume yet. Van and I are going as Shaggy and Daphne from *Scooby Doo*, but Fred and Velma are unclaimed. If you wanted to match with me, you could be Fred." She ran her fingers up and down the straps of the backpack he was wearing.

"Fred, huh? Aren't he and Daphne supposed to be a couple?" he smiled, obviously pleased by her suggestion.

Brenna shrugged. "Well, not technically, but I always hoped that they'd get together."

"That sounds great to me," he affirmed with a nod. Then he frowned. "But isn't he a blonde? You're not going to make me dye my hair or wear a wig are you?"

She ran her fingers though his hair, pretending to examine it. "I think we can leave it black. I have a feeling you'd make a wretched blonde." Then she rested her hand on his cheek. "Since we're agreed, I think that we should slightly modify our plans for Saturday. Why don't you pick me up for work in the morning, and we can hang out at the bakery? My boss won't mind. Then we can go to the thrift store and find some suitable clothes for you."

"And then back to my house for lunch and a movie," he finished. Mitch sighed and released her. "I guess you'd better get home to your uncle."

"Have a good night." She felt a twinge of sadness knowing that he was going home to an empty house. "You can call me if you want."

He nodded and headed towards his car. She turned to unlock the door, but then stopped when she felt him return. She twisted her body to face him and he leaned in so that his breath tickled her face.

"I'm planning to kiss you on Saturday. Just thought you might like to know," he whispered, teasing her.

But Mitch wasn't the only one who could play games. Brenna grabbed him by the straps of his backpack and pulled him the rest of the way, like she meant to kiss him, but at the last second, she angled her head to whisper in his ear.

"I'm going to hold you to that."

Chapter Twenty

Even though Brenna was tired when she got home and even though she had a ton of homework waiting for her, she headed out to her darkroom after dinner. The meal had run a bit longer than usual because she'd felt like she'd been abandoning her uncle. He seemed glad to have the extra attention, though Brenna couldn't help but notice that he seemed as tired as she did. It had passed through her mind several times during the week to ask him about the Columbia newspaper, but every time she came close to bringing it up, she remembered the fury that had been in Abraham's eyes and let it go. Like she told herself before, if there was something to be worried about, he'd let her know. Until then, she'd leave it in his more than capable hands.

Besides, the last thing she wanted to do that night was worry about the potential for bad things to happen. What she wanted most was to embrace her inner girl and develop the picture of her and Mitch. She brought her backpack with her so she could make a stab at her homework while she waited for the chemicals to process, but it was an exercise in futility as the only thing she could truly concentrate on was the thought of kissing Mitch.

Really, it was cruel to tell a girl you were going to kiss her and then make her wait. Now that he seemed to be certain of her feelings, Mitch seemed to enjoy making her suffer. Well, maybe it wasn't that bad since she only had to wait a few days and he'd been waiting who knew how long to date her. She'd gotten off relatively easy by comparison. Still, Saturday seemed an awfully long time from now.

Brenna had just loaded her film onto the reel and stuck it in the lightproof tank when there was a knock on her door. "Just a minute!" she called as she screwed the lid back on and flipped on the lights. Hoping it was Mitch, Brenna ran a hand over her hair and opened it with a smile.

Duke frowned when he watched her face fall. "Don't look all excited to see me," he said with a note of petulance.

"Sorry," she recovered, stepping aside so he could come in. "I thought you were someone else."

"The Sniffer?" Duke tossed out as he hopped up on the counter. He looked uncommonly bored, which meant that he'd pick a fight with her just for the sake of having something to do. It irritated her to no end that one shallow girl could wreak this much havoc on her friend. Well, Kelly might have ruined Duke for the moment, but Brenna wasn't going to let that mess up her relationship with him, which was why she smiled and patted his knee instead of getting annoyed.

"I told you, his name is Mitch," she reminded him, feeling like she w as uttering lines from an after-school special. "I'm sure that you'll like him once you get to know him."

Stubborn to the core, Duke frowned again. "I'm sure you're wrong."

Patience. He's your friend even if he is being an idiot.

Brenna smiled. "I'm not going to let you bait me, so don't even try it." Then she tweaked his nose.

Duke growled, one hand flying to his nose and the other

reaching out for her, but Brenna danced out of his grasp, laughing merrily. "I hate it when you do that," he cried.

"Well, if you weren't being such a sourpuss, I wouldn't have had to do it," she replied, still grinning.

Sighing, Duke rubbed his nose and let his shoulders sag in defeat. She was right and he knew it. Feeling that his ferocity had been disarmed, Brenna approached and resting her hands on his knees, she looked up at her friend.

"You can't keep letting her do this to you," she stated quietly. "You're so strong. I have no idea how she can have this much control over you."

He shrugged. "When you fall in love, you'll understand."

The concept of love wasn't a debate she was eager to get into again with Duke, so she tried a different tactic. "Do you like feeling this way? Do you like making Grandma Carrie, *Zio*, and me miserable on your behalf?"

"Of course not," he replied dejectedly.

"Then get back out there and live!" Brenna cried, shaking his shoulders. "Daniel James Ward has never been one to sit like a loser on the sidelines! You want the girl who treats you like crap back, then go get her! If you don't want her, then kick her to the metaphoric curb and be done with it! You are a man of action, so act!"

In response, his hand shot up and latched onto her nose, pinching it hard. He laughed good-naturedly as she smacked his shoulder in protest.

"You know you're only this optimistic because you have a boyfriend," Duke replied sagely.

"There could be some truth to that," she admitted with an impish grin. Grabbing the tank, she stuck it under the faucet and turned on the water for the required pre-soak.

A minute passed and she felt Duke move behind her. "Are

these the ones you took of me the other night?"

"No, I already developed those. They're hanging on the line."

Brenna pointed the string holding up a dozen photos of his grease-covered hands wielding mechanic's tools. He went over to examine them as she carefully poured the diluted developer into the tank, snapped the cap on, and started the timer.

"So what's on the roll you're developing?" Duke asked, taking his seat on the counter again.

Brenna turned the tank upside down and the righted it. "Just some pictures I took at school," she said casually.

Not fooled, Duke gave her a sly grin. "Pictures of you and the Sniffer."

"There might be one or two of those," she admitted. "But there are also pictures of students getting ready for the Halloween Carnival."

Ready for a shift in topics, Duke asked, "So what movie are you and Van watching tomorrow night?"

"*Dolls*. I think it's about people who are turned into dolls and forced to kill. Something like that." Brenna rotated the tank again, letting the developer completely coat the film.

"What, like baby dolls?" Duke sounded skeptic.

She waved dismissively. "More like action figures, I think. It was one of Van's choices."

He shook his head. "How does he even find movies like that? It's so random."

"Well, Van is random so it works. Plus, it's a vintage horror b-film, and we like those. You can come watch with us if you want," Brenna said, glancing up at him with a grin. "The Sniffer's not coming."

That made him smile. "Maybe I will."

He told her about his day as she continued developing her film negatives. After the allotted time passed, Brenna poured out the developer, replacing it with a chemical designed to stop the developing process. Then she poured that out and put in the fixer, shaking the tank for ten seconds every minute.

Duke kept up a steady stream of conversation as he watched her every move. He had always been fascinated by the process of developing film and photos but had never shown any interest in learning how to do it himself. Brenna suspected that actually doing it would take the magic away from it.

Once the film had been fixed and rinsed, she opened the tank, pulled out the reel and unwound her film. As she stuck it in the wash, a thought suddenly occurred to her. Had *Zio* mentioned the newspaper to Duke? If there was something larger going on than a simple prank, Brenna was sure that he would have – and quite possibly instructed him not to tell her anything. Still, it was worth a shot. If he knew nothing, that was a good sign.

While Abraham was a master at hiding his emotions on a daily basis, Duke most certainly was not. He could when he was in the right mindset, but if she sprung the question on him when he was unprepared, she could probably get a good idea of what he knew just from his reaction.

"What do you know about Eliza Kent and the Columbia newspaper that was left on my mom's grave?" Brenna blurted out, interrupting him.

The reaction she got was almost cartoonish. Duke's eyes went wide with panic and his jaw dropped.

Brenna kept her concern under her control and tried to sound casual. "That bad, huh?"

A heartbeat later, Duke was back to normal. "Nah, it's nothing to worry about. Just a silly prank." Remaining silent, she gave him a look that clearly conveyed her disbelief, which made him even more uncomfortable. "We shouldn't be talking about this, Biddy. If you have questions about it, go ask Abe."

"*Zio* isn't going to tell me anything."

"Because there isn't anything to tell!" He threw his hands in the air as if to say she was making a big deal over nothing.

She walked over to him and leaned against his knees as she stared into his eyes. They were unmistakably worried, which in turn worried Brenna. Whatever it was they were dealing with, it wasn't a mere prank. However, she didn't have time for it. Not with Mystery Girl still running around out there.

"Go talk to him," he pleaded in a low voice before she could press her request further. "I can't tell you anything."

Brenna knew what that meant. It was code for: Abe made me swear an oath of silence, so please don't ask me to break it. She felt torn. Asking her uncle would get her nowhere. If he didn't want to tell her, he wouldn't. If he had intended to illuminate her, he would have done it by now. However, if Brenna tried, she was pretty sure that she could get Duke to spill everything he knew. He wasn't the kind of person who liked keeping secrets. He was just too honest. However, she didn't think she could live with knowing that she'd made Duke violate her uncle's trust like that.

Weighing her options, Brenna drummed her fingers on his knee. There wasn't much she could do to figure out what was going on. What good would investigating Eliza Kent's murder do? She already knew it was unsolved, so what could she possibly hope to uncover about an eighteen-year-old murder that the police hadn't known at the time? She had no additional avenues to search either – just her enigmatic uncle.

"I'm not going to force you to tell me," she began by promising. Duke relaxed visibly. "But I do have a question that I need you answer. Should I trust *Zio* on this?"

In other words: Should she trust that Abraham knew what he was doing and would tell her if she was in danger? There had never been a time when Brenna's trust in her uncle had wavered, but it was harder this time knowing that there were things he wasn't telling her.

Duke put his hands on the sides of her face and held her gaze. "Absolutely," he affirmed with confidence. "He may not be the most informative person, but he always has your best interests at heart."

"I know he does," she said, her heart warming with love for her uncle. She could do this. Even if she didn't have all the answers, she could let the matter go and rest confident in Abraham. She nodded.

"There's a good girl," Duke smiled, releasing her.

CHAPTER TWENTY-ONE

It was Friday night, and dinner was over. Abraham had retired to his study to read a book on criminal psychology. Brenna was baking cookies while her best friend kept watch from his perch on the counter. On babysitting duty, Van held both Lloyd Dobler and Sophia Irene in his lap.

"Sara wasn't helping prep for the carnival. My source, also known as Keiko Martin, informed me that she was at work as well," he informed her, banging the heel of his shoe idly against the cabinet below him. "She went straight to the movie theater after the final bell rang."

Brenna scraped her spatula around the inside of the bowl, making sure that the ingredients were mixed in fully. "What's the rest of her schedule like? Is it fixed like mine or does it change every week?" If her schedule was the same, she might have an alibi for some of the Mystery Girl appearances.

"Keiko said it was a week by week thing," he answered.

"Then she could still be our girl," Brenna said as she turned on the mixer. She still wasn't convinced about Sara, though. "It's just so frustrating because I barely know Sara. She seems to fit the profile in some aspects, but maybe that's just my perception of her personality."

Van shrugged haphazardly. "Don't look at me. I didn't even know who you were talking about until you called her by her nickname – Second-hand Sara."

"Did you see anything else suspicious? Any girls behaving especially forward towards Mitch because I wasn't there?" Brenna had wondered if Mystery Girl might have been present yesterday but extra guarded in her actions. So with the girlfriend gone, did the mouse come out to play?

Van shifted, looking uncomfortable as he fiddled with the babies in his arms. "No, I don't think so."

She frowned. Did he honestly think that she wouldn't know that he was keeping something from her? The ability to detect falseness in their best friend ran both ways for the pair. They simply knew each other too well to be deceived. "You know you can't keep secrets from me, so spill it."

"You're not going to like it, and really, you don't have anything to worry about. Mitch handled himself quite well."

His words, which were meant to calm her, produced the opposite effect. It had to be bad if he didn't want to tell her. "What happened?"

"Alexis was a little inappropriate with your almost boyfriend," he sighed. Brenna could only imagine what *that* meant. "But don't worry! He completely brushed her off. Right in front of onlookers, too. You would have been proud."

Brenna decided that she preferred to spend the rest of her night proud of Mitch than mad at Alexis, so she asked, "What did he say?"

"Something along the lines of 'thanks but no thanks' and 'my girlfriend is way hotter than you, you whore.'"

"He called her a whore?" She was astonished. Mitch was always so polite. Maybe she *did* want to hear a full retelling after all.

Van shook his head. "Nah, but we all sensed that it was implied. Then he disentangled himself from her and went about his business like nothing happened. It was the coldest rebuff I've ever had the pleasure of witnessing. I had to resist the urge to applaud."

Grinning, Brenna emptied an entire bag of chocolate chips into the bowl. Both she and Van subscribed to the theory that a cookie could never have too much chocolate in it. While she found Van's story amusing, Brenna was sure that Mitch's rejection wasn't enough to keep Alexis from trying again. The cheerleader wasn't the type to give up without a fight even if it was over a boy she didn't really want. She wondered vaguely how Missy felt about that. It was one thing when a girl like Brenna, who Missy didn't like, was dating her former flame, but when a friend like Alexis, who knew the couples' history, went after him that had to sting a little.

"Hey, maybe Alexis is Mystery Girl!" Van came to life at the idea, his eyes widening to the size of dinner plates. "After all, she was there at Harvey's. She's the reason you went to the bathroom."

Brenna snorted in contempt. "Alexis wouldn't stalk a boy; she'd attack him head on. Plus, you told me that Mystery Girl had a slight frame. Does that apply to our curvaceous head cheerleader?"

"No," he sighed, wilting like a flower in the desert sun.

Chuckling at his disappointment, Brenna pulled the bowl out of the mixer and set it on the counter so she could roll the dough into balls. Nothing could relax Brenna quite like being with Van. She never had to worry about what she said or did around him. Even when life felt complicated, like it was now with stalkers and boyfriends, Van had a way of making all the stress just drift away with the mere sound of his laughter.

"So are you getting Mitch a present?" he asked while the cookies were baking in the oven.

"I developed the photo that Hannah took of us and framed it," she shrugged. Brenna had told Van about her plans to celebrate Mitch's birthday. He had been equally appalled that the Hamiltons were out of town, though his verbal recriminations contained more colorful language.

"That's a little narcissistic, don't you think?" he teased.

"It's all I have, and you know he'll like it," she replied.

Van sighed dreamily. "He'll probably sleep with it under his pillow." Brenna smacked his knee. Ignoring her, he held up the babies and stared into their tiny faces. "Now, children, let me explain to you about the importance of the Halloween Horrorfest. This is a night for Sir's mommy and Lloyd Dobler's daddy to watch scary movies and scream like sorority girls about to be gutted."

"Gross, Van," Brenna moaned, peering inside the oven to check the cookies. Then she patted the babies' tiny plastic heads. "Kids, you'll note that it's just Van who screams. I am not a screamer."

"Sir, your mommy can be annoyingly superior at times. I hope you didn't inherit that trait from her," Van told the little girl. The only answer he received was the slamming of the oven door as Brenna pulled out the cookie trays. Then she moved to the sink to clean up.

"Lloyd Dobler, let me tell you about the first time I met your mother," Van began, balancing the doll on his knee. "She was being chased by a psychotic killer with a chainsaw. In an incredible display of creativity and brute strength, I defeated the villain and rescued your mother. Exceedingly grateful, she declared her undying love for me, and we lived happily ever after until the day she left me for that demonic rodeo clown."

He pulled his head up sharply. "Does it bother you when I make jokes about deadbeat parents?" he asked, no doubt thinking of her own deadbeat father.

"No, because it's not real, and I know that if it was real, you'd never joke about it. Thanks for asking, though." Brenna handed him a cookie. "What do you think happened to Sophia Irene's daddy?"

Lost in thought, Van chewed on his cookie. "Your baby daddy was a firefighter who gave his life to rescue a family from a burning building. He died a hero. There was a parade in his honor, and the mayor gave you plaque to commemorate his sacrifice."

"That sounds like something a man that I loved would do." When she did think about it – which wasn't often – Brenna had always assumed that if she married, she'd marry someone who was brave and self-sacrificing like her uncle.

"That's because you're noble, and you love the nobility in others."

"You always say such nice things about me," she mused.

"Well, if you continue to make me cookies, I'll continue to say nice things about you," came Van's cheeky reply.

Plating the cookies, Brenna laughed. She carried them into the living room and set them on the table. There was a knock on the door and she went to answer it, suspecting that it was Duke.

"So you decided to give the homicidal dolls a try," she said, smirking.

Duke shrugged as he stepped inside the house. "I didn't have anything better to do, and even if the movie stinks, the food will be good."

"Hey Danny," Van greeted, shoving soda cans and robot babies into his arms. "Why don't you set the movie up, Brenna, and I'll get the popcorn."

"Okay," she agreed, grabbing the movie.

Duke set the babies down on the couch before settling himself in the armchair and popping his soda can open. "You going out with your boyfriend tomorrow?"

"He's coming to work with me and then we're going back to his place to watch a scary movie." She slipped the DVD into the player and pressed play.

"Which one?"

Brenna shook her head as she headed to the couch. "He didn't say."

"Well, he's in for a rude disappointment," he declared jovially.

"What's that supposed to mean?" she inquired.

Duke shrugged like it should have been obvious. "He's hoping that you'll get scared, get all clingy, and beg him to protect you. But you're not the scaredy-cat type."

"I'm good at pretending, though," she grinned mischievously. Duke didn't approve.

There was a moderately loud crash from the kitchen, the sound of a bowl hitting the floor. Brenna rolled her eyes. What was Van doing? "Hey!" she called. "If you make a mess in there, I'm not cleaning it up!"

Silence.

"Van!" she called again. "What happened?"

Still no answer.

Feeling slightly put out by his silence, Brenna got up to investigate. When she stepped into the kitchen, the first thing she saw was the overturned bowl and popcorn all over the floor. Then she saw the opened door and her heart kicked into gear. It looked like he'd left the house in a rush, spilling popcorn in the process, but why?

Brenna could only think of one reason: Mystery Girl. She

must have been lurking outside and he'd seen her. Instead of calling for help, he'd chased after the stalker by himself like an idiot. And after giving her a hard time for doing the same thing!

She rushed to the door and descended the steps, pausing at the foot of them to search for her best friend. "Van!" she cried, her eyes roaming the yard. She wanted to follow in pursuit, but running off blindly wasn't the best way to help her friend. "Where are you?"

There was no answer. No sound of his voice. Not the smallest snap of a twig or the rustle of leaves. Van was just gone. Had he been running that fast or had something more sinister happened? Maybe he hadn't seen Mystery Girl at all. Maybe she'd abducted him, and what? Vanished into thin air? Wrapped him in her ghostly essence and spirited him away?

What happened next followed in rapid succession. Something hit the ground behind her with a thud, hands grabbed her and a voice shouted, "Boo!"

Brenna screamed as she wrenched herself free from her attacker, who fell to the ground in a gale of hysterical laughter.

Wait. Laughter?

Her eyes processed the sight of her best friend rolling on the ground, clutching his side. Then she saw the ladder leaned up against the side of the house and realized what he'd done. He'd climbed up it and perched on the roof, waiting for the right moment to jump down and scare her.

"I got you! I got you!" he crowed, utterly delighted with himself. "I win!"

She suddenly recalled the bet they'd made two weeks ago, and how Van had been charged with the seemingly impossible task of making her scream. And he'd actually managed to pull it off.

Growling, Brenna threw herself on top of him, pummeling any part of his body that her fists could reach. "You jerk! I can't believe you did that!"

"You're a bona fide Scream Queen!" Oblivious to her assault, he continued laughing his heart out.

"You're cruel!" she declared, still punching him even though her fists hurt. "I thought something horrible had happened to you! Next time I'll let the ghost get you!"

Van kept laughing, which only made her angrier. He wasn't even trying to protect himself. Fine, she thought. Let's see what he thinks of this. She put her hands in his hair and rubbed furiously until it was a tangled mess.

"Okay, okay!" the boy cried out, sounding panicked as he tried to protect his head.

Duke stepped outside, ignoring the scuffle, said, "Van, your doll is crying."

"Lloyd Dobler, Daddy's coming!" he promised, extracting himself from underneath his best friend.

"And you're picking up that popcorn!" she shouted at his retreating form.

About twenty minutes later, Brenna sat on the couch, her arms wrapped so tightly around Sophia Irene that she would have been squeezing the life out of the baby if she'd been real. Looking pleased as punch, Van sat next to her, brushing his hair back to perfection and not caring in the slightest that he was in the proverbial doghouse. Especially since Duke was there as well. Brenna had been highly annoyed to discover that he'd been privy to Van's scare tactics. It crossed her mind to ditch them both, but instead of pouting, she calmed her nerves with the thought of revenge. Van was going to pay for what he'd done.

Brenna wasn't the least bit upset by how much the movie freaked him out either. About half way through the movie, Van moved Lloyd Dobler off his lap and set him against the bookshelf. Twenty minutes later, he flipped the doll around because he claimed Lloyd Dobler was looking at him funny. When Brenna and Sophia Irene went to the kitchen under the guise of getting more soda, she taped a butter knife into her doll's hand and then thrust the baby into Van's face. She was rewarded with a very satisfying shriek, which greatly improved her mood.

"Man, that was the creepiest movie I've ever seen," a wide-eyed Van admitted as he carried his dishes to the kitchen. "I think Lloyd Dobler's sleeping in the closet tonight."

"That's a good idea," Brenna agreed. "Tomorrow, you can examine the door and if you find tiny scratch marks, you'll know he was attempting to break free and kill you."

Van paled. "That's not even funny."

"It's hilarious," Duke put in. "It's a doll, Van. Get over it."

"Get over it?" he shrieked, thrusting Lloyd Dobler into Duke's face. "Look into his eyes and try to tell me his intentions are pure! His pupils look like daggers for crying out loud!"

"He looks happy to me," Duke replied.

Van was beside himself. "Exactly my point! No one should be that happy all the time! It's the same way with clowns!"

Duke looked at Brenna. "So when he comes over here, do you feed him sugar straight from the container?"

Brenna snorted. "Don't blame his insanity on me. It's clearly a result of breathing in too much hairspray."

Chapter Twenty-Two

Much to Van's delight, Lloyd Dobler didn't murder him in the middle of the night. Brenna thought it would have served him right if the doll had attacked him. She still couldn't believe he'd pulled that stunt last night after all the drama with Mystery Girl. Of course, that was what made his efforts so successful. Really though, if she looked at it objectively, it had been incredibly clever. Van had won their bet fair and square, even if he'd been cruel in doing it. After all, he *was* a boy. He couldn't help being heartless sometimes.

"When will you be home?" Abraham asked as Brenna took her cereal bowl to the sink.

"Before dinner," she said, coming back to join him at the kitchen table.

"And you're watching a movie at his house?"

She resisted the urge to smile. It must be hard for him, watching her go off with a boy and out of the safety of his guardianship. Brenna pulled out a piece of paper and handed it to him.

"Here's his address, cell phone number, and home number. Now you can reach him if you need to, which I'm sure you won't since you're not a man who overreacts to little things like your niece dating."

"You can do things here, you know," he said. The "under my watchful eye" went implied. "If you're going to keep seeing young Mr. Hamilton, it might be a good idea for me to get to know him better."

"You always call him that, 'young Mr. Hamilton,'" she observed.

Abraham cocked a quizzical eyebrow. "Do I?"

Like he didn't know that already, she thought. "It's very formal. Maybe that's your way of reminding me that even though he's a boy, he still has to behave like a gentleman."

"My girl is so very clever." He was smiling with his eyes.

Brenna kissed his cheek. "Don't worry, *Zio*. We'll both behave."

A few minutes later, when Mitch picked her up, she felt the unmistakable flutter of butterflies in her stomach. As much as she tried to calm herself down, she couldn't downplay the significance of the day. Not only was this her first real date, she knew that they were going to have the "talk" that would officially move their relationship out of the realm of make believe and into reality. All of which was sweetened by the promise of a kiss. So when she slid into the front seat of his car and he flashed her the infamous crooked smile, Brenna enjoyed the more decided beating of her heart. A girl could definitely get used to feeling this way, she thought as she returned his smile.

"Good morning," he greeted, sounding a little nervous but happy. Resting his arm on the back of the passenger seat, Mitch was wearing the most casual thing she'd ever seen him in – jeans and a red t-shirt. It was different, but he pulled the look off well.

"The same to you," she answered with a click of her seatbelt.

She set her backpack between her legs. Sophia Irene was peeking out of the top with Mitch's birthday present underneath her tiny, plastic feet. "Are you ready for today?"

He moved his hand from the back of the seat to her face, brushing a stray hair off of her cheek. "Absolutely," he affirmed with a quiet intensity before he had to focus his attention on pulling away from the curb. They drove in silence for a few minutes, stealing glances at one another and then grinning with embarrassment when they got caught. Yes, this was definitely going to be an excellent day.

"You're sure your boss won't mind if I hang out with you?" Mitch asked finally.

Brenna gave a dismissive wave. "I already cleared it with Berthal. She may put you to work, though, so consider yourself warned."

Alternative rock music wafted out of the speakers, which surprised her. With his button-up shirt and polished shoes, she would have thought that something like classical music was more Mitch's style. Guess that proved that surface appearances could be deceiving. People were often far more complicated than that. There was so much about him that she didn't know yet, but she was certainly looking forward to unraveling his secrets.

"You look nice today," he announced suddenly.

Clothes weren't something that Brenna paid a lot of attention to, so she saw nothing remarkable with her baby blue top and jeans. Her ponytail wasn't particularly exciting either, in her mind. The expression on her face must have been quizzical because Mitch felt the need to clarify.

"That color of blue makes your eyes standout. They're really pretty."

"Thank you." It came out as a mumble as Brenna fought the urge to drop her head so she could hide her blushing face. Great.

Why did she have to develop the awkward inability to accept a compliment now?

"Better get used to those, Brenna," Mitch warned. "I've been keeping track of all the things I want to compliment you about."

Pleased but embarrassed, she hid her face behind her hand. "You're making me feel like a giggling schoolgirl."

"Last time I checked, you were still in school, so it's okay. Plus, I like knowing I can make you blush." He pulled her hand down so he could see her face. She frowned sternly at him, and he laughed. "Very intimidating," he assured her.

A moment later, Mitch pulled to a stop in the back of Honey B's. Even though it was a mere twenty steps from the car to the back door, he still took her hand. When she sighed involuntarily at his touch, he chuckled, and she smacked his chest lightly. He was enjoying the effect he had on her far too much. She needed to calm down or she'd never make it through the day without embarrassing herself. Ignoring the boy trailing behind her, Brenna called out a greeting as they entered through the back door.

"Morning, honey," the older woman said, coming over to them. She gave Mitch an appraising look. "And here you are, Brenna's young man. I recognize your face. You are most welcome here."

"It's a pleasure to meet you, Mrs. Bean," he said, extending his hand.

Berthal shook it and fanning herself, gave Brenna an approving wink when Mitch turned to set her backpack down on the counter. Blushing furiously, the young girl swatted Berthal's hand away. It was hard not to giggle.

"I really appreciate you letting me stay with Brenna this morning." As usual, Mitch was the picture of politeness. His eyes roamed the kitchen, looking for something that needed to be done. "Is there anything I can do to make myself useful?"

The look on Berthal's face was far from innocent. "Oh, I'm sure that our girl can put you to work in here."

"Berthal!" Brenna chastised, her face a brilliant shade of red.

The old woman patted her cheek. "Honey, you need to lighten up. Have fun, kids. Let me know if you need anything." She exited the kitchen swiftly, leaving them alone.

"So what are we making today?" he asked, rubbing his hands together.

Walking over to the shelf, Brenna pulled down a binder full of recipes. "We're making a small, individual chocolate cake. It'll be five inches around, and perfect for two people," she said as flipped through the pages. Mitch peered over her shoulder. "We keep all of the recipes in here, so it's a very important book," she told him.

"It's your baking bible," Mitch summed up.

"Pretty much," Brenna agreed, pointing to a recipe. "This is the one we want."

As they got started, she was surprised to see how comfortable Mitch was in a kitchen. She'd grown up with an uncle who cooked, but Brenna had always figured that was one of Abraham's oddities, perhaps born out of necessity since there was no one else to do the cooking. Duke could barely tell the difference between flour and sugar, and the only cooking Van did was the creative kind, which usually resulted in inedible concoctions that were immediately thrown out. But Mitch knew exactly what he was doing and even had a sort of sense as to where ingredients were located in the kitchen without being told. Cooking with him was more fun than she'd anticipated.

"You're pretty good at this," she observed, watching him pour flour carefully into the running mixer. No novice could have done that without getting flour everywhere.

"With my parents gone a lot, I'm on my own for meals. Fast

food and microwave dinners get boring pretty quick."

Right. That made sense in a terribly tragic sort of way. She could just picture Mitch at the stove, cooking meals that he would eat by himself in an empty house. Even though she'd never met his parents, Brenna was already inclined to dislike them for the way they abandoned their son. It had to bother him more than he let on, especially today. Brenna had not been a huge fan of celebrating her birthday, but that had been her choice – not one of conscious neglect by Abraham. Maybe Mitch didn't hold much stock in celebrating his either, but to think that his parents wouldn't care enough to attempt to acknowledge the day was something completely different.

"You'll have to come over for dinner sometime," she said. "Aside from that making me happy, I think my uncle would like to get to know you better."

He smiled down at her. "I'd like that."

"Really? You're not intimidated by a man who carries a gun?"

Mitch shrugged. "The way I see it, the sooner we get used to each other, the better."

A variety of topics came up as they worked, but conversation always veered away from their blossoming relationship and Mystery Girl. Brenna guessed that Mitch didn't want to ruin the day by bringing up "business," or distract her from her job by delving into serious personal stuff. That suited her just fine. She would rather not have that conversation in the kitchen of Honey B's where they could be interrupted at any moment by Berthal. It was a private matter that should be treated as such.

"Now, this cake can't be iced until it has cooled down," Brenna told him as she carried the pan, fresh from the oven, across the room. "So we're going to speed up the process a bit by sticking it in the freezer." The walk-in freezer wasn't big – about six feet wide and eight feet long – but it *was* cold, set at about 38 degrees Fahrenheit. She set the cake down on one of the empty racks.

Mitch examined the door as if it were vital to his survival. "Don't you ever worry about getting locked inside this thing?"

Brenna shook her head, jiggling the knob. "You can open it from the inside, and if for some reason that didn't work, you just flip the switch. That triggers an alarm and turns on that light, so someone knows to come let you out." She pointed to a red light bulb above the door. "Safe as houses."

He didn't look convinced and backed out, shivering slightly.

"Are you claustrophobic?" she inquired.

"I dunno. Maybe," he replied, eyes wide. "I just don't like the idea of getting stuck in there."

Brenna rested her hands on his shoulders. "Don't worry. You don't have to ever go back into the big, bad freezer." Then taking him by the hand, she pulled him over to the mixer and taught him how to make chocolate frosting.

When the time came to ice the cake, Mitch didn't actually help, but he kept a watchful eye on the process, hovering right behind Brenna's shoulder as she worked. He oohed and ahhed appropriately as she piped a cursive "Happy Birthday" in green icing onto the cake. She couldn't help but smile at his enthusiasm and the secret fact that the cake was actually for him. As a fan of surprises, her boss was more than happy to square away not only their time together in the kitchen but the cake as well. The thought of giving it to Mitch made Brenna happy, and she congratulated herself on her own sneakiness. He would never see it coming.

When Brenna's shift ended, they headed to the thrift store in search of a suitable costume for Mitch. New to You was a large enough place that you could lose a person pretty easily behind the aisles packed with items, especially if she was short. The owners preferred to think of the store as well stocked rather than cluttered.

Like most shops of its kind, it had that pervasive musty smell that evoked massive sneezing attacks to those unfortunate folks with dust allergies. Brenna typically didn't spend a lot of time there until Halloween rolled around and the search for costume-appropriate items started.

Upon entering the store, she sent him in search of pants as she picked up a shopping basket to put Sophia Irene in. She meant to go look at the shirts but got distracted as she passed the toy section. Jumbled up in a box on the floor was a large assortment of Barbies and other knock-off fashion dolls. Van was a fool if he thought he was going to get away unscathed over that stunt he pulled last night. She knelt down to help herself to the box's contents, figuring that she'd find a way to use them in her plan for revenge.

Grinning wickedly, Brenna stood up a moment later and headed towards the men's shirts. Her eyes searched automatically for Mitch and found him working his way through the rack. And he wasn't alone. Well, technically, he was, but he had a shadow in the decidedly female form of Sara Xavier. Watching them made Brenna distinctly uncomfortable. Every time Mitch moved, Sara moved automatically as if she was tethered to him, but she never attempted to close the distance between them. The girl's mouth was moving as if they were having a conversation. Mitch wasn't aware of her presence and Sara, with her dreamy-eyed expression, hadn't seen Brenna.

Wow. Sara was head over heels for Mitch – Brenna was certain of it. When she'd seen Sara watching him on Thursday as they prepped for the carnival, the girl had obviously been more on her guard. She'd known Brenna was there, but today, her emotions were completely transparent.

Brenna immediately felt on the defensive. Given what she was seeing now, wasn't Sara the living embodiment of the profile she and Van had come up with? A quiet girl, hopelessly in love with a boy who didn't even realize she was standing four feet away from him. And now that she thought about it, Sara was a flutist in the band. That could explain the music Brenna had heard. It was possible that Sara had gotten her costume at the thrift store, too. After all, Van thought some of the clothes could have been vintage.

It was looking quite possible that Sara was Mystery Girl. So how was Brenna going to proceed now? Acknowledge the girl's presence? Maybe shoot her a "back off" glare? Pretend not to see her until after she'd embraced Mitch? Or simply ignore her altogether?

After a moment's indecision, she decided to stick with the plan that had been set in motion to drive Mystery Girl to the brink of desperation until she made a mistake. Knowing her identity now didn't change the game. In fact it made things easier since they knew who to watch for.

Plastering a big smile on her face, Brenna walked down the aisle, her eyes focused solely on Mitch like the adoring girlfriend she was supposed to be. Upon reaching him, she wrapped her arms around him, banging her basket into his side, and buried her head in his chest.

"Did you miss me that much?" he asked, returning her embrace.

Brenna placed her hand on his neck and pulled his head down to whisper in his ear. "I know we said we wouldn't discuss business, but I think Mystery Girl didn't get the memo." She smiled, hoping to mislead Sara into thinking they were sharing private words of love. "Don't look behind you and follow my lead. We just have to pretend for a little while."

"Promise?" he asked. He smiled at her but the telltale signs of frustration were in his eyes. He was tired of this game, and so was Brenna. Weren't they ever going to get some uninterrupted time to themselves?

She tapped his nose with her finger and nodded. At least, she hoped she wasn't lying.

Mitch held up the pants in his hand. They were blue polyester. "How about these?"

"They look perfect," she agreed, taking his hand. "Let's find you a shirt and get out of here."

"Why are you buying dolls?" he asked, glancing down at her shopping basket.

Brenna gave a dismissive wave. "It's a long story, the short of it being that I plan to give Van a heart attack."

"I love your sense of humor," he grinned. "Let me know if I can help."

A few minutes later, they were pawing through the shirts, searching for a suitable one. Mitch kept his eyes studiously on the racks as Brenna directed. She, on the other hand, managed to sneak some glances in various directions to see if Sara was still lurking. She had that sensation of being watched so she knew the girl had to be close.

And she was – peering at them as she tried to hide at the end of an aisle. It was undeniably disturbing, knowing Sara was watching them. Brenna could only imagine the type of thoughts that accompanied such behavior.

"Stay cool and I'll explain," she muttered to Mitch. He dutifully kept searching the rack and nodded. "When we were separated, I noticed Sara Xavier watching you in a very intimate and creepy way."

He frowned, no doubt trying to remember if he'd seen her. "Where was she?"

"Right behind you." She placed her hand on top of his, holding it steady. They shared a serious look, though both of them had slapped broad smiles on their faces. "Mitch, she fits the bill.

A quiet, unnoticed girl who's completely in love with you. Plus, she plays the flute, and I bet she picked up that costume of hers here. She shops here a lot, you know."

Everyone knew that Sara's family was dirt poor and had to buy a lot of their clothes at the thrift store. After all, she was called "Second-hand Sara" for a reason, albeit a cruel one.

"Are you sure?" he asked, continuing his search.

Brenna nodded. "I had my suspicions when I saw her watching you at the ASB meeting on Thursday, but I think she had her feelings under control then because I was there. She didn't know I came in with you today, so what she did was natural."

"What about this one?" In effort to remain unsuspicious, Mitch held up a long-sleeved white shirt to his chest. It looked good.

"Yeah, I think that's perfect," she confirmed.

"Should we try to confront her?" He looked ready to drop the clothes and tackle Sara to the ground. If only it were that simple.

Brenna sighed, "She'll simply deny that it's her. I think we have to stick with the original plan of catching her red-handed, but it should be simpler now that we've figured it out."

"Then can we go now? I don't want to spend anymore of my day with you on stalkers."

How could any girl resist such eagerness? Brenna smiled, nodding. "We're done. Chrissie's going to make your ascot and you're borrowing one of your dad's belts, so that covers it."

A few minutes later, they climbed into Mitch's car, shopping bags in tow, with their thoughts far away from Sara Xavier. Smiling, they fed off each other's excitement now that the much sought-after alone time was here. They just needed to make one more stop. As Mitch started the engine, Brenna put her hand on his arm.

"I have a confession," she began. "You know that special

order cake we made this morning?"

"Yeah?" he replied uncertainly.

"It's for you," she said, grinning. "Hannah let it slip that today was your birthday."

The gesture took him completely by surprise, which pleased Brenna. "You made a birthday cake for me?"

"Well, technically, you helped make it, too," she said. "I thought we should celebrate. Have our own little party or something."

"Believe me," he replied with assurance. "We are definitely going to celebrate."

A half an hour later, Mitch pulled into his driveway. Because they valued their privacy, the Hamiltons lived in a large, two-story house on the outskirts of Mount Vernon. Trees and vegetation, including cornfields, surrounded it, making it the perfect setting for a stalker. And while the white house was beautiful with its Greek Revival columns and dark green trim, it was too big for a boy to live in by himself. Brenna was willing to bet big time that it gave off a spooky vibe at night even to Mitch.

Inside, the house was immaculate which wasn't hard to pull off since most of it went unused. Mitch's room was on the second floor. She knew that his parents had money but his room didn't have the usual rich boy toys, except for a fairly impressive computer. The dark browns and greens with which he'd decorated gave the room a forested effect that Brenna found very peaceful.

Downstairs, the only rooms that showed any signs of life were the kitchen and the living room. With all of the photos hung on the walls, one would have thought a happy family like the Vaughns lived there. But the pictures were nothing but window-dressing to hide the fragmentation of the Hamilton family. Mitch bore a strong resemblance to his father, Robert, but the older man had a hard look around his eyes that his son didn't possess. Sylvia,

Mitch's mother, was a bottled blonde that didn't seem to fit in with the rest of her family.

But of course, Brenna could speak none of these observations out loud. All she could do was smile and say how lovely the home was, which was true.

The first thing Mitch did when the tour was done was shut the drapes and blinds to every window in the kitchen and living room. "There," he sighed upon returning. "Now we have all the privacy we need. Let's eat."

Now, most people might not find it fun to spend any part of a date in a kitchen – let alone time in two different kitchens – but they enjoyed it. Of course, now that they were in Mitch's house instead of the bakery, they were free to play around and flirt up a storm. Knowing that no one could see them or monitor their behavior was incredibly liberating. They could be themselves. Every time Mitch touched her, Brenna knew that it was real. To finally have such certainty in his actions was delightful. It made it much easier to return his affection.

Lunch was a simple affair consisting of sandwiches, chips, fruit salad, and chocolate cake. They sat at the table, savoring the opportunity to talk about anything that wasn't connected to Mystery Girl. Honestly, Brenna had figured that the first thing Mitch would want to discuss would be their relationship, but the boy didn't broach the subject at all. Not even after she gave him the photo – which he loved. Brenna wondered if she should bring it up. After all, girls these days made the first move all the time. She was confident and sure of Mitch's feelings for her.

The only problem was that Brenna sort of liked being pursued. In some respects, she was no different than Mystery Girl. She wanted Mitch to choose her, too. And who knew? Maybe he was waiting for the right moment and by jumping the gun, she'd ruin whatever big move he had in store for her. Truthfully, she wanted to see what it was.

"So which movie did you pick out for us to watch?" she inquired.

"It's called *Lady in White*. It's a ghost story and not quite your traditional horror movie," he told her.

Brenna cocked her eyebrow. "With all that's going on, you picked a movie about the supernatural?"

He shrugged casually. "What can I say? I like to live on the edge."

"Or you're a glutton for punishment," she smiled as she carried their plates to the sink. Mitch's chair squeaked as he got up to follow her. When she turned around, he was right there. He rested his hands on the counter, trapping her in place. It was an imprisonment that she didn't mind at all.

"Speaking of gluttony, that cake was amazing. Thank you." The smile he gave Brenna made her heart race. Even if she'd wanted to, she wouldn't have been able to tear her eyes away from his face.

"I'm sorry that it wasn't more," she said softly.

Mitch shook his head. "It was perfect. The whole day has been perfect. There's nothing else I would have preferred to do than spend time with you." He took a small step forward, eliminating what little space had been between them, and then he exhaled heavily. "Brenna, my mother's birthday is in February."

Her initial thought was one of confusion – what did that have to do with anything? – and then her confusion mounted when she remembered that he ordered a cake from her last month. Why did he pay for a birthday cake for his mom then? But the part of her brain that was becoming more adept at deciphering Mitch's behavior told her to stop being an idiot and not be so literal. The birthday had nothing to do with what he was saying.

"You were looking for a way to spend time with me," she

concluded, trying to stay calm. Now that it appeared that they were finally going to have the "talk," she felt queasy. Maybe as long as they kept talking like rational people, she'd be okay. "Why the subterfuge?"

"It was just the first stage in my plan to win your heart," he confessed with blatant honesty. "A five-pronged attack to be precise, but then that stuff with Kevin happened. That kinda messed things up, and I don't want to waste anymore time." That crooked smile was back again, and so was his self-confidence. She could tell that speaking his mind felt good to him. "Brenna, I've liked you for quite a while now, and with this being our senior year, I don't want to have any regrets."

"Me neither," she agreed, placing her hands on the crooks of his arms. She knew the kiss was coming, but she wanted to hear more of his thoughts, hoping that it would enhance the moment. "But are you sure you want me? I heard that Alexis expressed an interest in you."

Mimicking her, Mitch put his hands on Brenna's arms and rubbed his thumbs in small circles against her skin. When she didn't protest, he shifted forward, so close that she could feel his breath on her face.

"Now why would I ever want her when I can have you?" While his tone might have held some amusement in it, the look in his eyes made it quite clear that he was serious.

Suddenly thinking clearly became very difficult. She blurted out the first thing that came to mind. "How long exactly?" Her voice was unsteady, which might have annoyed her if she'd been aware of it.

"Have I liked you?" he clarified. Wow but he was amazingly self-possessed right now. She nodded. "Ever since Mrs. Wilson's class."

The name sliced through the fogginess in her mind, making

her laugh. Instantly she saw her school photo – a tiny little girl
with massively permed hair. She'd convinced herself that she
needed to have curly hair like Little Orphan Annie and couldn't be
dissuaded. Van's mom was a professional stylist and had done the
work herself, and while the technique was flawless, it had not
produced the most flattering effect on Brenna.

"That was the fourth grade!" she protested. "I had that awful
perm."

He nodded, growing serious. "Like I said, this has been a long
time coming."

It was one of those moments when everything faded away
until all that was left was a girl and the boy making her heart race.
The boy whose eyes she couldn't look away from. The back of his
fingers stroked down the side of her face, leaving a tingling
sensation in their wake, and her heart stopped altogether. When
his hand alighted on her waist, she forgot how to breathe. And as
he leaned in, her mind anticipated with giddy delight how it would
feel when their lips met.

Only they never did because a robot baby picked that exact
moment to let out a metallic-sounding wail.

"Sir!" Brenna blurted out in frustration and then corrected
herself belatedly, "I mean, Sophia Irene!" Mitch stepped back
automatically at her sudden movement. She snatched the baby off
of the counter and such was her annoyance that she jammed the
key into her back with a little more force than necessary.

Her eyes flickered down to the offending Sophia Irene, whose
plastic smile seemed all too innocent. Brenna's cheeks felt hot
with disappointment and embarrassment. Adding insult to injury,
Mitch headed into the living room. The moment was officially
lost.

Feeling dejected, she trailed after him, wondering if Fate was
personally conspiring against her or if she and Mitch merely had

the worst timing ever. There was something incredibly awkward about a failed kiss – even though it wasn't Mitch's fault. Any kiss that occurred right now would feel more like an effort to ease the tension of the moment rather than an act of passion. That wasn't what either of them wanted for their first time, so Mitch started the movie and joined Brenna on the couch.

While the opening credits played, he began the process of inching his way closer to her. It started with a small squirm – that got him about half an inch, she guessed. Then he leaned forward, pretending to stretch before shifting over another inch when he sat back again. When he did it again, she giggled.

"Like that?" Mitch inquired, his voice thick with inflated arrogance.

Brenna gave an exaggerated nod. "You're super smooth."

"The smoothest," he declared, throwing his arm around her. She snuggled into his chest, enjoying the closeness, and reached across his lap to take hold of his other hand.

The movie progressed, but Brenna wasn't really paying attention to what was happening. Her focus was on the boy sitting next to her. Mitch's fingers made up and down motions against her shoulder in a lazy way that suggested he wasn't even aware he was doing it. Every now and then, he'd rest his cheek against her head. It was nice, being with Mitch in that way. Much more than nice, actually.

But when it seemed like the movie was coming to an end, she paid enough attention to be able to discuss it should Mitch be interested. He'd been right – this wasn't your traditional horror movie. You could tell by the ending. The bad guy was actually caught, the young protagonist saved, and the ghosts reunited to head off into the afterlife. Basically, it was a happy ending.

The credits rolled, and they stayed on the couch, making small talk about the film and what they were going to do the rest of the evening. Both of them were planning quiet nights at home, making up for the studying they'd neglected of late. They both knew they wouldn't get any done if they tried to do it together. Spending the day with each other had been wonderful, but it was time to return to reality and the annoying problem that was Mystery Girl.

"We have to think of something to do about Sara," Brenna whispered.

Mitch sighed. "Maybe she'll see that we're a real, solid couple now and leave us alone."

Tilting her head, Brenna looked up at him. "Are we a real couple?"

"Well, yeah," he said, confused by her question. "What did you think that talk in the kitchen was about?"

"I didn't think that we finished that conversation," she replied.

Mitch stood up so suddenly that Brenna thought she'd done something wrong, but then he pulled her into his arms. She didn't even have time to prepare before their lips met. As first kisses went, it was sweet and tender with a hint of what would be in store for future ones. It wasn't like it often gets depicted in books with girls getting intoxicated by the very scent of their romantic male lead. Mitch smelled fresh like springtime, and he tasted like chocolate cake. It was real – *he* was real. The way her body responded to him was real, too. Everything – the heat radiating from his closeness, the pressure of his hands on her hips, the slight way her knees wobbled from nerves, how her heart was skipping in her chest – combined for a pleasing effect that made Brenna wish she'd tried this kissing thing a long time ago.

But such sensations couldn't completely overwhelm her feelings of self-consciousness. It sort of felt like she was taking a test she hadn't studied for because she didn't know it was coming. What if she was doing it wrong? What was she supposed to do with her hands? Standing there, hands by her side, felt silly, so she slid them around his waist and hoped that was an appropriate place. She didn't feel brave enough to put them anywhere else. And was she moving her mouth correctly? It felt awkward. Hopefully that feeling stemmed from kissing inexperience rather than poor execution.

Her worrying was needless. When Mitch pulled away, he was smiling like a kid in a candy store and he didn't let go of her. That was a good sign.

"Consider the matter closed. You are mine, and no one is going to come between us now," he vowed as his hands tightened around her.

Brenna found Mitch's air of confidence to be quite attractive. His previous lack of courage when it came to expressing his feelings had been incredibly frustrating. In the books she read, she always found herself drawn to the male characters who knew what they wanted and went after it. Not in a reckless way but with determination and foresight. Mitch's pursuit of her hadn't felt like that, but his boldness now was a complete and much welcomed turnaround. It made her feel more courageous as well.

"Sorry," she sighed helplessly, "but I'm still confused. I need you to convince me some more." She wrapped her arms around his neck and pulled his head closer to hers.

Mitch was still grinning when they kissed again.

CHAPTER TWENTY-THREE

When Brenna closed the front door behind her, lips still tingling from Mitch's goodbye kiss, she shut her eyes and sighed. It was amazing how a couple of kisses could make the world such a brighter, happier place. And magical. There was definitely more magic. Having a boyfriend was a wonderful thing. She was still grounded in reality enough to know that she wasn't in love. Honestly, she wasn't exactly sure *what* she was in, but it felt amazing and she intended to enjoy the sensation.

She was dating Mitch. She had a boyfriend.

Brenna hid her smile behind her hand. Wow. That idea was going to take some getting used to, and if it hadn't been for Mystery Girl, none of it might have happened.

"Oh no, it's far more serious than I'd expected."

Abraham's voice pulled Brenna out her reverie. Her uncle had just stepped out of the kitchen and was taking in her dreamy-eyed expression with grave concern. Bounding over to him, she threw her arms around him.

"I'm very happy right now, *Zio*," she declared with fervor.

"That's apparent," he remarked. "You look like you've been kissing."

Instead of wondering how he could sound so certain or pretending it wasn't true, she nodded unabashedly. "It was delightful. I plan on doing a whole lot more of it, too."

"God, grant me strength," Abraham pleaded, burying his face in his hand.

"Don't worry, *Zio*. I'm just teasing," Brenna said, letting him go so she could dance into the kitchen. She felt like Ginger Rogers. Too bad her Fred Astaire had English homework or else they could have danced the night away.

"No, you're not," he countered.

Brenna came to a halt in front of the fridge. "No, I'm not," she agreed, "but I promise to be good. I know how I was raised." She examined the contents of the fridge and found them wanting. "Would you like me to make dinner?" she offered, providing her uncle with a much-desired change in topic.

"I'll take care of it," he assured her. "You go do your homework."

That sounded like a wonderful idea to Brenna, who raced up the steps like one possessed. She spent the next few hours in a world of Spanish conjugation, solving derivatives, and dealing with a fussy Sophia Irene. Strangely enough, knocking out multiple homework assignments in one sitting was the perfect capstone to her day. Being productive felt good.

Her cell phone rang and she smiled when she saw Mitch's name pop up in the caller ID. "Hi, Boyfriend," she greeted playfully.

"Did you look at the photo you gave me?" No greeting. Just a question in a tone that bordered on panicked.

"Sure, I looked at it," she replied, confused. She searched vaguely for the copy she'd made for herself before realizing that she hadn't brought it in from the darkroom. "What's wrong with it? I thought we looked good."

"I'm not talking about us," Mitch clarified. "I'm talking about the background. She's there, Brenna. Mystery Girl is in the photo."

In an instant, Brenna ran down the stairs, assuring Abraham that everything was all right as she flew out the back door and up the steps to her darkroom. The white light clicked on and she pulled the photo in question off the line so she could examine it. She hadn't noticed anyone in the background because she'd been so focused on how she and Mitch looked. Now that Brenna was paying attention, though, she could see her. The photo was black and white so it would have been easy to overlook the half-girl in the background, but she didn't cut herself any slack. How could she have missed it? There was Mystery Girl with her stringy hair, her hoodie with the patchwork trim, skirt, and leggings – exactly how Mitch, Van, and Keiko had described her.

"I can't believe I missed that, and I can't believe she was there and we didn't see her!" she cried, massaging her temple. Knowing she'd missed spotting Mystery Girl on Thursday was going to eat at her for days.

"We were focused on other things," Mitch soothed. "Don't be too hard on yourself."

She ignored his words of comfort. "But we could have ended it then! This would have all been over!" Stupid, silly Brenna! Her thoughts had been completely wrapped up in Mitch. Romance was clearly hazardous to an investigation.

"Can you tell what's in her hand?" he asked.

Brenna stared at the object. It was long, thin, and blurry – the girl had been in motion when the photo was snapped. "I'm not sure. If she's in this photo, though, maybe she's in others."

Pulling the other photos off the line, Brenna spread them out on the counter so she could examine them. There was no hint of Mystery Girl in the close-ups she'd taken of Mitch's hands, which made sense. The girl would have had to be right behind him to make it into one of those shots. Brenna would have definitely seen her then. Mystery Girl wasn't in the candid photos she'd snapped either, but she *was* in the photo that Hannah had taken of Brenna, Mitch, Van, and Mr. Rose. That made sense because that picture and the one of just the two of them had been taken in rapid succession. In fact, Mystery Girl was less blurry in the second picture.

"It's a flute," Brenna decided. "That's what she's holding in her hand." Then she paused for a moment. "I think Mystery Girl just did us a huge favor."

In addition to being agitated, Mitch now sounded confused. "How so?"

"She thought she was being clever, trying to scare us by showing up in the pictures of us. She doesn't know that we suspect her of being Sara Xavier. All I have to do now is go back and look at the other people in the candid shots. If Sara's not there, then it's a good bet she's Mystery Girl. There wouldn't have been time for her to change between when I took them and when Hannah took our photo."

"But did you take pictures of everyone who was working?" Mitch pressed. "You could have just missed her."

He had a legitimate point, and therefore, she'd have to take her findings with a grain of salt. However, Sara's absence in the photos would further solidify Brenna's suspicions about the girl. They could still keep looking at her as Mystery Girl.

"No, but I deliberately took photos around the whole cafeteria to get as many people in them as possible. If Sara's not in one, then she most likely wasn't there when I took them."

Mitch waited in silence as Brenna examined the faces in the photos. Seconds ticked by and she could sense his apprehension growing. Finally, Brenna announced with pleasure, "She's not there."

"Are you sure?" he questioned.

"Positive," she affirmed, feeling her temper rise. Sara had cast a dark shadow over her perfect day, and Brenna was going to make her pay for that. "Okay, I'm done with this nonsense. Sara Xavier is going down. By the time the Halloween Carnival rolls around, Mystery Girl is going to be nothing but a bad memory."

"What are you going to do?"

It annoyed her that Mitch sounded so uncertain. Didn't he want all of this to be over? Wasn't he the one who had declared that no one was going to come between them? Why the sudden lack of enthusiasm?

"Mitch, we gotta make her crack, or she'll never leave us alone. She's been stalking us both and it's time to put an end to it."

"But what if it's not her? What if we go after her and she's innocent?"

Then they were nothing but total jerks, she thought, but what other option was there? Sara was hands down their best suspect, but the tiny sliver of doubt that existed was just enough to give Mitch discomfort. He always treated people with respect – that was one of the qualities he possessed that Brenna was attracted to the most – so the idea that they could end up tormenting an innocent girl, who was already teased for being poor, would upset him.

"I completely understand what you're saying. The last thing that I would want to do is cause Sara pain when she hasn't earned it," she assured him. "Is there anyone else that you think it could be?"

Brenna was pretty sure she already knew the answer. Investigations didn't seem to be Mitch's strong suit. She couldn't remember him ever committing to a suspect or a theory outside the possibility of a haunting. The only thing that he'd agreed to wholeheartedly was the dating charade, and he'd had ulterior motives at the time.

He was quiet for so long that she started to get worried. "Mitch?"

"Brenna," he began slowly. He paused, taking a breath. "What if Mystery Girl is a ghost? I still don't see why Sara would drag her flute around like that since it's such an identifier. Why would she want us to know it's her? It makes more sense if she's a ghost and she wants us to figure out who she is."

The issue he raised was valid. Well, not the ghost part. But why would Sara want them to identify her? The only thing Brenna could think of was that maybe Sara was tired of playing games, too. Maybe she was finalizing some plans of her own to put an end to all of this. Mitch wasn't a fan of that idea when she voiced it. He was against anything that might indicate Brenna was in some kind of danger.

"The bottom line is that we need to get this sorted out, so if you have no other suggestions," Brenna paused, allowing Mitch time to speak before continuing, "then we have to escalate our behavior in front of Sara. We have to deliberately seek her out."

"What do you mean? You want to taunt her and be mean or something?"

"Absolutely not." If there was any possibility that Brenna was wrong about Sara, she didn't want to make things worse by being openly cruel to her. "I mean, we need to be very affectionate at school when Sara's around. We should find out when she's working at the theater and go on a date there. That sort of thing. We have to shove our relationship down her throat. I think we should pay attention to her, too, so when you see her, say hi. It should drive her crazy to have your attention now when you're with me."

Whether Mitch liked the plan or not, he certainly didn't have a problem kissing Brenna in front of her locker on Monday. It was convenient that Sara's locker was in the same bank as hers. The girl got a front row view of the action. The couple kissed, hugged, and in general kept their arms wrapped around each other as they talked. Not wanting to get in trouble with Mr. Elliott, they didn't overdo it, but it was enough according to Van.

Van had stood in the distance, watching Sara watch the amorous couple, and concluded that the girl looked nothing short of devastated. She trailed behind them on their way to English, staring with glazed-over eyes as they kissed again before entering Mr. Rose's classroom together. The girl's demeanor shifted noticeably when Mitch greeted her – Sara sat one row over and a seat back from him in Rose's class. Then he turned away from her and waved at Brenna.

Things got interesting at break when Sara literally ran into Brenna and spilled her entire can of soda down the front of her white shirt. Of course, Sara apologized profusely and Brenna smiled, saying that it was no big deal. She ran to the bathroom to wash it off only to realize belatedly what bad idea that was since her white shirt basically became see-through when it was wet. Hugging her arms around herself, Brenna exited the bathroom in a hurry, ignoring Dylan when he asked her where the wet t-shirt contest was being held, and located Van, who graciously loaned her his acid-wash jacket.

With Keiko's help, Van found out that Sara was scheduled to work on Tuesday after school. In keeping with the plan, Brenna and Mitch made an impromptu trip to the movies, which unfortunately meant that she had to bail on Mr. Rose. Her teacher had looked decidedly disappointed in her as if he suspected her of shirking her commitment in order to be with her new boyfriend and wanted Brenna to know he had thought better of her. It couldn't be helped, though. While technically she *was* sneaking off to be with her new boyfriend, she was really trying to catch his stalker. But she had made sure to swing by and pick up the sophomore notebooks at lunch to show that she still planned to help him.

After her shift at Honey B's, Brenna had driven home to freshen up before Mitch swung by to get her. He hadn't been in a good mood when she got into the car. Mr. Rose had spent the better part of the carnival preparation time chewing him out over an incident involving Missy and a hot glue gun.

"I don't care if he isn't sleeping or if he's got too much work," Mitch bellowed en route to the movies. "He needs to back the hell off! I've done everything he's ever asked me to do, and I'm sick of his crap!"

Brenna had never heard Mitch talk about Mr. Rose like that. He was usually so calm and levelheaded. She figured that the combined stress of the carnival and Mystery Girl was finally making him crack. She placed her hand on his arm.

"It's done," she soothed, rubbing her hand against his skin. "You're with me. Doesn't that make you happy?"

"It would if our date wasn't Mystery Girl-inspired," he grimaced.

His mood improved, however, by the time they arrived at the theater. They put on quite a nauseating display for Sara who filled their popcorn and drink order. Then they sat in the dark theater, their heads suspiciously close together in case Sara should wander in. Honestly, Brenna wasn't even sure which movie they were watching. They just picked the one with the most convenient start time.

About halfway through, some excitement did occur. Brenna left to use the bathroom, and upon finishing her business, she discovered that the door had been locked. She was trapped inside.

For a few minutes, she pounded on the door, knowing full well that Sara should be able to hear her at the snack counter, but no one came to her rescue. Finally, she sent Mitch a text, hoping he'd check his phone even though he was at the movies. The door opened a few minutes later. Sara, with keys in hand, apologized profusely, saying she had no idea how something like that could have happened and would Brenna please accept the candy bar of her choice with the compliments of the theater?

"First the soda yesterday, and tonight, she locked me in the bathroom!" Brenna was the one in need of soothing on the car ride home.

"Well, you're the one who wanted to rile her up," Mitch reminded her. Because of that remark, he was only allowed to kiss her cheek when he dropped her off at home.

Wednesday was notable, but not in a Mystery Girl-related way. It stood out because Mitch, who was obviously still holding a grudge from the previous day, got into a heated debate with Mr. Rose about the concept of love in *Great Expectations*. It didn't last long – only a couple of minutes – but when Mitch remarked how love was closely tied to appearances, and therefore, to deception, Mr. Rose silenced him with a hand and changed the topic.

"What's going on with them?" Van whispered to Brenna as they left them room. Mr. Rose had detained Mitch after class.

Brenna frowned. "You know how stressed Mr. Rose has been. Well, yesterday, he sort of took it out on Mitch during carnival preparation, and Mitch was pretty mad about it."

"Weird. It's not like either of them to act like that," Van observed. "I think the sooner Saturday rolls around, the better. Everyone will feel better once the carnival is done." He looked down at Lloyd Dobler, a sudden thought occurring to him. "Hey, since we have 'children' now, does that mean we get to play the games and win candy?"

Rolling her eyes, Brenna linked arms with her best friend. "I think that only applies to children with pulses."

"Man, those technicalities will get you every time," he sighed.

Chapter Twenty-Four

"Brenna, would you mind hanging back for a bit?" Mr. Rose petitioned after they had finished cleaning up the carnival preparations on Thursday afternoon. "There are some things I'd like to go over with you."

Nearly every other student had already left for the night. They were all tired, but the good news was that everything was done. All of the ASB students and the volunteers could take Friday off to relax before showing up on Saturday to set up for the event.

"Sure," she agreed as she shut the last of the posters away in Mr. Rose's cabinet. She waved to Paige and Autumn as they left the classroom.

"You're staying?" Mitch asked, frowning.

Brenna nodded. "Just for a few minutes."

"Then I'll stay with you," he said, pulling off his backpack.

She moved the strap back up on his shoulder. "Go home," she said, pushing lightly against his chest. "You've had a long day and you're tired."

Mitch looked concerned and shot a furtive glance at Mr. Rose. "What if something bad happens?"

The fact that Sara hadn't been at school that day was a subject of much debate between Brenna, Van, and Mitch. Was she planning something diabolical or merely ill? Still convinced that Mystery Girl was a ghost, Van had taken matters into his own hands. He asked Keiko to stop by Sara's house under the guise of bringing her the homework she'd missed that day to see if the girl was really sick. Van's text had informed them that Sara looked about two steps away from the grave. Even so, Mitch was still nervous.

"I'll leave with Mr. Rose, and everything will be fine," she promised.

Privately, Brenna thought he had a very good point and vowed to be on her guard when she left the building. Sara could be pulling an elaborate ruse. After all, she seemed to be a fan of theatrics. At least, she sort of hoped that Sara was putting up a front. For all of Brenna's bluster on Saturday about catching Mystery Girl before the carnival, she was coming to the end of her rope. She hated to think that her enemy had bested her, but she had no idea how to catch Mystery Girl. She hadn't mentioned it to Van or Mitch yet, but if they hadn't caught Sara or whoever it was by Halloween, Brenna was going to take the problem to Abraham.

Her boyfriend didn't look appeased, but he sighed, "Fine. Just call me when you get home so I know you're safe."

Brenna nodded as Mitch bent down to kiss her cheek. Perhaps she should have been embarrassed by such a bold gesture in front of her teacher, but she couldn't have cared less what anyone else thought. In fact, she would have much preferred it if Mitch kept kissing her.

Once she watched him disappear down the stairs, she stepped back into the room and turned towards her teacher. "What would you like to go over?"

Mr. Rose stood at his desk, frowning. Unfortunately, much to Brenna's dismay, that look was becoming commonplace these days. She thought his mood had been improving, but that didn't appear to be the case since the residual tension between him and Mitch had yet to dissipate. Brenna hoped that everyone would feel better once the carnival was over.

"These," he said, tossing the sophomore notebooks down on his desk.

"Those are the ones I brought in this morning, right?" she asked, walking over to him. Picking up one notebook, she flipped through it and saw her familiar correction marks. Everything looked in order. She glanced up at him and instantly felt chastised. He was angry.

"Brenna, if I'd wanted half-assed work, I would have let Autumn be my TA this year," he all but spat.

If it had been anyone else, her temper would have flared at the insult. Brenna had never done anything half-assed in her life! But Mr. Rose was someone who's opinion mattered, and the sting of his words made her deflate like a balloon. Her favorite teacher thought her work was sub-par. He needed her help, and she let him down.

"Oh, I thought I got everything," she said haltingly. Had she made careless mistakes? Maybe she'd been too distracted by Mitch, trying to catch Mystery Girl, or the Halloween Carnival for that matter. With so many things competing for her attention of late, it wouldn't be inconceivable that she'd gotten something wrong. After all, she wasn't infallible. "I'll go over them again."

She tried to gather the notebooks up in her arms, but Mr. Rose knocked them out of her hands. A few skittered across his desk and onto the floor. Brenna froze, empty hands still outstretched. Her stomach churned at the sudden hostility she felt coming off of him. Her eyes refused to look anywhere but the ground. Getting yelled at by a teacher wasn't something she was used to, but this felt like something else entirely.

"Why? So you can mess them up again?"

She bit her lip. What was going on? The amount of anger Mr. Rose was displaying seemed out of place given her crime. Unease trickled down her spine. Leaving sounded like a good idea right about now, but she couldn't just run away while she was getting reprimanded from an authority figure. Surely the best way out of this was to make nice, and then everything would be okay. Her mouth was as dry as a desert, but she managed to get her words out in spite of it.

"I'm sorry."

Mr. Rose let out a disbelieving bark of laughter. "You're sorry? Don't lie to me. I hate when you do that."

Oh, so he was upset that she'd lied to him about why she couldn't help on Tuesday. "I'm sorry about Tuesday," she began, but he cut her off.

"This isn't just about Tuesday!" He wasn't yelling, but each word felt like a knife slicing through her skin. "It's about last Saturday, the Saturday before that, and Monday at the library. It's about you screwing that boy when you should be with me!"

A cold dread settled over Brenna as he crossed the line. As her teacher, Brenna's personal life was none of his business. It was bad enough for him to bring Mitch up like that, but to imply that she had a sexual relationship with him meant that Mr. Rose had been thinking about it. Something was very wrong here. The kind of wrong that should have had her running from the room. Unconsciously, she took a step back, eyes still on the ground.

Two heartbeats later, Mr. Rose exhaled. "My apologies, Brenna. I don't know what got into me. I didn't mean to make you uncomfortable."

It was the change in his voice that brought her head up, her body automatically relaxing. That sounded more like the Mr. Rose she knew. Yes, upsetting her had been unintentional. After all, he was under a lot of pressure and he hadn't been sleeping well. She could cut him some slack.

Then Brenna saw the look on his face.

The smile he was wearing was one she'd never seen before, and it made her skin crawl. It was too familiar and held far too many expectations. He liked this, liked seeing her scared. It was as if a veil had been lifted, revealing the real Avery Rose. The one she thought she knew, the one who had been the object of her schoolgirl crush, was a mere illusion designed to draw her in. That startling realization triggered a memory. She was standing in the library with Mitch. What was it that he'd said? If her instincts told her to run, she should run. Well, they were screaming at her now. It was time to leave.

Brenna bolted for the open door. She made it halfway out of the room before he caught her. Lifting her bodily from the ground, he threw her back inside with ease. She tried to prepare herself for the fall, but her left hand crumpled painfully as she collided with a desk. It toppled to the ground, and she fell with it. Immediately, Brenna tried to get up, but her left hand couldn't hold her weight without sending pain shooting up her arm. Gritting her teeth, she struggled to her feet, turning around in time to see Mr. Rose lock the door. Not to keep her in but to keep others out. Assuming there was anyone else left in the building, he didn't want to be interrupted.

Mr. Rose didn't give her any time to plan her next move. Catching her by the neck, he pulled her forward and slammed her face-first against the whiteboard. For a moment, Brenna saw stars. The board's ledge caught her painfully in the stomach, making it difficult to breathe properly.

"Do you have any idea the hell you've put me through these past few weeks?" he seethed into her ear. Brenna was uncomfortably aware of the way his body was pressed against hers. "Did you enjoy making me suffer?"

Terrified as she was, Brenna forced herself to understand what he was saying. His recent foul mood, he was blaming it on her. She'd hurt him, and if his actions were any indication, he was going to make her pay for it.

"No, sir," she said. There was no need to pretend to sound scared. "I didn't mean to. I didn't know."

Her words produced no change in him. "Don't play games, Brenna. I know how you feel about me. I've watched the blush creep into your cheeks, felt your eyes watching me, and seen the way your whole face lights up when I notice you."

So he hadn't been oblivious to her crush after all. He'd been aware of it and fed off of it. What she had felt for him was innocent, but he'd taken those feelings and twisted them into something dark and ugly.

"I know what you want from me." One finger skimmed gently across the bare skin of her back where her shirt had ridden up. Fighting to keep her emotions in check, Brenna bit her lip. "Do you know how long I've waited for you? I picked you out from all the others, cultivating your mind to be exactly what I want. You're mine, and no teenager is going to get in my way!"

He pulled her around to face him, one hand still firmly pressed against her throat, and slammed her back against the whiteboard. Grabbing her injured left arm, Mr. Rose gave it a twist. Brenna wanted to be brave. She didn't want to cower in front of him, but her eyes watered from the pain she felt. The whimper that escaped between her lips was tiny, but he still heard it.

"Hurts doesn't it?" he asked, eyes flashing as he leaned against her. "Imagine that pain magnified by a thousand times and you can begin to understand how I feel every time I see you with that boy. It's unbearable, what you've done to me."

"I'm sorry," she gasped.

"What?" he asked, feigning deafness. He cocked his ear closer to her lips. "I didn't quite catch that."

"I'm sorry." It came out louder and much more desperate as she repeated it. The tears were flowing freely now. She wanted to look away, but the hand on her neck forced her head to stay up. There was nowhere to look except into his eyes.

They say that the eyes are the window into a person's soul. If that was true, then Avery Rose's soul was dark and violent. Brenna had been scared for her life before – anyone trapped in a library with a gun-toting student would be – but this was a new kind of terror. She hadn't been the target of aggression then, and she hadn't been alone. Not like now. There was no one to help her. Trying to pry it away, Brenna scratched at the hand choking her, but it did no good.

He might actually kill me.

It was a cold, rational thought that sliced through her fear, not eliminating it but sectioning it off until Brenna felt herself spilt into two girls. One petrified by her emotions and the other calm and focused. The rational side hovered in the back of her mind, analyzing the predator before her and offering counsel on how to escape in a steady voice that sounded like Abraham.

This is about power and domination. He's using fear to control you. So let him see that you're scared, but keep your strength hidden. Save it for the right moment. Tell him what he wants to hear. Let him think he's winning, and then give him hell.

Oblivious to her internal conversation, Mr. Rose laid down the law. "You're going to break up with Mitch. I don't want to see you with him ever again or you'll regret it. Do you understand?"

She nodded, not bothering to hide her fear.

The pressure against her neck increased, constricting her windpipe. Mr. Rose frowned at her obvious distress but seemed to think she'd earned it. "I need to hear you say it, Brenna."

"Yes," she managed to squeak as she blinked up at him.

So many thoughts danced through her mind. What did he think was going to happen if she broke up with Mitch? That she'd carry on a relationship with him instead? Had Mr. Rose forgotten who her uncle was? Didn't he know that the first thing she'd do when she escaped was tell Abraham what happened? Perhaps he underestimated just how close niece and uncle were. If that was the case, Mr. Rose was in for a rude awakening.

The atmosphere shifted between them. What he wanted from her was written on his face, blazing like a neon sign on a dark night, and if that hadn't been enough, the way he moved his body against hers left little room for confusion. He let go of her arm and slipped his hand underneath her shirt. Violence was one thing. Getting felt up by your teacher was another. Brenna knew which one she preferred.

"Say you love me. I want to hear you say it." He wrapped his demand in a whisper that sent the hairs on Brenna's neck standing on end. When she didn't answer, his hand flew out from underneath her shirt and hit the whiteboard with brutal shudder. "Say it!"

"I love you," she answered. How could she feel so humiliated when there was only one person present to witness her disgrace?

With a sigh, he relaxed visibly and became a different man, switching emotions as quick as one flipped on a light. "See, everything is much easier for the both of us if you simply do what I ask," he smiled, kissing her forehead.

Tenderly, he stroked the neck he had been strangling a second ago, while the other one found its way back up her shirt. No, this couldn't be happening. It was a bad dream or a hallucination. It wasn't real. Brenna squeezed her eyes shut, willing herself to be anywhere other than where she was.

But it didn't work. She was still trapped, and he was still

touching her breasts.

Okay, now it was time to fight.

"You need to stop," Brenna commanded, interjecting as much authority into her voice as possible. "Please stop!"

When her plea fell on deaf ears, she turned to violence. She scratched at his hands, face, and neck, but he merely returned the favor like they were engaging in foreplay. When she tried to kick him, he pressed his thighs more firmly against her legs, pinning them to the wall. And the harder she shoved against his chest, the tighter he held her. No matter how hard she tried, she couldn't break free. Mr. Rose was simply too strong.

He pressed his forehead against her. "Don't be scared. It's okay," he whispered.

"No," she cried.

Opening her mouth was a mistake. He slipped his tongue inside with precision accuracy. His mouth kept her head pinned against the whiteboard, allowing the hand holding her neck to move between her thighs. The strength of the violation was mind numbing. All the fight Brenna had was suddenly directed internally as she struggled to keep her body from completely shutting down under the strength of his incapacitating assault.

And that was the point, wasn't it? Once he broke her, he would always have her under his thumb. This scene would play out again and again except that she wouldn't fight it next time. He would own her, body and soul.

But as his fingers worked to unbutton her jeans, the unexpected occurred. The lights went out, plunging them both in inexplicable darkness. Mr. Rose froze, neither letting Brenna go nor continuing his unwanted advances. The beam of light that passed through the window fell across his face, illuminating his eyes. They looked concerned.

Then the classroom door swung open and someone shouted, "I

told you to leave her alone, Avery!"

It was a girl's voice, but there was no one at the door that Brenna could see. Even as the disembodied voice sent chills down Brenna's spine, a glimmer of familiarity rang in her mind. She'd heard this voice before. Mr. Rose definitely had for he immediately let go of Brenna, backing away with wide eyes.

From out in the hallway, something passed by the open door. They could see it even in the darkness. It was large, maybe even human. Mr. Rose pivoted, unleashing a panicked cry of "Stay away from me!" Then he bolted out the door.

Brenna didn't waste time wondering what strange force had delivered her. She snatched up her backpack and ran as fast as she could out of the building. She didn't cross paths with Mr. Rose, thanks, perhaps, to whoever or whatever had intervened in the classroom. When she climbed into her car, she slammed the door shut with such force that the vehicle shook. Jamming the key in the ignition, she twisted it and the engine roared to life. The car peeled out of the parking lot with a screech.

There, in the safety of her car, the full weight of what happened caught up with her. Only then was she aware of the way her heart was crashing against her ribcage, how she was in danger of hyperventilating, and how she was trembling like a leaf in the wind. Gripping the steering wheel, Brenna tried to focus on slowing her breathing while she waited for the stoplight to turn green.

Breathe in. *You're safe.*

Breathe out. *He won't touch you again.*

Breathe in. *He'll be punished.*

Breathe out. *You're safe.*

It took effort and a steady stream of internal assurances to finally slow her breathing and her pulse down. Her arm was throbbing with pain. The adrenaline was wearing off, leaving

Brenna with nothing but a heavy weariness as she processed reality.

How had everything gone so horribly wrong? One minute everything was normal, and then the next, she had stumbled into some alternate universe where funny, intelligent, caring Mr. Rose was a sexual predator. Even though she'd been there, experienced the darkness within him firsthand, part of her still had trouble believing it. Never in a million years would she have believed him capable of such a despicable thing. But even as that declaration passed through her mind, a tiny voice contradicted it.

If you had only opened your eyes, you would have seen the warning signs. They were there, but you ignored them.

Yes, because she trusted him! He was a teacher, a responsible authority figure who was supposed to provide her with a safe environment. He was supposed to nurture her mind and help her reach her full potential. Not physically abuse her while feeling her up against the whiteboard.

Shuddering at the memory, Brenna automatically went to wrap her arms around herself, but her left arm gave a painful protest. She tried to flex her fingers, and while they did move, the effort hurt terribly. Probably not broken but definitely sprained. Fighting her misery, Brenna shook her head.

Hindsight made everything clear. She remembered the night they finished going over her entrance essay – the casual way he'd mentioned how overworked he was with no one to help him. And she'd volunteered like an idiot. My but he was clever. He made it seem like it had been her idea when it was what he wanted all along. More time alone with her. More time to have personal conversations. And that stupid book! He'd wanted to single her out and make her feel special. He'd even lured her into his car to buy more paint for the carnival. It was a clever trap into which she'd walked all too willingly. Like the perfect predator, he used her feelings against her.

Fury roared to life inside of Brenna. She slapped the steering wheel with her uninjured hand. See? This is exactly why she was better off not trusting people! Their smiles and kind words told nothing but lies. Regardless of the title they held, people shouldn't be trusted until they had proved themselves worthy of it, and even then, that trust should always come with a warning label.

Avery Rose – Likes to strangle students until they agree to have sex with him.

And what had happened with the lights? Who had saved her? She thought that the girl had run by the door, but it had been so dark that she couldn't be sure. The girl sounded young – Brenna's age, maybe – and there had definitely been something familiar about her voice. She couldn't decide if it was a voice she should have recognized or merely reminiscent of a voice she did know. One thing was for certain – Mr. Rose had known her or at least, he'd met her before. Regardless, Brenna owed her a debt that could never be repaid. But how had she known that Brenna needed help? And how did she open a locked door? She could have had a key or even picked the lock. Both Brenna and Mr. Rose had been too focused on other things to spare any attention for the door. Really, she supposed it didn't matter to some extent. She'd been rescued. She wasn't still trapped in that room, being pawed at by that evil man.

Without warning, someone knocked their knuckles against the car window. Jumping, Brenna cringed away from the sound, fearing the worst. Mr. Rose had found her. He wanted to finish what he'd started.

"Brenna?"

It took a moment for the recognition to kick in. She knew that voice. *Zio*. But what was he doing here? Had he driven to the school for some reason? She looked up and for a moment, had no idea where she was. Then things came into focus. Boxes. Tools. Her Vespa. It was the garage. The last thing she remembered was sitting at a stoplight. Somehow she'd driven home without even knowing it. That was a little unnerving.

Zio was calling her attention back to him as he rattled the door handle. She opened it for him. "Sweetheart, where have you been? You didn't tell me you were planning to miss dinner. I was worried." His voice sounded fuzzy, like it was coming from underwater. "I called your cell phone, but you never answered. I was just coming to look for you."

He called? Dumbfounded, Brenna pulled out her phone and saw that she had three missed calls from him, one from Van, two from Mitch, and a text from Duke. It was odd that they should have all been trying to get in touch with her – almost like they knew she was in trouble. Not only that, but it was nearing eight o'clock. She'd lost almost two hours.

"Brenna?" The concern in his voice was almost tangible. Still a bit confused, she stumbled out of the car. Abraham took a step back to give her room, his eyes examining her appearance. She knew she looked like a mess, a truth confirmed by his next words. "Brenna, what's wrong?"

Everything. Everything was wrong.

Abraham reached for her, his hand outstretched, and her body, remembering other hands, responded of its own accord and jerked away from him. Some automatic emotion flitted across her uncle's face as his hand halted in mid-air. Her eyes went wide as she realized what she had done. The wall that had been holding back her emotions came crashing down.

For a moment, Brenna simply stood there, tears streaming down her face, as she mustered the strength to speak. Even though she knew it wasn't her fault, she still felt like a naughty child in trouble. Giving up, she tried to explain through her sobs.

"He tried – he touched – *Zio*, I didn't want him to!"

Even as she said it, Brenna wished that somehow her uncle wouldn't understand what she was trying to say and that she'd never have to go over the humiliating details. But the Chief of Police was no idiot. She watched her uncle's face grow fierce as the meaning of her words sunk in. It scared her. Not because she thought his anger was directed at her, but because it validated the horror she'd been feeling.

"The Hamilton boy tried to force you?"

"No!" she cried, mortified. It was much worse than that. "Mr. Rose!"

That was one answer he had not been expecting. "Your teacher?"

She nodded miserably. As if there were any other Rose in Mount Vernon. But she couldn't blame him. She was still stunned by the revelation, too.

"I – I – I told him to stop, but he wouldn't listen!" She could feel his phantom hands holding her and resisted the urge to push them away. Hanging her head, Brenna's fingers flew to her eyes, trying to hold back her tears. It didn't work.

"He touched you?" Abraham's voice had a hard edge to it, hinting at barely concealed fury. Brenna told herself that he had to ask that question. His duty as uncle and cop demanded it, but that didn't make it easier to answer. Afraid of what she might see there, she couldn't bring herself to meet his eyes. She nodded.

"Brenna, I know this is difficult for you, but I need to know exactly what he did." He was working overtime to keep himself calm.

Sucking in a deep breath and closing her eyes, she attempted to pull herself together. She walked him through those horrible moments in the classroom, explaining how angry and violent Mr. Rose had been at first. She tried to distance herself from the events like she was merely relating a story to her uncle. That helped until she brought up her injured arm. She hadn't heard Abraham's approach, but she felt his tentative hands alight on her shoulder, testing her receptivity. His gentleness gave her the strength to look up at him. His eyes were filled with a pain she'd never seen before.

"May I see?" he asked. She held up her arm.

Abraham probed it gently with his fingers, eliciting a tiny wince from his niece. He performed a similar examination on her neck after Brenna told him how her teacher had held her by the throat. He swore when he saw the bruises forming and the scratch marks.

"He changed after that. He kissed me and put his hand under my shirt so he could touch my – so he could touch me." Brenna's gaze faltered, her courage waning. She couldn't take much more of this. "There was lots of rubbing and fondling, and no matter how hard I tried to make him stop, he wouldn't."

"Did he," he stopped abruptly and cleared his throat. Brenna had never heard her uncle stumble over his words before. She knew what question he was trying to phrase and moved quickly to spare him.

"He didn't get the chance. The lights went out and a girl's voice told him to leave me alone. He ran away." That wasn't going to make any sense to him – she knew that. It didn't even make sense to her. She had no idea what really happened in that classroom. All she knew was that she'd been saved, and right now, that was good enough for both of them. "But I think he was going to –"

Brenna couldn't bring herself to finish her sentence. Lip quivering, she'd reached a breaking point where all her strength had been depleted. Her uncle wrapped his arms around her and kissed her head. "You're safe now, and he will answer for what he's done," he promised as she cried into his chest.

Only divine intervention would save Avery Rose from Chief Rutherford now.

Chapter Twenty-Five

In the wee hours of the morning, Brenna woke with the vague impression that something had shattered downstairs. She sat up, instantly alert as all of the horrible events of the previous evening came flooding back to her.

After she'd told *Zio* all of the sordid details, Brenna experienced a new sort of horror in the form of an official investigation. It was bad enough when someone had to suffer through such a terrible ordeal, but then to turn around and immediately relive it under the scrutinizing gaze of police officers only made it seem much more real. Being under the microscope like that hadn't been Brenna's idea of a good time, especially since she'd known most of the officers from birth. The two that showed up at the house, Officers Fenton and Jones, were practically extended family. At least they hadn't patronized her. Under the watchful gaze of their boss, they stayed professional, asking all the right questions and taking extensive notes, but they hadn't been able to hide the sadness in their eyes.

Thankfully, Duke had been sent straight to the school with another officer. He hadn't been on duty, but it didn't matter. Abraham rounded up all the troops – just one of the perks of being the boss. Brenna sensed that sitting on the sidelines had been difficult for her uncle. A large part of him wanted to be hunting down the wayward teacher, but he understood that his priority lay with taking care of her. Neither of them had spoken much, but his hand had always been resting on her shoulder, providing comfort and support. Truthfully, it was all she needed.

But what was going on now? Straining her ears, Brenna heard voices, both male, coming from downstairs. But thieves breaking in wouldn't give themselves away by talking.

Slipping out of bed, Brenna crept out of her room and sat down on the top step to listen. She could hear them, *Zio* and Duke, moving around in the kitchen, no doubt discussing what the investigation had turned up. She desperately wanted to know what happened. Had Duke been the one to catch Mr. Rose? Did the teacher confess or provide an alternate account of the scene between them? Unfortunately, her ears only picked up snatches of their conversation. If she wanted to hear better, she'd have to get closer.

Might as well be direct, she decided. Grabbing her robe, Brenna slipped it on as she descended the steps. Stepping into the kitchen, she saw her uncle bent over, picking pieces of broken glass up and tossing them into the trash can Duke was holding.

"Hey Biddy," her friend greeted her somberly.

Abraham glanced up, and for a moment, Brenna saw the look of fury on his face but it vanished when their eyes met. "Did we wake you?" he asked, already knowing the answer.

"It's okay," she said. "What happened?"

"Abe dropped a glass."

Zio was breaking things, and Duke was avoiding the issue. That could only mean one thing – something had gone wrong. "I see that," Brenna replied, trying to remain calm. "What happened with Mr. Rose?" She couldn't even say his name without feeling sick.

Duke shot a look at Abraham as he threw the last piece of glass into the trash can. Clearing his throat, her uncle stood up. "I'm afraid that he eluded us."

"He got away?" It came out as a much more condemning shriek than she'd intended. All of the calm that had settled over her as she slept vanished. Rose was still out there? Would he come after her? Maybe try to finish what he started with either murder or rape? "You should be out there looking for him then!"

Duke graciously overlooked her annoyance. "Trust me, we are, but his disappearance has a weird feel to it. His car's still at the school, and his house was tossed in a rather interesting manner." There was more to be said, Brenna could tell, but Duke turned to Abraham, who nodded for him to continue. "There were things left out in plain sight that I think Rose would have destroyed or taken with him if he was fleeing."

Must he be so cryptic? It must be bad if he insisted on being vague. "What does that mean?"

"Photographs."

Duke's abrupt reply felt like a slap in the face. Instinctively, Brenna curled herself into a ball. Her head drooped. "You mean pictures of me."

"Not just you," replied Abraham as if that made it better. "There were others girls."

Other girls – ones who probably hadn't been as lucky as she had been. The thought repulsed her. She clutched her stomach, feeling nauseous. How had he lured them into his web? Had they gone willingly into his arms or fought and kicked the whole way like her? She was willing to bet that he'd made them cry. He seemed to like it more when fear was involved.

Uncertain of what to say, Brenna looked at her uncle. The mask had slipped off of his features, leaving pure rage blazing like a neon sign. Seeing it so clearly displayed, she wondered if maybe she'd been wrong in thinking none of it was directed at her. Maybe he *was* angry with her – angry that she'd been foolish enough to land herself in such a predicament, angry that he'd had to send his men out to clean up the mess, angry that she couldn't provide better answers to his questions. With all the trouble she'd caused, she couldn't blame him if he was.

Brenna was unable to stop herself from asking the question. "*Zio*, are you mad at me?"

For one heartbreaking moment, you could have heard a pin drop. Then the tears and words flowed from her with reckless abandon. "It's my own fault," she cried, edging near hysteria. "I shouldn't have let him do those things to me! I swear I tried to make him stop! Please don't be mad forever, *Zio*! I'm so sorry!"

She felt her uncle's hands on the side of her face, steadying her as he dropped down to her eye level. What Brenna saw in his eyes was an emotion far beyond sadness. "Listen to me," he said, holding her gaze. "What happened tonight was not your fault. You did nothing wrong. You were supposed to be able to trust him. He betrayed you, hurt you, and intended to do worse things than that. My anger is for him alone. Nothing he said, did, or tried to do could ever take my love from you. Do you understand?"

Sniffing, she nodded before burying her head in his chest. He stroked her hair, whispering comforting words to her as she beat back the tears. Certain of his love, it was easier to regain her composure. Sucking in a steadying breath, she stepped to the sink and splashed some cold water on her face. Duke, who'd been standing motionless for the past few moments, handed her a towel.

An idea occurred to Brenna as she patted her face dry. "Do you think the girl who saved me did something to him?"

"The thought crossed my mind," Abraham admitted as he reclined against the counter. "How did his behavior seem to you in the days leading up to tonight?"

"He was different, definitely not his usual cheerful self," she said. In hindsight, his unpleasant behavior made sense given his jealousness. It got progressively worse the closer Brenna and Mitch got to each other. There was one thing she couldn't explain, though. "He seemed unusually tired, which I think also attributed to his bad mood."

Abraham frowned, considering her words. "Did he offer any explanation for that?"

"His neighbor's dog was afraid of the thunderstorms. It barked a lot and kept him up at night." As Brenna repeated his story, she suddenly wondered about its validity. It could have been solely designed to elicit a sympathetic response from her, which it did. "That was a lie, wasn't it?"

Duke and Abraham shared a look, which made Brenna feel like a gullible fool. Mr. Rose had completely pulled the wool over her eyes.

"There's no dog, but he does have an interesting neighbor – Mrs. Watson," Duke replied. His tone implied a significance that she didn't immediately understand, and then she remembered the night Duke had come over for dinner. He'd related the complaint Mrs. Watson had made about a Peeping Tom. Well, wasn't that interesting? For once in her life, the old woman had been right. There had been someone lurking outside her home, but it was Mr. Rose who had been under surveillance. And he'd known he was being watched. That was the real reason he hadn't been sleeping properly.

"Wow. Our girl had her eye on him for a long time," Brenna breathed, letting the truth sink in. Then she remembered something. "Last week, I asked him if something was wrong, and he told me he was going through a rough break up. His girlfriend was having trouble letting go. I bet he was talking about her."

"That would probably be a fair assessment if she was harassing him," Abraham agreed.

But why, if the girl had known what kind of man Avery Rose was, didn't she try to warn Brenna herself? Why let things get as far as they did? Had she hoped that Mr. Rose would straighten up and therefore be able to spare Brenna from the awful truth about her teacher? Too many questions swirled around her head, leaving no room for her brain to attempt to answer them. She was completely drained emotionally, scrubbed raw by what was undoubtedly the worst evening of her life. Everything hurt. Eyes resolutely on the kitchen floor, Brenna picked at the black brace she was wearing. Merely a sprain but still a painful gift from her teacher. Duke's shoes greeted her, shuffling slightly out of eagerness. Then he handed her something.

Sophia Irene. She hadn't been in her backpack when she ran out of Mr. Rose's class earlier that night. In fact, she'd forgotten all about her until now.

Tears pricked at the corner of Brenna's eyes as she hugged the doll to her chest. After everything that happened, the fact that it would even cross Duke's mind to bring her to Brenna meant more than he could know. Maybe it was crazy, but it was comforting to have something to hold onto. It made her feel like a little girl again when the Boogeyman was nothing but a figment of her imagination. She felt his hand on her shoulder, and she looked up.

"Thanks," she said, giving him a small smile.

"She cried once, but I took care of it."

Words failed her, so Brenna wrapped her arms around him in a tight hug, Sophia Irene squished between them. His hands felt so different than the other ones that had held her tonight. The pressure of his touch conveyed warmth, comfort, and love. While Brenna didn't necessarily feel better, she felt at peace. Everything – eventually – was going to be okay.

CHAPTER TWENTY-SIX

When Brenna woke up again, it was nearly lunchtime. It took her a minute to realize that it was Friday. For the first time in her life, she couldn't have cared less about missing school. Part of her felt like if she never went back, that wouldn't have been such a bad thing. If only life was that simple and it wasn't against her nature to hide, she could stay in her bedroom forever.

Yeah, that wasn't going to happen.

Growling, she pushed back her duvet and climbed out of bed. The house was silent as usual, but she knew Abraham was still there. After what happened last night, there was no way he would let her wake up in an empty house. She found him at the kitchen table, going through the case file.

"How are you this morning?" he asked, holding his hand out to her.

Brenna leaned in for a hug and kissed his cheek. "Not perfect but better than last night."

Abraham nodded as if he'd expected as much. He closed the case file and folded his hands on top of it. "There are some things I'd like to discuss with you," he began, watching her carefully, "but I think you might enjoy some breakfast first."

At the mention of food, Brenna's stomach rumbled so loudly that her uncle heard it. When was the last time she ate? Yesterday at lunch? She offered to help, but Abraham had already mixed up the pancake batter. All that he had to do was cook them. As he stood at the stove, he told her funny stories about Amelia, proving true the old adage that laughter really was the best medicine. Even though it couldn't completely dispel the clouds, it cut through darkness, brightening Brenna's soul.

A short while later, when she'd eaten her fill, Brenna pushed her plate away and looked at her uncle. "Okay, what do you want to talk about?"

"While you were still sleeping, Van and Mitch came calling. It seems that they'd heard some interesting rumors flying around school about what happened last night, especially when Principal Travers told your English class that Mr. Rose was gone and wouldn't be coming back."

Brenna felt her stomach churn and wondered vaguely if eating had been a wise move after all. She had known this was going to happen. Things like this didn't occur in a vacuum. There would be ramifications. Gossip and rumors whispered in the halls at school. Curious looks sent her way. Her classmates wouldn't let her forget it any time soon. How humiliating. Mr. Rose was a popular teacher. Some people might even think she'd laid false charges at his door after failing to seduce him.

Abraham reached for her hand, bringing her focus back to him. "I hope you won't be too angry with me, but I decided to tell them the truth. I didn't want you to have to relive it again."

Sweet, glorious relief. She'd been agonizing over what to tell them, and now, her uncle had taken that weight from her. She could only imagine the looks on their faces during that conversation. "Thank you," she breathed. "How'd they take it?"

"About as well as you'd expect. Van was quite colorful with

his vocabulary." It must have been epic, because the memory of it drew out a smile in Abraham. "Mitch's ferocity, while every bit as intense, was quiet. They care about you very much."

Yes, Brenna knew that to be true. She was very fortunate to have such wonderful men – young and old – in her life. Sighing, she rested her head in her palm. "I'm surprised they're not still here."

"They wanted to stay, but since I had no idea how long you'd be sleeping, I told them that their time would be better spent at school." He smiled again. "Plus, the last thing I wanted was for you to wake up to a house full of people."

"Thanks for that," she grinned back. She'd have to deal with them once school finished, but now that the worst part was over, she felt she could handle it. Most of their initial anger would be abated by then, too. That was definitely a plus. A stray thought occurred to her. "I'm supposed to work today."

"You can call in sick," Abraham told her. "Berthal will understand."

Brenna shook her head. "No, I want to work. I can only take sitting around for so long. Is that all you wanted to tell me?" She had a vague notion that there was a lot more he wanted to discuss.

Abraham placed the case file in front of him and opened it. "Normally, I don't share information in an investigation, but these are unusual circumstances. There are some things that I think you should know and possibly, some questions you can answer for me."

Zio needed her clarification? Brenna might have been excited if she hadn't been victimized last night, but maybe talking about it from the angle of an investigator would help her work through it. If she could help catch the bad guy, that was a good thing. "Go ahead," she said, gesturing with her hand.

"I've come to the conclusion that your mysterious

benefactress is really more of a guardian angel." He pulled out a picture and slid it across the table. It was an infrared photo of her bedroom. She could just make out her prone figure lying in the bed. "Now look at the time stamp."

Obediently, she glanced down at the numbers. The picture was taken very early in the morning on last Tuesday. Last Tuesday. During that intense, never-ending thunderstorm. "Mr. Rose was outside my room when I ran out into the rain!" she cried, the pieces fitting together.

He nodded, looking somber. "I think she knew that he was targeting you and showed up that night to stop him. I don't think she meant to wake you or to lure you out of the house. You probably scared her to death, assuming she lingered long enough to see you run outside." He put the picture back into the folder.

So Mr. Rose had been prowling around her house late at night. No wonder he had been so tired and cranky. What a liar he was. A cruel, heartless liar. "She saved me more than once," Brenna breathed. "*Zio*, we have to find this girl. I have to thank her."

"Yes, and we have to find out what she did to Avery Rose."

"So you think she abducted him?" Brenna asked, watching her uncle's eyes.

For once, he didn't try to hide anything from her. "Yes, I do. What she intends to do with him, assuming he's still alive, I can only hazard to guess."

The idea that Mr. Rose could already be dead and gone struck Brenna to the core. Half of her thought the world was better off if he was while the other half hoped he was still alive – primarily because she wanted to be there to see him brought to justice.

"But if she did take him, how in the world did she pull it off? From what I could tell, she wasn't a big girl, and he's a full grown man! I don't see how she could have taken him down in a fight. Even if she did manage to incapacitate him in some way, how did she move his body? And for that matter, how did she know all of this? How did she know what kind of man he was and that I was his next target?"

"Those are excellent questions," Abraham agreed, which loosely translated meant he had no idea. Picking up a stack of photos, he separated them into three groups – one for each girl. One stack was devoted to her. Brenna had no desire to see what kind of poses Mr. Rose had managed to capture. The other two faces she recognized with the eyes of a younger girl.

"Do you know them?" he questioned.

Pointing to the first stack, Brenna said, "That's Rebecca Harrison. She graduated my freshman year." She couldn't remember much more about the girl other than that. At the time, she'd been more focused on figuring out how to navigate through high school than anything else.

But the other girl, that was a different matter.

"Jennifer Morgan graduated last year," she told her uncle, tapping the second group of photos. As she looked at the blond girl, she saw things in a new light. "Everyone thought that she was going to be valedictorian, but her grades dropped unexpectedly. Now I guess we know why. It was because of Mr. Rose and what he did to her."

Looking at the pictures, it was hard not to notice the similarities between them. All three of them were blondes with petite frames. They were pretty but not gorgeous like Alexis – definitely more schoolgirl than hottie. Thinking about Jennifer, she realized that the girl hadn't had a lot of friends. She kept to herself. In that way, she was sort of like Brenna. Rebecca was probably the same way, too.

"We're the same. Petite blondes with brains. I bet he picked us out when we were in his sophomore class," Brenna said, sinking under the weight of the realization. Unbelievable. Mr. Rose had his predatory skills down to an art form. She wondered which sophomore he'd had his eyes on before it all hit the fan. "Holy crap. He was nothing short of diabolical."

Abraham exhaled wearily. "Yes, I haven't come across the likes of him in a long while."

"Do you think one of them is the girl who saved me?" she inquired, looking at the faces in a new light. Had one of them found the nerve to go on the offense? "That might explain how the girl knew his secrets. She'd already experienced it."

He nodded. "It's a fairly good possibility."

Brenna looked down at the photos. Three victims over the past four years. Why hadn't there been one from her sophomore year? Had there been no girl who fit his type? Maybe there was but he had been unsuccessful in trapping her. But wouldn't he still have the photos? Maybe not if they were his trophies. He probably wouldn't want to keep a reminder of his failures.

Giving voice to her thoughts, she said, "I wonder why there's a missing year."

"I'm not sure there was," he replied, sifting through the case file again. "When Daniel searched Mr. Rose's home, he found all of the photos together. As you can see, there were several photos of each girl. Except for one." Abraham set a picture in front of her. "He could only find one picture of this girl. It doesn't appear to be one of the others because the initials on the back are different."

The second her eyes landed on the photo, Brenna's heart stopped. It was her – Mystery Girl complete with her red hoodie, yellow skirt, and blue leggings. The photo had caught her in motion, hands out at her side and one leg stretched forward as she walked. Her head was angled, providing Brenna only with a profile. Strands of blond hair escaped from out of her hood.

"Do you know her?" Abraham asked, hardly oblivious to the

recognition on his niece's face.

Brenna hesitated. "I don't know who she is, but she looks like someone Mitch and Van have seen around. *Zio*, this is the girl who saved me."

"How can you be so sure?" he inquired. It was a fair question.

"The night I ran out into the storm, I thought I saw a girl in a red hoodie. I think it must have been an outfit she wore regularly so Mr. Rose would immediately recognize her when he saw it."

As surprised as she was to see Mystery Girl, Brenna knew she should have expected it. If she had gotten around to thinking about it, the whole thing would have struck her as suspiciously coincidental. What were the odds that there were two mysterious girls running around Mount Vernon? Not very likely. No, there was only one girl. Of course, hindsight made everything clear. She had been watching Mr. Rose. She had saved Brenna last night. The warning note she'd received in her book – the assigned one for English – was warning her about Mr. Rose, not Mitch. Mystery Girl had never been her enemy. Like *Zio* said, she was Brenna's guardian angel.

The one thing that she couldn't make sense of was why the girl had been stalking Mitch, but she pushed that particular issue aside for the moment. Identifying the girl was far more important to her right now. Flipping over the photo, she saw the letters SW.

"SW," she mused. The letters felt important – like she should know them – but their significance eluded her. However, she had the resource to find out – hopefully. "Let me go get my yearbook."

Feeling a long-sought answer was in reach, Brenna raced up to her room and reappeared in the kitchen a minute later with her yearbook. She never made it past the first page. What caught her attention was a special photo collage dedicated to the memory of a student who'd died that year – Summer Winters. In one picture, the girl was decked out in the same red hoodie outfit. There was no doubt about it. Summer Winters was Mystery Girl.

There was a reason why Summer's name didn't surface in Van's search of murdered girls – she'd committed suicide. She died at no one's hands but her own. Nearly two years ago, Summer's death had rocked the school. How could such a smart, pretty girl with a bright future take her own life? Principal Travers had brought in a couple of grief counselors and held a special assembly to talk about the issue of suicide. Classmates who had never talked to Summer before mourned her death, setting candles and flowers by her locker because it was the appropriate thing to do.

"It appears that a dead girl has been haunting Mr. Rose." Brenna could detect the faintest trace of satisfaction in Abraham's voice. She remembered how scared her teacher had seemed when the lights went out and Mystery Girl's voice filled the air. Now it made sense. He'd been seeing the dead girl he'd raped for weeks. "I can only guess what seeing her must have done to him, knowing that he was the reason she took her life. The past is suddenly becoming clearer."

"What do you mean?" Brenna pressed, wanting to know the rest of the story.

He shot Brenna a look as if making up his mind and then nodded. "Summer was pregnant, and no one knew who the father was until now."

Poor Summer. Poor, poor Summer. Being repeatedly sexually assaulted by your teacher was bad enough but to find out you were pregnant as a result of one of those encounters was something else entirely. Brenna could only imagine how scared the girl had felt. Had Mr. Rose known about the baby?

"Are you sure that Summer committed suicide? Maybe Mr. Rose killed her. A baby would have ruined everything. People would have found out what he'd done."

Abraham shook his head. "No, it was most definitely a suicide. My guess, though, is that he used his velvet tongue to convince her of how trapped she was and what her life would be like if she tried to expose him. If Summer hadn't killed herself, though, someone like him definitely could have taken matters into his own hands." He sighed and spread his hands. "Since neither of us believe in ghosts, the question is – who wanted Avery Rose to believe that Summer Winters had come back to get him?"

"There's only one person who would care enough to do that," Brenna declared, turning to the sophomore section of the yearbook. Her eyes scanned the last page for the familiar name and jabbed her finger at the photo. "Her little sister, Autumn."

Brenna almost wouldn't have recognized the little blond girl smiling up at her. The Winters sisters looked alarmingly alike. In her Mystery Girl costume, it would be easy to mistake them. Autumn's transformation into a black-haired girl with a monochromatic wardrobe occurred shortly after Summer was laid to rest. It was an outward sign of her inner suffering – not a fashion statement.

"When she spoke last night, I thought there was something familiar about her voice," Brenna recalled. Now that she had a name, she recognized the girl's voice. "It sounded like Autumn's but the pitch was higher."

Abraham was on his feet in an instant. "It is imperative that I find Autumn immediately." He reached for his keys and then hesitated, looking back at her. Brenna shooed him with her hands.

"Go find her," she instructed. "I'm fine."

Seconds later, the door was swinging shut behind him. Brenna sat at the table, staring at Autumn's picture. She could only imagine the planning and effort Autumn had exerted to make sure Avery Rose never did to another girl what he'd done to her sister. She remembered that the teacher had made some comment about not letting Autumn be his TA. Maybe the girl had been trying to catch him red-handed by offering herself as bait. But he'd turned her down because he'd wanted Brenna. So Autumn had relied on her theatrics to punish the teacher by driving him crazy and keeping him away from his intended victim.

As tragic as the whole situation was, Brenna couldn't help but see a bit of humor in it. Van had been right after all. Mystery Girl *was* a ghost, and she was trying to protect Brenna. His theory had come the closest to being accurate. She was going to have to give him credit for that. Not that he'd really want it now.

Everything made sense except for one thing – why had Mitch been involved?

Okay, it was time to get logical about this whole thing. The answer was here. If she got her thoughts organized, she could find it.

Here was what she knew: Autumn had been appearing to Mr. Rose and Mitch for roughly the same length of time. She'd been trying to scare Mr. Rose away from Brenna, but it hadn't worked, so she started appearing to Brenna as a sort of warning to get her attention. But really, how was Brenna supposed to have been able to put the pieces together? Such a warning from Mystery Girl would only have been effective if Brenna had known Summer well enough to recognize the outfit or if she'd known of Summer's history with Mr. Rose. Well, Brenna didn't think she'd ever spoken to Summer, and she most certainly didn't know about Mr. Rose.

So logically, if Autumn had been trying to get Mitch's attention, the same reasoning would hold true. Brenna was pretty sure that he hadn't been friends with Summer, and the other option...

Mitch had confessed that his first thought was that Mystery

Girl was a ghost, which had always struck Brenna as odd. He seemed much more reasonable than that.

Quick to assume the worst, he had always seemed certain that Brenna was in danger and didn't like it when she was out of his sight. She couldn't remember him ever being concerned for his own personal safety.

When it came to naming a living suspect, Mitch had been reluctant, always finding a problem with Brenna's argument and inevitably pointing her back to the haunting theory.

He'd been fighting with Mr. Rose this week, the first of which occurred after Brenna said she couldn't help the teacher after school on Tuesday.

Separately, the facts didn't seem that suspicious, but when Brenna added all them up, she was faced with a very painful revelation. She didn't want to believe it – couldn't believe it – but she couldn't find a fault with her reasoning. Mitch had known the truth about Mr. Rose all along.

CHAPTER TWENTY-SEVEN

In a cloud of near-blinding fury, Brenna drove to the school. She paid no attention to the startled looks people gave her when she entered the building just as lunch was ending. Maybe it was her disheveled appearance or the fire in her eyes, but they all but fled from her presence as she stalked down the hall. Fine. Let the frightened mice run. She had no quarrel with them lest they get in her way.

She knew where he would be. Mitch always went to his locker right before fifth period, and today was no different. He didn't see her coming. He had his back to her, talking to Shane Duffy. It was the widening of Shane's eyes that alerted Mitch to impending danger. He turned around as the track star discreetly moved away.

"What's wrong?" Mitch asked, looking pale.

He reached out for her, but she knocked his hand away in a gesture that caught the immediate attention of those around them. Perhaps Brenna should have taken the discussion to a more private location, but she was beyond the point of reason, and she couldn't care less what anyone else thought about what was said.

"I'm only going to ask you this once, and don't you dare lie to me," she breathed, searing Mitch with the intensity of her gaze. "Did you know Mystery Girl was supposed to be Summer Winters?"

He went, if possible, even paler, but he answered her. "Yes."

That one simple word sliced through her like a knife, and that wasn't even the worst of it. "Did you know about her and Mr. Rose? Did you know what he did to her?"

The look on his face said it all, but Brenna needed to hear him say it. She waited, arms crossed tightly over her chest. After what felt like an eternity, Mitch spoke quietly, "I walked in on them after school once."

Chewing the inside of her cheek, she nodded and pivoting on her heel, bolted. She sensed his pursuit, could hear him calling her name, but she ignored him. Weaving in and out of students with reckless agility, Brenna widened the gap between them. They were creating quite a scene – everyone was watching Mitch chase her down the hall – but she couldn't have cared less. In fact, part of her enjoyed it. People would want to know why they fought and then the truth would come out about their less-than-shiny ASB President. Let him deal with the aftermath of that.

In blatant disregard for the rules, Brenna ran past the office and out the front door. Elliott could just try to stop her from leaving school. She hurried as fast as she could, but with his longer legs and the absence of obstacles, Mitch caught up with her in the parking lot. He grabbed her arm, which was a mistake.

Fist clenched, Brenna whirled around and swung as hard as she could. He stepped back, clutching his jaw. "Don't touch me! Don't ever touch me again!" she shouted. "You don't get to do that anymore!"

"Brenna, please. I'm sorry," he said, courage resurfacing.

"You're sorry?" Brenna cried. "What do you think this is? A game? Do you think it's funny what Mr. Rose did?" She couldn't fathom the boy standing in front of her. Maybe she'd misjudged him completely. Maybe he was a cruel boy who liked messing with girls' hearts. She thought of Missy, who he'd dumped after they'd slept together. Maybe that had been Mitch's idea of a joke, too.

As if sensing her thoughts, Mitch's eyes flashed furiously. "Absolutely not."

He seemed sincere in his denial, but who could say for certain? He'd pretended before. Now that she had him here, Brenna felt her curiosity grow. She wanted, no, she *needed* to know the truth. No matter how unpleasant the details.

"What I want to know is how a person can walk in on a scene like that and not say something," she said.

"Mr. Rose asked me not to tell," he said, words tumbling out of his mouth like falling dominoes. "He said that they were in love and that no one would understand."

Brenna waited, eyes narrowed in suspicion. There had to have been more to it than that. If Mitch had simply walked in on an amorous couple, why would Autumn have gone to such great lengths to get his attention? Autumn had been haunting or stalking him in order to provoke some kind of reaction from him. Most likely, she wanted Mitch to tell Brenna the truth. It seemed she'd only interceded because the boy had failed to do so.

"What aren't you telling me?" she demanded. "The lies stop now."

His mouth opened and closed like a fish out of water. Then he spoke so quietly that Brenna almost missed his answer. "But I could tell that Summer didn't feel the same way. She wanted him to stop." With one finger, he rubbed at his eye.

Under the weight of his admission, Brenna swayed on her feet. "And you said nothing? You knew what he was all along and you said nothing! Not to anyone! Not to me, and you knew what he was capable of!"

"I didn't know what was going on between the two of you," he blurted out.

Suddenly, things made sense. "Oh, I get it. Until last Saturday, you weren't sure that I was going to pick you. When I did, you thought that'd be enough to make him back off, but it wasn't, was it? That's why there's been so much tension between the two of you this week. You've been fighting over me!"

The whole thing was so awful that she could barely stand it. "It doesn't matter if I wanted him or not. Teachers and students aren't supposed to sleep together. You had an obligation to say something."

"What do you think I've been trying to do this whole time?" Mitch brought up, trying to deflect her rage.

In that moment, everything else slid into place. Knowing exactly what was going on, Mitch had come to Brenna with his "problem," confident that she'd investigate. He was counting on her to find all the answers and then stop Rose so he wouldn't have to. He'd wanted her to do all of the hard work while he played the hapless victim. Somehow, the realization made her even more furious.

"Well, thank you very much for your concern!" she bellowed, hands clenched at her side. She turned to leave again, but he stopped her.

"I was scared!" he implored.

Brenna rounded on Mitch. "No, *I* was scared! He threw me into the desks, twisted my arm, choked me, and then tried to rape me! The fear you felt was nothing compared to mine!"

Confronted with the rashness of his statement, Mitch swallowed. "No one was going to believe me. He was a teacher, and I was a kid. If I told you, you wouldn't have believed me either. You loved him."

"But you would have done your job! The truth would have been out there. If I hadn't listened to it, then that would have been on me, but now, it's on you."

"Brenna, please forgive me! I'm sorry!" Desperation was written across his face.

Fury seeped underneath Brenna's skin, wrapping her heart in its icy grasp. She felt nothing but coldness for the boy in front of her. "You made me care about you with your pretty words, but they were nothing but lies."

"No, that's not true. I care more about you than anything else!"

Repulsed by his words, she shook her head. "No, you don't or you would have said something. You never would have left me alone with him. You never would have let him violate me."

He was struck speechless by her words. She took advantage of his silence to clear her mind. "You know what I think? I think you're a boy who cares too much about appearances. I think you liked being admired by your peers. You didn't want to confront Mr. Rose two years ago because you didn't want to become *that* boy – the one caught up in a scandal that ended a popular teacher's career. It would have hung over your head like a dark cloud and Doug Porter would have been ASB President this year."

She was so angry, so disgusted that she could barely look at Mitch, but he needed to hear what she had to say. "Summer was pregnant with his baby. She was scared and trapped. All she needed was one person to stand beside her. She needed you." Brenna jabbed her finger into his chest. "If you had just told someone what was happening, Summer would still be alive today."

Summer would have found help. She would have been rescued from Mr. Rose – possibly never getting pregnant in the process. But even if she did, she wouldn't have been alone.

"The consequence of your inaction is not only the death of a girl but her unborn child as well; the academic failure and psychological torture of last year's victim, Jennifer Morgan; and the violation and broken heart of a girl you claimed to care about. All of which could have been avoided if you'd just opened your mouth."

Temper wearing thin, Brenna's voice wavered at the last second. If she didn't get out of here soon, she was going to start crying, and the last thing she would ever do was cry in front of this boy.

"After holding me in your arms and telling me how much you cared, you let me walk blindly into the same trap," she accused, rousing her strength for her final pronouncement. "Why? Because you are nothing but a spineless coward. What kills me the most is that I should have known better. A boy who doesn't have the guts to tell a girl that he likes her, who resorts to anonymously sending her roses on her birthday isn't the one for me."

Mitch frowned, looking legitimately confused. "I never sent you roses on your birthday."

"What?" Brenna was taken aback, momentarily distracted from the issue at hand. Van had been certain that they were from Mitch and convinced her, too. If the roses weren't love tokens from him, who sent them and what was their purpose?

Mitch capitalized on her confusion by taking hold of her arms. He pulled her close, staring boldly into her eyes. "You're absolutely right. It's my fault. Please, Brenna, tell me what I can do to make it up to you?"

She strained against him, pushing him away with a mighty shove. "You're weak, Mitch Hamilton. I cannot abide weakness. If you're so keen to make amends, start by saving Summer's life."

Storming away with her head held high felt good, but the second she slammed her car door shut, the tears started pouring. Driving to the police station without causing an accident was a minor miracle. Brenna wasn't one for dramatic entrances, but when she stepped through the door in the middle of a wailing emotional breakdown, all eyes turned on her. Crying females weren't something most of the officers were eager to deal with, so they hung back, shooting her concerned looks as Duke rushed forward to find out what was wrong. He followed her into Abraham's office, peppering her with questions that she didn't have the ability to answer.

What with the sobbing and hiccupping, it took awhile for Brenna to tell her story. She told Abraham and Duke about Mystery Girl, the investigation, the fake relationship that turned into a real one, and Mitch's knowledge of the whole affair. If her uncle was angry at the deception, he didn't show it. Brenna could tell that Duke desperately wanted to be mad at her, but she was so pathetic that he didn't have the heart to. He was plenty furious with Mitch and thought that the boy should be arrested on the spot. Abraham said nothing as he held his miserable niece, rubbing soothing circles on her back. When she seemed to calm down, he kissed her head and in an overly optimistic moment, promised that everything was going to be okay.

Brenna wasn't so sure, but a few hours later, she did feel slightly better when her best friend confessed his desire to beat the crap out of Mitch.

"I don't think I've ever been so mad with anyone before," Van admitted as he ran warm water over Brenna's hair. She was leaning over the kitchen sink. "That includes the time Stevie Ray shaved half of my head while I was asleep."

Given everything that had happened in the past twenty-four hours, Brenna felt remarkably at peace. Coming clean with her uncle had done wonders for her state of mind. Yes, she was still broken-hearted and it would take a while to heal from both Mr. Rose's and Mitch's betrayal, but Brenna knew that she would. She pulled herself together enough to work her shift at Honey B's and then gone straight home to Van, who was waiting to change her golden hair to an attractive – and temporary – shade of red. Her transformation into Daphne was nearly complete.

"I can't even imagine how you must be feeling right now," he said. "Seriously, Brenna, I know you can fight your own battles, but say the word, and I will clean his clock."

Her smile couldn't be kept at bay. Boyfriends might come and go, but Van was as constant as the sun. A special part of her heart would always belong to him. "Your offer is greatly appreciated, but don't waste your time. He's not worth it."

"Ain't it the truth," Van agreed with a definitive nod.

"Honestly, I'm just glad everything's over."

Van snorted. "Hardly. Autumn's gone and so is Mr. Rose."

It was true. Autumn had vanished – a trick she had been quite good at as Mystery Girl. Her parents, already bereft by Summer's death, had taken the news regarding Mr. Rose and Autumn's actions hard. Abraham had felt torn between wanting to applaud their daughter's heroic intervention and his duty to consider her a suspect in the teacher's disappearance. He and Duke were still out searching for both of them.

"Okay, so technically, it isn't over, but our part is. We don't have to worry about Mystery Girl anymore. We can just be high school kids again."

"Here, here," he affirmed as he turned off the water. Grabbing a towel, he soaked up as much of the wetness as he could and then led her to the bathroom, where he positioned her on the toilet. With a practiced hand, he began combing out the tangles.

"I don't need a boyfriend anyway. I've got work and school. Plus, there's college to think about." Brenna swallowed a sigh, realizing it sounded like she was trying to convince herself. If she was completely honest, she was going to miss Mitch very much. It wouldn't hurt so bad if she hadn't truly cared about him.

Their conversation was put on hold when Van switched on the blow dryer. Brenna closed her eyes, enjoying the hot air and the feel of his fingers in her hair. It was kind of nice timing – all of this badness occurring right before Halloween. She could set Brenna Rutherford on the shelf for a little while and become a cartoon character with a sexy purple dress, flashy red hair, and no problems.

"You have an amazing hair stylist, if I do say so myself," Van announced, eyeing her red tresses with satisfaction. He gestured to the mirror. "And now for your viewing pleasure."

Almost giddy, Brenna stepped in front of the mirror, and she wasn't disappointed. While she was fond of her normal hair color, the red Van had picked was flattering and a lovely change from the usual.

"It's perfect," she agreed. "Very Daphne."

Because he'd promised Chrissie he would, Van made Brenna try on her dress and other accessories just to make sure everything looked good. She disappeared into her room to change, and in the end, the outfit didn't just look good – it looked fabulous. The form-fitting dress was shorter than any she'd worn before and she rocked it. Add that to the light purple tights, headband, and green scarf, and her costume was complete.

"If I said you looked hot, would that have a negative impact on our friendship?" Van pondered wryly. After a second's thought, she shook her head. "Then call 911, because, baby, you are smoking in that dress!"

Feeling flirty, Brenna flounced her hair as she twirled in front of her mirror. "Why, thank you. I should have Chrissie make all of my clothes." She ran her hands over the material, savoring her moment of happiness. This might just be her favorite Halloween costume.

"I have a surprise for you," her best friend announced. "I put it together while you were changing." He vanished for a moment, leaving Brenna curious. Seconds later, she could hear the sound of his approaching feet. "Close your eyes," he called out.

Smiling, Brenna let out an exasperated sigh. "They're closed." She heard him enter the room and felt him put something in her hands. It felt like Sophia Irene. What was Van doing?"

"Okay, open them," he instructed her.

Sophia Irene was wearing a tiny orange sweater and red skirt. On her head was a homemade brown wig and tiny glasses. She had been turned into a pint-sized Velma. Not only that but Lloyd Dobler was wearing a Scooby Doo outfit complete with ears. It was the cutest, sweetest, most endearing gesture.

"Since we have to take them with us tomorrow night, I thought they should have costumes, too. Chrissie helped a little," he shrugged, smiling.

Brenna threw her arms around him, sandwiching the dolls between them. "Thank you," she said, kissing his cheek. Maybe what he'd done shouldn't have meant as much as it did, but after bad things happened, the little joys grew sweeter.

Van held her close in a tight embrace. They hadn't spoken of last night save for its impact on Brenna's relationship with Mitch, but in that moment, she could feel the depth of his concern for her wellbeing. Tears welled up in her eyes not out of sadness but appreciation. Whatever she needed from Van, he would give it to her just like he'd always done.

When they pulled away from each other, his blue eyes searched her face for signs of distress, but all he saw was her smile. "You know, I may be a terrible person for saying this, but I'm really glad we're watching *Nightmare on Elm Street* tonight," she admitted.

"And why's that?" he asked, a hint of smile tugging at his lips.

"Because the boyfriend dies," she confessed, her grin growing more pronounced.

Van laughed.

CHAPTER TWENTY-EIGHT

Halloween was a bright and sunny day – perfect carnival weather. In keeping with the spirit of the day, Brenna wore her costume to work and did her best to stay clean. As much as Brenna didn't want to think about Mitch, the boy kept stealing into her mind. Of course, it didn't help that she was baking the cookies that he asked her to bring the carnival. Watching the final entry in the Halloween Horrorfest with Van last night had been so much fun, but now that she was alone again with her thoughts, her temper resurfaced.

As she worked, Brenna wondered if he would have the nerve to wear the Fred costume they picked out together. If he knew what was best for him, he wouldn't dare. Then she wondered if he'd found someone to take her place at the center of the maze. She sort of hoped that he hadn't. The idea of him sitting all alone made her happy, and she didn't care if that was petty. Of course, Hannah would probably just take her place, and Brenna could sit with Van at the front.

Brenna growled in frustration as she slammed the oven door shut. Boys were more trouble than they were worth. She wanted nothing to do with them. *Zio*, Van, and Duke – those were the only males she would deal with from now on. The rest if them could take a hike. She would never kiss another boy, never go on another date, and never give her heart away.

Yes, dying a virgin sounded like an excellent idea.

Her shift ran a bit longer than usual because of the cookies she was making, so about mid-afternoon, she headed to the park where the carnival was being held. Fortune smiled on Brenna in the timely appearance of Keiko, who helped her carry the four bakery boxes to the snack table. By nature, Keiko wasn't a very sympathetic person, but she squeezed Brenna's hand and said that she hoped that Mitch would know unspeakable torture. That earned her a smile.

With the delivery completed, Brenna headed back to the car, keeping eyes trained on the ground so she wouldn't accidentally see Mitch. She kicked a pebble and watched it skitter across the parking lot. Stupid Mitch and his silence! The more Brenna thought about it, the more she failed to see much of a difference between Mitch and Mr. Rose. If she had her way, she'd punish them both.

Oh no.

If Brenna felt that way, wouldn't Autumn feel that way, too? In fact, there was a good chance that what Mitch did – or didn't do, rather – would be considered a greater offense in the girl's mind. What if Brenna had been looking at it all wrong? What if Autumn's appearances to Mitch weren't solely designed to make him help Brenna? What if she had been haunting Mitch to scare him or intensify his feelings of guilt because he was a target, too? Maybe Autumn wanted to punish him like she did Mr. Rose.

And if Autumn took Mr. Rose, Mitch might be next on her list.

For a second, Brenna allowed herself not to care. Summer was dead because Mitch didn't help her, so maybe he deserved whatever Autumn had planned for him. She could take a page out of his book and keep silent – especially since she had no idea if her hunch was accurate. But even as she tried to downplay her suspicions, Brenna knew she was right. Mitch was in trouble.

"This is so unfair!" she bellowed, wishing she had something to hit. Why did she have to save him? He hadn't cared enough to save her! Sometimes being a good person was incredibly frustrating. Mitch Hamilton deserved to rot, but unfortunately, Brenna wouldn't have been able to live with herself if she didn't try to help him.

So where would he be? Brenna ran back to the park, this time with her eyes in search of Mitch, but she didn't see him. However, she ran into Shane Duffy, who told her that Mitch was at the school, so she ran back to her car. En route to the school, Brenna placed a call to Abraham. Her uncle informed her that he'd already arrived at a similar conclusion and tried to offer Mitch protection, but the boy had refused it.

"And you let him do that?" Brenna asked, dumbfounded.

"It's his right," Abraham replied. "I can't force police protection on him. Instead, I'm throwing my efforts into apprehending Autumn before it gets to that."

The call ended and Brenna was left wondering what to do. If Mitch knew of the potential danger, her job was done. He could lie in the bed that he made with his eyes wide open. She didn't have to do anything.

And yet Brenna's conscience wouldn't let her sit idly by. She had to do her best to ensure his safety even if it meant dragging him to the police station. He wasn't going to get hurt if she could help it. Maybe she could literally slap some sense into him. She smiled. That actually sounded like fun.

But her efforts were thwarted again when she couldn't find Mitch at the school. Panicking, Brenna began to fear that she was too late and Autumn had done something to him. What if he was already dead? Her heart ached at the idea, making it very clear that as much as she might hate Mitch Hamilton and what he'd done, she still had feelings for him. How messed up was that?

"If you're looking for your boyfriend, he went home," Doug Porter called out, shattering her concentration. "He wanted to change into his costume while the rest of us did all of the work."

She stared at him a moment, torn between wanting to declare that Mitch wasn't her boyfriend and feeling the desire to defend his work ethic since that hadn't been faked. She must have looked confused because Doug rolled his eyes and stalked away, muttering to himself. Running back to her car, Brenna called Mitch's cell phone, but it went straight to voicemail. She didn't leave a message, settling instead for tearing out of the parking lot at an alarming speed.

On her way to Mitch's house, Brenna called to update Van, who didn't understand why she was wasting her time to help the idiot. She hadn't expected encouragement from him – even though she knew that if he'd had the brain wave, he'd be doing the same thing – but his words made her feel foolish, and her already frazzled temper snapped. She hung up the phone, promising that she wouldn't trouble him again and she'd see him later at the carnival. Then Brenna chucked her phone into the backseat where it collided with a thud against Sophia Irene's head.

Screeching to a halt in front of the Hamilton home, Brenna bolted from the car and raced up the path. She pressed the doorbell repeatedly until a very surprised Mitch opened it.

"Brenna? What are you doing here?" he asked. He was wearing part of a bear suit – the kind you'd see a cartoon character wear at a theme park. Under different circumstances, it would have been charming.

There was no time for pleasantries. "You're in danger.

Autumn's going to make you pay for letting Summer die."

Disgrace colored Mitch's cheeks but he held his ground. "Your uncle already talked with me. I told him that I didn't want protection."

"Well, I don't care what you want," she informed him plainly. Feeling ashamed over rudely disregarding his wishes was the last thing on her mind. "You're coming to the police station with me right now."

"Why do you even care what happens to me?" he asked with quiet astonishment.

That was an excellent question with a potentially long and complicated answer. Not wanting to open that can of worms, she boiled it down to one simple response. "Because I'm not like you. I can't sit by and let someone get hurt. No matter who it is," she answered, injecting a small amount of contempt into her final words.

He nodded, almost smiling. "Wow. You're not pulling any punches, are you?"

She shrugged. "Just being honest. Come on. We need to get you to the police station."

"But the carnival is starting soon," he said. "I'm supposed to be there."

Mitch's sense of self-preservation was frustratingly lacking. "Look, we'll go down there, talk with my uncle, and get some officer to come to the carnival with us. You can still work the event, and I can go back to pretending you don't exist."

He winced at her harshness but nodded, resigned. "Fine. I have to get my head," he said before vanishing down the hall.

Okay, Brenna sighed. Crisis averted. Mitch would go down to the station where *Zio* would talk sense into him. She didn't really concern herself with what her uncle might do to protect Mitch. He could lock him up in a jail cell for all she cared. Maybe

Zio would dangle him as bait to draw Autumn out. Regardless, now that she'd expended effort, her job was done. This was the last time she'd deal with Mitch Hamilton.

Being back at his house, the place of their first kiss, stung more than she cared to admit. The afternoon they'd spent here last week had been wonderful. What a difference one day could make! Now, all she wanted to do was leave this place as fast as possible. Of course, she couldn't do that until Mitch returned.

Brenna tapped her foot impatiently, wondering what in the world he could be doing. Stupid boy, she thought as she went inside. Pausing for a moment, her ears picked up the sound of movement in the living room. Brenna frowned, put out by his lagging. Didn't he understand that his life might be in danger?

"Mitch, we have to go. Quit fooling around," she called out as she rounded the corner.

But Mitch wasn't the one making noise in the living room. It was Mystery Girl. Brenna only had time to register her own shock before the intruder raised her weapon and fired.

"What's wrong with you?" Keiko asked as she glanced sideways to assess Van's frown.

They were kneeling in front of Fisher's massive DJ turntable, sorting through the various cables that needed to be plugged into speakers. DJ Ghost, as Fisher called himself, was running through the approved playlist with Hannah and Shane. Not surprisingly, the boy had dressed up as a ghost, playing up the fact that he didn't need any make-up to look pale since he was albino. Lloyd Dobler lay at Van's feet, looking very content in his Scooby Doo outfit.

When Van had arrived at the park, Keiko had recruited him even though he knew very little about setting up a sound system. He had no aversion to learning, though, when his teacher was the

Bride of Frankenstein. Keiko's costume was so incredible that when Van saw it, his jaw actually dropped. Her hair was a good ten inches tall with two jagged, white streaks going up the length of it. The white dress she was wearing had a choir robe feel to it, but it was attractively drawn in at the waist with a wide black belt with a black rose on it. For an added effect, she'd excessively powdered her face, turning it almost as white as Fisher's, and painted her lips ruby red.

Honestly, Van had felt out of place next to her in his green shirt and brown bellbottom pants. But he didn't feel too shabby, thanks to his Shaggy-esque Afro, which was held up by liberal amounts of hairspray and styling gel.

He shrugged, trying to downplay his emotions as he answered her question. "Brenna and I had a disagreement." Fighting – real, legitimate fighting – wasn't something they normally did. He hated the tension between them.

Keiko nodded knowingly. "What did you do?"

"Why would you assume it's my fault?"

"Because you're male," she replied with a smile.

He rolled his eyes but kept talking. "She thinks that Mystery Girl is going to come after Mitch, and she went to warn him. I may have implied that she was stupid for helping him when he didn't bother to help her. Brenna got mad and hung up the phone."

"See? I told you it was your fault," Keiko told him. Her hands moved swiftly, the task of anything technical was practically second nature to her. "Even if I am inclined to agree with you, that was a really dumb thing to say to Brenna."

"I know," Van sighed, "but I have all this pent up anger towards Mitch that's clouding my judgment."

Keiko frowned. "The guy is a Grade A douche bag, but that won't stop Brenna from helping him. You should know that."

Of course, he'd told her all about Mystery Girl, Mr. Rose, and

Mitch. After everything she'd done, Van figured she'd earned the right to know, and he knew that Brenna would feel the same way. Keiko, who was friends with Autumn, was shocked to learn the truth, but shock quickly transformed into appreciation. Now the girl was ready to throw a parade in Autumn's honor. Van wasn't far behind seconding that motion.

"Or you either," Keiko added, glancing at him with a smile.

Van snorted. "Yeah, but it's kind of hard to do that now when she won't answer my calls."

"Let's go find her then," the girl said, standing up. "Our work here is done. Fish, you're all set."

Fisher flashed her a smile. "Keiko, you're awesome."

"Yeah, I know," she agreed, turning to Hannah and Shane. "Have either of you seen Brenna or Mitch? We need to find them."

Hannah shook her head. "I haven't seen him since this morning. He should have been here by now."

"You know those two," Shane said, giving a dismissive wave. "They're probably holed up in the school somewhere, making out. Brenna went there to look for him a while ago. Bet they lost track of time." The boy laughed and Hannah hit him in the stomach – a clear demonstration that not everyone knew about the whole Mr. Rose-Brenna-Mitch triangle.

Van ignored the comment and thanked the pair, asking them to call him if Brenna turned up. "We'll go check the school," he told Keiko as they walked away. "She's probably handcuffed herself to him so she can watch his every move. Autumn probably won't try anything if she's near Mitch."

He didn't say it, but it bothered him that no one had heard from Mitch yet. It was odd that someone who was so responsible – in some areas at least – wouldn't be here up to his neck in carnival preparation. This was Mitch's carnival after all. No one seemed concerned that he wasn't around. Of course, it was highly probable that he was finishing something up at school and would come tearing in at the last second.

Together, he and Keiko moved through the throng of students putting the final touches on their carnival games. Though the event start time was still thirty minutes away, eager children were already lining up in preparation for the fun.

"We're taking my car," Keiko asserted, dragging the boy by the hand to her Honda. "I don't trust your van or your driving to get us there in time."

"I think I should be offended by that remark," he replied.

"You can be offended later," she told him as she unlocked the door. "Now get in."

Keiko had a lead foot – that was just one more thing Van could add to his growing list of observations about the girl. Riding shotgun with the Bride of Frankenstein, he felt like he'd been caught up in a high-speed car chase that would undoubtedly end in either a spectacular crash or a shoot-out with the cops.

The Honda came to a screeching halt in front of the school just as Doug was exiting the building. Van rolled down the window and leaned out of it.

"Hey Doug! Have you seen Brenna and Mitch?" he shouted.

The boy frowned. "What do I look like? Mitch's secretary?"

"Dude, it's important," Van clarified. "Have you seen him or not?"

"I'll tell you what's important," Doug said, stomping towards the car. "This carnival is important! But is our President here? No! He's off hooking up with girlfriend while I do all the work! And does anyone thank me for my sacrificial attitude? No!"

Figuring he could catch this fly with some honey, Van resisted the urge to roll his eyes. "You're absolutely right, Doug. You totally should have been President over that idiot. He has no concept of responsibility."

Doug threw up his hands. "Thank God! There's one person in our class who hasn't been duped by that moron!"

As much fun as it was hearing Doug bash Mitch, Van had more important things to do. "Hey, buddy, it's really important that I find Brenna. Shane said she came here looking for Mitch. Did you happen to see her? I don't like the idea of her being alone with that guy."

Suddenly, Doug was much more cooperative. He leaned against the car like he was an old friend. "She came around earlier, and I told her that Mitch was at his house. She didn't stick around, so I guess she went there."

"You're a hero, Doug." Van held out his hand for a high five, which the boy was all too eager to give him. Then the car peeled away seconds later with Van still hanging out of it.

"Do you even know where you're going?" he inquired of the driver as he buckled his seatbelt.

Keiko nodded. "We did a project together last year for Spanish class. He lives in a big house on the edge of town."

As she drove, Van debated the wisdom in calling Abe. His gut was telling him something wasn't right, but the last thing Van wanted to do was turn into a Drama Queen. There was a very good possibility that Brenna was at Mitch's house, babysitting the idiot. So why get Abe riled up if there was no need to? He didn't want to give the man a heart attack. However, Van's gut wasn't appeased when they pulled up to the house and he saw Brenna's car in the driveway.

That means nothing, he thought. They could have driven in Mitch's car or they could still be here.

Keiko waited at the wheel while he ran up to the door. He pressed the doorbell, paused, and then pressed the doorbell again when no one came running. His fist was raised, poised to deliver a shattering blow, when his phone rang.

"Hello?" he answered, hoping to hear Brenna's voice.

"Hey Van, it's Hannah," the girl greeted. "I just wanted to let you know that Brenna and Mitch arrived. They're already in the maze."

Brenna was sitting with Mitch? She was taking the whole protection thing a little too far in his opinion. And why hadn't she called him herself? Was she still so angry that she didn't even want to talk to him?

"What happened to her phone?" he inquired, heading back to Keiko's car.

"Her battery died," Hannah informed him. "So what is Brenna supposed to be anyway? I didn't quite get her costume."

It was downright criminal that people didn't know the *Scooby Doo* characters. That was an iconic television show. "She's Daphne from *Scooby Doo*," he clarified.

"Oh," the girl replied, sounding confused. "I thought Daphne was a redhead, but it's been forever since I saw that show."

Van stopped dead in his tracks – in part due to confusion over Hannah's comment and in part due to what he saw in the back of Brenna's car. Sophia Irene. His best friend wouldn't have gone anywhere without her. This was not good.

Hannah was still chatting away in his ear. "Her red hoodie is super cute. I've never seen anything like it. Did she add the trim herself?"

"Sorry, Hannah, I gotta go." Van hung up the phone without waiting for her reply. He needed to get to Abe. Brenna and Mitch were in trouble, but at least he knew where they were. Mystery Girl was making her final stand at the Halloween Carnival.

CHAPTER TWENTY-NINE

When Brenna regained consciousness, she heard people screaming.
Wait, that wasn't right. They weren't screaming, they were
laughing. What was going on? She strained to make sense of the
cacophony as her vision swam into focus. No, they were
screaming and laughing – except the screams weren't coming from
real people.

Sound effects, her brain told her. Haunted house sound
effects.

And what was that smell? The strange mixture of scents was
familiar, but she couldn't break them down so that they were
recognizable. There were too many things clamoring for her
brain's immediate attention.

Brenna blinked and everything around her suddenly became
clear. She was sitting on the ground, hands bound behind her
back. There was hay everywhere. Add that to the sound effects
and the laughter and Brenna knew where she was – inside the
maze. More specifically, in the middle of the maze. There was a
bowl of candy on a rickety wooden table. Behind it, a coffin stood
upright with a mummy, his hands folded across his chest in eternal
slumber, inside of it. Next to that was a witch's cauldron, a long-

handed ladle bobbing gently in some kind of liquid. Strategically placed around those items were a couple of hay bales and multi-colored gourds. A bevy of bats created a canopy above it all. They swayed gently underneath the black and orange lights as if they were in mid-flight. It was all set to receive happy children, except none of them were ever going to find their way to the center because the entrance had been sealed off with hay bales.

She wasn't alone, though.

Sitting tied to a chair, duct tape around his mouth, was Mitch. He didn't acknowledge Brenna's presence or the signs of life around him. His head drooped, but not due to lack of consciousness. It was a sign of acceptance. Whatever was going to happen to him, he knew he deserved it every bit as much as the man sitting across from him.

Similarly bound, Mr. Rose was still wearing the same white shirt and black slacks he'd worn on Thursday, but wherever he'd been the past two days, he hadn't been taken care of. His shirt was torn and soiled with dirt and something that looked very much like blood. His pants were similarly filthy; his normally adorable curls were a tangled mess. But all of that was nothing compared to his face. Mr. Rose's eyes were bulging with panic – like he'd seen the dead rise from the grave.

His fear might have had something to do with the petite blond girl straddling his waist. Mystery Girl. On top of her head, like she had just slid it up off of her face, was a clear, plastic mask. So that was what had given her a featureless appearance the night Van saw her. Finally seeing Autumn up close in her costume, it was alarming how much the girl resembled her older sister. No wonder Mr. Rose was freaking out. Brenna wondered what horrors Autumn had subjected him to over the past few days. Nothing he hadn't earned.

Certainly the wicked-looking hunting knife the girl was

wielding wasn't helping him stay calm.

Okay, so Autumn had them bound and gagged. What was her endgame? It had to be violent, so why not assume the worst-case scenario? Mitch and Mr. Rose were dead men walking. But what about her? Brenna's mouth was free of tape, which had to mean that she was free to speak. Most likely, Autumn intended to show her that the people who'd hurt her were being punished, but clearly, she hadn't been trusted not to interfere because her hands were bound.

So what should she do? If Brenna screamed for help, what were the odds that the people running around the maze would take her seriously? More than likely, they'd assume her scream was just another sound effect. Even if someone did try to help, Autumn could kill all three of them in a matter of seconds. Brenna wouldn't be able to stop her if her hands weren't free.

Right then, no screaming. Talking, however, was a different matter. With all that had happened, Brenna felt an undeniable connection to Autumn, which she was sure ran both ways. Why else would Autumn have invested so much time and energy to keep her safe? Maybe Brenna could play upon that bond, get the girl talking, and figure out how to get out of this situation with no one dying. If she was completely honest with herself, she didn't care about Mr. Rose's life so much as she didn't want to see Autumn become a killer.

"Autumn?" she said, stirring from where she sat. "What's going on?"

"Hi, Brenna," the girl greeted her as casually as if they were merely passing each other in the hall at school. "I'm sorry I had to knock you out."

"That's okay," she assured her, attempting to straighten up. She tried her question again. "What are we doing here?"

"Fall was Summer's favorite season," Autumn replied, her

eyes misting over. Everything else faded away – the noise, their location, even the man she was straddling. "She loved to watch the leaves change color and the sound they made when she crunched them underneath her feet. It made her happy."

The mournful sound of the girl's voice made Brenna's heart ache. Not a day went by when Autumn didn't feel the agonizing loss of her sister. "I'm so sorry," she said. "I know how much you loved her."

"Summer was my best friend. My secret keeper, my inspiration, my sunshine." Then she turned to Mr. Rose. "Until the day you slipped inside of her and stole her light." Without warning, Autumn struck the man across the face. It didn't draw out a muffled scream, but he shook his head, blinking his eyes.

"You're a bad man, Avery Rose," Autumn drawled, tracing a finger over his taped lips. "You like smart, pretty blondes. The ones who've gone unnoticed by the boys their age. They're delicate, pure roses just waiting for you to pluck."

She slid her hand down between their bodies. From Brenna's vantage point, she couldn't see where it had disappeared, but she had a pretty good idea. When he jumped, Brenna found it incredibly hard not to feel a sense of satisfaction. Seems Mr. Rose didn't like getting fondled against his will, either.

"You're so handsome and charming. And so very clever! How can such innocence resist your allure?" Autumn's wandering hand moved to the teacher's hair, her fingers twisting themselves in the curls that Brenna used to find so adorable. The man strained helplessly as he tried to get away from her. "They blush and smile at your compliments, feeling pleased that their teacher would notice them."

She leaned forward until the tips of their noses touched. "When they look at you with such adoration, you feel pleasure. When you get them alone, you feel strong. And when you break their will, you feel like a god. There is nothing you can't do to them. No one can stop you."

It was hard not to be mesmerized by the sound of Autumn's voice, especially when everything was dead on. How long had she been watching him? Studying his every move? She couldn't have known immediately what had happened to her sister or she would have intervened last year with Jennifer. Brenna was certain of that.

"What's the matter, Avery? Don't you recognize your Summer girl? That's what you called me, isn't it?" Autumn cooed, kissing his duct-taped lips. "You said you loved me, so how could you forget me? I never left you, Avery, not even when I died. And you want to know why? Because you stole a piece of my soul! It's right in there!"

It happened so fast that Brenna almost thought it was too late. Autumn brought up her hunting knife, jabbing it into Mr. Rose's chest. The girl stopped short of actually stabbing him in the heart, though the teacher could definitely feel the tip of the blade – his muffled screams gave him away. He squirmed underneath her, but Autumn never moved, never lifted the knife. She sat with her eyes closed, tears streaming down her face. Then she turned her face upwards, like a child gazing with love and trust into the face of her parent.

"Yes, I'll do it, Summer," she nodded. "I'll set you free. I'll save you."

Oh crap. If Autumn thought she was talking with her deceased sister, then she was well on her way to Crazy Town. All bets were off when it came to what the girl would do next. Staying tied up wasn't an option. Brenna looked around, desperate to find anything that might help her cut through the tape.

Something glinted in the light, immediately attracting her attention. It was a piece of glass. Brenna had no idea where it came from and she didn't care. As far as she was concerned, it was a gift from God. Stretching her hands behind her, she grabbed it and went to work. Trying to cut through the tape was hard. She sliced her fingers more than anything else. Now that she was bleeding, the task was even harder to do, but Brenna refused to give up. She just needed more time.

"Autumn," she spoke loudly, calling the girl's attention back to her. "How did you know?"

Smiling dreamily, the girl looked up at the sky. "Summer told me. She said I had to save you."

"You *did* save me," she replied with sincerity. "I was so scared until you showed up. Thank you for helping me." It didn't feel like enough, merely saying thank you. Even though she planned to stop Autumn from carrying out her murderous intentions, she still wanted to do something nice for the girl. It was an odd juxtaposition of desires.

Her words produced an unintended outcome. "I only did what any decent person would have done," Autumn smiled. Then she slid off of Mr. Rose and moved in front of Mitch, keeping the knife in a white-knuckled grip. The fury Brenna had seen previously from the girl paled in comparison to what she saw now. "I don't know which is worse: the monster who preys on girls or the boy who lets him."

Now that was an excellent question, Brenna thought as she worked to free herself. After thinking about it, she knew Mitch's betrayal had hurt more, but it was hard to quantify the behavior since the boy hadn't actually done anything. That was the problem, though. She fought back a wince as the glass slipped in her now bloodied-hands, cutting her fingers once again.

"Okay, so you didn't know my sister well. She was just some senior girl to you. There was no incentive for you to do the right thing, but I know how you feel about her." Autumn said to Mitch as she pointed at Brenna. "I thought, surely he'll say something to

Brenna. He cares about her. He won't want her to get hurt. He'll protect her. But you said nothing. You let the monster touch her."

Mitch didn't make a sound. He never moved.

No doubt aggravated by his lack of reaction, Autumn grabbed the corner of the tape covering his mouth and ripped it off in one clean jerk. His eyes watered from the pain, but he didn't cry out.

"Say something," she demanded.

He looked up at her, silent tears streaming down his face. "I was weak. I'm sorry."

"That's it?" Autumn all but exploded. "Where's your defense? No grand speech to justify your actions?"

Again, he was silent as he met her gaze unflinchingly. Nothing he could say would make things better. Suddenly, Autumn looked over at Brenna. "Do you know what sloth is?"

Of course, she knew what sloth was – it was one of the seven deadly sins. Just like wrath. In the back of her mind, a warning bell went off with that realization, but she didn't have time to analyze it. Autumn was waiting for her reply.

Brenna tried to appear unsuspecting as she nodded. "It's laziness."

"It's more than that. It's knowing what the right thing to do is and choosing not to do it," the other girl clarified. "I've been studying it. There was this author, Samuel Butler, who said natural amiableness is too often seen in company with sloth, with uselessness, with the vanity of fashionable life. I think that fits Mitch pretty well, don't you?"

She had a definite point, but Brenna felt that agreeing with anything Autumn said might be detrimental to her escape plans. The girl didn't need any encouragement from her.

"All you had to do was say something and my sister would still be alive, and for that, I hate you more than him," the girl sneered, pointing at Mr. Rose. She paused deliberately, giving

Mitch a chance to speak, but he didn't. "Still silent? Why am I not surprised? After all, you're so good at that."

By now, Brenna had sliced through half of the tape. She attempted to pull her hands apart but the tape wouldn't give. Speed was of the essence now. Autumn was moving between Mr. Rose and Mitch, as if deciding which male she wanted to turn into a human pincushion first.

"Autumn, whatever you're planning to do, please don't do it," Brenna pleaded. "Let's get out of here. Mr. Rose will answer for what he's done. Mitch did wrong, but hurting him won't make things better."

"Brenna, you don't understand! I'm trying to help you!" Autumn cried. "The men in your life are liars! Don't you want them all to stop lying to you?"

Ice cold dread filled Brenna's veins. She had a sinking feeling that Autumn didn't just mean Mr. Rose and Mitch. "What are you talking about?"

"Ask your uncle and your cop friend about the lead pipe Kevin Bishop used in his attacks. Ask them whose blood they found on it. Then ask your uncle how your mother *really* died."

Brenna's heart might have actually stopped. Was her brain malfunctioning or did Autumn just imply that Abraham had been lying to her about Amelia's death? There was no way he would do such a thing. It was utterly inconceivable. Trusting anything that came out of Autumn's mouth was dangerous, and yet, the girl had piqued her curiosity. "What do you mean?"

She didn't elaborate but followed up with another earth-shattering revelation. "Your uncle is no better than Mitch. If he'd told the truth about Eliza Kent's death, your mother might still be alive today."

Brenna felt like she'd been slapped. There was only one way Autumn could know about Eliza Kent. "You left those roses on my mother's grave."

Autumn nodded. "I wanted to help you uncover the truth. Your uncle, he's a bad man. You can't trust him."

No, no, no! She couldn't be hearing this! Autumn – the girl who thought she was receiving directions from her dead sister – had to be wrong about *Zio*. Whatever the girl thought she knew, it couldn't be true. Brenna desperately wanted to dismiss Autumn as unreliable, but then again, she'd known about Eliza Kent. Plus, there was so much she didn't know about her uncle. Abraham was so private, and hadn't he sat on the couch and told her that he wasn't as saintly as she assumed? There was a fine line between privacy and secrecy. She had always considered Abraham to be on the private side of the line, but perhaps that had been a mistake.

"Just as you did nothing to save my sister, no one will do anything to help you." Autumn pointed a condemning finger at Mitch. "Our classmates are all around us, and you can scream, but no one will help you. You will suffer as Summer suffered." Autumn held up the knife. "You watched that monster destroy my sister, so watch this."

"No!" Brenna cried, realizing what the girl intended to do.

With a mighty yank, her hands pulled free and she stumbled to her feet, but it was too late. Slipping behind Mr. Rose, Autumn grabbed a handful of the man's hair and slit his throat in one fell swoop, coating Mitch in a spurting shower of blood.

Someone was screaming a guttural wail that sounded like a dying animal. It took Brenna a moment to realize the sound was coming from her. She couldn't stop screaming, couldn't move, couldn't do anything but watch her teacher die. She hated Mr. Rose, but seeing this, watching his heart pump his blood out of his body, was the single worst experience of her life.

Then she saw Autumn move towards Mitch, bloody knife in hand, and her instincts kicked in. No one else was dying tonight.

She launched herself at the girl. Fists swinging, she punched every part of Autumn that she could before grabbing her in a chokehold. Showing no mercy, she twisted her arm behind her back, and the girl cried out in pain, dropping the knife. Shoving Autumn to the ground, Brenna picked up the weapon and ran to Mitch's chair to cut him free.

"Brenna," he began.

"Shut up!" she commanded as she sawed through the tape. There was no time for apologies or thanks.

"Brenna, look!" he cried with unmistakable fear.

She obeyed, turning to see Autumn dump over the cauldron. A clear liquid spilled across the ground. What in the world was she doing? Then Brenna saw the lighter in her hand and understood. Gasoline – that was one of the things she'd been smelling. Autumn intended to set the place on fire.

"I'm sorry, Brenna, but Mitch isn't leaving here alive," she stated calmly before tossing the lighter into the liquid. Flames erupted instantly.

"Fire! Call 911!" Brenna screamed, panic creeping into her voice as she finished cutting Mitch free. She yanked him from the chair. Her thoughts weren't merely for herself. There were children running through the maze, and there was an excellent chance that Autumn had just condemned them to death as well. "Fire! Run!"

Brenna had turned her back on the flames to free Mitch and when she turned around, her stomach dropped. Half of the wall was already engulfed, a tall black cloud rising to the sky. Above the roar, she could make out the sounds of genuine terror. People had realized they were in danger. Good. Maybe tonight wouldn't turn into a complete massacre.

"We have to get out of here!" she shouted at Mitch just as Autumn slammed into her.

Caught off guard, Brenna fell to the ground and dropped the knife. Recovering, Autumn quickly stepped over her to pick it up. Brenna raised her head in time to see Autumn slash her knife through the empty space where Mitch's head had been a second ago. He jumped back, eager to avoid her thrusting motions, and fell on Mr. Rose's corpse. In his haste to get away, he rolled off of the body and onto the ground, giving Autumn easier access with her knife.

There was no time for this! They were all going to die if Autumn wasn't immediately taken out of commission. Scrambling to her feet, Brenna grabbed Mitch's chair and swung it at Autumn with as much force as she could muster. The girl fell and the knife went sailing through the air.

"Grab that!" she yelled to Mitch, who obeyed.

Tossing the chair aside, Brenna ran to the only wall of hay that wasn't on fire. She shoved against one segment repeatedly until it toppled over. She had no idea how to get out of the maze, but with the fire raging, knowing the way probably wouldn't have done any good. No, the shortest way out of the maze was to barrel straight through it.

"Please help us! We're trapped!" she screamed into the night, hoping that someone would hear her and offer assistance.

Behind her, Autumn shrieked, "Summer, I'm coming! Summer!"

Brenna turned to see Mitch wrestling with the girl. They were too close to the flames. Autumn's hand was outstretched, reaching towards the fire like it was her dearest friend as he pulled her away. Without warning, she slammed her elbow into Mitch's face and he lost hold of her. She darted towards the fire, intent on succumbing to it. Brenna ran after her, but Mitch got to Autumn first and threw her back. Then he hit her squarely in the face. Autumn staggered, and he let his fist fly again. She fell to the ground.

"Get her out of here!" Brenna yelled, pointing to the hole she'd made. She helped Mitch hoist Autumn onto his shoulders and gave him a push. She couldn't say what made her do it – maybe just a nagging sensation that something wasn't right – but at the last second, Brenna turned around to look at the fire. Through the flames, she saw the coffin standing empty.

Wait, hadn't there been a mummy in there when she woke up? Where was it now? How could it have vanished?

Before she could mull over an answer, a wall of heat slammed into her and Brenna doubled over under the staggering assault of the smoke that had suddenly increased tenfold around her. The mummy could wait. She had to get out of here or she was going to die. She turned, running towards the hole, but the flames were everywhere now. In her panic, she doubted her sense of direction. Was she going the right way? She couldn't tell! Black, acrid smoke stung her eyes and filled her lungs.

Quit panicking! Your body was positioned right in front of the hole when you turned around, so just run straight!

She obeyed, ignoring the flames and running at full speed. Nearly blinded, she collided with the fallen hay bales and tumbled to the ground. On her hands and knees, she crawled over them and staggered to her feet. Where was she supposed to go now? Orange flames were everywhere. She couldn't see anything but black smoke and impending death.

Overcome by the need to cough, Brenna fell to her knees, shouting, "Help me!"

CHAPTER THIRTY

Brenna's head was down, so she almost missed it, but she looked up just in time to see a figure leap through the flames with the dexterity of an Olympic hurdler. She couldn't see his face thanks to the smoke stinging her eyes, but she felt strong arms pick her up. Then he was running through the fire. Brenna clung to her savior, recognizing her uncle by the way he carried her and the collared dress shirt underneath her fingers. She buried her face in his neck, hanging on for dear life. The heat was overwhelming, so hot that she was sure it would melt her skin off, and then, all of a sudden, it was gone. Cold air surrounded them, soothing her burning skin.

Abraham dropped to his knees, coughing furiously as he dumped her out of his arms. "Roll!" he commanded. She obeyed, rolling over and over to smother any lingering flames just like she'd been taught in school. She could hear Abraham doing the same thing.

Rolling over one last time, Brenna looked up at her uncle, who was leaning over her. All around them, people were screaming and crying. She could hear the fire truck siren in the distance. It was complete chaos, but she ignored everything but him.

"Are you hurt?" he asked, his hands assessing for injuries. He grabbed her hands, eyes concerned by their bloodied state.

"I'm okay," she wheezed, hugging him. He squeezed her much too tight, indicating the strength of his concern. She pulled away. "Mitch and Autumn?"

He nodded. "With Daniel. They're both relatively fine."

"She killed Mr. Rose," she told him, fighting a shudder at the memory. Her gaze turned towards the flames. "His body is in there."

She opened her mouth to say more but clamped it shut when the tears threatened. They weren't for the wicked man who'd met a wicked end but for the loss of innocence that had occurred. Autumn had become a murderer; Brenna and Mitch had witnessed the act. None of them would be the same again.

Abraham pressed a firm kiss to her forehead. "I'm so sorry that you had to see that. I should have gotten to you sooner."

"I'm glad you showed up when you did," she stated, smiling softly at him. If he'd been a minute later, there probably would have been another dead body in the maze.

But there were more important things to dwell on than her brush with death.

"*Zio*, Autumn mentioned sloth," Brenna said, focusing on the critical issue. "While she wanted to get revenge on Mr. Rose, she was more keen on punishing Mitch because he didn't help Summer. Last month, we were dealing with Kevin's wrath; this month, it's Mitch's sloth. That can't be a coincidence. If anything, it looks like a pattern."

She watched her uncle's eyes carefully. They didn't look surprised at her words, meaning the thought had already occurred to him. Once again, she was a step behind him, but there were a few things he didn't know yet.

"Autumn left the newspaper and roses on Mom's grave," she

said, "but I can't see how she would have known that about your past."

"She told you that?" he asked. Was the smoke still affecting her eyes or did *Zio* actually look fearful?

Brenna nodded. "There's no way she got me, Mr. Rose, and Mitch into the maze all by herself. She had to have someone helping her – someone who knew about Eliza Kent and Mr. Rose. Not a high schooler but an adult. I think he was here tonight, too."

That drew him up quickly. "What?"

"There was a mummy in a coffin. I thought it was part of the decorations, but when I was trying to find my way out of the fire, I noticed that the mummy was gone. I think it was someone who'd been watching to see how things turned out."

Immediately, Abraham raised his head, eyes searching for any sign of the mummy, but with all the people running around in costumes, it was a futile gesture. Plus, Brenna wasn't done yet. "*Zio*, Kevin said that it wasn't over. I think this is what he meant. More of the seven deadly sins were going to appear. There's no way he could have known that unless someone, like the mummy man, told him. The mummy must be helping students carry them out. But if that's true, why is he doing it? What's his end goal?"

"That is a very good question," Abraham told her.

Brenna couldn't help but notice that he didn't contradict her theory, so her thoughts must not have been too far off the mark. It upset her to think that there was some mastermind out there, turning her classmates into puppets as he pulled their strings, but what bothered her even more was that she had a pretty good idea what this all about – the deaths of Eliza Kent and Amelia. Why bring up the past if it had no bearing on the present? There would be no reason to otherwise. So, if they *were* looking at the second installment of a high school crime spree, then it had to be somehow connected to her uncle's past.

Confronted by this realization, it was hard not to remember what Autumn had said about Abraham being a bad man. But Brenna couldn't believe that was true – the man had literally walked through fire to save her. A bad man wouldn't have done that. But the other accusation about the true nature of her mother's death wasn't so easy to dismiss. She only had her uncle's word on the matter, and there had never been a reason to doubt it until now. She desperately wanted to know what Autumn had meant when she mentioned the blood on Kevin's lead pipe. From the moment she'd read about the manner of Eliza's death, she'd seen the similarity in modus operandi. Was it possible that there might actually be a physical blood link between the two crimes? Is that what Autumn had meant? Or did the blood belong to someone else – like her mother? But how could that be since Amelia died in a car crash? Someone had obviously lied.

Brenna had Autumn's assertion on one hand and her own knowledge of Abraham on the other. The two most certainly didn't jive with each other, so there was only one thing left to do. Brenna had to uncover the truth for herself.

Chapter Thirty-One

"I miss Lloyd Dobler," Van sighed as he and Brenna trudged down the cemetery path. It was a Saturday not unlike the last time they were there, but this time, they were here to visit the grave of a different girl.

The Monday after Halloween, they had given their simulation babies back to Mrs. Johnson and some people, including Van, were still dealing with their own variation of postpartum depression. As much as Brenna enjoyed having Sophia Irene around, she was definitely glad to give the doll back. She needed her life to return to normal, which meant no babies or boyfriends.

She smiled. "I thought you were looking forward to sleeping through the night again."

He shrugged. "I guess I got used to the lack of sleep. Lloyd Dobler was such a good listener, and a welcome distraction from the unpleasantness of life. I could really use one of those right now."

That was most certainly true. One week had passed since Halloween and the impact of that fateful day was still being felt. The Rose scandal, as people were calling it, had shocked the school to its core. Learning that a popular teacher had sexually assaulted his students would have been devastating enough, but follow that up with his murder and the knowledge Mitch Hamilton had knowingly concealed the teacher's dark secret and the school was in turmoil.

In an odd twist of fate, Mitch had become even more popular. Not because people approved of what he'd done, but because they liked talking about his startling fall from grace. Such sensational gossip was even bigger than the Lucas Nash incident from last month. The Golden Boy wasn't so golden anymore. He still sat at a full table every day at lunch, talked with his friends, but Brenna could tell he was a mere shadow of his former self.

Very few people approached Brenna for details, but they made no attempt to pretend they weren't whispering about her when she walked down the halls. Alexis made a few snide remarks about Brenna's love life, and Dylan had the nerve to ask if she was interested in hooking up since things with Mr. Rose and Mitch didn't work out. She would have hit him if Van hadn't gotten there first. Mr. Elliot happened to be standing nearby when her attempt at violence occurred, but he walked away as if he hadn't seen it. Brenna appreciated the assistant principal's show of support.

Funny enough, Sara Xavier, having seen Mitch's true colors, was now offering Brenna pitying looks, sad smiles, and had even gone so far as to hug her. Like most high school love affairs, the depth of Sara's affection for Mitch turned out to be as shallow as a wading pool. Of course, her generosity of spirit probably had something to do with the fact that she could currently be seen walking the halls hand-in-hand with Ricky Garcia.

"I still can't believe Mr. Rose is dead," Van said with a shake of his head.

Brenna closed her eyes, trying to push the memory of his demise out of her mind. She'd been reliving that moment in the maze every night since it happened, but she hadn't told Van that. She didn't want him to worry even more about her mental health.

"He had it coming, but I wish Autumn hadn't done it," he added. "What's going on with her anyway?"

"She's getting a psychological evaluation, but I think *Zio* feels pretty confident that her lawyer will plead insanity and win. She needs help."

It might have been wrong since the girl was undeniably guilty, but Brenna was sort of glad that Autumn was crazy. She preferred thinking of her as mentally ill rather than a cold killer. It seemed like there was more hope for her future that way because she wasn't broken in the same way that Kevin Bishop had been. She could get better with counseling. Perhaps that was incredibly naive, but given everything that had happened, Brenna was looking for comfort anywhere she could find it.

"You know, you were right about Mystery Girl after all," she told him. "We *were* dealing with a ghost who was trying to save me."

Van let out a low chuckle. "And here I was thinking that I'd gotten it all wrong. She wasn't a dead girl, and Mitch wasn't your knight in shining armor." He shook his head. "We were dealing with Tess."

"What?" Brenna asked.

"It's *Tess of the d'Urbervilles*," he explained. "Summer personified Tess, the poor girl who gets raped and pressured into a sexual relationship by Alec, or Mr. Rose. Summer's story doesn't end with her death, but with Autumn's assimilation of her identity. The new Summer sacrifices her life and future by killing Mr. Rose and thus ridding the world of a horrible monster. Not a perfect comparison, but the similarities are striking."

"I hated that book, and now, you just made me hate it even more," sighed Brenna. "It's intolerable that the innocent suffer only to be twisted into criminals."

Lost in thought, Van was quiet for a moment. Everything that had happened was weighing exceptionally heavy on him. Brenna suspected that it had something to do with feelings of helplessness and guilt. He hadn't been there to help her fight off Mr. Rose or stood by her in the maze – which, in his mind, he might have been if he'd bothered to help when Brenna thought Mitch was in danger. Because he lacked the first-hand experience, he didn't know what his best friend had gone through or how to help her recover.

Brenna had tried to assure him that she didn't blame him for anything. In fact, she was certain that she'd be dead if Van hadn't gone looking for her. He was the one who called Abraham and sent him to the maze. But he was still beating himself up over the whole mess. Since Brenna's words were useless, she decided the best way to help him get over it was to keep moving on. She refused to let herself wallow in depression when Van was around. She went about her day as usual to prove that she wouldn't be defeated by what had happened. It was working – slowly but surely.

Today was just another step towards closure. Ever since Brenna had found out about Summer, she'd felt an intense desire to visit the girl's grave. Even though Summer was no longer alive, they shared a kinship that she wanted to acknowledge. In her hand, she held a bouquet of red roses just like the ones she'd left for her mother. It seemed a fitting honor to bestow upon the poor girl.

"What does Abe say about your whole Puppet Master idea?" Van asked suddenly. "It's so very conspiracy theory to think that there's some great mastermind turning high school kids into criminals."

"*Zio* is keeping his cards close to his chest, but I think he agrees with me. There's just no way that Autumn could have pulled off everything without help. She's a small girl. She'd have trouble moving me let alone Mr. Rose. Plus, there's the whole matter of how she even found out the truth."

Brenna had been disappointed that her uncle hadn't seen fit to share that important detail from Autumn's interrogation with her. However, he had cleared up a matter of interest for Van. The night that he'd chased Mystery Girl through the woods, Autumn – or maybe the mummy man since Brenna wasn't certain a girl riding the sanity line could have come up with the idea – had been prepared for him. She placed portable speakers in the trees, each with its own MP3 player that had a track of her giggling on it. Since they were remote controlled, she could set them off without being near them. Definitely a clever move. How Autumn had known about the whole stakeout date, though, remained a mystery.

As usual, Van wasn't willing to commit to such a grand theory, but there were some points that he simply couldn't dismiss. "Well, I don't see how Autumn could ever have found out about Eliza Kent."

"Exactly," Brenna nodded. "Only someone who was present at that time in my uncle's past would know about her."

Scowling, Van kicked a rock. "That's why it doesn't make any sense to me! If someone's got a grudge against Abe, why isn't he just going after him? Why mess around with high school kids at all?"

Because the Puppet Master wants me to know the truth about my uncle, Brenna thought. He wanted her involved in whatever it was he was doing. She was also fairly convinced that he was the one who'd left those white roses on her birthday as a kind of warning – possibly of impending death since white roses were typically used at funerals. Whose death he might be foreshadowing was a question she'd avoided altogether. She hadn't told Van about the things Autumn had said about Abraham or her new brainwave about the roses. She knew what he'd say – Autumn was crazy so of course, nothing she said was true. It wouldn't be worth her time to investigate. Brenna thought he was probably right. At least, she hoped he was. Regardless, she was going to find a way to uncover the truth and put the matter to rest.

"I'm not sure," she replied evasively. "I guess we'll find out, though, since there are five of the seven deadly sins left."

Van buried his face in his hands. "You'd better be wrong. I don't think I can take five more experiences like this."

Brenna was uncertain of what she could say to appease him, so they walked in silence towards Summer's grave. As they drew near, though, they saw that someone else was already there – Mitch. Standing at the foot of the grave, Mitch stared at the tombstone, his hands in his pockets. At his feet was a bouquet of daisies.

Seeing him there, Brenna felt a wave of pity wash over her. The emotions she felt for Mitch had been fluctuating between anger, sadness, and pity all week. It was complicated, the state of her heart, and she had a feeling it was going to stay that way for a while, because, in spite of it all, she still cared about the boy.

Van looked at Brenna, ready to take his cue from her.

"Just give me a few minutes," she said. She walked quietly up to Mitch's side, and he turned his head at the sound of her approach.

"Hey," she greeted him with a small smile, letting him know that she didn't want to fight. Not here at Summer's grave. That wouldn't be right. "How are you feeling?"

Mitch flexed his arm, which up until yesterday had been bandaged. He hadn't escaped the fire unharmed. "Not great but I deserve much worse."

She didn't know what to say. Part of her wanted to agree with him but part of her remembered him in the maze, braving the flames to save Autumn. She preferred things that were black and white – a person was either good or bad. But Mitch was varying shades of gray. Sure, he was mostly white but the black mark against him was pretty strong. She didn't know how that should impact her feelings for him. To be fair, she could search the world and never find a perfect person, but that didn't mean she should forgive and forget and jump back into a relationship with Mitch. Honestly, she wasn't sure if they had a future together. They weren't friends, but they weren't enemies, either.

"You did a good thing, though," she told him. "You saved Autumn."

"I'm not sure she appreciated the effort," he replied, dropping his gaze to the grave marker. "Besides, it doesn't change anything. Summer is still dead, and now, Mr. Rose is dead. You could have died, too. It's all my fault."

Brenna remembered with perfect clarity that she'd essentially blamed Mitch for Summer's death, and while there was some truth to that, it wasn't quite fair to lay all of the responsibility on him. Ultimately, Summer had acted of her own volition. There had always been other options besides suicide.

"No, it's not," she said, injecting certainty into her voice. "Mr. Rose was evil and he chose to do those things. Summer chose to end her life rather than to confide in someone like her sister."

Unconvinced, he shook his head. "But if I'd said something, Rose definitely would have been stopped and Summer might not have killed herself. Yeah, they made their own choices, but I made mine, too. Mine resulted in the death of two people – three counting the baby. I have to live with that knowledge for the rest of my life."

His exterior cracked and whatever wall that had been holding back his emotions came tumbling down. "There were so many times I almost came clean, but I didn't know how to after misleading you for so long. I thought the lie would make it better, but it only made it worse," he managed through his tears. "Brenna, I know that I hurt you and that you hate me, but you have to believe me when I say I'm sorry."

"I don't hate you," she assured him. Amazingly enough, she knew it was true. It would be easier to get over Mitch if she *did* hate him, but the heart didn't always make things that easy. "I still have feelings for you, but I'm not sure what that means."

He nodded miserably and turned his full attention back to the girl they'd both come to visit. Brenna laid her roses next to the daisies Mitch had brought and stood beside him in silence. Mitch made no attempt to control his emotions but let his tears flow freely. Moved by his pain, Summer's death, and her own sadness, Brenna gave in to her own tears. She wasn't certain what tomorrow held in store for them – if anything – but today, they were joined in grief.

Reaching out, Brenna took hold of Mitch's hand and squeezed it.

"Thanks for coming with me tonight," Brenna whispered to Duke as they snuck through the brush later that night. It was midnight, and they were on a secret mission to deliver some much-earned revenge. The house they were creeping up to was completely dark, its sleeping occupant completely unaware of what they had in store for him. It was great.

"I'm always up for some excitement," he replied with a grin. "Plus, he has this coming."

When Brenna had recruited Duke earlier in the week, he'd agreed wholeheartedly, which was good since she needed his hands to pull off the plan she'd concocted. His mood had seen a significant improvement of late because he had patched things up with Kelly. That didn't necessarily make Brenna happy, but she was pleased that her friend was no longer depressed.

Upon reaching the desired spot, Duke set the box he'd been carrying down on the ground and looked at Brenna. He had a serious look about him that clued her into what was coming. "I know we haven't really talked about it, but I wanted you to know that I'm really sorry about how things with Mitch turned out. I don't want you thinking that I don't care because I didn't like the guy."

Oh, the topic of Mitch had come up between them, but it had always resulted in Duke airing his temper out. Brenna had heard him spew out some pretty impressive rants about the boy and what he'd like to do to him. Oddly enough, she'd found it comforting, and she let her own hostility live vicariously through his until it had almost diminished.

"I know you care," she nodded, looking away. After seeing Mitch earlier at the cemetery, Duke's spontaneous tenderness was making her overly emotional. She didn't want him to see her sudden tears.

He wasn't fooled. Taking her chin, he pulled her head up so he could brush her tears away with his fingers. "It'll take a while, but you'll heal. I promise," he smiled like one who knew about broken hearts. "You'll find a boy who's far more deserving of your affections."

"Maybe, but I think I'm going to swear off dating for a while," Brenna told him. It wasn't lost on her how this conversation bore some resemblance to the talk they'd had in the garage a few weeks ago when Duke was fixing Abraham's car. Only this time, the roles were reversed. "I'll stick to revenge. Let's string them up."

The fashion dolls that Brenna had purchased at the thrift store were inside the box Duke had carried. One long piece of twine had been wrapped around the dolls' waists so that when Brenna held it up, the dolls dangled sideways down it in a long line. There were two such arrangements, and she meant to hang them down Van's window as the first part of her scheme.

Without warning, the back door opened and Max Vaughn stepped outside. "Hey guys," he greeted amicably. "How's it going?"

Of course, Brenna had consulted the Vaughns about the prank she planned to pull on their son. No one appreciated a prank like Max, and he'd graciously volunteered his assistance.

"Great. Thanks so much for putting up the nails," she replied.

"You know me, I love a good joke," the man chuckled, rubbing his hand across his bald head. "He's out like a light so you're good to go."

Smiling, Brenna tied the first string to the nail. The dolls bounced lightly against Van's bedroom window before Brenna pulled the string taut and tied it to the nail at the bottom of the sill. Duke followed her example with the second string. With the way they were strung up, the dolls were lying on their sides, with their smiling faces pressed against the window and their arms raised over their heads like they were trying to break through the glass.

"Okay, that looks good. Let's proceed to phase two," Brenna instructed them.

Nodding, Duke followed Max into the house with a large, police-issue flashlight in his hand. Brenna pulled down her hood so her face could be clearly seen. With the use of heavy amounts of makeup, she'd given herself doll-like features and styled her hair, which still bore traces of red, like a glamorous Barbie.

The moon shone brightly overhead, spilling its light into Van's room. From where she stood at the window, she could just make out the sleeping form of her best friend in his bed, arm draped over the side of it. He looked so innocent and peaceful. Scaring him to death was going to be so much fun.

Van's bedroom door opened slowly and Brenna pressed her fingertips against the window. Then Duke turned on the flashlight. Its powerful beam slashed through the darkness, illuminating Brenna and the dolls. She raked her nails down the window, drawing out a long, agonizing screech. Van stirred from sleep, turned his weary eyes towards the window, paused for a second, and then screamed bloody murder as he tumbled out of bed. She fell, too, hitting the ground as she nearly died laughing.

Recovering, Van bellowed with a voice that rattled the windowpane, "BRENNA!"

Yes, there was nothing quite like a little good-natured revenge to get a girl back on track.

The End

HERE'S A SNEAK PEEK AT THE NEXT BRENNA RUTHERFORD MYSTERY:
ON ICE

Damn but it was cold outside. He hadn't expected to feel the bitter chill so strongly through his thick coat and gloves, but with the way the wind was whipping through the alley, he might as well have been naked for all the good they did. The only part of him that was warm was his head. No, strike that. Warm wasn't quite a strong enough word; it felt like a sauna underneath his helmet. He wanted to take the damn thing off, but he had promised that under no circumstances would he remove it. That was just one of the many things that had been drilled repeatedly into his brain.

Out on the streets, a few shoppers stumbled out of closing stores, arms laden down with bags that they carried like spoils of war. Another Black Friday had been vanquished. Thanks to the darkness and their own fatigue, they didn't see him crouching behind the boutique. He waited for the last group to pass by before standing up.

By now, Trendsation had been closed for nearly thirty minutes. The only people that were inside were the employees, and there were only two of them. Moving quietly through the shadows, he headed for the back door that he knew would be unlocked. As he reached for the door knob, he paused to settle his nerves. He shook his shoulders, loosening them up even as his hand tightened reflexively around the stun baton it held.

The costume he was wearing might have been lame, but the stun baton was completely badass. Twenty inches long, it was five hundred thousand volts of pure electricity. According to the website, if you touched someone with it for three to five seconds, they would be dazed and temporarily paralyzed. It would also deliver a shock at six inches from the tip so that no one could take it away from you.

In other words, it was totally awesome.

While he had been excited about tonight, it was a big step from talking about committing robbery and actually doing it. Thankfully, he hadn't had to come up with the plan on his own. Everything had been spelled out in perfect detail until he knew it all backwards and forwards. Go in through the back door, stun Mrs. Dixon, and order Missy to give him the cash. After she did, he was to get the hell out of there.

It sure sounded easy enough. Almost like a game.

He gave the knob a turn and smiled when he felt it move with his hand. As quiet as a mouse, he slipped through the back door and halted in his tracks. Mrs. Dixon was at the end of the hall, her sweater-clad back to him. That wasn't right. She was supposed to be in the storage room. That's where he was supposed to stun her so that he could lock her inside. The plan had made that very clear.

Sweat ran down his face in tiny rivers as he forced himself to stay calm. Okay, he'd been in situations like this before where things didn't go exactly as planned so there was no need to panic. Running away wasn't an option now that he'd come this far; it was time to punt. Who said he couldn't just stun her in the hall? After all, the older woman had no idea he was even there.

Confidence guided him forward. He was almost there, stun baton at the ready, when something alerted the woman to his presence. She turned around, her eyes going wide with shock. For two heartbeats, they stared at each other before he remembered that he had a weapon. His hand shot forward, the tip of his electrified baton hitting her stomach. The shop owner's body twitched under the contact and she let out a pitiful squeak before it finally silenced her.

Okay, that hadn't been too bad. Hurting people wasn't something that he was interested in – all he wanted was the money – but he recognized the need to incapacitate people so that he could get it. That's why they'd settled on the baton rather than a gun.

He stepped over her body just as Missy Jensen rounded the corner. "Mrs. Dixon?" she called, no doubt wondering if her boss needed help.

When her eyes landed on him, she froze. He could have sworn that she was trying not to laugh. He couldn't blame her; he knew how silly he looked in a Santa costume topped off with a helmet similar to one a Star Wars geek would wear. But it kept his identity a secret, which was all that mattered in the end.

"Give me the money," he demanded. The helmet's voice modulator made his voice unrecognizable even to him. Truth be told, that was also pretty awesome. He jabbed the air with his stun baton to encourage the reluctant Missy. She stepped back, uncertain.

"Now," he pressed, injecting some hostility into his voice as he made a swiping motion with his weapon. He missed her body by an inch, maybe less. He didn't have his finger on the trigger this time, though.

"I'm going," she cried, moving forward but always looking over her shoulder at him. She stopped in front of the register, fingers poised to open it, and looked up at him. "You're not going to hurt me, are you?" It almost sounded like she was daring him.

He kept the baton between them. "Just give me the money." From his belt, he pulled a sack and tossed it on the counter. "Put it inside."

Missy complied, opening the cash drawer. As she slipped the bills inside, she shot furtive glances at the armed figure behind her. He gestured with his weapon, but this time, his finger slipped on the trigger. The baton sparked for a second, close enough to catch Missy in the side, before he quickly jerked it away. Missy hit the counter hard, catching herself before she fell. Thankfully, she didn't pass out.

"That was a warning," he told her, covering up his mistake. "And don't look at me."

Silently, she went back to shoving money into the bag. He watched the rapid rise and fall of her chest. Her body was reacting to him, and he liked it.

Task finished, Missy held out the bag, careful to keep her body facing forward. "Go to the storage closet," he instructed as he took it from her.

"Are you going to hurt me?" she asked again as she walked towards the closet.

"I will if you don't hurry," he cried, smacking her in the back with his bag. Missy stumbled, falling against a shelf. "Move faster."

She opened the door, and raising his foot to her butt, he pushed her inside and slammed it shut. Almost immediately, Missy was pounding against it, screaming profanities at him. Smiling, he grabbed a chair and shoved it underneath the knob to keep the door closed. He turned away, enjoying the heft to his Santa sack, and as he stepped over a groaning Mrs. Dixon, he sighed and stabbed the stun baton into her side again. The old woman went limp.

Man, this robbery stuff was fun.

Unravel the mystery in October 2013

ABOUT THE AUTHOR

Ann K. Shepherd graduated *summa cum laude* from Biola University with a degree in Psychology. Currently, she lives next door to Mickey Mouse in Anaheim, California, where she can usually be found seated in front of her computer with a Diet Coke or curled up with a young adult novel. She prefers werewolves to vampires, is highly imaginative yet anal, hates heights but loves to fly, and firmly believes that there can never be too much cheese in any dish. Visit her at www.annkshepherd.com.